A Heavy Chest of Dreams

by

Emmy Culley

Grosvenor House
Publishing Limited

All rights reserved
Copyright © Emmy Culley, 2008

This novel is entirely a work of fiction. The names, characters and incidents portrayed in it are solely the work of the author's imagination. Any resemblance to actual persons, living or dead, events or locations is entirely coincidental.

A Heavy Chest of Dreams copyright Emmy Culley published in 2008 by Grosvenor House Publishers.

The Author asserts the moral right to be identified as the author of these works.

All rights reserved. No part of this publication may be reproduced, stored in a retrieval system, or transmitted, in any form, electronic, mechanical, photocopying, recording or otherwise without the prior permission of the publishers.

This book is sold subject to the condition that it shall not, by any way of trade or otherwise, be lent, re-sold, hired out or otherwise circulated without the publisher's prior consent in any form of binding or cover other than that in which it is published and without a similar condition including this condition being imposed on the subsequent purchaser.

Book cover photography copyright Paul of Alternative Images, Nottingham.

Cover photographs of Emmy Culley: www.emmyculleyswebofdreams.com
ISBN 978-1-906645-15-1

*For my precious son, Anthony,
Thank you for being my rock through
good times and bad.
I wish you all the success, luck and love
that you can possibly bear.*

*Enjoy this tale, 'me hearty' and may the memory
of many fearless pyrates
stay with you through a very happy
and exciting life!*

A Pyrate's Prayer
*Prithee, Capt'n most gracious and
charge of the sea,
Bless all of thy sailors, wherever we be!
Bless all shipmates, our cabins an'
weapons we carry,
An' rid us of morsal, pox, flux and scurvy!*

*May our bounty be 'bundent
when Spaniards meet fog,
With Doubloons a plenty, 'baccy and grog!
We end this fine prayer as yer
servants of course…..
If…….. ye send dozens of wenches
Lest we take 'em by force!
Arrrrrrrrrrmen!*

Glossary

Aqua Vitae – a strong, expensive spirit

Bawd/ bawd house/ bawdy den – prostitute/ brothel

Belike – perhaps

Bodhrán – a handheld, shallow, goatskin drum (Irish)

Bowsprit – a spar projecting from the bow of a vessel

Bubbies – Breasts

Comfits – sweets

Cunnie – vagina... derived from the Latin 'cunnus'

Doubloon – a gold coin, the highest value Spanish coin in circulation

Drabber – prostitute's punter

Fie! – A general exclamation of disgust

Flux (bloody Flux) – Dysentery

Pillcock or pillicock – penis

Pinnace – a small, light sailing ship used for communication between ships and shore

Poitín – Irish moonshine, a liquor made from potatoes

Pox / The 'French welcome' – syphilis

Morsal – gangrene

Nonpareil – beauty

Quiver – vagina

Scurvy – a disease caused by vitamin C deficiency, common in the 15th century amongst sailors on long voyages

Sweating sickness – acute, infectious epidemic in 15th century England

Swive – to have sex

Mammaries – breasts

Manchet loaves – fine white bread popular in Tudor times

Mummers – actors

Perchance – possibly

Poop deck – a small deck at the rear (stern) of the ship, over the captain's cabin

Prithee – please

Verily – truthfully

Vihuela – a 15th century Spanish guitar-like string instrument

Translation from Spanish to English: '¡Puede dios castigar los bastardos que mataron mi ángel hermoso!' –

'May God punish the bastards who killed my beautiful angel!'

Acknowledgements

I dedicate this book to my only child and wee bro, Anthony John Patrick Carter who I totally adore. We have been through some extremely difficult times together and you always manage to give infinite love and support to me and our close little family. You are the most wonderful son a mother could possibly ask for, honey!

Abundant thanks to Mum and Dad; the most supportive and loving parents ever. You have both helped me and Anthony through some incredibly hard years. I will never be able to repay your kindness!

Thanks also to my God Father, uncle and most loyal friend and counsellor, chief proof reader and fellow writer, Dave Brown. You are just like your Dad... simply the best!

Huge appreciation goes to my sweet Nan and soul twin, Micky and her beloved Pat, my wonderful Granddad. Sadly Gramps, you now have to watch and guide me from the Otherworld... I love you both sooooooooo much!

My sincere gratitude also goes to my good friend and photographer, Paul Alexander of 'Alternative Images' for your patience and hard work in producing excellent cover pictures.

A massive thank you to Kev Shercliff, proprietor of Midland Tattoo Centre in Cannock, Staffordshire for your bear hugs, all of my lovely ink-work and plenty of laughs during good times and bad. You are one of my oldest friends, honey and I think the world of you!

Thank you to all of you who have supported me in pursuit of my crazy dreams, especially Nick Potter. You have helped me find my way and stuck by me through thick and thin; you are a total treasure! Thank you for all of our wonderful times!

Cheers to all of my Myspace friends for your support and encouragement. Be safe and happy, all of you!

'Some books are to be tasted, others to be swallowed, and some few to be digested: that is, some books are to be read only in parts, others to be read, but not curiously, and some few to be read wholly, and with diligence and attention.'

Sir Francis Bacon (1561-1626)

Bon appetit! x

Love always,

Emmy (proud descendant of the MacNichols clan of the Scottish Highlands and the Culley clan of Ireland) x x x

Prologue

Ever since I was a young girl barely able to walk, I have had the most vivid and wonderful visions of pyrates. Bedtime stories that my Mum would read to soothe my hyperactive mind, told of days when swashbuckling, dandy and handsome heroes ruled the high seas. My eyes would light up at the mention of treasure chests full of jewels and glittering gold. These caskets were probably buried somewhere exotic by a peg-legged old character wearing an eye patch, armed to the hilt with the most elaborate weaponry. Brandishing a cutlass, he would be wearing a costume that any Prima Donna would envy! These exciting stories fuelled my wildest fantasies. My dreams were dominated by breath-takingly dangerous, erotic adventures. Clad in tightly laced corset, bosom heaving and long, flowing hair being whipped by the wind, I travelled the seven seas in the arms of my pyrate lover. Childhood sexual fantasies reigned high in my dream-world, but there were none more erotically charged and enticing than those involving my pyrate heroes. I treasured them so highly that they have remained with me ever since.

Contrary to the popular romantic notion of pyracy, the idea of loveable yet villainous rogues could be no further from the truth. So now, I invite you to close your eyes and take yourself back a few hundred years. Put to use all of your sensory skills and imagine the most foul mouthed, violent and murderous thieves. Add to this, filthy, stinking creatures who would rape and pillage without a second thought and there you have your average pyrates. Mix this realistic perception with willing, hardy but rough sailors, able to stay awake through long days and nights working the ship's sails, whilst performing vigorous and heavy duties through the fiercest of storms and attacks. There we have a little more insight into the true identity of the characters who commonly chose pyracy as a trade... fiendishly dangerous and so different from the romantic tales that we have all been fed!

The story you are about to read, with its tantalisingly wicked characters, has been buried in the depths of my mind like a hidden treasure chest. I have woven much historical detail gathered from documents of the time of my main character's birth in the filthy, disease ridden port town of Plymouth.

Sushana Culley was born at six in the evening of a hot summer day, the twelfth of July 1538, the year when King Henry the eighth ruled England and forcibly claimed his place as head of the Church. Miss Culley's future was fated to be adventurous and colourful. Unravelled piece by piece, we will share some extreme and sordid details of her life. I shall begin with an unsettled time when pyrates were loathed and feared along the shores of England. Hatred had brewed amongst commonfolk and there were few more popular entertainment spectacles in the town squares than the latest public hanging... especially when the condemned was a notorious pyrate.

CHAPTER 1

Beauty is a Curse

Sushana scanned the intriguing array of colourful characters which had amassed in front of the courthouse. An impressive gathering of English citizens had eagerly chosen to join her in such a foreboding and dreadful scene. Miss Culley's head started to spin as hollow and uneasy echoes bounced off wattle walls in the narrow, cobbled streets of Plymouth. The stench was even more offensive than usual, as pungent and putrid odours of sweat, sewage, smoke and decay mingled together: an apt perfume to create the flavour of this day, Sushana thought with a rueful smile. She was surprised to see that a hunchback had managed to gain a cramped, but prime place amongst the reeking, death-hungry mob. Such freakish, deformed folk were usually banished to the outskirts of any social gatherings, no matter what their status. The sad creature attempted a rallying grin when he noticed her eyes alight on him.

Queen Elizabeth now ruled over England, the island had been in turmoil during Bloody Mary's reign but was at last growing steadily in wealth and power. Legalised death still stalked the squalid streets and Sushana hid a wry smile as she thought that ironically she was about to die for the same deeds that gained knighthoods for others!

'Beauty is a curse!' Sushana's foster mother, Bess had often told her. Now, as she stood proudly in front of the bloodthirsty audience, these wise words came back to her. She bit back tears as filthy familiar hands tightened the rough noose around her delicate neck. A shiver crept down her spine as the executioner's touch lingered on her skin. He made no secret of his sexual attraction towards his prey. The crowd roared with morbid excitement as the gruesome, tantalising but sickening show played out before them. Sushana could smell the foul stench of her captor's breath as he pressed his body hard into hers, squeezing an ample breast between his gnarled fingers. His grin was hideous and it only made the woman he was about to legally murder look more beautiful. She lifted her piercing eyes of sapphire towards the setting sun and sneered insolently in a final rebuke.

Sushana's lips began to move as she mouthed an unheard monologue, her heavy chest heaving as she drew breath with increasing difficulty. A thick, specially made rope tightened around her throat as she struggled to make her words audible. The unprecedented crowd fell into a hushed stupor. Thousands of folk, some of whom had travelled many miles to watch the infamous Sushana Culley hang, stood in the dying heat of day straining to hear her final plea. However, the gorgeous woman who stood proudly before them didn't beg for her life. She coolly surveyed her onlookers with calm interest, waiting patiently for them to give her the respect that she both deserved and desired. The crowd was mesmerised by her detached demeanour.

Front rows were always the best place to witness gruesome execution scenes and Shana, as her lovers had fondly called her, gave the lucky few hundred nearest to her a superb performance. As she felt the opium take effect, she looked deeply into each person's eyes and her mind whirled in a hurricane of wild and wonderful memories. Her whisper was barely audible; '...no regrets...' Nearby, a toothless woman repeated Shana's words loud enough for many of the crowd to hear... The crone's yelled lisps were quite comical, yet the echoed words caused a stir of different emotions. Cries for mercy were heard as a priest offered her the cross to kiss. Men began to panic as the final minutes of their icon's fantastic life ticked slowly away. Surely some hero would turn up hacking his way through the guards, sweep up his heroine and free her from the noose? Shana's admirers were ready for anything. They had been faithful followers of her incredible antics and adventures during an impressive ten year reign of the seas. Her infamy had spread over vast waters and foreign lands... No one expected to see their legend in a state of submission... everyone was waiting for a spectacular rescue! None could accept that this alluring woman with such power and strength would allow anything or anyone to break her spirit.

The foul stench of shit, puke and blood that lingered after the executions of less famous victims gradually faded as Shana's gaze glazed over. She focused on the bluest eyes she could find in the crowd. The chosen man was almost swooning in the heat, cocking his head like a pining puppy as he became even more mesmerised by this incredibly sensual woman. Anthony was the blacksmith's son and had stood all day in the scorching midsummer sun to witness the last moments of his fantasy woman's life. In his young and adventurous mind, he longed to be the man who would whisk her into his arms and ride away, back to her awaiting galleon. Despite his heroic delusion, he had frozen when he had seen her... In life, she was far more beautiful than words could describe. The engravings on the rough posters calling for her capture had failed to represent Sushana's incredible beauty. This woman had such a sexual presence and allure; many of her male audience stood before her feeling aroused beyond belief. It was almost unbearable to witness the snuffing out of such an intensely sexual flame!

Sushana 'had it' and her guardian, Albert had always told her so. He had recognised her gift of indescribable magnetism early in her life. The fact that she was blissfully ignorant of her allure made her all the more enticing! As Shana stood proudly on the rough, wooden platform her guardian's words played over and over in her drug-addled mind... 'She's one in a million is our Shana.' She missed him beyond belief. Shana's blood rushed to her heart at the thought of Albert. He had always been so good to her, treating her like his own daughter. Shana bit her bottom lip and her eyes welled with tears as she remembered a happy childhood.

'The blue eyes... focus... must not pass out!...' thought Shana, then a spiteful twist of a stiffened nipple and the strong scent of smelling salts dragged her mind back to reality. She stared deep into the soul of the blue eyes that had stayed in fixed focus when her own had failed her. The smith's son, Anthony stood in absolute awe of her beauty and bravery. He had often witnessed grown men blubber at the mere sight of the scaffold awaiting them, yet this woman stood tall and proud as she was groped and humiliated before so many! Inner strength was what had kept Shana going for years, that and the love for her only man-child, Patrick. Her son awaited his mother's return on shores far away... Now she drew on all the inner strength that she had taken a lifetime to build.

The noose had been loosened to prolong the entertainment and agony. Now the crowd began to jeer again, disappointed with the executioner for allowing his prized prisoner to swoon. Master Olaf Hickford's cruelty was well known amongst regular execution watchers. He was an arrogant bastard who took pride in his terrible profession, often bragging in his cups of his hanging skills. His speciality was to entertain fans by taunting the bound and helpless victims; his favourite prey being a terrified woman. Most men loathed him but, as always, there were a pathetic few who held him in awe. His sycophantic following of fools beheld him as some kind of perverse icon. Later in the White Swan, this meagre gathering would ensure as always that their sadistic role model's tankard overflowed with a steady supply of ale.

Sushana had no interest in the overweight, unkempt, foul-breathed fool who made a living from others' misfortune, feeding his over-large ego by bragging in the taverns about his latest 'kill'. With a final look of contempt, Sushana shook her head proudly at the oaf who offered her a silken scarf. The soft pastel scarf had been donated by a wealthy gentleman who wished a dignified and speedy death for his fantasy woman. The refusal of the elderly dignitary's makeshift blindfold sent the crowd into a frenzy; they were now on the verge of hysteria. Hickford had lost control and did not feel his usual, confident self.

This day, the twelfth day of July in the year of Our Lord 1578 would haunt Master Olaf for the rest of his miserable life. It would go down in history as the day when he lost face before the largest gathering he had ever 'performed' in front of. It totally finished him. His career was over and his life from that date would not be worth living. The bitch of a wench standing before him, who he had forcibly and brutally taken the night before, had won. He had raped this impertinent strumpet on the stone floor of the cold, dank cell beneath the courthouse in the City of Plymouth and she was about to serve him his just desserts. Little did he know what revenge the infamous and cunning pyrate queen had prepared for him. Almost in a nervous reaction, a pathetic and futile retaliation to her non-compliance, he spitefully pinched her nipple again and pushed the tiny bottle of pungent salts up to her nostrils... he was not going to allow his captive another fainting spell!

The Executioner by appointment of the King was forty eight on the day that Miss Sushana Culley reached her fortieth year. The uncouth brute stood before the woman who he firmly believed he had managed to tame with his sexual dominance the previous eve. The condemned woman merely gazed into his pig-like, pale, watery blue eyes as they narrowed in wasted defiance.

Anthony felt his heart skip a beat and he had to steady himself as Shana turned her head with dramatic purpose and looked his way once more. Perfect rosebud lips gently parted to reveal a silken, pink tongue that slowly traced her upper lip in a vulgar, but incredibly arousing manner. She glanced sensually through thick, dark eyelashes at the spellbound youth, still avoiding eye contact with the frustrated Hickford. Her strong, but feminine hands were tied in front of her crotch and Shana was able to hitch her skirts high enough to bare her beautiful, long tanned legs. Her performance was fantastic and how refreshing it was to see humiliation rebound! Olaf Hickford would not be the only man affected by the whiles of this wild, free-spirited pyrate wench that day. Shana's uninhibited sexuality entertained the audience beyond measure as the reign of the High Executioner fast approached its end.

Chapter 2

Early Years

Thomas Culley had been widowed young. His delicate and sickly first wife lost her life to the same tragic disease that, unbeknown to him, would one day claim his own. Before the locally accepted mourning period was over, Thomas had found comfort in Elspeth's arms. This caused a stir amongst the community because Elspeth was well known in East Teignmouth as the most beautiful of the unmarried women. Yet she was extremely choosy when it came to menfolk. Many eager suitors were keen to please the pretty wench, but none of their elaborate gifts or fanciful dates impressed her. Fate had been kind to this intelligent young woman and she had enjoyed a very happy, cosseted youth.

Unlike other women of her time, Elspeth was both able and permitted to engage in interesting conversation with men who she met at church and traders who visited her family home to do business with her father. Master Elijah Culley was a well respected and wealthy spice trader, keen to see his teenage daughter married to a respectable and suitably free gentleman. When Elijah became a widower, he was blissfully unaware that his wild natured teenage daughter would fall in love with a man almost fifteen years her senior.

One fateful winter's eve, when the night was drawing in, Elspeth heard the muffled sound of male voices in the room below her bedchamber. As usual, she had retired early to her room so that she could read in relative peace. Her father's late night visitors often disturbed her and occasionally succumbing to temptation, she eavesdropped on their conversations... a rare opportunity for a woman of her time. Most male business was conducted far away from female ears. Men took great care to prevent women from overhearing or worse, repeating the latest tales of debauchery, smuggling and pyracy. The last thing needed was fear to be spread amongst the city folk.

Something about the gentle purr of a new voice caught Elspeth's attention. The glass beaker that she held to the floorboards during her eavesdropping sessions was not a good conductor of the pleasurable tones through the thick wood. Disappointment only fed her curiosity. Elspeth's upturned nose crumpled with frustration as she rose from the floor. Drawing her heavy cotton night dress up and over her knees she put her ear to the thick, oak door... Nothing... absolute silence...

'God's Blood!' cursed the pretty wench. Her heart skipped a beat as she suddenly fell forward through the opening door. Her father, red faced with disappointment, annoyance and a touch of anger, stood in the narrow passageway at the top of the wooden stairway, his hand still on the door knob. 'Elspeth!' the elderly spice merchant gasped, rolling his eyes in despair at his daughter's language!

'How d' ye expect me to react when ye use such foul an' blasphemous speak? Thy tongue is comparable to a fishwife's!' The pretty maiden's cheeky grin and delightful, well- practiced wink calmed the old man's temper. She swept confidently past her weary, wrinkled old father to the top of the stairs. 'Another suitor, methinks?' the womanchild asked eagerly as her father eyed his daughter with bewilderment laced with a tad of frustration. Yet, he could not help but smile with pride. Without doubt this adorable wench would grow into a woman destined to take the world by storm and probably teach men a few tricks into the bargain! Old Elijah Culley pondered on this and then answered Elspeth with a hidden smirk. 'My dear child, thy beauty thankfully matches thy impudence. I am entertaining a friend of mine this eve, so methinks ye can relax and lose thy sen in one of thy fantastical tales.' Elijah's blue eyes twinkled as his curious daughter stretched over the balcony, trying to catch a glimpse of the mystery guest. This scene amused the old man as he had never before witnessed his daughter acting with such keen interest where menfolk were concerned. Elspeth craned her slim neck further until the oak banister began to creak. She pulled back and whirled around excitedly to look into her father's eyes.

Elspeth was a tall, slim wench blessed with a stunning hourglass figure. Breathtakingly beautiful with pale blue eyes and soft, wavy blonde hair, her skin was always tanned... unusual for well-bred females. Peasants had dark, weather-beaten skin from hours spent labouring under the summer sun, whilst ladies were encouraged to stay in the shadows, holding delicate parasols that helped keep a fashionable pallor to their skin.

"So, ye have an interest in my visitor do ye?" Elijah looked deeply into his daughter's eyes. She recognised her father's melancholy and her own eyes narrowed, silently questioning. Her father looked down as he explained, 'Alas, this gentleman has no interest in any wench other than his recently deceased wife. He loved her deeply.' No more words were needed between the two kindred spirits and seconds ticked away in silence as they imagined the sorrow felt by the visitor.

Weeks flew by, and whilst Elspeth held the utmost respect for the deceased wife of the mysterious visitor, she still longed to meet him. Since the night on the stairway, father and daughter had held no further conversation about the man whose identity was yet to be revealed… that was, until one bleak winter's eve when Elspeth could wait no longer.

Snow lay thick on the ground the night that Elspeth planned to finally learn the identity of the man with the wonderful voice. Her clothes were neatly folded and ready by her bed, so the teenager could dress quickly when she heard her father retire for the night. Her heart thumped hard against her ribs and she felt an excitement that she had never experienced before. Cheeks warm and rosy, eyes sparkling with delight and a heart full of eager anticipation, the feisty young wench rose from her bed and pulled on her thick woollen clothes. She opened the heavy door and peered over the banister where she had stood on the night that her fantasy man had first caught her attention. Elspeth closed her pretty eyes and breathed deeply; the spices that her father had purchased from the Spanish trader that day smelled divine! The young woman took in each of the scents, rich and pure… cinnamon, nutmeg, cloves, cardamon, ginger, cumin, cayenne pepper and her favourite of all, anise. Each had its own exquisite, exotic aroma. The perfume cocktail made Elspeth feel quite light headed… a feeling that she had grown to enjoy.

The candle flame flickered throwing long, menacing shadows before her into the well of darkness below. As she descended the creaking steps, a mischievous smile played on her lips. How handsome she imagined her unidentified beau to be! Warmth spread over her body, a sensation that made her feel quite frustrated, yet she knew not why. Elspeth's pace quickened when she reached the parlour where she was grateful to feel a little warmth. A hearty fire had been kept burning for ten of the twelve days of Yule. This year's Yule log had been a fine choice, thanks to old Albert, their faithful gardener. The young woman smiled as she remembered happy childhood days when, wrapped in warm clothes she ventured out into the woods with kind and gentle Albert. The unlikely pair would spend hours seeking out the most suitable log to drag home and burn on the hearth throughout Yule. Elspeth's basket was always full of red silk ribbons with which to decorate the fine log. This tradition was a mix of pagan and Christian ceremonies and the 'Twelfths' were eagerly awaited as the rule was that no work was to be carried out by land labourers during that time. Their only task throughout Yuletide was to tend to the animals. When the two had found their perfect Yule log, they would return home dragging their prized find behind them. Once safely back, they would follow the ancient tradition of kindling a fresh fire with a handful of charred remains that Albert had saved from the previous year's Yule fire. The old hand would always allow his young charge the honour of striking flint onto tinder. The youngster was usually successful first time and would proudly light the taper.

Elspeth's mind suddenly returned to the present as she smelled the aromatic posy that she had placed on her late mother's spinning wheel. This was another tradition that she enjoyed. It was supposed to deter women from spinning through the 'Twelfths', although sadly the old and faithful spinning wheel had not been used since the passing of her mother two years since. With a thoughtful sigh, the pretty maiden hitched up her skirts and made for the kitchen.

Back doors were mostly used by serving folk, the likes of Bess, the family cook and her brother, Albert. However, Elspeth often used it as a safe escape route on nights like these, when she planned to go out for a few hours without her father knowing. As a precaution, the crafty wench always took the heavy, black iron key from the key hook. Bess was a light sleeper; her dry old bones ached on winter nights. Years of walking on legs bowed like willow branches by the rickets that poor Bess had endured since adolescence, had finally taken their toll. The lame woman would hobble down to sit in front of the hearth in the early hours, but her deafness was a blessing for the late night escapee.

Elspeth's candle flame flickered as she opened the kitchen door and entered the refreshingly cool room. The delicious smell of Bess's mince pyes tempted her and she crept over to the pantry and helped herself to one of the fine seasonal treats. Her mouth watered as she bit into the pastry and closed her eyes. She savoured the rich, sweet taste of dried fruits and minced mutton. Quickly, she broke the tip off a cone of sugar and away she went, closing the pantry door behind her. Popping the sweet treat into her mouth, she scooted out of the back door and into the darkness.

The roughly cobbled street was newly laid and some stones had not yet settled. Snow and ice had lifted a few of them, making the path uneven and treacherous. A cold breeze gently caressed Elspeth's face and blessed her with a tingly kiss as she tiptoed carefully along. Her senses became aroused beyond any of her wildest dreams as she pulled her cloak around her slim, but curvaceous body and braved the icy night. It took almost an hour to walk to the church and the determined woman-child just made it in time to see the first of the men leaving after Evensong. Positioning herself on the corner of the narrow street, the pretty stalker pulled her hood close to her face to conceal her identity and found a handy place to hide her lantern.

Most of the merchants and regular attendants of St. Editha's knew Elijah Culley and his beautiful daughter, so she took no chances. Ten minutes seemed like an hour until finally a tall, dark figure emerged slowly from the door. His steps were steady and sure as he walked along the tiny path through the churchyard, pausing before the lych gate. Strong, broad shoulders... dark, wavy hair and a full beard... Elspeth drank in every detail of this gorgeous being that, she had no doubt, was her mystery man. Her heart quickened and her breath caught in her throat as she felt that familiar feeling stirring in her crotch. This man was incredible! From the shadows, the watcher looked on in awe as her target knelt before the last gravestone in the churchyard. Elspeth could hardly hold back her tears as she began to feel guilty looking in at such an intimate, private moment. The feeling soon passed as she watched the man who she had fallen for when she had heard his voice.

Excitement overcame Elspeth and she no longer felt the chill in the air. When all was clear and she was certain that everyone had left, she retrieved her lantern and tiptoed over into the graveyard. Her shoes were sodden, absolutely soaked and her thick woollen stockings were also wet through. Amazingly, the young wench felt no fear as she passed beneath the lych gate. Gravestones stood in neat rows, snow covering their bases and tops, making them difficult to read. Crouching in front of the headstone nearest the gate, a wet and cold young woman lifted her lantern.

It wasn't the cold, or lack of fluid that made Elspeth Culley faint that night in the quaint little graveyard, but the words revealed when she had brushed the snow aside. Luckily, a local spice trader had attended service that Sunday eve and had hung back only to pay respect to his deceased wife, who had died of consumption a few months earlier. The concerned gentleman had lifted the young woman from the snow and carried her to the local surgeon's house. Dr. Prindle dosed her with aqua vitae and his wife helped the poor child take off her wet clothes. After fetching some of their daughter's fresh clothes, she made Elspeth comfortable near the welcome, roaring Yule fire and sent a servant to give word to her father of her whereabouts.

The whole affair remained a mystery to all but old Elijah Culley. Only he knew why his daughter was out alone in the graveyard that night long ago and he would take their secret to his grave. Elspeth never felt any regret about her actions when she finally learnt the identity of her beau... at least, if fate was kind, she would be able to keep her Irish surname! For unbeknown to her, she had fallen madly and helplessly in love with Thomas, husband of the deceased Mrs. Louisa Culley and second cousin to Elspeth's own father! Like old Elijah, Thomas was a successful spice trader. He and his ailing wife had moved to live closer to his only remaining relatives. Poor Louisa had insisted that Thomas should be near to loved ones for support after death had claimed her. Sadly, she had recently been diagnosed with tuberculosis, the dreadful killer disease.

Word travelled fast about the young wench's graveyard faint and Thomas Culley felt rather flattered to have such a beauty interested in him. He made a point of visiting Elijah's house the following day to enquire after Elspeth's health. As soon as he laid eyes upon her in daylight, he knew that she was the woman for him. They became betrothed soon after their first meeting and the Culley couple courted happily. Thomas's fiancée was eager to please her man and just as keen to learn exactly how best to please him! Innocent but sensual pleasure took her beyond anything she had ever dreamed and each time they met, Thomas would wonder what he had done to deserve such an incredible woman. In his eyes, she had everything; intelligence, wit, lust, beauty and desire, but most of all, she had so much love! He was besotted with his bride-to-be and neither wanted to wait long for betrothal. Townsfolk were gossiping and disgusted by the match. 'Absolute and down right disrespectful', was the word going round and Elspeth soon gained the name of harlot. Not that she or the other Culleys cared. Her mother was long gone and her father and new man rather enjoyed the drama. After all, they were of Irish stock and had never quite felt at home in England. Celtic blood runs strong and this pair would make sure that the Culley name would carry on.

Nights of sheer, unadulterated passion between two wild and hungry lovers only made Elspeth more lustful for her soul mate. The chemistry between this man and woman was incredible, their bodies thrashed and entwined in a tangle of sexual delight each time they had chance. Daring trysts became a habit and the aroused couple would gain ultimate pleasure. They had surely met their sexual match.

Time passed too slowly and the forbidden bond reached the heights of passion until the blessed day arrived. Mr Thomas and Miss Elspeth Culley had aptly chosen the pagan day of fornication and procreation, Beltane as their Wedding day. The bride wore the most beautiful silken white robe, heavily embroidered with lavish gold, floral patterns. Her posy was filled with spices, so the aroma drifted around the church and flowers were everywhere possible on this happy day. Thomas and Elijah looked handsome in dark green doublets and hose with matching velvet bonnets. But the most dapper guest attending St. Editha's Church on that blissful day, was proud Albert, who blew his large, hooked nose on poor Bess's only kerchief throughout the ceremony. The kind hearted soul cried buckets of joy and gave his wee friend a special gift... a compass that he had inherited from his father who had been a sailor for most of his life. Delighted with the heirloom, Elspeth vowed to pass it on to their first born son within the blissful union.

Honeymoon night that Beltane back in 1537 was a delight to remember at the Cock Inn. Elijah Culley, having guessed the couple's secret trysts, had searched for the perfect venue with a name fitting for its randy guests' desires. At last the frustrated lovers could fornicate legally. No more snatched sexual encounters or secret liaisons! As Elspeth lay in the narrow four poster bed with her new husband, her head resting on his chest, she reached under the cotton sheets and held his erect penis. Instantly responding, Thomas Culley softly kissed his beautiful bride, tracing his tongue down her delicate neck. His wife groaned with sheer pleasure and she squeezed her hand tightly, just as he'd shown her, as his tongue and lips teased the flesh of her stiffened nipples. He caressed her firm, pert breasts and entered her with a groan of ecstasy. Finally, the passionate couple could enjoy each other all night and into the early hours... without any inhibitions or feelings of guilt... and make as much noise as they wanted! There was no need for false modesty in the inns of the time. All knew that they were newlyweds and a certain amount of creaking bed ropes and cries of shock or ecstasy met with hearty approval and lifting of tankards by the rowdy guests drinking directly below.

Thomas Culley was incredibly happy. New love and contentment had been the last feelings that the middle-aged man had expected since the loss of his wife. He still visited his first love's grave and never once felt self-conscious as he crouched close to her final resting place, whispering his news. His late wife, Louisa would have been pleased that Thomas had met mischievous Elspeth. The two women possessed a similar temperament, each being head-strong and passionate about everything they believed in. Both of Thomas's wives would fight for what they deemed right and often voiced strong opinions when others would shrink from confrontation. The tall, proud but gentle spice trader knelt on the icy ground and placed a posy of violets on his dead wife, Louisa's grave. A sudden rattling cough caused him to fall forward, so he steadied himself and stood slowly upright, regaining his balance. He reached for the kerchief that Louisa had given him and held it to his lips, closing his eyes as he smelt lavender, her favourite perfume. His dry cough had become a nuisance and he would be glad when winter gave way to spring that year. Tiny spatters of blood on the soft white cotton were hardly noticeable to the colour blind merchant. If only he had known, he would never have become betrothed to his Elspeth.

That winter was long and hard for the Culleys as unbeknown to them, Thomas's late wife had left him a horrific legacy. The couple were destined to suffer terrible misfortune. All too soon, the dreaded symptoms of the debilitating disease that had carried off Louisa, became evident as Thomas suffered more distressing coughing fits and his fine, muscular body began to waste away. Love kept him and his new wife close during the precious few weeks that they were destined to share. Fate was being so cruel to the couple who adored one another with absolute unconditional love. Bravely they made the most of Thomas's final weeks and on the eve of his death he managed to whisper a dying wish to his heart-broken wife. Her man had suffered greatly in the time she had known him and his face now showed the strain. His stunningly green eyes still sparkled when they met his true love's gaze, yet the hollow darkness beneath put years on his true age.

Elspeth and her young cook, Bess had carried the matrimonial bed into the parlour, so that Thomas could stay warm by the hearth. Bess had been a loyal servant to the Culleys since Elspeth was a child and they had become firm friends. Unlike Elspeth, poor Bess had no hope of meeting a partner for she had been cursed with rickets and her young limbs bowed ugly beneath her skirts. The disability made Bess sway as she walked and local children often made fun of her gait. But Bess would waddle on with her stick and pay no mind on the surface, yet inside she hurt like hell.

One night late in January in the year 1538, Elspeth Culley was lying in bed with her head close to her husband's, next to a roaring fire. Every time Thomas fought for his breath, the young woman winced. It was as if her heart was being pierced every time her man inhaled. The fresh herbs that she had dried and preserved in warmer days smelled so good and pure. She had hung silken bags filled with lavender, rosemary and thyme on the bed posts and the aroma seemed to calm her love. Elspeth kissed Thomas's sweat- beaded brow and gently bathed it with a cool cloth. His eyes opened and he looked at her for the last time. A single tear ran onto the feather-stuffed pillow as the choking began. Turning him onto his side, Elspeth wailed his name and told him of her undying love. Struggling for breath, the sound of Thomas Culley's last moments were not pleasant. The blood from his collapsed lungs was thick and darkest red. He pressed his face to his beautiful wife's breast and held it firmly there, pulling her weight on top of him. Elspeth let out a despairing cry that echoed eerily through the small room and up into the eaves of the sad home.

Bess returned to her mistress's house the following day and found her weeping and exhausted with her husband's body held close to her own. Tears streamed down her face as the loyal cook waddled off to fetch Dr. Prindle before more heartache and bad luck could befall her special friend. Thomas had made clear to both women that his final request was for them to do everything in their power to ensure that his wife was looked after well. Their precious only child must be brought into the world safely with no more turmoil. Bess was determined to respect her late master's wishes. If the newborn was a man-child, his father's wish was to call him Master Tom Culley but if the child was a pretty, wee wench, she was destined to go by the name of Miss Sushana Culley.

Chapter 3

Premature Arrival for a Little Treasure

Bess and Elspeth managed to turn the tiny house into a pretty home during the months that followed Thomas's untimely death. The two close friends made sure that Thomas's spirit remained in the peaceful cottage despite his bodily absence. He had left his widow the deeds to his business and the heavy, precious spice chests would ensure a tidy income for her, Bess, Albert and the child-to-be. Elspeth's pregnancy had been uncomfortable since conception. Although her belly swelled healthily, sickness and exhaustion wracked the poor woman's body. She had been strong so far in her life, but the shock of her husband's ill-health and dreadful demise had shattered her spirit beyond repair. Occasionally Bess managed to make her mistress smile, but the wonderful, contagious laughs and giggles that Elspeth had always been known for, had rapidly diminished in her grief. Time would tell whether the spark would ever return, but Bess feared the worst as she sat with Elspeth one summer's eve in July.

The birds were singing late that evening and the smell of freshly baked bread lingered in the air. Bess had baked four manchet loaves to last the week. Old Elijah visited his daughter every night and Bess's brother, Albert had promised to drop by the following day to tend to the garden. Since Elspeth had taken to her bed in the fifth month of pregnancy, Bess had carried out all of the chores and found little time for gardening. Her older brother had been quick to offer his services; he had always been protective of his unfortunate sister and helped whenever possible. The last of the loaves had cooled and Bess began to place them in the ark to protect them from mice and damp. She started when she heard the almighty crash and hobbled as fast as she could towards the source of the noise.

Bess's heart raced when she saw the crumpled heap on the parlour floor in front of the fire. She noticed the upturned piss pot and skewiff bed and realised with dread that Elspeth had fallen whilst trying to carry the pot over to the window. How many times had she warned the weak woman not to try to do things that Bess was quite capable of doing! Rushing over to her aid, Bess noticed blood on Elspeth's nightgown and panicked... The baby! By all accounts, wee Culley was not due until September time! 'God's teeth! Pray let it not be now!' Bess whispered as she checked the other woman's pulse. It was weak, but she could feel a flutter. The tiny, bent woman grabbed the taller wench under the armpits and heaved her backwards onto the bed. With a kiss and comforting word, Bess grabbed her shawl and made for the door. If her gut feelings were to be trusted, this baby was not going to wait much longer.

Twenty minutes had passed since Bess left the pregnant Elspeth safely on her bed. Now she watched from the parlour door as Dr. Prindle and the old midwife fussed around their patient. It was unusual for a doctor to be present at a birthing, but the family doctor was taking no chances where Elspeth was concerned. If only she had fallen for his fine and healthy eldest son, he thought as he held the pewter cup to his patient's lips, encouraging her to drink some of the sweetened mead and milk mixture. Bess had prepared cotton sheets and water from the well simmered in the heavy pot over the hearth, but when it came to assisting in this matter, the squeamish cook kept her place by the kitchen door. Every few minutes, Bess disappeared into the scullery to scrub the pots, trying to remain sane. The woman wrung her arthritic hands with worry... Surely God would not take another of her loved ones?

It seemed as though days had passed rather than hours. The painful and distressing labour dragged on for almost ten hours and Bess mouthed a silent prayer of thanks when at last, she heard a healthy vibrating cry from tiny lungs. Without a thought, Bess threw away the scrubbing brush and rushed into the room. Colours merged in a swirl of blurred confusion as the cook's eyes darted, wide and petrified between the tiny bundle of life and the white cloth that covered the curves of her best friend's lifeless body. The surgeon's hands and lower arms were still covered in Elspeth's bright red lifeblood but the midwife had bathed the body before she had wrapped it. Dr. Prindle was deeply saddened and stood staring at the scene with helpless disbelief. Bess suppressed her grief momentarily and aided the good man by wiping her friend's life blood from his shaking hands. He was weeping but his tears were in vain. Elspeth had gone. Hopefully she had already joined her soul mate, but for the time being at least, the tiny babe needed to be loved and nurtured by someone special. The future care of a child left motherless by death during childbirth, all too common in these hard times, was usually decided long before the due date. Elspeth had paid heed to this tradition and had arranged for Bess, her loyal servant friend, to adopt her firstborn.

The devastated spinster managed to calm her inner turmoil and closed her big, brown eyes for a few seconds. Slowly, she approached the newborn baby. A stray tear rolled down the grieving woman's cheek as she peered beneath the swaddling cloth and caught the first glimpse of the tiny creature. Eyes tightly shut, the baby wriggled its delicate form within the small, wooden cot that her Grandpa had carved from the finest walnut. The baby girl had been hastily checked for imperfections by the old midwife. Not a single flaw could be found on her delicate wee form. The newborn babe was bathed in the softest glow of firelight. Flickering shadows cast from the candlelight danced across this delightful child. She had battled a traumatic birthing and lost both parents, yet there was an undeniable aura of strength within her fragile being. Bess gazed tenderly at the miniature figure who was the image of her beautiful mother. 'So...' thought the newly appointed Aunt Bess, 'this is little Miss Culley'. With a deep, heartfelt sigh of both sorrow and relief, Aunt Bess took hold of tiny Sushana and held her close. Before she settled payment, the new surrogate mother asked the midwife to fetch the wet nurse immediately. Bess turned to the exhausted retired ship's surgeon and begged him to report the premature birth and her friend's death to the priest. Time was precious and the superstitious Irish wench would not settle until the bairn had been baptised. The Culley clan had already suffered way too much misfortune and she would be taking no chances with her new charge.

Mrs. Turnbull arrived half an hour later. Two well cared for, plump boys with rosy cheeks followed close behind their buxom Ma. The room seemed to light up with colour and vibrancy as the pretty, tall and heavy-set wench bustled in, large skirts flowing with the sway of her wide, child-bearing hips. Bess took an instant liking to the newcomer and had no qualms about handing Sushana over to suckle from her ample, milk-filled bubbies. The tiny head lifted, eyelids fluttered and rosebud lips parted, then basic instinct took over. Mama Turnbull smiled and plumped her wide behind onto a stool that appeared much too small to hold her. A warm, comforting feeling of relief spread over poor Bess as she began to feel hope at last. Some of the burdens would soon be lifted, she felt sure of this.

The two women giggled like teenagers as they shared tales of their youth and local kinsfolk. They purposely avoided any morbid talk in front of the children, but equally they were protecting each other from further pain. Ma Turnbull was only twenty years old but had been bearing children since her arranged marriage at fourteen. Her body was well used to childbirth and suckling; it had hardly had a break from either since she fell pregnant the first time she had lain with her husband. Benjamin Turnbull was a farm hand, a sturdy, strong and ruddy young fellow who had fallen for the buxom virginal milkmaid the first time he set eyes on her. Violet was her name but, since giving birth to her firstborn, her natural maternal instinct took over and everyone called her Ma Turnbull. She took to babies like no other wench and produced more milk than even her robust fifth son, Jacob could ingest. He was a greedy wee whipper-snapper by all accounts! So, Ma Turnbull had swapped her days as a milk-maid for wet nursing and was always the first wench on the list of every pregnant lass in the city. Sadly she often breastfed motherless wains due to the high risks of childbirth. Bess believed that Ma Turnbull was fated to be Sushana's wet nurse. Had the baby gone full term, Ma Turnbull would have already been busy feeding the butcher's baby who was due to be born that week.

Unbeknown to kindly Bess, the rabbit's foot and lucky silver coin that she had placed in Sushana's cot awaiting her birth on the twelfth day of July that fateful summer, would remain with Sushana many nights of her life. Bess would swear for years to come that these good luck charms were the reason for the unexpectedly happy days that followed the devastating times within the walls of the house that had seen such sadness that year.

CHAPTER 4

Growing up in Henry's England

The morning sun lit the tiny room where young Sushana Culley slept. Her tiny form lay still as Bess looked in on her for the third time that Spring day. Bess liked to let the child sleep as long as possible and that Beltane would be no exception, even though she and her brother were keen to take her to enjoy the popular celebrations. The prettiest frock imaginable lay on the wooden child's chair in the corner of Shana's bedroom. Bess's arthritic hands were sore, yet still surprisingly dextrous. A smile spread across her lined face as she imagined her late friend's joy at the sight of her beautiful daughter dressed in such finery.

Walking over to the window where her Elspeth used to sit and brush her long hair, Bess sat on a high backed chair and watched as the little girl slept. The resemblance between the tiny wench and her deceased mother was uncanny, thought Bess as she took in every facial detail. She made a silent prayer of thanks that at least there was not much wrong with her eyesight, despite numerous other bodily ailments! Her giggles turned into a rattling splutter of a cough. That instant Shana stirred and turned her face towards the source of the disturbance. With wee nose crumpled, she opened her speedwell blue eyes and looked straight at Bess. Yawning widely, the toddler stretched her arms skyward and scanned the room; Shana had made a habit of this daily check. Her sharp eyes quickly noticed the gorgeous frock and lit up with glee.

The previous night had been Beltane Eve when Albert and Bess had sat together, as they had every night since Shana's traumatic birth. They had these late night discussions about the progress of their unexpected family addition. Neither sibling had married and certainly never expected to rear a child, so it had been a steep learning curve for both parties. During candlelit evenings, over a glass of mead, the pair earnestly discussed the progress of their precious charge. They would consult Ma Turnbull over the tiniest deviation from what they deemed normal child development. The homely wet nurse listened to every word earnestly and treated them all seriously; however she later shared many a gentle joke with her husband in the privacy of their tiny overcrowded but clean and happy home.

Both Bess and her brother had gained a fair amount of weight since becoming Shana's surrogate parents. To say that they were a 'little portly' was no exaggeration. Both had been determined that their little girl would want for nothing and spent money made from the spice trade on wholesome food and the best of everything. Albert made a habit of sharing the delicious meals that his sister prepared to tempt Shana's appetite. He would arrive at the house early every morning and leave as late as possible each night. His protective instinct was very strong and he felt responsible for the safety of Bess and Sushana.

Times had been extremely hard since Elspeth died. News of the Culley couple's death had provided the parishioners of East Teignmouth with plenty to discuss. Although the majority of visitors were well meaning, Bess and Albert quickly tired of the seemingly never-ending stream of townsfolk. The tiny bairn was unusually patient when grabbed from Ma Turnbull's succulent bosom, all too often mid feed. Aged spinsters displaying comically tragic expressions on their wrinkled faces clutched Shana to their shrivelled, empty bosoms. Ironically, the steady flow of visitors provided some amusement to the grieving Albert and Bess with their displays of sincere yet exaggerated misery. Many offering their last respects and condolences had never even met either of the deceased. Amongst them, Bess recognised the very women who had maligned poor Elspeth when she fell hopelessly in love with Thomas. Despite their insincerity and morbid curiosity, she provided cold meats, fresh bread and mead aplenty for the steady flow of mourners which she thought would never end. Elspeth and Thomas' closest friends and family were thoughtful enough to stay away and deal with their personal grief. The sensation seekers began to dwindle when news of the latest condemned prisoners reached the taverns and they were distracted by the prospect of a new execution spectacle.

Sushana seemed to be canny of folk as she lay in her cot observing each in seemingly great detail, as if fully aware of their intentions. Albert made sure that he was ever present as he and his sister were well aware of the risks of exploitation. Baby Culley had been left a tidy inheritance. Thomas had built an extremely successful spice trade which would soon be the only one in the area. Devastated by the news of the loss of his daughter, old Elijah had been utterly grief stricken and took to his bed soon after. Not even a visit from Bess with his tiny granddaughter could lighten his spirits but he managed to summon enough strength to hand over the deeds to his property and thriving spice trading company to Doctor Prindle. The old man was exhausted with grief and disappointment. He knew that his friend would safeguard Sushana's inheritance and prevent Petrus Gregorie, his devious apprentice, from cheating her out of her livelihood. Elijah Culley had battled so much tragedy in his long life and was tired and ready to meet his maker. The loss of his Elspeth had been more than he could bear. As a devout Christian, Elijah sent for the priest and was given his last rights. Loyal friends gathered around his deathbed and Dr. Prindle bled his broken-hearted patient hourly, although his efforts were in vain. As the clock struck midnight welcoming the first day of May, Elijah Culley breathed out his final breath.

As Bess played peek-a-boo with Shana whilst dressing her in the delightful Beltane costume, tears welled in her sore eyes. Dr. Pringle's wife had called in shortly after midnight when she noticed smoke billowing from the chimney. She was promptly met at the heavy oak door by Albert who invited her inside for a jug of warm broth. As they sat together around the hearth, Mrs. Pringle broke the news. Bess and Albert were sad to hear of Elijah's death but also somewhat relieved. The old man was well into his forties; a fair old age and losing Elspeth had finished him. Humming a traditional harvest ditty while her gnarled fingers laced little Shana tightly into her May Day costume, Bess did her best to keep her spirits high. This was to be a day for much merrymaking and Elspeth's Grandfather would not have wanted his passing to spoil his Granddaughter's first taste of the May Day celebrations.

Bess had expertly made Shana's farthingale as light as a feather. Once in place, it held out a kirtle made from fine, delicate linen to keep the child cool. Layer upon layer of the prettiest yellow silk skirts were added to make an outfit in the style of top fashion. A chemise of purest white silk exaggerated Shana's plump peachy coloured cheeks and her blue eyes had lit up with absolute glee as she was adorned with the layers of silk. If Bess had not have been sewing the long golden tippets to the shoulders of the richly embroidered bodice late the night before, she would not have been aware of the latest Culley family loss… so she was determined to give Shana a happy day. Besides, the child was far too young to understand death even though it had touched her short life too many times already!

Bess looked at the lovely maiden with immense pride and wished that her Granddaddy could have laid eyes upon her before he'd gone. 'Our sweet maiden! Ye are verily a nonpareil May queen in the making! Ye should be crowned this May Day methinks, belike ye have the need of a pair of stilts?' Shana smiled at Bess' delight and toddled unsteadily towards her, burbling away in a language of her own. The tired woman took the child into her arms and held her close, kissing the top of her head gently as she began to braid her hair. Almost forgetting the tiny replica of her May child that she had fashioned from a wooden clothes peg, Bess reached into the deep pocket of her skirt and brought out the wonderful doll to the toddler's delight. She had even managed to make a tiny posy and mayflower headdress for the miniature likeness and the tiniest string of pearls around its neck. The little girl was delighted and mesmerised by the tiny effigy and she immediately began to play with it. Bess watched the child lovingly and soon they were both lost in the magical world of make believe.

Once Shana's hair was neatly braided, Bess placed a ring of woven may and bluebells on her crown and a string of her late mother's pearls around her fragile neck.

The little girl did nothing to conceal her excitement and Bess thanked God for the perfect child whose nature was so like her mother's. Whooping with delight, Shana toddled over to the bedroom window and pulled at the curtains, lifting herself a little higher so that she could peer through the dense glass panes at the scene below. Falling back into Bess' thick skirts she laughed at the sound of the horns and was intrigued by the colourful blur of the parade that she could only glimpse in the streets below.

Albert's voice added to the commotion, prompting Bess to make sure that she and Shana relieved themselves in the privvie before joining the Beltane procession. Her brother had been busy all morn decorating the house with fresh smelling garlands of leaves, blossoming hawthorn and bluebells. His eyes were still sore from crying the night before. He had had to steel himself away to join a group of townsfolk for the traditional collection of a tall, strong birch tree from the woods. Fond but painful memories of past Beltane Eves spent with Elspeth filled his mind. The close friends had enjoyed years of celebrations together and were always keen to follow pagan tradition. Having helped to erect the May tree that year, poor Albert could not bear to stay and watch the womenfolk and children bedecking the Maypole with brightly coloured ribbons. He left as soon as the tree stood proudly in its position in the town square as the centrepiece of the following day's festivities. He had joined his sister and was glad of it. He had always believed that things happened for a reason and that night, it almost felt as though he was being guided by Elspeth from the Otherworld. His friend had always looked up to him and never worried about class rules. Greedy for Albert's knowledge, which had been passed down by word of mouth for centuries, Elspeth would spend most of her time with him and was never put off by the disapproval of others. All that she had ever given him was unconditional love and he had never taken that blessing for granted. The unlikely best friends rarely had secrets and he remembered how happy she had been when she had finally married her soul mate...

Attaching a basket of wild flowers, gathered in memory of Shana's Mama, to the door knob for her delightful daughter to discover, Albert's attention was drawn towards the Jack o' the Green. Dressed in a green outfit covered with leaves, he led a steadily growing procession of joyous folk along the road towards the centre of town. Amongst the many costumed revellers Albert saw people dressed as bears, stilt walkers, fire eaters, jugglers, minstrels, jesters and mummers. Robin Hood and his merry men danced alongside George and the dragon as mummers capered in competition to promote their play on this special day. A gentle tug at his coat caused Albert to start and a pretty grinning face looked up at him adoringly. She was perfect... no less. Shana squealed with delight as Albert picked her up and swung her around. Unable to stop her laughter, she began to hiccup and Bess chuckled to herself. Soon the little girl noticed the basket and carefully placed her peg dolly on the bed of flowers. Grabbing Albert's strong, rough hand, she took charge and pulled him through the door towards the animated parade. With Bess following close behind, the little family wove their way into the heaving crowd, leaving sadness behind them, for the meantime at least.

The noise was terrific, like nothing that Shana had ever experienced. She lapped up every gleeful moment. Lively festival-goers were determined to ensure that spring had awoken and if not, they would surely awaken it! Frolicking couples, still horny from their encounters the previous night, skipped along hand-in-hand to the melodic sound of the hurdy-gurdy. The Master of ceremonies urged those still indoors to join him. Blasting his trumpet as a final demand, he yelled for all to unite in joyful merriment. Shana was mesmerised by the whole affair. Playing out before her was a scene that she would carry into her adulthood and she took in every single detail. Everyone who saw Shana sighed and commented on her undeniable beauty. Albert implored his sister not to take any back-handed comments about Shana's parents to heart. He was well aware of Bess' over-protective nature and was hurt himself whenever he heard the distasteful mutters.

Once they had arrived at the town square festival-goers were treated to all kinds of delights. Shana was overcome with the sights, smells and sounds of so many different things. The young child was in utter awe at each new experience and Bess and Albert soon noticed that she was afeared of little. Even the brightly painted marionettes that moved in a frighteningly humanlike manner failed to scare little Miss Culley. The child showed her appreciation by laughing out loud with the cutest chuckle imaginable. Throughout the day, Shana insisted on being ridden back high on Albert's tired and aching shoulders to witness the show with the little puppet man wearing a jester's motley. The child was fascinated by the play, laughing at the main character's nose which almost touched his hideously jutting chin! Sushana's laughter seemed to be contagious and the old Italian puppeteer sought her out after his show to give her a handful of freshly made comfits and a huge wet kiss. The skilful man introduced himself as Signor

Bologna, his plump, red cheeks glistening with perspiration. Mopping his brow with a silken kerchief, he chortled with glee and gratitude and admitted that the bag of coins collected after that performance was the heaviest ever. He was convinced that his luck was due to 'ze leetle bambina and her laaaaarv of Pulcheeeeno.' Shana gladly accepted the old man's gratitude, managing to charm the crowd once more by mimicking the evil little puppet Pulcino's squawking tones. The crowd roared, totally smitten with the natural entertainer and poor, humble Albert could do nothing but blush and hold his little May princess higher so that she could be seen and admired by all. Even Pulcino's huge stick, easily as large as himself, failed to put off the fearless wench. Throughout the show Pulcino freely used the weapon to beat down each character. The nasty little chicken-voiced puppet even beat his own baby, shrieking his gleeful cackle; 'That's the way to do it!' Nothing seemed to deter the confident toddler; in fact she embraced the horrid wooden hunchback when he was brought out of the tent by his master to greet his newest and greatest fan. Bess loathed the whole concept of the show and chose to spend time with her servant friends, carding wool in a tent on the outskirts of the market square. She had never been one to enjoy cruelty and neither had her brother, but kind natured Albert was putty in the child's hands and would do almost anything to please her.

Bess left the mischievous carnival-loving pair and observed with affection the uncanny method of communication that they shared, needing to use no words... they had the same kindred connection that Albert had shared with Elspeth. The aging and tired woman sighed with envy at their unusual rapport and turned to leave them to enjoy the merriment. A last minute dread prompted Bess to warn her brother... 'Ye have a care to avoid tempting our wench with 'fulthy' pye meats, bre'r! Ye know full well how the rat meat and barbers' beef finds its way 'tween pastries at these festivities!' Bess was very glad that she was not alone in rearing the child but, even so, she had taken on the maternal role rather comfortably.

Gathering her heavy, mud-splattered skirt up in her twisted fingers, Bess rolled her eyes skyward when she realised that her brother had not heard her heed. Turning on an unsteady heel, she prepared herself for the battle through the hot, sweaty crowd. Shouldering her way past a drunken halfwit, she ducked just in time as he puked semi-digested oatcakes and stale ale over the unfortunate folk standing too near. Bess was carried with the flow of scattering spectators, luckily in the direction of her friends' tent! Her warnings about bad food had gone unheard and she could not help but worry about Albert and the child. They had suffered too many losses and she had understandably become rather paranoid about death. Living in such deadly times, Bess knew only too well that the strongest alone survived. Her friends had warned her weeks before Beltane that poisonous meats were being baked into pyes. Barber-surgeons had been struggling for trade since the King had made beards fashionable for menfolk. Word was out that they had begun to trade limbs sawn from suffering customers with some food traders. Bess believed every word of it and had good reason to, since meat was said to have been scarce due to an unusually high loss of livestock that year! Sucking her cheeks in comically, Bess' stomach turned as she shuddered at the thought of eating human flesh! 'Fie! Rat meat is all too common amongst the hoodlum bakers, but feastin' upon 'uman flesh! By my troth, if ever so much as a finger passes our princess' lips, I'll 'ave 'im in the stocks!' Bess mumbled, cursing her poor brother's lack of common sense as she fought her way through the drunken partygoers. She barely noticed the cutpurse following her closely behind as she hurried into a darkened alley to piss.

The crowning of the May queen always proved to be a spectacular event. This traditional highlight of the day drew crowds almost as well as a good hanging! This year was no exception and Mary, the May queen, loved all the attention. Soon after midday, a beautiful floral throne was uncovered in front of the tall phallic Maypole. 'A fine sample' thought Albert as he surveyed the Maypole with inward pride. Still riding atop of his shoulders, Shana blankly refused to let go of the little basket with her doll tucked safely inside. No matter how many times Albert offered to carry the treasure, the stubborn child refused to hand it over. She began to wriggle, trying to gain a better view of the popular event. Albert hitched her higher and felt tiny fingers grab onto a generous tuft of hair as Shana instinctively realised that he was helping her up for a better view. The wench was clever! Pointing a chubby finger toward the May queen as she was led into the market square, the gleeful girl held onto Albert with her strong little legs.

This year, Mary Wood had been chosen as the prettiest wench. Mary was so very fair and had a beautiful, well developed body for a girl so young. Her long golden locks spilled onto her shoulders, over plump ripe breasts covered only by a sheer white dress made of finest linen. Exquisite embroidery embellished the simple frock and Shana yelled with delight as the May queen was crowned with an intricately woven rowan twig and may blossom crown. For a moment, Albert could not believe that he had heard Shana talk, but when she repeated the words over and over, he could not contain his joy. He jumped up and down, spinning the little girl around with delight. Her yelps of glee made the crowd cheer as she shouted Pulcino's line, 'Azzzawaya do it!' she cried, giggling uncontrollably at the reactions she invoked around her. She was a natural born entertainer and Albert was so very proud. As he imagined how proud Elspeth would have been, he hitched his little companion back onto his shoulders just in time to see eight handsome young men battle for the coveted honour of lifting the May queen onto her floral throne. Only two lucky winners would have the honour of carrying their queen around for the rest of the day… at her command of course. The people could not have chosen a more fitting Beltane queen, as Mary had managed to keep her virginity intact. Happily she had joined the other youngsters the night before in front of the May fire and stayed out all night in the open with the boy she loved. They had not succumbed to temptation and managed to avoid the traditionally expected fornication antics.

Before sunrise on May Day, many rosy-cheeked teens had returned to the towns brandishing blossoming May branches with which to decorate buildings and celebrate the season of renewal and growth. A few went back to their family with a ribbon marked by their Beltane lover in a pagan Hand fasting ritual. Their hands had been bound together with two ribbons, signed or marked by each and they had agreed to enter into a relationship for a year and a day. Every Beltane Eve, all who had previously been joined in a Hand fasting union were able to renew their vows... and commit to their lover for another year and a day. As was the custom, young people enjoyed having sex out in the open and 'blessing' the fields where they lay. It was sure to be a good harvest this coming year!

Unusually, this year the May queen actually represented purity, unlike some of her predecessors who had produced fine 'Merry-be-gots' exactly nine months later. The may blossom symbolised female fertility and every year, young men were keen to sew their seed during a night of frolicking with a maiden before a raging Beltane fire, under the watchful eye of the moon. Many a girl, flushed with memories of newfound passion the previous night, awoke to bathe in early Mayday morning dew. It was believed that a wench who washed her face in this powerful dew would enjoy undying beauty and a woman who did the same could retain a youthful glow to her skin for years to come. 'Twas also said that the precious droplets could rid the skin of freckles and even cure neck ache! Any aspiring sailor, who washed his hands in carefully collected May morn dewdrops, would be assured that the knots he tied would always be the best.

Albert's feet ached as he walked from one entertainment to the next. The town was buzzing with adventure... He had stopped outside the tavern when he noticed a small group of people standing on tiptoe, pushing each other to gain a better view. Shana's whoops of excitement told him that the sight was worthwhile. With his little May princess guiding him, his curiosity soon paid off. An old crone sat on a wooden block and a beautiful brightly coloured bird sat atop a pole next to her. This bird was huge and had the brightest blue, yellow and green feathers! Tiny piercing eyes surveyed their audience and it appeared as if the creature wore a whitish skin face mask. Shana was smitten by this new find and cooed excitedly. Folk were ranting and calling for the old woman to be hanged as a witch and her cursed familiar drowned, yet others just stood in awe at the spectacle.

A cackling voice squawked periodically, 'Ye pox-riddled cheatin' gudgeon!' The line was repeated over and over, word perfect every time yet the crone did not appear to speak the offensive words. Surely this bewitched creature was the culprit, 'but how?' thought Albert. The fast-growing mob was becoming angry and out of control, urging each other on in their mounting aggression, threatening to take the crone and her 'monster' to the stocks. The old woman was confused and simply looked around helplessly, eyes wild and wide with bewilderment.

A piece of rough parchment had been tacked to the bird's pole and not one of the spectators was able to decipher the words. Albert squinted as he tried in vain to recognise some of the symbols that his Elspeth had taught him in years gone by. Nothing jogged his dwindling memory and he was relieved when he spotted young Master Gregorie emerging from the tavern. Hollering above the raucous crowd, Albert managed to catch Petrus Gregorie's attention and he wove his way over towards the ruckus. Shaking hands with Petrus was something that Albert tried to avoid because the man physically gave him the creeps. Standing about five feet tall, the fellow looked sickly. He had a grey tinge to his wax-like skin and had always reminded Albert of an undertaker. Greasy hair flopped over his eyes and his hat always appeared too small for his overlarge head. With an inward snigger, Albert realised that the hunch on Master Gregorie's back reminded him of the marionette Pulcino. Clearing his throat with embarrassment and feeling slightly guilty, Albert tried to explain what was going on over the jeers of the ever-raging crowd.

Master Gregorie was only twenty yet looked much older. The apprentice spice trader had been trying to worm his way into his Master, Elijah's business. Petrus had worked for old Elijah Culley since he was a young lad. Elijah had been kind enough to take the sickly orphan in and give him some dignity and the opportunity to learn a trade. Nevertheless Petrus had taken advantage of the generous man and had hoped one day to marry his only daughter… but his plans were ruined when she fell in love with the widower. Bess loathed Petrus Gregorie as much as Elspeth had and had been appalled when she recently realised that he had set his sights on Elspeth's newborn for future betrothal! It was a wonder that she even allowed him anywhere near the home since she had learned his intentions. Unfortunately having no alternative choice, Bess and Albert had been forced to accept Petrus' help with running a business in which they had no experience. Bess was keen to ensure that Petrus had nothing to do with the baby and all business needing his guidance was conducted in her brother's presence. Albert thought the weasel-like weakling perfectly harmless, but his sister trusted him less and less. Petrus read aloud the message on the parchment to the old crone's glee… It was soon learned that even she had no idea what was written. The mob began to settle as Petrus' monotone voice read out the well scribed message:

'To whom it may be of concern. Prithee take heed that I hereby pass into the possession of the holder, the rightful ownership of my parrot, Captain Crackler. Ne'er have I known such loyalty from any so strong as is within him. I am greatly sorrowed to be forced to part with him to settle a quarrel during a card game with Charlie Grotten.

Captain Crackler has been in my company since 1525. To whomever it may concern, prithee feed him well with fruits and nuts aplenty and offer him protection, as he may aggravate some with his unfavourable tongue.

Lest the unfortunate occurrence of ownership may rise, the bird is worth naught less than two Doubloons.

Yours under Command of King Henry VIII of Englande, Captain Henry Trefold; in obedient service of His Majesty the King of Englande.'

On mention of the King's name, the crowd scattered, thugs included and the old woman stood and stretched her crooked spine as straight as it would allow. Her relief was plain to see and she reached a filthy hand toward the prized bird which immediately squawked and took a bony finger between its vice-like beak. The crone's screams attracted new spectators and the sight was one that would not be an easy one to forget. It became quite clear to mild natured Albert that the old woman had been mistreating the poor creature that had been waiting for the chance to strike in a revenge attack. Shana found the whole thing utterly hilarious as blood and feathers flew through the air and cries of disgust and fear were heard. Not a single soul dared to help the woman until Albert took pity and passed Shana to a homely looking wench nearby. With one hand he took firm hold of the bird's chained legs and with the other, he expertly manipulated thumb over lower beak, fingers under the upper and prized the cruel bill open. Quite suddenly, the Macaw became still and peered at Albert with what seemed to be total respect. The crowd was amazed and clapped encouragingly as the large bird stepped onto Albert's shoulder. Shana also clapped her chubby little hands together and opened her arms wide asking to be passed back to him. The crone had taken her seat back on the log and was crying with pain and relief. Albert grabbed his child who immediately reached for the bird's head… gasps of fear were heard as the bird again opened its sharp beak, offering a dark grey lump of a tongue to the tiny fingers. Gently, Shana stroked Captain Crackler's feathered head and repeated her newly learned words… to everyone's delight. Oblivious to the newfound friendships, the crone managed to hold out her uninjured hand and demand payment. Unfortunately for Albert, he was not carrying enough coins to pay for Shana's new pet, but the conniving Petrus quickly took the parchment and offered to settle payment with the old woman. Slyly, he took her arm and led her in the direction of the barber-surgeon's house. Albert sighed with wary relief knowing that he could expect a visit from the creep the following day. He decided to show Shana the stocks as her final treat of the day. As they made their way through the staring mass of townsfolk, Albert mused as to how he could explain to his sister how he had acquired the new pet and even worse, the unavoidable visit from her most loathed bête noire! The three friends were an amusing sight as their three wildly different heads bobbed as one through the crowd toward prisoners' corner.

The stocks were full that day and housed the best pick of scoundrels, cut-throats and vagrants that the mob could find. Albert treated his princess to a bucket of rotten leftovers to hurl at the culprits. She was fascinated by the wooden device that held the ankles, wrists and necks of the captives. Each provided entertainment of a different kind.

A comely wench was getting a seeing to by a sex-starved sailor whilst trapped in one set of stocks and her neighbour was not so lucky with his head being pummelled by pebbles. Shana loved the whole scene and made sure that she made the most of her peneth's worth of slop.

A handsome looking young man was chained to a whipping post that had been erected at the centre of 'Vagabonds Corner' as displayed on a rough, makeshift sign. Shana pointed at the man and Albert put her down gently, not too near to the villain. Albert's mind wandered as he observed the young man who was chained with heavy iron shackles that ate into the ripped, swollen infected flesh of his ankles. Maggots were eating their way through the rotten stinking pulp and the man's eyes stared hauntingly ahead, seemingly oblivious to the whole situation. As Albert gazed at the scrawl, unable to interpret, but aware of the crime that the man had committed, he jumped with the sudden realisation that Shana was drawing a fresh crowd to join in her newly found fun... 'Azzzawaya do it!' the addictive little personality sang as she tottered toward the prisoner with her bucket of swill... Even the young pyrate broke his silence and told the crowd that they would be sorry if they even thought about hurling any filth his way. Laughing at the tiny child's nerve, the man took a low mock bow and rewarded Shana's nerve with a kiss on the forehead. Poor Albert managed to grab the child just in time and whisk her away from the scene before a big, drunken oaf stumbled up onto the platform and kicked the prisoner in the groin. Shana giggled as she was lifted back up high on Albert's shoulders, out of mischief... for the meantime at least!

The town was packed with folk enjoying watching an assorted array of performers. Bear-baiting drew the largest number of gamblers, but cock-fighting ran a close second place. Shin-kicking was a popular sport and the winner was usually the smith's son who wore the best iron tipped boots. Many cider dosed lads were carried out of the ring with their lower legs hanging limp like snapped branches. Each scene caused Shana to react in the most dramatic way and a few of her newly found fans followed her around for sheer entertainment value. Following a particularly gruesome shin injury caused by the May queen's beau, Albert decided that his little maiden had seen enough and carried her over to the soup-making stall. Carefully picking out the least mouldy pieces of bread, he paid the cook and received a big bowl of broth in exchange. The pair found a place to sit and share the welcome meal.

Come what may, Shana refused to part with her treasured doll and was still holding the basket handle in a vice-like grip when she fell asleep later that night in front of a dying fire. Albert watched the child's eyelids flicker showing signs of deep, satisfying slumber. Popping his fourth 'last oatcake' of the day into his mouth, Albert decided to carry the May princess up to her sleeping quarters. What a wonderful day they had enjoyed together. Wearily, he climbed the stairs and smiled as he heard the late night revellers singing drunkenly 'Robin Hood in Sherwood stood, hooded and hosed and shod. Four and twenty arrows he bore in his hands...' Their slurring voices grew fainter as Albert tucked his beauty into bed and noticed with a smile that the child was still holding tightly onto the basket with her peg doll securely inside. Looking at his timepiece he wondered where his sister had got to... It was so unlike Bess not to send word if she was going to be tardy in her homecoming.

Chapter 5

Discoveries in Adolescence

It was not until the day after Bess's brutal murder that poor Albert was informed. He was said to have broken down and word in the local taverns was that Ma Turnbull and her family had moved into the Culley home to help him care for the unfortunate little girl. There was also talk of a curse on the Culley family which passed from generation to generation. Petrus Gregorie had been very kind and taken over the running of the spice business, asking only for a meagre wage together with food and lodging. Many townsfolk rallied round to help the Turnbulls manage the home that Bess had kept so immaculately. Even Ma Turnbull regularly lost control of her emotions throughout the day and she was well used to dealing with bereavement and despair.

Albert refused to allow Shana out of his sight but the child had also grown extremely concerned about him. Whenever she played with the Turnbull children, she would ensure that she could see Albert and if they took her outside, she insisted that he joined them. The pair had always been inseparable but during their seemingly unending bout of dreadful losses, they had grown ever closer. Albert refused to talk about Bess and was not happy that Petrus had moved into Shana's home. He heeded his late sister's warning and was determined that no harm come to their Shana. Contrary to Albert's expectations, Petrus had managed to gain at least a little of his respect by offering to arrange Bess' burial.

Strangely, the sickly-looking apprentice could not do enough to help the newly formed 'family' with whatever they needed. Albert soon became obsessed with church services and the only time that he would leave Shana was to attend the late night vigil for men. Even then he would wait until his little girl was safely in her bed and sound asleep before leaving their house.

The unexpected change in Petrus' attitude toward Shana Culley had put Albert at ease, for the meantime at least. His totally indecent proposal to become betrothed to the young child had been out of the question from the very beginning. It was well known that headstrong and independent Elspeth Culley had avoided his advances for years. She had found the man utterly repulsive, both in manner and appearance. Petrus Gregorie was the last person that she would have wanted her daughter to marry.

Albert had accepted that the painful memory of his sister's foul murder would never leave his tortured mind. Without any word to the folks who had suddenly become Shana's extended family, Albert planned to take his little princess away for a while. That would allow Ma Turnbull to rearrange the home to her liking. His Bess had kept the place in tiptop order and he was well aware that women had different ideas about housekeeping. He had thought it best to let her prepare everything in the home without him around plus it would give the whole Turnbull family time to adapt to a new home and a different way of living. Albert frowned in deep thought as he made his way slowly upstairs. He had not been back to Ireland, the land of his birth, since he and Bess had left as young children. As floorboards creaked under his weight, he listened to the whispers of prayer coming from Shana's bedchamber. The sight that met his eyes when he reached the top of the landing almost made him break down in tears. His exhausted mind was bombarded with a strong surge of emotions. Agonising grief, total love and an overwhelming feeling of protection all hit the broken-hearted man at once. Through the open door of Shana's bedchamber, Albert could see a woman kneeling at the base of the maiden's bed. Three little figures knelt at the side, each not quite tall enough for their tiny elbows to reach the soft feather-stuffed mattress. Bess had made the fluffy, down mattress for the little girl when she had outgrown her wooden crib and moved into her new bed. He and Elspeth had carefully chosen the timber to make the crib as soon as they learned of her pregnancy. Albert remembered carefully fashioning the wood into a lovely cradle... Elspeth had been delighted.

'Papa! Pway tum hiver'... Shana's sweet voice pulled him from his trance-like state and he motioned for her to come and kiss him goodnight. The little girl looked up at Ma Turnbull for permission to rise. Quickly she rushed out of the room in her thick, floor length white nightgown and bedcap. Albert's weary eyes welled with tears as he took the tiny child in his strong arms, picked her up and swung her around much to her delight. Silently the two exchanged kisses and Shana pressed Bess' doll to his lips then her own before padding back to her bedchamber. Ma Turnbull smiled reassuringly at Albert and he smiled back with unspoken gratitude.

The Turnbulls were a loving family and had welcomed Shana as their own. Albert trusted the honest couple beyond measure. They would always be welcome in the Culley home, of that he was quite certain. Ma Turnbull's twin girls, Flo and Abi were almost two years older than Shana and their brother Arthur just a year older. They had all enjoyed playing with her ever since their Ma had become her wet-nurse. Shana loved her tiny companions as though they were her own siblings. Well accustomed to meeting all kinds of babyfolk, the Turnbull children were very patient with each newcomer but had shared an instant rapport with little Miss Culley. Wee Arthur Turnbull had been smitten at first sight.

The day that Albert and Shana left for Ireland was miserable and wet. Ma Turnbull had packed plenty of warm clothes for the excited little girl. Albert ensured that they took the little doll that Shana had named Bess. The coach that picked them up at The Vine tavern looked sturdy much to Albert's relief. He had never enjoyed travelling of any kind and he and Shana faced a long and dangerous journey by road. Had Bess not been murdered, Albert would never have entertained the idea of returning to the much missed Emerald Isle. Lifting Shana into the carriage, Albert hurled their bags onto the board behind the coachman's wooden seat then jumped inside to join his princess.

Shana was a natural traveller and nothing deterred her from enjoying every part of the appallingly long journey to Ireland whilst poor, pale faced Albert puked most of the way. The travel-sick soul almost suffered heart failure when one of the carriage wheels buckled beneath them. An extra overnight stop in a pleasant inn with a roaring fire and welcoming landlady almost convinced Albert to abandon their ambitious venture. His conscience overcame his misgivings as he had promised to take some much needed spices to an apocathory in the Celtic land.

Once in Ireland, Shana charmed her kinsfolk. People were thrilled that she bore the Culley name together with a temper to match that of any Celtic warrior. The couple were welcomed into the exquisite home of a newly discovered Romany kinswoman, Eileen Conachy. Her tiny horse-drawn caravan was delightful and very snug. Shana spent many a happy hour examining every treasure so lovingly collected and beautifully displayed. Each nook and cranny revealed a new delight waiting to be discovered. Shana was fascinated by the brightly coloured silks, sequins and tassels and was highly honoured when Eileen allowed her to dress Romany fashion. Every night, after the girl had fallen asleep the gypsy woman would sit and sew tiny costumes which she duly presented to Shana as a goodbye gift.

Widowed Eileen and her only child, Richie were sad to see their companions leave after an unexpectedly lengthy stay. Had Albert not had the charge of Shana, he would have chosen to remain in Ireland. He had fallen head over heels in love with the comely Irish woman who had given him more pleasure in two months than he could have ever dreamed of. A kiss and a promise sealed a fond farewell and the worldly widow tearfully waved Albert and Shana adieu on their way back to England.

For the newly formed clan, life in Henry's England was good and Albert made sure that Shana's thriving spice trade continued to do exactly that. Loyal to their King, the monarch who had been chosen by God Himself to rule their country, Shana's adopted family enjoyed all of the pastimes that he encouraged during his reign. The fact that she was a girl never deterred the little maiden from attempting boys' sports. She soon became a fantastic horsewoman and an archer second to none. Swordsmanship came naturally to her but she had to learn and practice in secret as the local townswomen were already disapproving of the young lady becoming a tomboy.

Dissolution and destruction of local Catholic monasteries enabled traders to become landed gentry and the aging Albert took advantage as soon as possible. He was glad of Petrus' advice in the matter of purchasing land from the Crown. On Shana's behalf, they extended the family's small plot to cover forty acres which stretched from Thomas Culley's original spice house far west to the banks of the river Teign. Land was dirt cheap and the newly self-appointed family treasurer, Petrus Gregorie calculated that Shana's vast funds would provide for stables to be built on the new land. Buying and breeding good bloodstock could be another opening to expand the Culley's fast growing business.

Delighted by Petrus' proposals of how to best make use of Shana's new land, Albert had plans of his own but they were far more daring. Albert was well aware that smuggling was a dangerous yet rewarding trade. Their new land ran right to the banks of the River Teign and was perfect for smugglers to disembark and land their contraband without being spotted... Respect for the Crown only ran skin-deep for wise and cunning Albert. Understandably, public opinion was beginning to sway against the King. Taxes had been raised yet again and although wealthy spice traders did not suffer too harsh a loss of their well earned profits, Albert and Petrus agreed that the ageing King Henry VIII had become bitter and was ruling by the chopping block. Powerful parliamentary ministers continued to raise taxation to fund England's wars against France and Scotland. A strong naval presence protected England's shores from further invasion and the Scottish posed no threat following their defeat at Solway Moss when King James V was killed in battle... but strong defence did not come cheap so taxation charges footed the bill nicely.

After much thought, Albert and Petrus made the most of the newly purchased land and allowed regular passage of desirable wares that the Crown taxed highly. An assortment of vessels carried contraband to and from 'Culley's spiceland' as it became widely known within the black market. Soon after the route had been deemed as safe, illegally imported goods began to arrive. Even opium reached the town of Teignmouth via 'Culley's Cut'. Shana's businesses thrived and she grew up playing in the fields whilst eagerly learning every detail about the illicit trading across her land.

Like her mother, Shana possessed an uncanny intelligence and excelled in all subjects that her tutor, Master Edward Lyley taught. By her seventh year the girl was fluent in Latin, French and Spanish... yet the latter had been learned, with little doubt, from Portuguese spice and opium traders who enjoyed chatting to the feisty wee maiden. A skilled horsewoman, they admired the way she rode without fear. She gained the utmost respect from many of the men who played deadly games of chance in order to gain wealth.

Whilst smugglers helped Shana's purses grow heavier, King Henry VIII of England invited another wife to his bedchambers... and then another soon after he called for the other poor soul's execution. Katherine Parr became His Majesty's queen of the moment and took on the unpleasant duty of bathing the puss-filled, open wounds on his grossly swollen leg. Rumour had it that the great

Henry was riddled with the pox and stank like an old whore as he lay rotting in his bed. Gossip in the taverns told of his ever-enlarging codpiece. The most popular yarn spun a hilarious rumour that the conceited King's impressive accessory helped keep clothing away from an agonisingly sore and raw glob of skinless flesh. This was apparently all that was left of his once virile and impressive but misused and abused manhood. Citizens once terrified of being executed for treason suddenly felt safe to mock their ailing and bitter King.

Albert could not believe how his Shana grew more beautiful every year. She possessed many of her mother's graces and was even more ferocious when challenged! By the time Shana had reached her ninth year she was aware of the entire workings of her thriving spice trade. This intelligent wench was streetwise, had more than her fair share of common sense and also displayed a shrewd business mind that she had surely inherited from her father. Shana had many friends, her best being Flo and Abi Turnbull... fondly known as 'the terrible twins' on the Culley estate. Their chubby, befreckled brother, Arthur was still smitten with Shana and his sisters loved to tease him as he would blush from collar to hairline with embarrassment every time he saw her. Usually the most talkative of the Turnbull siblings, Arthur would clam up in Shana's company and just sit staring ahead of him. Cruel as sisters can be, they had made up a ditty and would sing at the top of their voices whenever their unfortunate love-sick brother walked by:

'T'was nay so lang ago when Art eyed Shana fair,
'Tis such a pity tho' she hates his curly hair!
E'er did ye see a boy so smitten,

He'd like to fondle her sweet kitten!
Yon puny, rump-fed urchin boy
Shall ne'er dip into Shana's pye!'

The girls' pronounced the final word as 'poy' in their Devonshire accents to make a perfect rhyme. If Shana ever heard the girls' cruel taunts, she would chastise them and kiss the poor lad on the cheek, which made him blush even more! Henry Crimpling and Liza Knights were two local children who made up numbers in Shana's little gang. Shana and Henry fancied each other and Liza had a serious crush on Arthur. Of the six close friends, Liza was the odd one out. Jealousy and envy ruled the girl's heart and she wanted nothing more than to see Shana's demise. Four years older than her rival, Liza should have known better but her unfathomable jealousy bred evil hatred. Shana was well aware of the animosity that oozed from her so-called friend but preferred to keep her worst enemy close. She knew full well that the young woman only came around so that she could ride one of Shana's horses and roll in the hay with a stable boy. Unbeknown to the little harlot, Shana was aware of her wily habits... nothing went by without her knowledge.

Although Shana knew most folks' secrets, she had one of her own that she shared only with her most loyal friend, Albert. Since Shana had grown tall like her mother, she had been able to dress as a boy and venture out into the town incognito. Trade was still a man's game and despite her sole ownership of the Culley Spice Trade, as a woman, Shana was still not accepted as a trader. Petrus was the one to strike the deals with smugglers in public. Albert dealt with the sales and pricing of the valuable spices within the legal business. Behind closed doors was a different matter as all of the dealings that her loyal Albert carried out had to first be approved by Shana. Little had improved regarding the rights of womenfolk since her mother's day but Shana was not one to accept rules... she broke them often and her power gave her such an incredible feeling!

For years, Shana had been well aware of the plight of orphans and abandoned children. Few had much chance of enjoying even a half-decent life. Ma Turnbull had given the young wench the idea to open an orphanage a long while back. Her charitable idea had become even more attractive when Shana realised that an orphanage could also provide her with perfect cover. What better place would allow a young boy to mingle with other urchins, many unknown and all dressed alike? One of the rules that she laid down was that the children were to be given the freedom to come and go as they pleased, within reason. This enabled Shana to go as she pleased with no-one paying much interest in her character's identity or business. To most, orphans were simply viewed as vermin; in their desperation many would turn to crime for survival. Some of these poor rejected creatures lined the main horse roads swinging in cruel iron maidens or hanging from primitive gibbets.

Since the Catholic monasteries and convents had been destroyed, few folk bothered about orphan children and alms were no longer available. Shana had the opportunity to give these children a chance in life. One day she decided that the whole project could easily be funded by the lucrative smuggling trade that she had been keen to become involved in. With Albert's help... and Shana allowing the slimy Petrus to think that he was involved so that he could not interfere... Shana managed to organise for a functional, comfortable orphanage to be built to house ten boys and ten girls. A large building, separated by a courtyard, was erected around the small yet well designed stable block built by Albert's friend Mansell, a local carpenter. The project was ambitious, especially for such a young person let alone female, yet Albert thought it a wonderful idea and backed Shana in every possible way.

On the day of completion, following months of hard labour and plenty of public support, Shana and Albert were satisfied that they had done the right thing. The wise pair stood before a sprawling and simply designed piece of sturdy architecture that was to provide a home for twenty lucky children. Albert recalled sitting with Shana, exactly two years earlier, as they drew up plans around the very table where he and Bess used to sit and discuss their young charge's future. Shana rarely shed a tear but that first day of September 1547 she stood in front of 'The Orphanage of Mary Magdalene' with Albert and cried tears of relief, sadness and joy... tears that had been pent up inside for many years... for her dead parents who she had never known, for Bess who had loved her like her own daughter and for Albert who had loved and cherished her throughout her days. Shana had become a very successful womanchild and was determined to survive and live life to the full. Albert's eyes poured with tears as he held his daughter in his arms. 'Ne'er allow a single soul tell ye yer cannee do whate'er thy heart desires, my wench.' whispered the aging Albert as Shana kissed his cheek with silent gratitude. Later that eve they joined the Coronation celebrations at the Cock Inn where Shana had been conceived. King Henry VIII was dead and his sickly only son became the sixth King Edward to rule the land.

The Turnbull family were able to move straight into the orphanage and Ma Turnbull had no problem finding little ones to inhabit 'Mary Maggy's' as it soon fondly became known. Assigning each of her family to a suitable duty, the kindly woman excelled in managing the happy children's home. To everyone's surprise, even bitter little Liza became a well respected figure as she cared for the sickest of the children. Soon they were all celebrating the first anniversary of Mary Maggy's and twenty happy, well-fed and promising children began their second year there. The year that followed was hard but came as no surprise as Abi and Flo had the risky duty of nursing sick children under Liza's watchful eyes. Despite the cleanliness and excellent care that the orphanage workers offered following Liza's strict instructions, nature took its course. Disease passed swiftly from one child to another and it was inevitable that the carers would fall ill sooner or later. Unfortunately both twins caught smallpox at the same time and Ma Turnbull was beside herself with worry. The dreaded illness struck and the young girls suffered for five appalling months together with two orphans who unfortunately died. They were swiftly replaced by two of the hopeful tykes who begged daily for admittance.

Insisting on staying together, the twins were confined to a single room where they sweated the sickness out of their pain-riddled bodies. Thankfully both survived but poor Abi was left hideously scarred, whilst her sister's skin stayed pockmark-free. Luckily the twins were extremely close and adored one another... neither had ever felt any pressure of competition and knew that their parents loved them both equally. Fate had dealt a cruel blow to only one of the identical sisters yet, despite her disfigurement, Abi carried on her duties happily. Her unfortunate experience helped her to counsel a boy who had been scalded as a baby and there was no prouder mother around than Ma Turnbull. As soon as the twins had grown strong enough, Shana and their mother organised a huge party with no expense spared. As an extra surprise Albert managed to hire every travelling act that Shana and he had enjoyed each May Day… he even built a set of stocks and played victim so the children could bombard him with rotten fruit. The walls of Mary Maggy's Orphanage echoed with laughter and merriment that happy night. Even the sly-faced weasel Petrus Gregorie cracked a smile… for a second or two at least! Shana's knowledge of the man whom her mother had despised had widened recently and he had been up to some filthy tricks. Shana was determined to confront him someday and tell him exactly what she thought of him. As she eyed the lily-livered slime-ball, her mind worked busily away, planning how she would expel this malicious man from her life once and for all.

CHAPTER 6

Simply Simon

Most of Shana's newfound trading was carried out at night when she was able to roam free in the guise of Master Simon Stempton... 'Simply Simon' was the term she and Albert used when referring to their closely guarded secret. Shana's trade-runs disguised as Simon quickly became an extra source of income for the ever-improving orphanage. Master Simon gradually became a very well respected middleman for Culley Spices. New customers included the likes of Madame Josephine Chatte-Colossale who ran the local brothel; she bought the ever-popular pomanders that the children made at the orphanage. When wealthy gentlemen who frequented the brothel sampled the delightfully perfumed pomanders, they too became regular buyers. Soon market traders ordered a smaller version of the wooden pomanders to sell at executions. As Simon, Shana was able to use her shrewd business mind to her advantage and was never afraid to barter for a good price; a lot of work went into the production of the pomanders.

Shana taught the children and Ma Turnbull how to grind herbs and spices, mix them together with gum to make a scented hardened ball. These balls were inserted inside the beautifully carved wooden holders that the children had produced. Suitable ingredients were carefully chosen to meet individual requirements and word soon spread of the aromatic creations that dispelled the most revolting odours. In no time at all Ma Turnbull had organised a busy little production line and new orders were coming in before the last batch had been delivered.

Master Warnock, the apothecary was a hard, tight-fisted businessman but Simon managed to persuade him to buy lavender and cloves on a regular basis... it amused Shana when the snotty nosed apothecary told her that 'Miss Culley possessed ample 'nuff sense in her pretty head to hire a fine young man to deal with her business.' Dandy Master Warnock, well known for his penchant for elaborate dress, regularly teetered around town wearing ridiculous high heeled shoes, ordered from the most skilled cobbler in the fashionable French Court. His shoes would cost the conceited fool as much as the first horse that Albert had bought for Shana... and a months worth of feed to add to that! Clutching a heavily perfumed white French lace handkerchief to his nose, he enjoyed staring at the boys from Mary Maggy's a tad too keenly for comfort. A bachelor by choice, old Warnock definitely had an eye for the lads. To folks' disgust, he managed to get away with his alleged homosexual tendencies because most lived in fear of repercussions. As a wealthy member of the community, the man was also renowned for his ability to use magic, so no-one dared pass judgement... plus he would cure them of their ailments for a reduced fee if they swore to keep their mouths shut! Besides, as long as he never hurt the boys, where was the harm? Few cared about orphans, so he could pretty much do what he wanted with them! At least that was the attitude of most people when it came to the heinous crime of homosexuality. Most people lived by the rule that if they were not personally affected then there was no harm done!

Under the name and guise of Simon Stempton, Shana learned the most horrific details about the practice of buggery, a hangable offence. Mostly, these horror stories were told by macho men who frequented Madame Josie's whorehouse. Oddly, those regular punters who professed blatant homophobia, preferred to hire sweet, flat-chested young Daisy; a popular wench who offered anal penetration to her clients... more money was to be made this way and there was rarely risk of pregnancy.

Pretty Daisy D'arse, as she was fondly known due to her 'anal allowance', adored the new trader Simon and told her closest friend all about him. 'Two' was a huge, muscular black man who had been pinned down as a teenager and made a eunuch by a surgeon. The handsome African slave had been unfortunate when he had accepted a 'freebie' from one of Madame Josie's girls, who wanted to see what it was like to have sex with a black man. Her unusually loud squeals gave the game away as he entered her with his enormous rock-hard penis. Immediately dragged out and beaten beyond recognition for daring to 'violate a white woman', the slave was given two choices of punishment hence the name 'Two'. Sadly he chose to have his manhood completely removed rather than allow a white man to place a noose around his neck. Taken down to the cellar and laid on the cold stone floor between cold barrels of ale, Two was subjected to the most repulsive disfigurement imaginable to any man. Luckily he had passed out before the sadistic surgeon completely removed his genitals. The poor devil had never spoken a word since.

Two and Daisy had become close friends after she trusted the gentle giant with the details of her dreadful past. Still refusing to break his vow of silence, Daisy remembered being squeezed so tightly by the gentle man that she was not sure what to do. Then he released her and gave her a reassuring smile and their bond had grown stronger ever since. Shana looked forward to her visits to the brothel. Loving every minute of freedom, she always made the most of her nightly trips into the world where she was accepted as her alter ego, Simon. Growing up amongst adults who held little from her, she had often heard tales about after-dark misdoings but they were never as exciting as experiencing them in reality. Acting as Simon, the young woman was able to conduct all sorts of illicit activities as she mixed with folk that a young woman of her class should never have deemed suitable.

In 1554, when Queen Mary reigned on the English throne following her young brother's death, Catholicism returned to England. Regularly white-washed whorehouse walls were built higher to keep out raiders who could arrest prostitutes and clients, then close down the bawdy dens in the name of the Crown. Suddenly a brightly painted sign appeared overnight, swinging high on the old brothel front wall. The newly-advertised theatre house was to show monthly plays. Skinny old Madame Josephine had decided to run her disreputable business under the guise of a playhouse since establishments like hers were no longer legal. Along with many of the Madame's regular customers, Petrus Gregorie was seen frequenting the new playhouse far more often than once a month.

As Simon, Shana enjoyed the privilege of knowing most peoples' business and soon found out that Petrus' favourite prostitute was none other than Daisy D'Arse. Daisy's incredibly clear green eyes sparkled with tears of disgust as she shared her loathing of the 'stinky brefft pervert'. One dismal evening Daisy told Simon, 'Master Gregorie cannie get his prick hard' lest 'e watches me play wiv anover wench's cunnie... 'e 'as the need of vat 'whatsit' 'e eats afore 'e can get it up ...' Shana frowned in wonder as the girl confided in her male alter-ego. 'After vat 'e follows wi' a speedy swivin' of me arse'ole. 'Vat's when 'e wallops me and t'uvver wench. I tells ye, Simon, e's pure evil! An' ter fink 'ow vat kindly wench, Miss Culley took 'im on an' 'e sells that stuff with 'er not knowin' nuffin' 'bout it!'

All of a sudden, Shana shuddered with a sense of the power that she now held over the foul man whose cards she had marked long ago. Later that night, Shana enjoyed the most peaceful sleep she could remember. Fond memories of times long gone filled her dreams and she woke with renewed determination to uncover the truth about Master Gregorie.

Regular trips to the theatre, disguised as Simon, allowed Shana to grow closer to Daisy who openly shared her own and Two's sad life stories. Daisy had been happily married to a man twenty years her senior and grew extremely unhappy when the poor man lost his mind. In desperate need of love, she began a blatant affair with the local candlemaker. Such an attractive young woman caused quite a stir in the community with her insensitive behaviour. Many women living in Daisy's village had long been jealous of her wealthy marriage and indisputable beauty. When her senile old husband finally became completely deranged, a few local ladies organised an evil plot against the unfortunate girl. Followed one night by several upright church-goers, Daisy was caught at her lover's home. Dragged out onto the streets and stripped of the few clothes she was wearing, she was dragged home so that her wealthy old husband could decide her fate. Overcome with anger at being woken by complete strangers, the old man's ranting and raving was 'conveniently translated' by the mob. Insisting that the confused old fool had given his permission for his wayward wife to be auctioned at the cattle market the following day, the men in the group forced her to the ground and brutally raped her, one after another. That night, Daisy's body and mind were abused beyond repair and she longed for the morning to break.

When her allotted time arrived, poor Daisy stood naked and bloody before a rowdy crowd so people could bid for her. Humiliated and frightened for her lover's life, Daisy prayed for salvation. After a few minutes of bidding that seemed to last a lifetime, she was finally bought for a handsome sum of two pounds by Madame Josie. The hard-hearted old hag bid on her prize as if she was one of the beasts for sale. A bargain not to be missed, Daisy was sure to attract many gentlemen with her dainty features and gentle, ladylike manner. Rubbing her bony hands together in triumph and glee, Madame Josie had made a fine purchase that day. She had made an exception to her normal rule and ordered two of her African slaves to carry their mistress to the market on her purpose-built chair. Poor Two watched with disgust and despair as the fine white woman was sold into prostitution by her own people. When bidding was over, Daisy was led like an animal by a heavy chain to her new madam. Two was ordered to attach the shackles to the chair handle and they all returned to their prison in Gropecunt Lane. From that day onward, Two decided that he would look after and protect Daisy for the rest of his days.

Every drop-off that Simon made at the brothel took Shana closer to the demise of Petrus Gregorie. On the night when Shana finally learned the sickening truth about Petrus, she decided to trust her two friends with her secret and revealed her true identity to the shocked pair. As usual Two was standing guard at the theatre door, when Shana arrived at the premises where she had learned that Petrus paid regular visits to deal with Madame Josie. The one-legged harlot always looked forward to Petrus' call because he brought along the spice that made her richer. That night, Shana was determined to learn exactly what Petrus was up to and knew all too well how much Madame Josephine loved a visit from her handsome Simon. Winking at Two, Shana stepped inside and lingered in the foyer.

Impatiently awaiting Simon's arrival, the hideously painted strumpet sat with a large man's kerchief covering her crooked nose in a vain attempt to disguise the vile stenches of sex and unwashed bodies that wafted around her. Yelling obscenities and lashing wildly at any unfortunate person who dared pass too close, Madame Josie thrashed her pox-riddled body around on her special wooden chair like a crazed and extremely ugly monkey. Shana felt her spine tingle with disgust at the pathetic sight of the foul-mouthed bully of a woman. Following closely behind Two, Shana adopted Simon's usual gait and knelt before the hysterical pussy-pedlar. Madame Josephine's weak eyes narrowed when she caught sight of the young man. A few awful seconds passed by until she recognised the boy and thankfully adopted a more ladylike air. Reluctantly Shana pressed her full soft lips against dry leather-like skin. With subtlety and speed she managed to wipe away the flakes that had come away from the vile wench's cheek. There was a high price to pay for dressing and behaving as a handsome young man!

Shana noticed that the crone had been busy applying pale paste to her yellow tinged skin. Madame Josie had obviously spent ages stuffing bits of cotton into the cavities of her few remaining teeth caused by over consumption of valuable sugar. She was eager to look her best for Simon! Two hid the grin on his face behind a silk fan and began to wave it in gentle rhythm over his mistress' head. Shana flinched as the old cow swiped the side of poor Two's face with her weighty bone-handled stick that she used purely as a weapon. Since her slowly rotting flesh had caused her to lose a leg to the surgeon, she had refused to move from the comfortable well-padded chair that her girls nicknamed 'Ma'am's throne'.

Madame Josephine had been born with a freak disfigurement that made it impossible for her to appear naked in front of anyone. Since birth, Madame Josie had been mocked and abused because of a serious defect. The bitter and tormented woman had been born with both a vagina and penis. The very few who had seen her nether regions had been disgusted. Those who had caught a glimpse of her embarrassments had done so either whilst she was drunk, or on the extremely rare occasions when she was forced to bathe. She avoided washing as long as she could, until there was no option but to remove the sticky mass of infection that had formed on the stump where there was once a puny leg. Building up a firm and friendly business relationship had been easy for Shana who knew that the old bitch loved to be swived by young boys... it was impossible for her to display her naked body in front of a man because of the small, shrivelled penis that lay limply above her clitoris. As a teenager, desperate to be normal, Josephine had taken a knife and tried to hack off the offensive member that made it impossible to live without fear of discovery. This lame attempt at surgery left her badly mutilated and it was then that she decided to prostitute herself to the sailors who did not care which sex they swived. Embittered and full of loathing, Josephine began to take money for sexual favours and never refused a request, no matter how perverse. A monster had been born...

Once Madame Josephine had made enough money to hire a place to house and control other girls, she began to reap the benefits and no longer had to prostitute herself. When Daisy moved into the brothel, she recalled how sickened she had felt when Madame Josie had taken in young Tom Fisher, an orphan boy from the poorhouse, to attend to her sexual needs. The poor boy was expected to care for the old tyrant in every other possible way too. Since Tom's 'retirement' as everyone had been told, Simon had taken over the job of tending to Madame Josie's stump and would regularly rub soothing salves and oils into her rotting flesh. In return for the unpleasant favour, Madame Josie allowed Simon to enjoy the girl of his choice 'on the house'. Simon hastily accepted her kind offer and grabbed Daisy, pulling her into the nearest room. Once the door was locked, the two mischievous teenagers collapsed onto the bed in fits of laughter. Shana was glad to escape from the stinking, sadistic old dame who lusted after her as Simon and Daisy was grateful to her friend for rescuing her from horny punters. They played cards whilst Daisy made suitably satisfied sounds to avoid any suspicion. In the adjacent room, Mouldy

Moll was riding a large fat man with particular enthusiasm and whooped loudly when she heard her colleague's yells of pleasure. Moll had earned her nickname by the foul-smelling discoloured discharge which regularly seeped from her slack cunnie... Madame Josie took a higher percentage from her takings to pay for the pastes the apothecary suggested might cure her from the 'French welcome'.

Pussy-licking Pru was well-known as the wench with an expert tongue who Petrus often hired to give Daisy oral pleasure. When Pru heard the sounds of undeniable ecstasy from the room that Simon and Daisy had taken, her expression showed obvious envy. Allowing a believable amount of recovery time following such an impressive performance, Shana and the blushing Daisy re-emerged as Simon and his whore to the sounds of cheering and clapping. In Madame Josie's eyes Simon had exceeded her expectations beyond doubt. Grabbing a bottle of rhum that she had been saving for a special occasion, Madame Josie summoned her aids to carry her into her private chambers. Calling for Simon to follow, she jiggled the portable chair to hurry her porters along.

Once inside the dark candlelit room Shana made herself as comfortable as possible considering the unpleasant company. As the grog flowed steadily, the hideous hag's ulcer-riddled tongue loosened as she shared some truths almost as ugly as their narrator. Hours passed by and Shana listened intently as the vile facts were unravelled by the drunken whore, telling of Petrus Gregorie's miracle drug that the uneducated bitch called 'effonium'. Shana knew instantly that the woman was referring to the valuable spice pepper called Aframomum that could enhance and sustain erectile function if the correct dosage was taken. Sickened by Madame Josie's blasé attitude to her frankly abhorrent confession Shana listened carefully and was shocked that the crone appeared to be proud of her despicable actions! The Madame confirmed Daisy's account, bragging about taking in the orphan Tom Fisher who she then forced to give her sexual pleasure. By giving the boy regular doses of aphrodisiac pepper, she was able to exploit his body for lengthy sessions of sex. Shana clenched her large fists, trying to suppress her anger long enough to learn as much as possible. It was not easy to fake amusement whilst she listened to how the young boy was subjected to vile sexual acts to satisfy a sadistic and bitter fiend.

It was Madame Josie's final secret that she was most proud of and did she wallow in self-praise as she went into great detail telling the handsome young Simon how his whore of a mistress Missy Sushana Culley, was born into great wealth that she did not deserve. She explained how she could not refuse the chance of taking some profit from the spoilt little bitch when Petrus Gregorie initially approached her. His cunning proposition was simple: he promised to provide her with as much Aframomum as she could sell to her droopy-dicked clients. If she agreed to help him to settle a matter of grave importance, he would make it extremely worthwhile... Madame Josephine's slurred words began to hum in Shana's ears as her mind deciphered the information that she was revealing piece by despicable piece... 'Tom... Bess in the way... closer to the wench Shana... Albert could be persuaded...'

When she finally heard the horrific truth, the room seemed to spin around her and Shana saw red. Unable to wait another second, she leaped up and flew at the shocked woman who tried to reach for her stick in a lame attempt at last-minute defence. Grabbing an open jaw, Shana forced her clenched fist into the filthy germ-coated mouth of the most successful yet incredibly stupid Madame in East Teignmouth. Miss Sushana Culley made sure that the terrified woman's bolting eyes recognised her true identity as she choked her to death. When the struggling freak's body finally shuddered and lay quite still, Shana pulled her puke-covered fist out of the gaping mouth. Cocking her pretty head, Shana smiled at her work... 'a job well overdue', she thought as she coldly closed the dead woman's eyes and wiped the vomit from her tingling arm. Cleaning up was an easy job and Shana felt no need to hurry. It was not unusual for Simon to spend time with the mistress of the brothel and no-one would ever suspect foul play... the woman was ill and often drowned her sorrows in a bottle of rhum and nothing had been stolen. Feeling no remorse, Shana placed Simon's cap on her head and calmly left the room, closing the door behind her.

Two waved as Simon left the brothel later that night and headed towards the King's Head where Petrus Gregorie was still drinking ale. The drunken fool was pleased to have Simon's company and did not notice each time he poured grains of glass into the tankard of ale that he greedily supped from. Earlier that night, before leaving her first victim, Shana had carefully taken a pestle and mortar and ground the smallest shards of glass from the shattered rhum bottle into fine grains. As the whore peddler fought for her measly life, she had broken the rhum vessel and thus provided her murderess with an inventive plan for her next target. Carefully, Shana had ground the glass into fine grains, tipped it onto a kerchief which she folded and placed in the purse on Simon's belt. Knowing that Petrus was terrified of catching the killer virus that took her father's life before Shana was even born, she had decided to surprise him with a scare that would prepare him for the bitter taste of his own dangerous medicine.

Chapter 7

Precious Revenge

Simon and Petrus stayed at the tavern until the early hours of Thursday the thirteenth day of June 1554. Polly Perkins, the landlady was used to the backhander that Petrus gave her and she always looked forward to his late night binges. An added bonus for Polly was when the bribe included a generous packet of 'gator pepper that made her Henry's member stand up like a baby's arm holding an apple. Staggering back home in the early morning the two figures were greeted along the way. Many would remember Petrus' farewell celebration later that week and recognised the kind boy from Mary Maggy's who helped him along.

Petrus awoke with a blinding headache and found it difficult to focus on the figure who sat on the rickety stool in the corner of his bedchamber. Wiping the vomit from his face with the back of his hand, he yelped in panic when he spotted blood. He began to cough and spluttered up even more. Shana sat in perfect silence and watched as her prey suffered with the thought of being infected with Tuberculosis. Revelling in the pathetically sickening scene, she leant forward to allow the piss-soaked man to catch a glimpse of her bare skin. Dressed only in a thin linen nightgown, Shana's large dark nipples showed clearly through the fine cloth. Puking suddenly, Petrus quivered and just managed to recover enough to reach down under the sheets. At that moment he realised that there was another person in the room and sighed with relief when he recognised one of the Turnbull twins. Hoping that the third party was Flo in preference to her unsightly sister, Petrus reached under the crap-caked blanket, stiff from the warmth of the sunlight that streaked through the windowpanes. The girl moved forward and gently stroked her fingers over Shana's cheek, tracing the line of her neck and down onto her shoulder. Pausing to loosen the lacing on the see-through garment, the girl was becoming clearer in Petrus' vision. She was unmistakably the scarred twin sister, Abi but she would do, just one time. Unable to resist the sight of another girl fondling Shana's bare flesh, he pumped away at his hardness with a steady rhythmic motion.

Shana and Abi loved each other and had already been sexually attracted to one another long before they agreed to perform in front of Petrus. The man was a sorry sight and the stench in his room was putrid. His vanity amazed the two girls as they fondled and petted each others' intimate places in full view of the foul letch. Beckoning Petrus over to join them in a ménage à trois, Abi turned her back on him and bent over to show him her pert round buttocks. Shana touched Abi's breasts and continued to kiss her as Petrus stumbled out of bed. The offending weapon stuck out about six inches from his cadaver-like body. To her surprise Shana started to feel aroused as she focused on the purple headed member that was moving closer to her friend's pretty backside. Waiting for the perfect time to pounce, Shana pushed her accomplice to one side and produced a sharp cut-throat razor. Her muscular arm swiped a perfect curve in the thin air until it struck flesh, slicing though the infected throbbing member with a cut-throat razor. In a frenzy of bloodlust the hatred that had built up inside Shana Culley was released in that tiny stinking room. Abi ran outside and Shana heard her friend's heaving as she slashed at her victim's face. With gritted teeth and a warrior's cry, she pulled out his eyes and rammed them into the open pumping hole where his ugly prick had once been. Not yet satisfied that Petrus had received his just desserts, she ripped off his bollocks and shoved them into his mouth. The evil fool made such a noise as he choked on his own testicles. To mute his banshee screams, she took his severed member and stretched it around his mouth like a gag. When Petrus finally stopped struggling, Shana calmly took his body into the kitchen and sang 'Greensleeves' as she chopped the body into pieces for Simon to take to the pye makers. Abi kept away and everyone else was busy at the orphanage whilst Shana cleared up the mess that was once Master Petrus Gregorie... the bastard who had conceived the foul plot and hired Madame Josie to arrange for Bess to be murdered. In her cups, the hag had revealed to Master Simon how she had beaten innocent orphan, Tom Fisher almost to death when he had refused to kill harmless Bess.

Later that night, Shana broke the news to Albert that Petrus had left a hand written letter to her explaining that he had left for France. He wanted to learn the process of extracting oils from aromatic plants and herbs. Knowing that Albert had finally managed to find some happiness since his sister's humiliating death she chose not to reveal the truth. Bess had been squatting in an alleyway passing a motion. So close to safety only about twenty measly yards from the Pulcino show where Albert stood with Shana on his shoulders. They had both been laughing at the stupid little wooden man whilst poor Bess lay dying from multiple shallow wounds that desperate Tom Fisher had caused in a botched attempt to stab a vital organ. Ironically victim and attacker had both been terrified that tragic day long ago. Tom Fisher's body, black and stiff with rigor mortis, was found under a bridge with wrists badly slashed. He had almost cut right through to the bone before he had passed out through blood loss... the poor boy had even botched the taking of his own life.

A smiling Shana counted the cash that she had made from selling a good quantity of quality meat to the baker's stall in the market. She had bartered for a fair deal and the woman was sure to make a tidy profit from the pyes she intended to bake using the lean flesh. Shana planned to allow Simon a final night on the town to find a replacement trade since word was on the street that Madame Josephine had finally met her demise. She had suffered 'a fate dat was verily de Arlmoity Faarder's will and laang overdoo' as Father McGilacuddy said. Shana took the body and blood of Christ that day feeling no guilt whatsoever thanks to the priest's wise words. 'My mother's Catholic faith ran deeper than I ever realised', she thought as she pondered whether eating the flesh of an abusive, lying thief would be a sin in God's eyes. Father McGilacuddy had been overjoyed when she had asked him to baptise her into the Catholic faith and had taken her under his wing ever since.

Shana made sure that every last trace of Petrus Gregorie had disappeared. It was as if the man had never set foot in her precious family home. She battled with the thought of how much she should reveal to Albert of the gudgeon's part in poor Bess' murder. Their relationship was akin to that of father and daughter. She decided with deep sadness that he should know the whole hideous truth. Taking a large bottle of grog from the cellar, Shana grabbed a heavy cloak that Albert had brought back from Ireland. Pulling the hood over her head to shield her face from the cold autumn wind, she grabbed her skirts and headed towards the orphanage with an overburdened heart.

Stopping at the stables Shana reassured the horses and lifted her lantern to check their state. All seemed to be fine and she continued along the worn path that she knew so well. On reaching the simple gated entrance to the largest building on her estate, Shana paused to gain her wits. This was surely the most painful duty that she had ever had to face. As the heavy iron gates slowly creaked ajar, Shana's keen ears picked up the sound of an approaching wagon. Her horses became agitated and she turned to see a light flickering along the banks of the river by the smugglers' jetty. Acting on impulse Shana laid down the bottle, discarded her cloak and hitched up her skirts. Running for the stables, the beautiful woman's strong legs took her quickly and safely across uneven ground. Her horses were unafeared of their confident mistress and did not object when she entered their shelter. Stroking her favourite gelding, Flurry on his velvety soft nose, she undid his reins and mounted him bareback. One horse was always ready to ride at night in case of emergency. Shana rode each of her beauties bareback so they were well-used to it.

The wind whistled loudly as she galloped the eager horse over the field toward the flickering light. As she rode closer her heartbeat steadied as she saw a woman standing atop of a wonderful contraption. Shana steadied Flurry and shouted 'Who goes yonder?' and was surprised to hear a male voice answer, 'Tis Richie and me mudder Oileen here. We're sarchin ferr....' His words were cut off by Shana's yell of delight as she jumped from her mount and bounded over to her friend. She had been very young when she had met the gypsy and her son but fond memories of a wonderful time spent in their delightful horse-drawn home flooded back. Leaping up onto the seat where Eileen stood whilst Richie held the reins to steady the caravan, she welcomed the Irish woman with a huge hug. Eileen was overjoyed and her deep laugh rattled comically as the van creaked over to the left. Richie sat still with a keen grin on his face at the sight of the pretty girl who clearly adored his Mama. At last Shana turned her attention to the dark-haired, grey-eyed muscular young man and smiled openly as he gallantly kissed her hand. Maybe it was love at first sight for the couple… time would tell. More likely the feelings that the pair had for one another was pure, unadulterated lust and the air became heavy with sexual tension.

'Jesus Mary and Joseph Richie! Ye are in de foin company of a lady! Behave loik I taaart yers!' Eyebrows raised in wonder the culprit and his new fancy-woman burst into laughter and the three of them quickly relaxed in one another's company. Choosing to ride with the caravan, Shana led Flurry beside the wooden home. Once he was safely back in the stable, Shana walked over to rejoin her friends where Eileen Conachy had set up camp… right in front of the orphanage. Shana could not wait to see Albert's face when he learned that his Irish sweetheart had travelled to see him and rushed inside to find him. Suddenly the realisation hit her that it would be far easier for the man who she called father to hear the dreadful news with Eileen by his side.

That night celebrations were in order and the children were permitted to meet the new members of their ever-growing clan. A good sized fire was lit and the cider that Richie made flew freely. Ma Turnbull and Eileen partied and sang together like long lost friends and Richie played his bodhrán whilst Eileen played her harp. Albert was totally smitten with his dark-skinned beauty and infatuated by her exotic allure. Richie was pleased for his Ma' and got along famously with the man who intended to propose a life-long relationship with her. Sharing stew which had been cooking slowly in a huge pot, everyone learned all about Ireland through music, stories and dance as the night went on. Richie delighted everyone with his collection of many different instruments that he played for hours, entertaining them all. At one point, Shana and Richie managed to slip away to become better acquainted. During moments of recovery between passionate kisses, Shana managed to explain the ordeal that she faced. Richie helped her to collect her thoughts and together they planned to reveal the foul truth to Albert the following night.

The newly-united lovers returned to a dying fire and a display that sent the children into fits of hilarious laughter. A tiny baby monkey wearing a miniscule crown was performing acrobatics atop of the caravan. As the couple approached the wildly comical scene, the little tyke jumped with glee when he saw Shana. Richie rolled his eyes at the small ape and called his mother. Before Eileen realised that her son had summoned her attention, Shana felt a tiny hand grab a hardened nipple. Roaring with laughter, the children mischievously held their hands over their eyes and mouths feigning embarrassment as Richie prized the rascal from his girlfriend's tender bosom. All retired to their beds contented and delighted to have Albert's new Irish friends join their unique family.

Richie prodded the last dying ashes of the fire whilst Eileen shared the tale of her tiny baby pet monkey that had been given to her by her closest Irish friend Grace O'Malley. With her soft Celtic lilt, the gypsy recounted the story of how Grace desperately wanted to bring a pet back for her soul sister 'Oileen' and how Grace's own intolerance of animals very nearly won over in the end! Eileen's pretty eyes glazed over as she fondly recollected the day her friend returned from her latest adventure and walked proudly over to her with 'Flint de turd' perched on her shoulder, his long skinny tail wrapped tightly around her thick neck. As soon as the friends had embraced each other, Eileen remembered them sharing a particularly enjoyable passionate kiss which was rudely interrupted as wee Flint immediately broke rank and leapt onto his new mistress' shoulder. Sneaking a tiny hand beneath her blouse, he shocked Eileen by giving her bosom a friendly squeeze… 'Taught oid train de urchin ter please yers whilst oim away arn me travels.' Grace had then winked and reached behind her to take a large amount of Eileen's ass in her strong hand, squeezing it beneath the cloth as if testing the ripeness of a large plump fruit. Eileen continued to entertain her audience by imitating her friend Grace's manly voice and stood with hands upon hips in a masculine stance as she said, 'Oi was only too aware dat widout a doubt any animal was ter get arn me bubbies arn de' return voyage… So's oi caught tree of de flea-bitten filches knowin' full well dat oid shoot em if day caarz'd me or dee crew any bodder… Boy de toim we dropped anchor oid shat two o de feckers an' was left wi' de luckiest wan for ye, sweet Oileen!'

As Richie had sensibly advised, there had been no need to dampen Albert's surprise reunion with news of

Bess' murder. Albert and Eileen had spent the previous night together inside the cosy caravan whilst the young couple had chosen to stay awake under the stars. Richie had lit a new fire and had strong coffee brewing when his Mama emerged from their tiny home. Joined by Albert shortly after, Shana thought it best to reveal the disgusting facts that she had learned from Madame Josephine. She began to explain the unwelcome truth about Petrus and how he had arranged for Bess' murder. Without pausing, she went on to tell how Madame Josephine had forced the young orphaned boy to carry out the evil deed. Albert and Eileen froze where they sat. Eileen took her new man's hand in hers then held him in her arms. After she had revealed each vile fact, Shana took hold of Richie's clenched fist and led him gently away from the grieving man and his lover. On reaching the orphanage, their hearts ached with deepest sorrow as they heard unearthly screams of unfathomable pain. Albert had finally been able to let go.

CHAPTER 8

Fate Melts Two Hearts

The Culley estate buzzed with life. The year in which Shana Culley turned sixteen had been a vengeful one, yet in the young woman's eyes justice had been done. Summer passed into autumn and Queen Mary lost her first child. A barren landscape matched the plight of England's ruler and although the mood of the age was generally grim, this was not so at Mary Maggy's. Anyone who entered the orphanage doors was welcomed by an encouraging sight, way before its time. Children worked alongside adults in a therapeutic, fair environment. Amidst the healthy, happy and industrious groups of young folk were intelligent children who had been given the chance to make something of their lives. The orphanage provided a relaxing, stress-free atmosphere and members of the public were able to purchase the wares produced during a weekly open-day. Empowerment enabled the children to grow confident and feel no shame about their backgrounds and Ma Turnbull and her family ensured that they understood that their situation was by no means through any fault of their own. Eileen even managed to persuade Father McGilacuddy to say Mass at Mary Maggys' 'for de powor wee buggers who needed a fait and what bedder fait was der dan de Cattolic fait?'... so the good priest duly arranged for the children to take strict instruction in the Roman Catholic faith. Eileen and Richie were glad to help the Turnbulls out with instruction for the youngsters and were delighted to take on the role of

Godparents to the newly baptised. As time passed, the wares produced at Mary Maggy's filled the church markets and were making a steady profit for both orphanage and church. Eileen and Ma Turnbull took advantage of a perfect business opportunity and asked the dextrous Richie to teach the children how to whittle wood. Shana provided them with Sandalwood from India and Richie showed them how to carve small wooden beads in the shape of roses. Strung together, they made perfect, heavenly scented Rosary beads that Father McGilacuddy took away to have a sacred cross added. He blessed every one and even had one sent to Queen Mary on the news of her miscarriage. The highly religious queen wrote a letter to the Irish priest to thank him for the delightful gift and to 'bless all thy dear children at the orphanage'. Shana and Albert were delighted at the news and organised a party to celebrate. Queen Mary's letter was duly framed and admired by all visitors when they saw it hanging in pride of place in the main hall.

Eileen and Albert took charge of the festivities which happened to coincide with Yule. Albert was slower than he used to be and arthritis had set in his bones so he was glad to have Richie around to help that year. Flint provided more entertainment for everyone, as always, and the children found pleasure just watching the mischievous monkey up to no good. Unbeknown to Shana, Flint had found the spice cabinet and had begun to help himself to Aframomum... 'Grains of paradise' as they were known amidst the pyrate community. The tiny terror knew the peppered spice well from his days spent with his captor, Eileen's friend, Grace O'Malley. Eileen had only recently broken the news that Grace had become a pyrate after many years of legitimate seafaring.

During the particularly hyperactive night, Ma Turnbull pointed the wicked wee monkey out to Eileen. Her gypsy friend roared with laughter when she saw wee Flint above them, his little prick standing to attention... he chuckled craftily at the women's reaction, proudly baring his tiny pointed teeth.

The story told by Eileen as they sat around the campfire that Yule night was all about her best friend Grace O'Malley and her extraordinary life... Recently Shana had heard that the woman had become infamous in the world of pyracy. Eileen plucked away at her harp strings and told how her best friend had brought back some harmless-looking reddish brown seeds from West Africa. Eileen ground the strong-smelling seeds into a pepper. When she added some of the potent ingredient to food, Flint gobbled his meal like there was no tomorrow. Within minutes the little monkey's eyes widened with surprise and delight and his tiny manhood popped up for action before the two women had even finished their meals! As Eileen told her audience about Flint's first taste of the aphrodisiac, Shana and Richie sneaked inside the caravan for a kiss and cuddle. Soon after, the two lovers rolled around laughing at the excited ape's jubilation... they heard him jump up and down on the roof... the whole caravan began to shake and not one soul could keep a straight face. Even Arthur Turnbull giggled through his shyness at the sight of the horny ape's antics...

Albert could not stop howling at the thought of his Eileen and her bisexual lover coming up with a plan to sell the powerful aphrodisiac to Irish clans. They promised that the new product would increase livestock numbers and indeed breeding did increase tenfold. Flint was the perfect advertisement for a product that definitely raised a few eyebrows amongst other appendages! Unfortunately Flint became addicted to the 'alligator pepper' as it became known and the tiny ape earned the nickname 'Eileen's wee wanker' wherever the gypsy family roamed.

A communal bout of hiccups followed Eileen's hilarious story so she decided to offer the children a Tarot card reading to help calm things down before bedtime. Ma Turnball and her husband took the youngest children to bed, so Eileen allowed a few of the older ones to sit with her in the caravan two at a time. Richie had lit the tiny queenie stove to keep the small room warm and Eileen pulled out a tiny table that had been expertly concealed between two drawers under the seat where she sat. She took out the Tarot cards from their box and passed them over to be shuffled by each questioner. Each person was amazed by her accuracy with things past and present as she revealed things to them that she could never have known without her divination tools. Some girls giggled excitedly on hearing the word 'love' and sprang out of the tiny home with such energy and glee. Others fell silent when the cards that Eileen turned over suggested theft. A clip around the ear from the gypsy ensured that they would keep their hands firmly in pockets in future. Richie's home-brewed cider flowed freely as always on such celebratory occasions and all who entered the caravan came out smiling or blushing with embarrassment. When Shana and Richie went inside for a couple's reading Eileen smiled at them and told them to enjoy their time together because it was not meant to last. Disappointment was written all over poor Richie's face and he joined Albert by the fire to lament in his cider keg.

Shana decided to stay inside and asked for a personal Tarot reading... Eileen asked her to pick three cards, then turned each over in turn... the gypsy's face paled. She told Shana something unimportant and then turned another card... Death... In her happily intoxicated state Shana did not notice her companion's fearful expression...'New beginnings fer ye my lass'... Her second choice revealed the Lovers... At the flick of her wrist, Eileen's voice became harsh, panic had set in... the third card was the Devil and Eileen quickly replaced it in the pack and told Shana to go and spend some time with Richie 'befarr me poor son is overcome wi' de sickness of de haaart!' With a mock look of concern, Shana bounced up from the small stool and ducked her head through the small door. Calling Richie, the young woman ran off into the darkness with her pining lover in tow. Eileen thanked the pagan gods and goddesses and all her ancestors... then said a quick 'Hail Mary and Our Farder' before she returned the beautifully illustrated Tarot cards to their drawer. Fear and despair were clear in her wide deep-set eyes. Shocked into sobriety, Eileen stepped out into the field to join Albert who was singing softly and tending the fire.

Everyone outside still buzzed with animation and gathered around the lovers asking Eileen how the magic cards worked. Eileen humoured the children for a while until she had an idea that would help to end the night well. With her tortured mind still spinning with confusion about the message from Shana's reading, Eileen tried to put aside the image of the damning cards. Shana had innocently drawn the two cards that rarely appeared together but when they did, they foretold certain death and terrible misery...

Gathering the children around the fire, Eileen began to tell them about a ghost that she felt roaming their land... 'a man from toims laang ago, verily oi tells ye! Hark! 'E approaches noi!....' Some of the boys gasped and started to look around them in sheer panic and a girl let out a short shrill shriek. Eileen began to describe the spectre that she claimed to be able to see approaching them from the stables. Dressed in clothes from the days when knights fought one another for land, Eileen began to beckon the ghost... she kept calling into the dark misty field until finally she said loudly; 'Prithee, come hither me daaaarlin! Flint has some of dat dare hard-on powder dat ye caught di scent of! Dat' ul be two whole shillins t' ye, koind sir!'

The children's relieved laughter could be heard in the church on the other side of town as Father McGilacuddy sang Mass, thankfully with his back to the congregation so they could not see his smile. He had grown up with lovely Eileen and knew full well that she had been up to her late-night ghost storytelling. Popping a comfit discreetly in his mouth, he made a mental note to drop by the caravan the following day to share tea with his cousin and have a Tarot reading.... He was keen to learn whether the bastard daughter of the witch Anne Boleyn had any power over the throne. Since her sister Mary had miscarried, she was growing weak with one phantom pregnancy after another. The canny Irish priest wanted to be sure that he would be safe to stay on English soil for another year before returning to Ireland. Father McGilacuddy had heeded the written warnings from his homeland. Elizabeth was determined to take over the crown on her sister's death and allow England to become a Protestant country once more as it had been during her father's reign.

Following Eileen's tale of the wandering frustrated ghost, the children retired to bed after a perfect day. When Shana and Richie began to argue about the seriousness of their friendship, Albert decided that it was time to open an aged bottle of whisky. Eileen toasted the confused lovebirds and welcomed the dawn fairies. The four figures huddled together under a thin watery moon. As if fate was willing him on, Albert spotted a shooting star and it was at that magical moment that he told Eileen that he loved her like he had never loved another soul. Kneeling unsteadily before her, he produced a gold ring that he and Sushana had secretly bought from a gold merchant the previous week. Eileen was delighted by the surprise proposal and edged over to show Shana her ring. Respectful old Albert asked Richie for his permission to wed his mother and the two men embraced like father and son. Richie was absolutely euphoric that his mother had found such a wonderful man and started to cry tears of pure joy. Even Flint came out to see what all the fuss was about. Everyone burst out laughing when they saw the mischievous monkey slowly emerge from the caravan, rubbing his sleepy eyes and wearing a miniature fez that he had collected on his travels. Yawning and stretching like a little old man, the impertinent monkey tutted at the reception he had received and returned to the comfort of his velvet cushion.

Living with his fiancé in the pretty horse-drawn home fulfilled all of Albert's needs and desires. Although occasionally he felt pangs of guilt that it was he, not his sister, who had lived to find love and watch Sushana become a woman. The new-found family was loved and accepted by the Turnbull clan and the children adored their new baby brother... in the form of a particularly impish monkey. Flint regularly stole nuts and comfits and kept a secret stash of booty under his decorative purple velvet cushion that was trimmed with gold rope and pretty tassels on each corner. No-one had ever been allowed to touch Flint's pillow... that is until caring Albert moved into the caravan. Flint adored his mistress' new man and the old fellow felt the same about him. Wherever Albert went, his little friend was sure to be found. Flint often rode around perched on Albert's shoulder and both characters took up smoking when Eileen gave them each a clay pipe... she had a fine selection of all shapes and sizes brought back from countries all over the New World. Grace O'Malley referred to the pipes as 'nose-warmers' which always made Flint burst into fits of uncontrollable laughter. To Shana's delight, the lucky gypsy even owned an ornate bong from Turkey.

Whilst Albert and Flint struck up a relationship second to none, Shana and Richie played and canoodled with each other in every nook and cranny they could find in the derelict monastery within the grounds of Mary Maggy's. Shana was glad that she had made the sensible decision to leave the derelict building as a landmark on her property. She and her beau spent many a lust-filled hour canoodling between the broken-down stone walls that once housed supposedly celibate monks. That Yuletide, life could not have been better for all who lived at Shana's place.

On the third day of advent, Shana took in Sarah Hobsbawn who was a sorry sight to behold. It took four days for her to be able to stand without aid. The woman had been abused beyond belief and was in a wretched state. Sarah had been accused of adultery by her aged and grotesque husband. His bitterness had taken over his life and he had become obsessed with the notion that his pretty young wife was sleeping with the blacksmith, Saul Newton. The sad and sickening truth was that Sarah still loved her husband but also loved Saul. She had known Saul since she was a young girl and they had loved each other from the beginning. Being of noble birth, Sarah was not permitted to marry a blacksmith's son and was betrothed to a local nobleman when she was thirteen years old. A loyal and loving wife, Sarah made the huge mistake of admitting to her aged husband that she had befriended her old beau. Her husband soon grew insecure and gradually began to hate the handsome younger man. Finally the day came when Sarah's husband could stand it no longer and accused his innocent wife of adultery.

Sarah Hobsbawn was paraded around town on the ducking stool and then ducked in a river where the waters were not running high enough to provide any entertainment for the crowds. She took her humiliating punishment fearlessly and refused to admit to any crime. Following weeks of suffering severe degradation, Sarah was eventually locked into a cage that had been erected in the town square. She was made to wear a brank or scold's bridle; a cage-like torture devise that encased her whole head... a spiked metal bar pressed on her tongue so that she was unable to talk. Sarah was left like this for days whilst Saul had been forced to forge an obscene phallus-shaped branding iron. The blacksmith was made to watch as she was branded and then hauled away to be tortured. Saul Newton refused to degrade his childhood sweetheart by repenting for a sin that neither of them had committed or even considered! With the most incredible bravery, he protected her name until his torturers lost interest, dragged him away and boiled him alive in a vat of scalding oil. The poor man died in absolute agony.

Disgusted by the fate of a woman who, in her eyes, had been tormented enough, Shana decided to help. Due to the prisoner's weak state, she had no choice but to involve Richie. She shared her carefully thought-out plans with him and together they decided to rescue poor Sarah. Late one night, the two lovers prepared themselves for the attempt to free the trapped woman. Richie borrowed tools from Albert and Shana took a horse blanket to wrap Sarah in. It was a frosty night and when they arrived at the town square there was no-one to be seen. Two wild dogs had chosen to sleep behind the cage. They growled as the strangers approached but were soon pacified when Shana threw them some generous chunks of salted pork. Contented snorting and chomping noises gave Richie the signal to begin filing the padlock. Seconds seemed like minutes as the young man worked away at the metal, his fingers aching with cold. A snap was heard so Shana took over and prized open the heavy door with an iron bar that Albert used for removing horseshoes. The sudden sound of footsteps made the pair start and they leapt into the cage, quickly covering themselves with the blanket. Richie could only just make out the form of Sarah's crumpled body which lay in the foetal position in the far corner of the cage. Shana whispered to him to stay still until the footsteps had passed and he did exactly that. Thankfully the pair enjoyed a little warmth as they lay huddled next to the exhausted prisoner. It seemed to take forever for the passer-by to walk the length of the square and the two rescuers were relieved that Shana had brought enough meat along to keep the dogs quiet.

Luckily the disturbance had probably been caused by a vagabond who was undoubtedly drunk by the sound of the irregular pace of his footsteps. Only a vagrant or a fool would brave the bitter cold so late at night. Unfortunate vagrants were forced to search for food when there was nobody around... if caught, they could expect to be thrown into the stocks for at least three days, then face a good whipping. Vagrants were sadly quite common then and would try to gain work but with few skills they could only find jobs like repairing the roads. If caught a second time, they would be forced to live and work in bridewells or correction houses. If they kept getting caught, they were likely to be sent overseas to work in the colonies but some of the unluckier ones were hanged. Shuffling along, the poor intruder had whimpered with cold and pain and passed by without checking for food... no doubt he knew that the dogs and pigs would have cleared the square of any scraps. When all was quiet once more, Shana wrapped the young woman in the blanket and whispered reassuringly in her ear. Hearing no reply, Shana pulled the woman to her feet and Richie helped to carry her to the safety of Mary Maggy's as quickly as possible.

Sarah never spoke again but soon settled into a life of caring at the welcoming orphanage. Ma Turnbull made sure that the poor wench never wanted for anything and Eileen and Richie became particularly fond of their new charge. Shana befriended the once beautiful woman and would read her stories of hope and love but never once did the poor wretch smile... not even when Flint made his debut appearance. Scratching his little head in disbelief, even he seemed to understand how much pain this woman had endured. It was a heart-wrenching sight to see the tiny creature wrap his skinny arms around her delicate neck. He would kiss her dampened cheek which was permanently covered in sores because it was never dry of tears... a sorry sight to behold. Sarah now had people around her who loved her... only time would tell if she could ever find happiness again.

Albert was the one most affected by Sarah's mental health for he knew only too well how devastating life could be. He decided that a diversion may distract her from her grief. Since Sarah seemed to enjoy spending time with Eileen in her pretty caravan, Albert decided that he would surprise them both with a well overdue redecoration. Without anyone but Richie knowing what he had planned to do, Albert collected brightly coloured paints and even managed to get hold of some gold leaf from an aged scribe who had once been a monk. Eileen had moved into a small bedchamber in the orphanage since Sarah had arrived. The two women would sleep together in one bed as Sarah had the most disturbing nightmares and her bloodcurdling screams would wake up the children. Eileen's presence appeared to calm the poor soul, so Albert and Richie stayed out in the tiny home. Shana and Richie no longer slept together since his Mama had foreseen their separation, besides there was something about Sarah that Richie wanted to conquer and he was falling deeper in love with her every day.

Two nights before Christmas, Albert and Richie sat before a wonderful blazing fire drinking cider. Richie had spent the day at the orphanage with his mother and Sarah and he began to share his deep concerns about the wretched wench with Albert. The old man had spent a long day with the horses and had arranged a last minute drop-off through Culley's cut but he never felt too tired when loved ones needed him. Richie poured out his heart and the old man listened as a father would. The younger man was feeling very emotional that night and needed support and love... there was no better person than Albert to turn to. Eventually, too much stew and cider got the better of Richie and the men laughed as he began to fart. The noise of the wind expelled from his arse became louder as he laughed, forcing it through in spurts as if his bottom itself was chortling. Eventually even Richie had had enough and Albert suggested the poor lad take a good long crap before the gases seeping from his rear caught alight. The two men roared with laughter as they enjoyed a harmless release of childlike humour together. Taking some large dock leaves with him, Richie wandered off over the crunchy ice-covered field. Albert smiled as Richie disappeared behind a hedge to find a suitable place to take a good long dump.

Albert took the lamp inside Eileen's caravan and chose a bright scarlet paint to start on the outside. The wood was in excellent condition considering it had been neglected recently. The journey to England could not have done it much good but how happy he felt that his true love had come to him. Reaching for the large barrel of cider and his leather tankard old Albert felt a sharp pain in his chest. Grabbing hold of a curtain to steady himself, he realised that he had lost the feeling in his left hand. The old man stumbled forward and knocked into the cider barrel, clutching at his chest. The lamp dropped to the floor and Albert fell with it, knocking his head on the wooden drawer beneath the small bed. Blood trickled from the gashing wound on his temple as he lay unable to move, watching the flames erupt around him. Attempting a shout, Albert began to panic when nothing but a groan escaped his lips. The pack of Tarot cards dropped onto the floor and he stared in disbelief as the packet blackened, flames licking at the thick paper. Searing agony forced Albert to squeeze his eyes shut as he began to pray... for forgiveness for lying with Eileen before they had married... Albert begged God to look after his Shana and Eileen before his soul gave up the agonising battle to survive long enough for his body to be rescued.

Eileen awoke to the sound of screaming the like of which she had never heard before. She hoped to God that she would never ever hear that horrific sound again. Richie could not be calmed and sobbed for days following the devastating event. It had taken Shana, Benjamin Turnbull and Eileen to hold Richie down and prevent him from entering the raging fire to rescue his friend... his mother's special love. Those who had the dreadful misfortune of seeing Albert's charred remains never got over the scene. Even in his final hour, this fine man had been trying to make others happy.

As an owl hooted a haunting lament, Eileen broke down next to her son and screamed that she had been warned but could never interfere with fate's hand. Wracked with pain, Ma Turnbull took her sobbing friend back to the orphanage leaving Shana to calm Richie. The poor fellow kept mumbling about a curse and wishing to God that she had never told Albert how his sister had died. Richie had gone mad with guilt and had to be taken inside by Benjamin and two stable hands who had been woken by the commotion.

Feeling as she had never felt before, Shana silently fetched Simon's clothes. Numbness filled her very soul as she made her way slowly to the tavern where she and Petrus had shared their last drink... The only way she knew how to cope with her father's horrific death was to become Simon... She had no idea whether the landlady would open up when she heard the banging but she was determined to try... Shana left the foul stench of charred flesh behind her and walked slowly towards the King's Head.

CHAPTER 9

An Unforeseen Journey

Mrs. Bradshaw had been worried about the young orphan lad for days and was pleased to see that he had finally met with some company. Stifling a snigger, she imagined the boy must have been hollow to take the vast amount of ale and gin that he had consumed in the past two days and nights. Considering his age, Simon had impressed the landlady of the King's Head with his ability to hold the grog. She was all too used to throwing out men twice his age who were totally slaughtered having drunk only half the amount that Simon had. The aging widow had allowed him to stay room and board for both nights and he had soon cleared the boards of food that she had supplied without a problem. Simon had been popping into her establishment now and then for a few months and she had warmed to the polite lad. If it were not for her two own sons, she would have taken him on as a spare hand but she could not afford another mouth to feed since her husband had died of consumption two years earlier.

Shana smiled at the three men who had been in her company since the previous night. Kirk, Leonard and Heath had taken her mind away from Mary Maggy's and she had learned much about the New World from the strangers who were fast becoming friends with Simon. Laughing, she whistled for Mrs. Bradshaw to bring over a fresh pitcher of ale for Simon and his welcome guests. Shana's drinking pals had been very impressed by the clay tankard that he had bought from a local potter. The clever tradesman made tankards with whistles baked into their handles so ale-lovers could summon the innkeeper for a refill. Shana needed to relieve her bladder so she stood up and headed for the door. Out back there was a narrow alley that reeked of piss and punters had to watch where they stood to relieve themselves. Many a drunken lout had taken more than a piss between the tavern and the merchant's house that backed onto the property. Nestled comfortably between the wattle walls, Shana untied her breeches, dropped them to her knees and squatted above the clearest spot of ground.

When Shana woke up, she felt dampness between her legs. Disgusted by her actions, she cursed herself for the careless aim and grimaced at the strong pungent stink of her clothes. At first she found difficulty opening her dry sore eyes and then reality set in. A swaying motion made the girl nauseous and weakly she allowed her heavy head to drop straight back onto hard timber. Shrieking cries of hungry gulls offended her hearing so she put two hands to her ears in a vain attempt to block out the annoying sound. A rather pleasant smell of tar wafted over to where she lay. At least it helped a little to disguise the stench of puke and other bodily excretions. Seemingly from nowhere, a gush of water covered Shana from head to toe. Its coolness felt pleasant yet the force of the water slapped her face hard, rudely awakening her confused mind. Determined to regain her wits, Shana wiped her wet face on her shoulder to help ease the sting... Licking her salty lips, she remembered the sudden pain on the side of her head... how could she have been so naïve especially after what had happened to Bess?

On her first attempt to stand, Shana yelped as the thick rope pulled her back onto the deck. Clenching her strong hands into tight fists, she grimaced and looked around at the man to whom she was bound. Still fast asleep from heaven knows what he was sleeping off, the thug who was tied securely to Shana made an unpleasant snorting noise. Attractive patterns decorated the darkened leather-like skin of his upper arms. A long black silky ponytail that grew from the centre of his otherwise bald head immediately told her that he was from another land. As her volatile temper reached boiling point, Shana decided that she would take no more and yelled at the top of her voice, 'Whichever foot-licking arse-swiver dared t...' The words caught in her throat as she felt the first cruel swipe of the lash. Before she could draw in breath, a huge fist hit her straight between the eyes.

The next time Shana awoke, she instantly regretted her blind bravery. Lying on what felt like a briar bush, the bruised, battered and bleeding woman could not even summon enough strength to lift her head to see where she had been taken... or more likely thrown! The feel of her broken body caused her to feel absolute dread and a sense of utter helplessness crept over her. Shana burst into tears and lay sobbing in the rat-infested bowels of The Falcon. Around her lay bodies, some showed signs of life whilst others were rotting away amongst them. Shana Culley had no idea how long she had been on the craft that sailed steadily towards a destination unbeknown to her. She hoped to God that she was still in her sixteenth year and that somehow she could find a way to get out of this dreadful mess.

During the time she had spent with the dead and dying brown-skinned slaves, Shana had learned the art of true survival. Unable to communicate by speech, the gutsy maiden had developed a way of signing using hand movements and soon managed to communicate with the people who did not yet understand English. Over time a small group of slaves, the strongest amongst the chained and fettered captives, managed to learn pigeon-English. Gradually they began to view Shana as their leader. Dark brown eyes glowing with respect, the other captives looked to her for guidance. She was the only white person amongst them and it took a great deal to gain any trust from people who had been abducted by the white man. The slaves watched as the boy made himself stronger by stretching as much as the small hold would allow and lifting his heavy chains to strengthen weakened muscles. When their inhuman captors living above them remembered to throw down meagre scraps of rotten food, Shana sorted it out in equal rations.

Separation of the dead from the living kept the sharp-toothed vermin away as much as possible. Each time some poor weak or diseased soul died in the cramped crawl-space in the depths of the slave ship, the rats ate away the flesh until the bones could be broken free from the chains. That way, Shana's gang were able to throw the corpses over to a far corner. In no time at all, the bones were stripped clean of flesh and the rats became fat and satisfied enough to leave the living captives alone. The smell was horrendous... absolutely diabolical... like nothing Shana had ever experienced. The newly formed group grew stronger every day; one woman had even successfully given birth in the foul dank hell under thick oak boards.

Precious was a tall black man from African lands, he had been renamed by Shana because his given name was so long and impossible for her tongue to master. His name and those of his kin consisted of a series of gibberish and clicks; or so it seemed to her. It had become essential for Shana and the five survivors from the original hundred slaves, to work together. The crew above believed Shana to be a white lad who they had abducted to take over the duties of captain's cabin boy. As far as Shana could gather, the slave ship had docked in Teignmouth port whilst the crew collected sacks of grain and woven cloth to take with them to Antwerp. There they planned to trade the meagre amount of slaves who had miraculously survived the arduous journey from Africa. In danger of running out of food during the long journey, the crew had rationed what they could muster amongst themselves, knowing that the strongest of the slaves would probably survive a few weeks of starvation. Once the ship had reached Belgian shores they planned to sell the slaves, pick up fresh supplies and more wares to trade. Most sickening was the fact that these men were well used to treating their captives with mindless cruelty and thought more of the ship's cats than another human life. Shana had seen plenty of villains and hoodlums hang or suffer torture as punishment for crimes that they had knowingly committed but this kind of abuse of men, women and children was totally unforgivable in her eyes. No crime had been committed by her newfound friends and they had grown to love Simon as their own kin.

Accustomed to the dark, filthy quarters the six survivors plotted to escape once they reached the port of Antwerp. Shana had told her friends that they were welcome to live and work in the orphanage if they could make their way to England. Over the weeks she managed to teach them how to ask directions. By repeating the words 'Ma Turnbull', 'Mary Maggy's' and 'East Teignmouth', the slaves would surely find someone back in England who would help guide them to sanctuary. Shana tried her level best to put them at ease for the time being but they were beginning to grow restless and fear for their lives. Judging by the reaction of her attacker the day she had awoken on board the sorry vessel, Shana was all too aware that she would never be able to escape alone. Precious, his wife Kia and their baby, Taru had all survived thus far and she was determined to make sure that their little family found the peace and safety they deserved. Precious had been so grateful to the young man who had helped him deliver his son and he was never going to forget that kindness. To them, Simon was one of their family. 'Gift' and 'Princess' were the names that the other two survivors had been given by Precious who enjoyed learning English words and their meanings. Gift was older than Precious but a strong man despite his appearance. Standing around five feet tall, the wiry man had no bottom teeth and a milky layer appeared to have grown over his eyes. Despite his unhealthy appearance, he had managed to outlive many who had seemed much fitter. Princess was about the same age as Shana and used to cuddle the white boy who she had grown to love. Since they had both grown stronger, they had began to explore each other sexually and Shana had found it difficult to keep Princess' wandering hands off her body… she was not yet ready to test her new clan's views of sexuality. Well-used to men becoming offended at the very idea of a woman being in charge of anything but babies or hairstyles, she thought it safest to stay disguised as Simon… at least until they were free.

Soon the day arrived when The Falcon reached the port of Antwerp. Anchored offshore, the ship swayed in a gentle summer breeze. Her crew prepared rafts to row ashore in order to buy fresh supplies and merchandise to bring back to their ship. It was essential for them to load the vessel with as many goods and wares as possible to trade at their next port of call. Although the slave trade brought good money, most of the slaves had died in transit.

Below decks, Shana pondered for a short while... had she not suffered at the hands of the heartless crew; she would probably have enjoyed a stint at sea with the chance to explore new countries. Once again, anger stirred inside her but she had learnt from her hard lesson. The thought of her new family's fate and a possible chance of freedom soon quelled any hasty action. Listening in silence to the sounds of busy sailors moving above them, Shana and the others awaited their chance of escape. She had devised a plan and each person had been told exactly what part they had to play in their bid for freedom. Tiny Taru suckled contently at his mother's swollen breast. Shana's days spent with Ma Turnbull had taught her all there was to know about baby and mother care. She had made sure that Kia had eaten the largest portions of slop and the others had willingly agreed to take a smaller ration both whilst Kia was pregnant and feeding her new baby. Tenderly, Shana touched Taru's forehead and smiled reassuringly at his pretty mother. It was almost time for them to make their move.

Captain Edward Thurlow continued to shout orders to his crew as they rowed away from the Falcon on rafts. It would take a couple of hours at least whilst they purchased goods from the docksides. Standing idly with three men who he had chosen to stay aboard, the cantankerous oaf of a captain would allow no one a minute's peace. Shana was finding it difficult to work out exactly where each man was positioned. She pushed her face right up to the circular iron grid in order to see where the captain stood... he was her target. Precious had insisted on dealing with the two largest of the remaining crew and the last blaggard was Gift's. The task of unpinning their leg irons had been assigned to Kia and Princess. It was therefore essential for someone to gain either a weapon or tool during the struggle. The two women needed to hide with baby Taru until Shana gave them the all clear. Whilst the slaves in the hold waited for an opportune time to attack, the skeleton crew relaxed and enjoyed the sunshine whilst they waited for the others to return with news and wares from the busy port.

Beads of sweat collected on the silken brown skin of Kia's breast as Taru suckled hungrily on her nipple. Huddled close together, the little group listened to their abductors as they enjoyed the last of the rhum in ignorant bliss of their captives' plan. To Shana's relief, she recognised the slurring tones of 'Fingers Trawford', a one-armed member of Captain Thurlow's crew. Bragging about his days spent serving under King Henry VIII, he was repeating a well-worn story of the day he sailed on the King's favourite ship, the Mary Rose. She had been named in honour of the King's youngest sister. Grumbling at having to listen to the boring tale, his long-suffering colleagues joined in with the final lame joke... 'Mary Rose went out like me dear ole wife... she looked fine and top heavy as I rode her out to sea but sank into the depths of hell when she 'ad too many men insoid 'er!'... Trawford cursed his tormentors and turned his back on them, slamming a booted foot onto the trapdoor where the prisoners lay in wait. 'Whoresons!' shouted Trawford as he stamped his foot and spat straight into Taru's face.

Shana knew at once that it was time and Precious yelled in his native tongue as he punched the bars that separated the strong black man from the pathetic bully. Precious' anger boiled inside as Shana shot him a warning look... this could easily be their one and only chance of freedom! As Simon, Shana's main aim was to keep her small team focused, alert and alive. Simon gave Kia the sign she had been waiting for and she threw herself into fits of convulsion, frothing at the mouth, eyes rolling wildly and bolting from their deep sockets. Her performance was terrifyingly realistic and had the others not known its falsity, they would never have doubted the reality of her suffering. Wasting no time, Shana called Trawford and begged him to open the hatch. 'She ails of the sweating sickness and we will all surely die if we catches it!' she yelled with convincing terror. Making as much noise and banging as they possibly could, the little gang thrashed about in the bowels of the ship as if they were crazed... Kia never once stopped the violent throes of a woman possessed and the crew above began to feel uneasy. As Simon, Shana jabbered about voodoo magic and witch-doctor's curses, feeding the ever-nervous sailors an impressive yarn. The superstitious sailors began to feel uneasy. She kept up her act until Trawford suffered a sudden pang of guilt and fetched a huge ring of keys from the captain's cabin. Angry at their mate's action a fight broke out on deck. Precious readied himself, crouching like a panther in the murky darkness of his prison. Admiration shone in his deep brown eyes as he watched Kia thrash uncontrollably next to him. He was the only one who stayed alert, silent and still amidst the chaotic melée. Suddenly Princess screamed. The horrific, blood-curdling scream caused a chill shiver to run down Captain Thurlow's spine. Wild-eyed with hysterical fear the beautiful black woman pointed at the demented face of the prisoner closest to her... Precious held a corpse's leg to his mouth and ripped a healthy slice of meat from the calf, grinning insanely as he began to chew the flesh. Looking at his new meal, he faked the sudden dawning that Princess looked tastier than the rotting flesh. Throwing it aside, he leapt at Princess and appeared to sink his teeth into her neck.

Sailors are renowned as being superstitious in the extreme and the act of cannibalism was the final straw for the men. Captain Thurlow had reassured his crew when he explained that the natives that they captured and transported to be sold as slaves were no more than animals being taken to slaughter. For years it had been deemed unlucky to carry women onboard any craft so the intelligent captain ensured that female slaves were seen by the crew as no more unlucky than a female cat or monkey. Since many sailors chose to keep cats and monkeys of both sexes aboard their ship, it made perfect sense to them that holding female slaves as cargo would pose no threat of bad luck as they were just livestock. In actual fact, the slaves lived amongst male and female rats so all were considered to be vermin.

Captain Thurlow had not taken into account the fact that these 'natives' were pagan creatures who worshipped the devil or worse! The mere thought of having no less than a witch doctor amongst them made him uneasy and to say that his men were panicking would be an extreme understatement. As the drunken Trawford fumbled and juggled with the huge bunch of keys, the other men turned into gibbering idiots, their maniacal shrieks adding to the confusion. Keeping up the commotion, Shana steadied herself for the pending attack and mentally urged the oaf Trawford to find the right key. 'Stay calm'... 'not too soon'... 'be ready'... Precious and Gift clenched their large fists tightly, anticipating their long-awaited revenge.

In the event it all happened quickly; a chaotic blur of violent struggle. Shana and her gang had the advantage over the terrified and confused crew. A petrified Trawford had panicked and made the impulsive decision to free the white boy from the company of a vile, cannibalistic witch doctor and his possessed victim. Captain Thurlow had completely lost control. In a desperate attempt to stop Trawford from rescuing Simon, he ordered his men to seize the demented sailor. With a dread of being cursed, the crew refused to go anywhere near the prisoners so Trawford was forced to unlock the hatch himself. Captain Thurlow fired his pistol as Trawford struggled with the trapdoor. The minute the hatch was wrenched open, a lucky shot from the captain's pistol hit the femoral artery in the sailor's thigh. The lead shot caused a torrent of blood to spurt all over the wooden boards as the stunned man skidded across the deck in agonising death throes. Managing to grab hold of a knife from the dying man's belt, Kia used its tip to unlock the others' shackles, then her own.

Gift was the lightest and fastest of the prisoners and when Kia had released his shackles, sprang from his trap like an enraged leopard. Following closely behind, Precious picked up Trawford's sprawling body and threw him with unbelievable force. It hit the captain who fired a stray shot from his second pistol that skimmed the tall slave's head leaving an ugly gouge of open flesh on his glistening forehead. Without as much as a flinch Precious leapt at his first target, grabbed him around the neck and began to crush his throat between immense bulging muscles. Fending off an attacker from behind, the big African man retaliated with an upward elbow jab that hit the man perfectly on target. A sickening crunch of bone breaking under the force of the powerful blow met with an unearthly scream as the victim's nasal bone embedded into his brain. Precious had struggled to keep hold of his initial target with one arm but lost grip of him as the captain fired another shot. Shana had managed to overpower her shocked victim and grabbed his cutlass, slashing it across the base of his throat with one clean sweep. Bloodlust overcame the woman whose heart was full of pent-up hatred and loathing of her captors.

Gift and the women watched in amazed disbelief as Simon attacked his victim over and over with cold unadulterated violence. When the captain finally slumped lifelessly to the floor, Shana dropped down with him, punching and kicking the body in an uncontrollable frenzy. With no further threat of attack, everyone but Shana hastily continued their escape but she seemed to have lost any fear of discovery. In a final repulsive act of revenge, Shana took hold of the cutlass and grabbed a clump of Thurlow's ginger hair. Carefully tracing the sharp blade in a neat line starting under the dead man's bearded chin and all around his battered face, the young woman finished her final cut and ripped the captain's face clean away from its skull. Covering her small baby's face, Kia stepped forward as if she was going to approach the enraged Simon but her husband held her back.

Realising that it was far too late to calm the boy, Precious made sure that his family had the best possible chance of escape before the remainder of the crew returned. All he and his little family could do was watch with horror as their leader and friend hacked off the faces of their captors with unfathomable rage. It was a sorry and sad final sight to behold as the women climbed down the ladder into the waiting rowing boat. Now they would most likely have to prepare for their next ordeal without their special friend and saviour. As Precious kissed Taru and passed him to his mother who waited in the boat, he looked up the rope ladder and wondered whether he would be successful in persuading poor Simon to leave with him. His wife looked at him in despair as she realised his intentions. Holding her sister tightly, Princess gave the signal to Gift to start rowing. Precious never looked back and began his ascent back to join his crazed white friend. His sacrifice was large but he had faith.

Madness had not taken hold of Shana Culley's mind; quite the opposite in actual fact. As she sat on the main deck of the Falcon, sewing the weather-beaten faces of its malicious crew together in a sick display of horrific bunting, she calmly whistled a sailor's ditty to her mask-like audience. Neatly stitching each face securely onto the next, Shana looked up at her friend and gave him a triumphant smile.

CHAPTER 10

A Woman's Scorn

When Shana had finished sewing her gruesome creation, she explained to Precious that she had decided to stay in the Falcon until the rest of the crew returned. Busy nailing the horrific banner to the masts of the vessel, she explained herself to the utterly bemused Precious. He stood and stared at Simon's handiwork, listening intently to his friend's explanation. Once she was satisfied with the display, Shana turned to her friend and began to untie her shirt. The poor man thought that the boy had lost his mind. Baring her small, pert breasts to the surprised man, Shana suddenly felt an indescribable sense of power. Dropping to his knees with exhaustion and shock, Precious just stared at the woman standing in front of him. Laughing aloud, Shana threw back her head and breathed the fresh sea air deep into her lungs.

After a few minutes, Precious began to snigger then roared with laughter as he spotted the neat little pile of jewellery that his friend had carefully taken from the victims. Pointing at a pair of gleaming gold hoop earrings, the African man pointed to her ears and the large sail needle that his friend had used to sew the vile facial collage together. Grabbing the earrings at once, Shana lay down in front of her African friend and handed him the needle. Pressing her earlobe down and holding it firmly onto the wooden board beneath her, Precious pushed the thick needle through Shana's flesh followed by the earring. After he had pierced both ears, Precious lay down next to Shana and holding her in his strong arms, kissed her forehead in a protective paternal way.

Collecting weapons and ammunition was easy for the two friends and together they stripped their victims of clothes and dressed themselves in outfits fitting for the outlaws that they had become with little choice. Precious stood tall and proud wearing a brightly-coloured head scarf that completely covered his closely cropped hair. He had chosen a loose-fitting white shirt, a finely embroidered silk waistcoat and a pair of black leather boots made of the softest kidskin. Looking at her handsome companion with a hint of pride, Shana tied a scarlet silken scarf around his neck to complete the look. Considering the lack of female clothing aboard the slave ship, the handy young woman had managed to create a spectacularly eye-catching creation for her attire. She had taken a pair of one of the dead men's hose and cut off the legs to produce an extremely short garment that was sure to shock. The shortened trews gave her the freedom of movement that she was surely going to need. Tucking in a well chosen shirt that disguised her sex once more, Shana tied silken scarves around her small waist and over one shoulder to carry her chosen weapons. A fine cutlass rested at her slim hip in an ornate scabbard that displayed status and wealth. The two friends had shared out the jewellery equally and were suitably adorned with the finest pieces of gold. Had neither known the other, each would have had the impression that they faced men of great importance who were without doubt within the pyrate trade.

When the unsuspecting crew returned to their ship later that evening, they were met with a violent welcome. Drunk and satisfied with bellies full of food, twenty sailors started to board their vessel with no idea of what awaited them. Blind with fury, Shana leapt at the first three men before they even set foot on deck. Precious was close behind her and thrust his dagger deep into the ribs of an unsuspecting sailor. The shrill battle cries surprised the men still climbing the rope ladders and they watched helplessly as dead and dying men plummeted past them into the chilling depths below. Panic ensued and to the attackers' relief not one sailor turned back. In their drunken state the men became confused yet determined to regain rightful charge of the Falcon. On seeing their adversaries the sailors were filled with dread and offered little retaliation. Hacking and firing at will, Precious and Shana fought a bloody battle back to back against a bunch of foul-hearted cowards. Their faces gave away their fearful thoughts as each spotted the grotesque banner that stretched above their heads. Such a gruesome act could surely only have been performed by pyrates or witch-doctors... the men were terrified and their vulnerability gave the Shana and Precious even more of an advantage.

Making the most of their excellent position, the pair faced their enemies with incredible courage and strength. Leading their opponents to areas where they had laid down prepared, loaded pistols and spare weaponry, they battled fiercely against ridiculous odds. Falling before the two attackers, some begged for mercy others shouted abuse but every man fell under their combined and unforgiving wrath. Finally the last three sailors stepped onto the ship and faced the blood-thirsty escapees. Before Precious had a chance to recover from his last struggle he received a heavy blow to his left temple and dropped to one knee. With cutlass still held firmly in hand, the strong man hit his attacker across the mouth with the butt of his spent pistol. Following through with a low stabbing thrust, his opponent's guts spilled onto slippery, blood-saturated decks.

Shana last saw Precious as he slumped forward onto his victim's body. A bright flash exploded in her face and the traumatised woman screamed in agony. It was a sorry sight to see as Shana reeled around in intense pain. Before her attacker realised, she thrust a short sharp knife into his groin and stabbed with seemingly unceasing energy. Then all of a sudden her vision and hearing failed and Shana collapsed in a heap. Ironically she had fallen onto the hatch door that had trapped her and her friends inside the small stinking cramped cell. There, below the decks, she had remained for five miserable months out of sixteen years of her life.

A cold winter breeze caused Shana to stir. A steady stream of warm fluid sprayed steadily against her face. The bitter taste caught at the back of her throat as she breathed in too deeply. She could see the sun shining brightly behind the silhouette of the man standing above her. With a start she shook her head and puked up the piss. Recognising the bellowing, jeering voice of the quartermaster Shana realised her plight. Frightened for Precious' fate, she called out in vain. They had fought together side by side and skilfully battled unfair odds only to be captured once more. Reaching her hand up to touch her cheekbone, Shana realised with sickening dread that Precious was still alive and being whipped mercilessly. Each lash that tore away his flesh made her heart ache with regret that she had not insisted her friend join his family. What in the blazes did she think that they could have possibly achieved? The sound of the African man's final grunts was weak and low as the lash tore into his broken body. Tears poured from Shana's eyes as she banged her fists against the wooden boards that formed the side of her prison. Biting her tongue until her mouth filled with blood Shana head-butted the hard wood until unconsciousness finally rid her mind from torturous turmoil.

A freezing breeze whipped at Shana's sore skin when she regained consciousness. Blue skies freckled with sporadic white wisps of cloud pulsated into vision. Slowly she opened her bruised and swollen eyelids allowing her stinging eyes to become accustomed to bright daylight. Redundant sails flapped against their masts as the ship still lay idle in the calm waters. Gulls screamed their whining lament and Shana tried to focus on the blurred faces that surrounded her. As she strained her eyes a faint glimmer of hope filled her heart when she spotted the dark face amongst her audience. Straddling the pole to which she was firmly tied, Shana found it difficult to stretch her stiff body to an upright position. As her vision became clearer she stared back insolently at her enemies. Then, with sudden horror, she realised why her motley audience were so intent on seeing the reaction of the boy who they had strung up for a thrashing... they wanted to see Simon's reaction... when he saw... what they had done... to...

A thick stream of bile sprayed over her spectators as Shana took in the dreadful sight. Precious had been hauled upside down by ropes on the mast. His large kind brown eyes were open and fixed on Shana. Had she not noticed the cat chewing at a large piece of her friend's brain, she would have believed him to be still alive. All looked perfectly normal had it not been for the hole in the tall man's skull which was displaying part of the greyish matter. Every time the foul moggie took another bite from her companion's vital organ his heavy muscular body swung around to bare its fatal wound.

If only she had gone with the others to the safety of the shore... each time that Shana felt the lash of the cat o' nine tails she cursed her own vengeful soul... crack... the cruel whip slashed her soft flesh... mercilessly the crew cheered as Simon received his punishment... crack... no tears of pain but anger and sorrow for Precious' wife and baby... slash... The men roared with delight as leather tails whipped past their heads. Shouting out the count, the quartermaster watched gleefully as Shana took every slash in silence. Her mind was set on paying her final respects to a brave and precious man whose name had been totally apt... he would never be forgotten. As Quartermaster Watkins shouted 'Fifteen!' the crew began to complain that no-one had won the wager... 'Yon boy be made of iron or 'e 'as took leave of 'is senses like 'is friend!' came a sarcastic remark made by some fool whose voice Shana gladly recognised. Her last thought as the salt water hit her agonising open wounds was one of determined revenge... 'On my honour, the heathen will rue the day he slandered Precious.' Shana felt a scalding pain spread over her entire back as she collapsed and hung suspended against the thick wooden pole.

CHAPTER 11

Simon's First Duty aboard the Falcon

As if none of the incidents over the past few days had ever occurred, Shana woke to find that her surroundings were most unlike those which she had previously been accustomed to whilst aboard the Falcon. The ropes of the hammock creaked as Shana lifted her battered head to scan the small room in which she was confined. Breathing out a sigh of despair, Shana realised that she had managed to deprive herself of even the slimmest chance of returning to life ashore. Through a tiny porthole she glimpsed the vast sea stretching to a blurred horizon. Once again she found herself trapped in a ship that was well on its way to Heaven knows where. Rough rope cut into her wrists as she clenched her fists together trying to relieve the numbness in her hands. Her legs were not tied but nevertheless she was unable to move from the hammock cocooned around her battered body. Relieved to see that her clothes were still intact, including the shredded shirt that had been torn to ribbons by the lash, Shana strained her ears trying to decipher the muffled voices over many other sounds. Her back stuck to the material of the makeshift bed and if she moved suddenly, the sticky scabs that had formed tore away from the small areas of undamaged skin… not that there was much left on her raw flesh! Nothing could be done for the time being but rest. Soon the rolling waves rocked Shana's exhausted body into a deep slumber.

Surprised to find herself turned on her side, Shana woke to the sound of waves lashing at the ship's boards. Panic set in when she realised that she had lost all feeling in her arms and hands. For one dreadful moment the poor girl believed that both had been amputated by the callous crew. Once she had regained her wits and satisfied herself that her arms were still attached, she noticed the shadow of a figure seated on the small fitted bed adjacent to where she lay. A deep voice told her, 'Thou art most fortunate to be breathing young man!' Recognition dawned on the young woman and she felt her blood curdle within her veins. Quartermaster Watkins was sitting upright on Captain Thurlow's bunk. Second in command the pumped-up little Welshman had, without doubt, taken the position of captain. It was he who had ordered that her friend be tortured in such an inhumane manner.

Shana gritted her teeth and clenched her bruised jaws tightly together with sheer anger and hatred. She answered her captor in a manner intentionally devoid of emotion. Compliance was most essential if she were to have any hope of survival. A passive role was the one to be played by Simon from now on, Shana decided with renewed hope. 'I intend to serve thee well kind sir.' Summoning as many sad memories as she could, the clever actress wept pitifully and begged for forgiveness. Pleading innocence and explaining how she had been inflicted by a dangerous voodoo curse, she blubbered a confused but convincing tale of how Simon had been under the spell of the dark witchdoctor. Praying to God as she begged for mercy, she feigned absolute regret and self- disgust for daring to communicate with the 'filthy heathens' let alone join in an attack on her own people. Her performance as Simon fared well once again and

Shana shuddered with disgust when the newly appointed captain's intentions began to dawn on her.

Once satisfied that his desires had been clearly understood, Captain Watkins approached the swinging hammock in which Shana lay, frozen with apprehension and dread. She could smell the rhum on his breath as he stood above his new cabin boy. Slurring words of encouragement, he attempted to lull the poor wretched boy into a false sense of security. Shana was in no way naïve and had heard of the tactics used by sexual predators all too often... the last time she had encountered such a beast her position had been strong, but now she lay helpless before this monster. Determined not to show any signs of fear, Shana began a frantic plea for mercy... Captain Watkins started to undress as he made promises that Shana did not want to hear... 'Now my boy if thee pleasure me well thou shalt one day gain a worthy position aboard my ship.' The repulsive man made grunts and soft moans as he readied himself for the assault... Shana bit deep into her bottom lip and squeezed her pretty eyes shut... if she was lucky this could be over very quickly. Her heart pounded against her ribs like a caged bird desperate to escape. As she felt her breeches being untied and gently eased down to expose her soft young bottom, Shana shuddered with disgust. At least her new master was taking the soft approach with his victim... 'Have to focus on happy times'... Shana's determination to take her mind away from the diabolical truth... 'Rid thy mind of this atrocity...' Desperately trying not to feel the spit that was being spread around her tight anus... Forcing herself to believe that it was poor Simon, not she who was about to be assaulted in such a degrading manner... Shana took herself away; back to a beautiful day when she and Richie had lain together and explored each other in such a loving way... the pain that Simon felt wrenched at Shana's heart... she was unable to help the poor boy inside her mind... Simon yelled and tears streamed from his eyes as he became a victim of buggery on the Falcon, in the middle of an ocean he knew not where... Richie kissed Shana gently on the lips, lowering his hand as he caressed her firm breasts... unbelievable pain wracked Simon's lower body as the perverse act became more aggressive. The vile rapist grew harder and more aroused... Richie's large hand massaged Shana's nipples between his fingers and he lowered his head to meet them with his moist tongue... Simon's blood soaked the captain's shirt as he thrust his large thick shaft deep into his anus... Shana's concentration broke when she could no longer block out the pain... she was no longer able to stifle the tears... 'Simon... Simon... ye'll be fine in no time... it always feels uncomfortable at first...' The sibilant sound of Captain Watkins' soothing tones sickened both Shana and Simon and they huddled together in one body and mind. Quietly weeping, Shana lay as still as she possibly could and imagined holding Simon close to her breast. The captain stumbled away in a drunken stupor, totally satisfied by his new boy's compliance. Smiling with relief and pleasure, Captain Watkins plonked his short body onto the cabin cot and soon fell into a peaceful slumber.

CHAPTER 12

Alea Iacta Est...

Two seemingly short years passed by speedily and Simon Stempton celebrated his twentieth birthday whilst serving as Captain Watkins' submissive cabin boy aboard the Falcon. Shana had gradually come to feel more at ease in the guise of the boy who had allowed her to gain respect in a time when women were rarely taken seriously in a predominantly man's world. Despite her dread of night time, when Simon was subjected to the increasingly sadistic captain's sexual abuse, Shana loved her new life at sea. Quickly and efficiently Shana was able to master the ropes and had soon gained respect from the majority of the crew serving aboard the sturdy carrack. Life at sea suited the wench remarkably well and as Simon, she fast became a well-trusted member of a tight-knit team of hardy men. The sailors relied on each other's skills, as well as their own, to stay alive and Simon had already earned a respected place amongst them although he had yet to be promoted to a full crewmember.

The men of The Falcon continued to battle the elements and bravely charted new courses across infrequently sailed and often unknown seas. Trust was paramount amongst the crew and they made the most of the all too rare occasions when they were able to relax aboard the busy ship. Singing together in her belly, their harmonious voices produced an eerie echoing melody which sounded as if they were in a cave. Moments like these had kept Shana sane and more able to cope with the nightly abuse that Captain Watkins dealt out to his obedient and passive servant, Simon Stempton. Shana vowed that one day she would wreak terrible revenge and for Simon, that day could not arrive too soon. Meanwhile, back in England, on the 17th November 1558 Elizabeth, the daughter of King Henry VIII and his 'whore queen' Ann Boleyn, became queen.

Dice games were popular aboard the Falcon and Shana was often lucky with her throws. Never without her own bale of bone dice that she had won from a Cathayan sailor in a game of Hazard, Shana would often invite select members of the crew to a gambling session. Everyone knew that dice and cards were Simon's main vices and all respected the poor lad for not wanting to get involved with women. To Shana's relief, that was one less thing for her to worry about... at least whilst Simon was Captain Watkins' plaything there was far less chance of her true identity being discovered. Most of the crew understood how hard it was for cabin boys and would generally spare them from any further unnecessary degradation... Previous 'servers' had been torn to shreds by over-rough anal intercourse and at least one poor urchin had flung himself into the dark, icy depths when he could stand no more.

In most civilized countries homosexuality had been ruled to be a heinous crime and anyone caught practising the 'ungodly act of sodomy' would be sure to swing from the gallows. Aboard the Falcon, the men would often speculate whether their captain had chosen a life at sea to enable him to satisfy his homosexual tendencies... whilst on land he was able to remain safely married. Like many other sailors' wives, poor Mrs. Watkins had taken in a black cat who she named 'Mr. Kins'. Superstition dictated that women who longed for their husbands' safe return should give a black cat a home and whilst the animal was fed, watered and kept from harm, their men's safety would be ensured. Little did Mrs. Watkins know that her husband had always been revolted by her feminine body and there was no chance of her bearing any offspring in their celibate union. One long journey followed another until the loyal wife finally accepted her position and took a lover. Of course that suited Captain Watkins perfectly, everyone was happy and any bastard offspring would bear his name.

Two men in particular, who served with Simon on the Falcon, had taken the lad under their wing. 'Irish' was the boatswain and amongst the most skilled in his trade. Shana was very fond of the man who was proud to have come from 'the English Dale' as Dublin was fondly known. Everyone who met the amusing, happy-go-lucky Irishman was treated to a detailed account of his royal Celtic bloodline and his wonderful well rehearsed script never altered. An immensely loveable character, Irish showed extreme loyalty to a trusted few. To say that the man was paranoid where Englishmen were concerned would be a gross understatement. In charge of dropping anchor, weighing and handling the sails amongst other ship maintaining duties, Irish often called Simon to his aid. Shana had felt flattered the first few times that the rough but handsome ship-hand had asked Simon to help him but she soon realised that her keen listening and speedy learning skills were much sought after. Many of Simon's fellow mates had been slow to master the ropes and regularly annoyed the skilful crew with their tardiness and failure to communicate adequately.

Lashings were a common deterrent aboard the Falcon as her captain refused to suffer fools gladly. However marooning was Captain Watkins' preferred punishment and a goodly number of new crew members suffered an unknown fate on some isolated island with no more than a bottle of water, one pistol and a single shot. Since Simon had been his cabin boy, the captain had ordered no less than eleven unworthy seamen to be dropped off at uninhabited isles along one of the Falcon's many trade routes. Apprentice boys were dispensable as it was no trouble to pick up fresh young blood at any port. Armed with cosh and sacks, a thuggish team of men would be sent ashore to press-gang any stragglers from local inns. A generous toddy of rhum and a pipe full of tobacco would ensure that there were plenty of volunteers keen to help in hijacking innocent lads.

Some crimes that Captain Watkins deemed punishable by the lash were stealing, fighting, smoking tobacco in the hold with no pipe cap and carrying a burning candle without a lantern. Moses' Law meant that the culprit would receive forty stripes lacking one on his bare back. The more serious the crime, the harsher the whip chosen. The cat o' nine tails was the most severe of these and had taken more than its fair share of lives. Its lashes tore many deep wounds into the victim's naked flesh. These wounds could bleed for days and often festered and became infected. The nine leather thongs with a wicked barb at each end cut so deep into a poor man's body that bones or organs were often exposed. Not once was a man allowed a reduction in lashes, even when his body hung limp and lifeless the complete sentence would be carried out. Smith, the ship's cook collected the blood of the unlucky culprits to sell to butchers ashore. A good price would often be paid for fresh blood. A sprinkling of good red blood was regularly used to disguise rotting and stale meat. Without an ounce of pity, the sadistic cook had been known to squeeze every last drop of life-blood from the unconscious victim's vital organs if the poor sod had been unfortunate enough to have committed his offence near to a port town. The bitter disabled seaman had lost an arm during a scuffle with pirates in a tavern in Nueva España or New Spain. In place of his missing hand, he wore a beaklike metal contraption that fitted tightly into a leather cup-shaped cap tied onto his wrist. With this unsightly gadget, Smith was well able to prepare and cook food for the crew. When it came to close combat, it became a fearsome and effective weapon capable of disembowelment and the gouging out of eyeballs.

Tripod was a picturesque character who had been a vagrant before his seafaring days. Like Shana, Tripod had been forced into service one night in a life long since forgotten. Shana admired her best mate for his nerve and determination. Orphaned from birth, Tripod's father had been a sailor who manned number seven gun on the Man o' War, an impressive galleon in the King's fleet during the first half of the century. An old prostitute had boarded the craft for business at Liverpool docks and had happily served no less than seven gunners the night her unfortunate son-to-be was conceived. A year later when the Man o' War made its annual return to Liverpool, the haggard crone thrust a filthy bundle into the arms of the first sailor to disembark. Back on board, the sailor took the infant to the gunner's deck. No-one claimed the infant to be their own offspring but gunner number seven peered closely into the baby's face and fancied that he could see a resemblance to himself. Taking pity on the grubby baby who seemed to have a similar mischievous glint in his already wanton eyes, the gunner put his number and ship on the birth certificate clutched in his tiny fist. Arranging for a trustworthy old widow to care for the child until he reached working age was easy. Widows were glad of a lump sum to enable them to care for unwanted children and perhaps provide the odd toddy or two to help forget the bleak future that lay ahead. Unbelievably, Tripod's surrogate father returned yearly to drop a fat purse off into the grateful widow's hand. The young lad's early years were uneventful but by the age of six Tripod became a dextrous cut-purse and fell in with a notorious gang in the dock area. An incredible run of luck ensured his freedom for many years but inevitably in time his luck ran out. Whipped within inches of death, Tripod vowed never to steal again. In desperation he turned to vagrancy for a whole year, tramping the country mud tracks, relying on handouts from coach travellers and kindly farm labourers.

A harsh winter drove him back to the mean city streets of Liverpool where he scavenged among the waste heaps, eating rotten food thrown out with the shit and piss. Living such an unpleasant existence led to the breakdown of his health when he fell ill with cholera. He and a bunch of other vagrants were dragged to the city square where they were punished and warned never to return to the area again. If any amongst the vagabonds dared to set foot in Liverpool just once more, they would be hanged immediately. Against the odds of survival, Tripod lived and volunteered to serve aboard the next vessel that was willing to take him. A life at sea proved to be a welcome treat for the grateful cabin boy who quickly became an indispensable crewmember. Feeling somewhat akin to Simon, Tripod soon became Shana's closest friend and the pair regularly shared stories of their past experiences as lowly vagrants. Shana found it easy to invent a feasible life for Simon Stempton, which she based on a selection of the orphans who had sought shelter at Mary Maggy's… her memories of the orphanage were still very clear but it seemed as though another lifetime had passed since she had spent time within its welcome walls.

Tripod's yell brought Shana's mind to attention and she instinctively leapt to her feet, knocking over the leather bucket full of soapy sea water. Inwardly cursing her clumsiness, she began to mop up the spilt fluid but soon burst into relieved laughter at the sight of her jovial, ever-smiling friend. Breeches pulled high and belted with an ornate buckle that he had undoubtedly purchased in Nueva España, Tripod stood in front of Shana with hips thrust forward vulgarly. Having gained his nickname by his unusually long and large appendage, Tripod was well-known for fucking anything with a pulse… and on more desperate occasions, without! Jokes aboard the Falcon were rife, especially where Tripod was concerned. Many a night, just before most of the crew took to their sleeping places, gags about the sporting gunner would be heard echoing around the ship. Sarcasm reigned amongst the crew and warnings to ensure that all livestock were locked safely in the pens below deck in case Tripod felt the need… or telling men to sleep with their arses well covered, would be favourites amongst the sailors' jibes. The good-natured man would always take the piss-taking scenarios well within his stride and Shana had quickly warmed to this benign and loveable character.

Shana smiled up at her friend's weather-beaten face as he pulled at his right ear signalling that he was up for a long night of serious gambling. Tripod had never admitted to anyone aboard that the large hole in his right ear had been cut by a group of townsmen when he had been accused of vagrancy… but most knew what the sign meant as it was a common punishment ashore in their day and age.

Night had begun to close in and the men aboard the Falcon were steadying her for anchorage near to the Cape Verde Islands. Well-known for its foreboding coastline with volcanic rock formations jutting jaggedly from inky blue waters, Cape Verde displayed its victims in the form of broken wrecks scattered around its shores. The Falcon's crew was alert and ready and orders could be heard from another approaching vessel in the cool evening air. A bright full moon lit the coastline and the captain had prudently laid at anchor there on that well-lit midsummer's eve. This trip had been a successful one so far and Captain Watkins had proved to be far luckier keeping his cargo of natives alive and healthy in appearance for trading. Insisting on impeccable cleanliness at all times, the cold-hearted little Welshman ordered his men to ensure that the black people kept their pens clean. Feeding them fresh goats' milk daily meant that they stayed strong and appeared to have been well fed at a surprisingly low expense. Biscuits that had become over-infested with weevils were lowered down to the slaves in leather buckets and the 'blighters were always pitifully grateful' to receive such privileges. This bunch had survived the long hard journey well and looked fresh as the day they had been captured. Dysentery had not reared its ugly head in months aboard

Captain Watkins' ship and he was determined to keep it that way. Orders that afternoon had been to scrub the animal and slave holds and lay fresh hay or sawdust if hay was short. New animals would be brought aboard the falcon for fresh milk and meat on her onward journey to the Coast of Guinea where trade stations offered a good selection of slaves for sale.

Ever since the untimely death of his predecessor, Captain Watkins had carefully planned regular trade routes between West Africa, Europe and America and was well-known as one of the major dealers in the slavery trade. Few buyers complained of the condition of the black natives, many of whom became excellent workers in the cotton and indigo plantations in Cape Verde. Other natives were taken to North Madeira, Spain or Portugal where they were sold to cloth merchants. There they learned to weave and dye cloth produced from cotton grown in 'Verde' as it became affectionately known. Cloth would then be taken on to Guinea where it was traded for more slaves. It was common for vassals to be sold for cash to slave ships, especially those that had lost many of their human cargo to disease or starvation. Sadly the Falcon was unique in its delivery of fit slaves and Shana and Tripod felt proud to be serving with such an efficient company. The sea bed was littered with so many bones of poor, perished black slaves.

Tripod helped Simon with his final chores before rejoining the crew to help manoeuvre the Falcon into the best position for anchorage. Many a ship that had anchored too near to Cape Verde's rocky, forbidding coastlines had been damaged beyond repair. Wooden skeletons jutted awkwardly from the darkened waters. Sun bleached limbs of broken wood pointed splintered fingers away from the isles as if warning vessels to keep a safe distance. Shana joined the crew as they expertly worked in unison, working well-oiled pulleys and cables to draw in the sails. In Shana's mind, sailing had become a wonderful fine art to which she felt a total connection. Shana took her allotted position and performed her role with speed and immaculate skill. Her sleek movements blended perfectly with ship and crew in a flawlessly coordinated routine that soon brought the ship safely to rest. The sound of her captain's confident call gave the well-earned all-clear to those serving aboard the Falcon. Tightly secured ropes creaked under the weight of weighty sails as the wind gently teased the thick cloth. Waves lapping against boards made a pleasant sound in contrast to the past weeks of ill tempered seas.

Although the weather had not been too bad, the craft had been put to the test once or twice during this passage and all felt relieved to be in sight of land. Wasting no time, men fell into rank and carried out duties according to their trade. Maintenance checks were carried out so that general repairs could be documented and appropriate materials ordered. Nothing was rushed and the clockwork precision and expert examination of all workable parts of ship, weaponry and ammunition was thorough. Jock Mackenzie, Master gunner and close friend of Irish sifted through barrels of gun powder ensuring that it was being kept dry enough to ensure separation. Under the huge Scot's watchful eye, his mates checked the cannonballs and weaponry for any sign of rust or malfunction. When everyone was satisfied with condition and quality specifications all reports were taken to the captain's cabin and the crew was duly dismissed. Cheers erupted from the Falcon's stout belly and excitement filled the atmosphere. Those left aboard to keep guard watched as candle flames grew smaller, flickering in a steady trail of small boats heading towards the shore.

Twilight had been Shana's favourite time in the lush tropical lands that she had grown to love. Captain Watkins was indeed no fool and insisted that Simon stayed on board whilst he and the rest of the crew went ashore to visit the trading colonies. Buggery was punishable by hanging and Portuguese settlers had heard tales of kidnapped children who were used as sexual slaves by depraved sailors. Simon would rarely be allowed to explore anything beyond the shores and the captain ensured that his boy was substantially rewarded for his compliance in such delicate matters. Shana had only just begun to realise the abusive captain's vulnerability and her mind had become busy with plans to wreak revenge for his abhorrent crimes against Simon.

Deep in thought, Shana stood on the main deck with the moonlight shining brightly on her pretty dark gold locks that she wore tied back from her face. Simon made sure never to be seen hatless and was always dressed neatly. Sun-kissed golden skin made Simon's slanted elfin eyes appear bluer than the ocean. Stars blinked above the ship as it swayed gently in a calm sea whose waves lapped lazily at the wooden vessel. Only a few men had been ordered to stay on board and the captain had ensured that fresh supplies had been brought back so they could enjoy a well-earned substantial meal. Below decks, the slaves had settled after eating an unusually decent meal of salt meat, oatmeal and butter cheese. Since the captain had entrusted Simon with social and communication training duties where the slaves were concerned, Shana chose to wait until they had been suitably fed and watered before she joined her fellow gamblers. Below her in a make-shift tabling den on the lower gun deck, Irish, Mackenzie and a few others could be heard making wagers in an intense game of Hazard. Rolling her pair of lucky dice between strong fingers, Shana made a few final checks before she signalled to the boy who had drawn the short straw and was keeping watch high in the crow's nest. When she had taken a closer look at the sleeping slaves, Shana felt satisfied that all was as it should be and went below decks to join the private gambling party.

Rhum flowed freely into the dawn hours and dice rattled against wood as players cast round after round. Monies rapidly changed hands and Simon held his lucky dice for a final throw that had been called when the rhum barrel was near empty. In this friendly group there were no cheats… no-one had to watch out for weighted dice or dice with high cuts as were often used by scoundrels in many gambling rings. All participants knew that Simon had the luck of the Irish and were not surprised with his winning throw. Jock gave Shana a congratulatory slap on the back that almost knocked her face-first onto the dice board as she reached for her winnings. Taking out a small pipe and a leather bag of tobacco that she had been saving for this very occasion, Shana shared some jokes with the others and offered her stash around. Soon the atmosphere was smoky and the mood chilled and mellow. 'Sauced' tobacco was a rare and much appreciated treat that Shana usually enjoyed alone. She would savour every last inhalation of the expensive but delicious brown leaves that had been enhanced by the addition of hemp from the Netherlands. When under the influence of this delightful mixture, Shana would be taken to a blissful, relaxing place that was akin to no other that she had experienced. As the men lay back on the boards or climbed into hammocks, they became engulfed in the euphoric mist of drugged smoke. Only just managing to make out a particularly curvaceous blurred shape that was steadily bobbing up and down atop of Tripod's lap, Shana giggled openly at the sight, her inhibitions and guard totally down in a rare state of utter relaxation. For all she cared, at that very moment, the men around her were welcome to fondle her gorgeous plump breasts and play with her delightfully tight little cunnie to their hearts content... She was stoned beyond doubt and in another world where she felt totally at ease and willing to do anything for the sake of unbounded sexual pleasure.

Awaking groggily, Shana felt stiffness in her shoulders and turned her head from side to side to try and ease the aching muscles. Scanning around her, she saw a heart-warming scene... her trusted friends lay scattered around in their gaming den, drinking vessels upturned or still clutched in hand and dead to the world. Gulls screeched their lonely morning calls and circled above the Falcon, disappearing momentarily in the brightest orange sun. Pipe in hand, Shana blinked sleepily as she noticed the only movement as horny Tripod pounded away at the prostitute who had come aboard to offer sexual services the previous night. Smiling happily to herself, she realised how aroused she had been feeling lately and actually thought that she would like one day to feel a man's hardness enter her in a pleasurable way. Groans of growing frustration could be heard between the small cannons that Jock kept in perfect order. 'Tripod, ye drabber! Have ye nay feelin' in thy pillcock? By my beard, I shall drag yon crusty-cunnied trull from thy yeasty crotch if ye foin her quiver once meer!' Jock's Scottish voice boomed out mock threats as the whore started to shake with orgasmic delight. Grabbing a bucket to take a morning shit, Shana winked at Tripod with faux admiration as he often showed genuine concern that Simon's lack of experience with women would have long-lasting influence on the boy's sexual preferences. Exposing a monstrous, shiny reddened appendage with the girth of Shana's own forearm, the well-ridden prostitute rolled off Tripod and fell instantly into a satisfied slumber... apparently blissfully unaware of the applause that she had earned from randy spectators. Blushing with what ought to have been embarrassment but was admittedly pure envied lust, Shana felt the tingling wetness between her legs and longed to be touched in an intimate way. Had she had a choice at that exact moment, Irish would have been the man she chose to satisfy her carnal needs. Gathering her wits and quelling desires that had been long denied, the young woman climbed the narrow wooden ladder to the upper deck.

A yell of disgust came from the waters below as Shana realised with amusement that she had flung a full bucket of her freshly expelled crap over poor Tom, the swabber's mate. He had been busily scrubbing the shit from the Falcon since early morning. Throwing an old rag way short of his target, the young lad started to swing the boson's chair on which he was perched precariously. Warning the boy not to swing the roped contraption too vigorously, Shana peaked her hat at the cheeky ship's hand and emptied a nearby bucket of stale piss overboard to stop his dangerous antics. She smirked to herself as she bared her arse and wiggled it cheekily at the ship's apprentice. If only Tom knew that Simon was really a girl! Without a care, Tom shouted obscenities and grabbed another rag to dip into the bucket of sea water that had been tied securely to the wooden plank that formed his seat. Captain Watkins had assigned the unpopular job of cleaning the beak head of faeces to Tom as punishment for his constant lying in order to avoid his duties. Laziness was a sin that the captain could not abide and he made sure that the worst duties were given to the idlest members of his crew. Amongst many dislikeable traits in the captain's personality lay one or two virtues that the crew appreciated and fairness was one of these.

Stretching her fit, lean body over the railings of the gun deck, Shana gazed over towards land and watched the steady stream of rafts and small boats make their way to and from the larger vessels. Shana was keen to continue on the journey to São Tiago, the isle to which the Falcon took its cargo of slaves. Riviera Grande was the city where the bulk of fresh supplies would be bought. Growing in size, population and wealth, the city had become a popular port of call for many slave ships. Since Shana had been serving aboard the slave carrier, she had heard sailors who went ashore talk about the city's encouraging development. Pyrates had become aware of the fast-growing richness of the isle and a few attacks had caused the Portuguese settlers, Riviera Grande's main inhabitants, to set up stronger defences. Shana was eager to view the exciting life of this bustling city albeit from the confines of the Falcon.

There were many thick heads the following day when the Falcon cast anchor and made its onward journey to São Tiago where the slaves were unloaded and sold. It broke Shana's heart to watch from the ship as traders bartered for the human beings of whom she had grown rather fond. She always found it extremely difficult not to become too attached to the African people who she could never regard as mere cargo.

Barrels full of salted fish, beer and crates of spices, coffee, tea and chocolate had been stacked on the main decks ready to be taken down into storage. Rhum and tobacco was due to arrive later. The slaves' dens were cleaned when the African people had been taken ashore earlier. Chores left to do before the captain's return had been allocated and Simon's main task was to repaint the code of conduct that Captain Watkins liked to have displayed in a prominent place aboard his ship. Even though some of the crew aboard the Falcon were unable to read, the captain made sure that all knew the rules by heart and often tested his men on spec. Simon took on the responsibility of teaching all new crew members each written rule. The complete muster, from cabin boy to bosun, called them out loud and clear every morning as they worked.

Pulling the weather-worn plaque from the wood where it had been displayed for a good while, Shana whistled a sea-shanty as she worked. The air was dry and an ochre sun shone high and bright in a clear blue sky. Captain Watkins had given Simon permission to work alone in his cabin and Shana was glad of that. A second skeleton crew had replaced the first and Simon was the only member who had not been permitted to venture ashore. Shana never minded spending time aboard the Falcon with only a few others and would make the most of the rare privacy, bathing and washing with no fear of being discovered nude. Happy in the knowledge that she would have a good few hours now that her closest friends were all ashore and enjoying their leisure time, she could relax. Although their company was extremely enjoyable, the young woman needed time to be herself for a change. Simon Stempton was a wonderful character to bring alive but Shana still existed and was determined to ensure her emergence from time to time. With lists of chores that had to be done before the captain's return, the men aboard saw Simon disappear into his cabin where he started work immediately.

Within the cabin, Shana scanned the small sleeping quarters that she had shared with her master since Precious' death. His rank had long gone to the Captain's already conceited head and his appearance had always been important to the unpopular Welshman. Regularly using boot-black to cover the grey speckles in his once dark hair, the aging fool had begun to perform a little self-dentistry. Simon was aware of all his captain's grooming secrets and encouraged him in his quest to improve his unfortunate appearance. The vain man faced a difficult task and it amused Shana greatly to see how seriously the foul abuser took himself. In her opinion Watkins was lower than any spineless creature imaginable. Each time he lost a rotten tooth, Simon would help his master to wire another onto the adjacent molar. Captain Watkins owned a good selection of spare teeth of all shades, shapes and sizes that he had purchased from surgeons on his trips ashore. Each tooth had been pulled from the decapitated heads of corpses and had made enterprising surgeons a tidy extra income since it had become fashionable for folks to refill the gaps in their gums. Teeth had become more difficult to come by of late and one of poor Simon's more macabre jobs as captain's personal cabin boy had been to prise teeth from the skulls that his master had purchased. Many surgeons had become lazy since the tooth market had rocketed. They would rather sell whole heads to save time removing the precious commodities when people were willing to do it for themselves. Shana had even heard tales told of heads being stolen from the bodies of hanged criminals that lined the coach tracks as a deterrent to would-be offenders.

Shana had managed to complete the sign with plenty of time to spare and had made an excellent job of the lettering. Satisfied with a day's hard work, she helped herself to a tot of rhum and lay on the hammock with her large eyes closed. A recognisable guffaw interrupted Shana's rest and she smiled with the knowledge that her, or more accurately Simon's best friend had returned safely. Jock was drunk and his attractive Scottish voice boomed through the floorboards making them vibrate as he laughed. 'Simon! Yerr wee tyke, come hither and yerr'l be amazed at what Irish and I have for yers!' Shana could not help but laugh and her heart was filled with immense love for her two Celtic shipmates. Together, the amusing pair had made her piteous life at sea worth living. Pulling on a thick, loose shirt that helped to hide her ever-growing breasts, Shana cleared her throat and gave a hearty cry to alert her friends of her whereabouts. She could already hear Irish's sing-song voice spreading the news of a volcano on a nearby isle that was, in his humble opinion, bound to erupt one day soon.

Nothing could have prepared Shana for the surprise that Simon's friends had bought as a belated birthday gift. Lit by the flickering light from their lanterns like a group of comical players, jester and all, the delightful bunch of seamen stood on the main deck of the Falcon awaiting the cabin boy's company. Standing unsteadily at the front of the little gathering, looking extremely pleased with himself, stood the sex maniac, Tripod. Either side of him loomed Jock Mackenzie and good old Irish, faces blushing bright red as a result of almost a full week's alcohol consumption in one day. Profits from the slave sale this trip must have been high and the taverns were ever eager to lighten the purses of newly paid sailors. Shana could not help grinning but thought better of cracking a warning joke about any of her friends standing too near to a naked flame for fear of spontaneous combustion. Kidding aside, she could smell the strong spirits on their breath from a fair distance away... and they were standing upwind!

Shana stepped closer and as Simon, asked them what they had been up to. 'No good I can well imagine!' she added with a cheeky grin. Applause met Simon's surprised but apprehensive response to their unexpected summons for his company. Shuffling with coy embarrassment, the two tallest sailors were pushed apart by a stumpy little hand. Shrimp, the tiny sailor with shortened limbs and an enlarged bulbous forehead, fought his way through the muscular bulk and emerged with sweat beaded brow and the prettiest bird imaginable perched atop of his hat. Bright white feathers covered the small parrot's belly and its wings and tail feathers were the brightest green. A tiny black head rubbed away at the clean, almost flawless material of Shrimp's smart hat, but the little bird was rapidly making a good job of changing its appearance. The comical avian character looked as if it was wearing egg-yolk coloured trousers. Small, bead-like orange eyes kept looking Shana's way as its strong hooked dark grey beak tore at the hat cloth. Suppressing an instinctive feminine desire to rush over and pet the tiny creature, Shana stood as she imagined Simon would and laughed at the sight of the short, stumpy man with his lively and affectionate new head adornment. Giving a sudden, piercingly loud wolf-whistle, the small, clown-like, feathered entertainer became even more frisky and animated as its audience roared with laughter. Shrimp gave a shrill scream as the little parrot wriggled his tail feathers in a humorous display, gripping his scalp through the cap's cloth with cruel sharp claws. Once it had expelled a generous amount of paint-like white and speckled grey turd from its rear end, it flapped its pretty wings and headed for Simon's hat. Not amused by the sickly sweet smell or with his freshly spattered shirt, Shrimp waddled off toward the quarterdeck to find a cloth. He needed to wipe off the gooey deposit that had landed right in the centre of his large bulbous nose.

Shana stood as still as she possibly could whilst her friends roared with hilarious laughter. Offering a hand up to the tiny bird, everyone was surprised to see the creature step confidently onto Simon's finger and rub its fluffy underbelly over his rough hand in a strange mating-like ritual. "Ere! I was thinkin' at least ye'd bring me back a freshly cooked chicken!' Shana remarked as the little bird rubbed away at her work-hardened hand. Stopping to lift its pretty head, the parrot shrieked, 'Micken!' in a high-pitched mimicking of Simon's tenor tones. The miniature friend of Simon Stempton and new pet for the well-loved cabin boy aboard the Falcon had chosen his own name. From that night on, Micken and Simon became inseparable and the amorous bird soon became a popular member of the tight-knit crew. The small parrot's ability to make even the grumpiest man smile with utter glee was priceless. Micken learned no words other than his own name and 'Yeeeeaaaahhhh!' which he yelled at the top of his comically child-like voice each time he saw Shana approach. By mimicking peoples' laughs perfectly but usually a full octave higher than its source, the sweet bird also cleverly managed to chuckle at exactly the right moment.

Soon after Simon and Micken had become fully acquainted that happy night, his friends presented him with another gift, Geoffrey Chaucer's 'Canterbury Tales'. The book was one that Shana had wanted to read for a long time. Touched by her friends' generosity and thoughtfulness in their choice of gifts, Shana made a promise to read them a chapter every night until the stories were finished. Holding Simon firmly to his promise, come rough, stormy or still seas, the cabin boy's calming voice could be heard reading aloud Chaucer's well-penned tales. Each told by a group of colourful characters including Chaucer himself, the tales revealed how a party of wayfarers kept each other amused along the pilgrims' route to the Shrine of Thomas a Becket in Canterbury Cathedral. Set in medieval England, the journey brought the eager sailors no less than twenty four tales. Shana felt elated to have introduced such literary delights to a bunch of largely uneducated men. Tales which ranged from rather comical to quite serious, kept them entertained marvellously during many a hard journey aboard the trading ship. A maternal instinct developed within Shana, as she took her place by the warm brazier every night, surrounded by her surrogate family who were eager to hear the next chapter in the skilfully woven stories. During these nights, they all experienced the most comfortable and pleasant bonding times. Shana had forgotten these welcome feelings that she had known long ago when back in England with her clan.

Captain Watkins always insisted on a safe, immaculate craft which was repaired, updated and adapted regularly for a more efficient and financially viable service. Under his strict instruction, the ship's carpenter had expertly constructed seats of easement within the beakhead to avoid any further unnecessary soiling of his precious Falcon's hull. Consisting of a wooden board with six generous sized holes, the seats that he had designed allowed sailors some comfort whilst defecating and their waste dropped conveniently straight into the sea. During long, uncomfortable months serving aboard a ship full of males, Shana had fashioned a horn into a tube covered with pink pig-skin leather to enable her to stand alongside the men from time to time so that she could piss. Before trying out her new appendage, Shana made sure that the contraption looked realistic. Her test run succeeded and she managed a convincing job of spraying a steady and well-aimed stream of piss overboard in full view of the crew. This contraption would surely dispel any possible unwanted curiosity as she had learned to be extra cautious, especially with new recruits. Practising on watch duty one night when she knew that she would not be disturbed, Shana soon became used to her new tool. Soon she was even able to defecate at the same time as pissing without a thought. When not in use the faux penis tucked neatly into her leggings. Interestingly, Simon's mock prick never excited or enticed her molester. Captain Watkins enjoyed the sight of young boy's soft, firm and peach-like ass cheeks. He had become obsessed with control and found nothing more arousing than his young, submissive boy bent over offering the forbidden orifice for his master's taking. Not in the slightest bit concerned about giving the recipient any pleasure, the captain was not as curious as Shana might have expected. Noting every weakness that the unsuspecting monster possessed, Shana became determined that her revenge would be even more horrific than her previous murderous conquests.

Upon reaching the age when most young women began to menstruate, Shana had little choice but to bind her large breasts with linen bandages and make her figure appear less like an hour-glass. Poor food and heavy work had helped delay her monthly periods long enough until one annoying and hair-raising day she noticed blood on the chair where she had sat eating her stale, tasteless rations. On inspection of the seat of Simon's trousers, she discovered a large blood stain. Fortunately, it could not have happened on a more suitable day. Ropes were being tarred to prevent them from rotting, so she was able to lean against the sticky, black matter and cover the wretched blood stain. Apart from this narrow escape, Shana had been lucky so far and had found it relatively easy to pass herself off as Simon, the unfortunate cabin boy. Her disguise had enabled her to sail thousands of miles, learning an invaluable trade as a sailor and preserving total anonymity as an undiscovered woman in a predominantly male world. Taking her soiled clothing into the captain's cabin, she cut the spoiled material into small rags to use for soaking up her monthly bleeding. With a heavy sigh of frustration, Shana decided that the time was fast approaching when she should take action and make some important changes in her life.

It was a clear starry night in September 1559 when Simon Stempton finished reading the final chapter of Canterbury Tales to his eager audience. Contrary to normal arrangements when his regular group of gamers joined him in a gambling session whilst anchored near to land, Simon had planned a gaming evening below decks, in the belly of the ship. The Falcon was at full sail and well en route to Africa. With the knowledge that only the most cunning and desperate of sailors would join her in the depths of the ship, Shana prepared the temporary gambling table amidst the stinking bilge waters that had collected over months at sea. Kicking a dark-haired rat into a shadowy nook, the young woman calmed Micken who, as usual, clung onto her shirt with strong vice-like claws. The cowardly parrot quivered with fear, his tiny back hunched like an arthritic old man and claws clinging for dear life onto his mama's shoulder. Fluffing his white chest feathers, pulling his delicate green wings back and thrusting his coral and gold coloured neck forward in an act of unconvincing bravado, the little tyke became angry and embarrassed when Shana sniggered at the sight of him. Rebuffing her with a guttural jabber akin to an adolescent child's insolent reply, the small parrot turned his back on his mistress and lifted his beak high. Laughing out loud, Shana petted her little friend knowing that he would soon forget his injured pride.

During years spent aboard the Falcon, the wise bird had learned to stay close to Simon. Living amongst the ship's cat and dog population was not easy and the clown-like bird was well-known for leaving a trail of exotic feathers as evidence of dangerous encounters. Eddie, the lucky ship's cat had undoubtedly earned the coveted place as top moggie amongst the feline population and he was Micken's worst enemy. Eddie's double-clawed paws meant that he was more skilled in rat-catching than any other ship cat and his climbing skills had yet to be matched. The large cat's thick, black fur was believed to bring good luck to the superstitious sailors hence Eddie was rewarded handsomely for his natural skills with a bowl of milk. Every morning, when Shana and Tom milked the goats, they always made sure that Eddie had the first taste of the creamy, frothy delight. Micken loathed it when Shana allowed the cat to rub its sleek yet thick-set body against her calves and would screech to high heaven until she could no longer stand his awful racket. When Micken felt sure that he was well out of danger, the impish bird would chuckle an evil laugh and nibble on Shana's ear. Whenever the two were alone, the lonely woman was able to mother her tiny baby pet without any inhibitions and was determined to make the most of the time she had to coo and fuss over her fluffy companion. Although she had some loyal and close friends aboard, Shana longed for passion and it grieved her to have to live as a boy. She had decided that her life was passing by too quickly and she alone could change her circumstances. It was time to act and Shana Culley felt ready at last. She was pleased that her pet, Micken had flourished and had fast become an incredibly happy little parrot during the months that he had passed living aboard the busy vessel.

Very pleased with the turnout at Simon's secret get-together, Shana ensured that all cups were regularly filled with rhum as the dice rolled. Irish had volunteered to keep an eye out for weighted dies or missing 4's and had warned the crafty Tripod to steer clear of any trouble since he was well aware of his oldest shipmate's dire financial situation. Having spent most of his earnings on whores and booze, the tough old sailor was fast losing respect amongst his peers. Shana had been grieved to watch as her loyal friend had told the ship's surgeon to pull out every tooth in his bony old head so that he could sell them to Simon for the conceited captain's collection. Two months back, Tripod had shocked even the most hardened of the crew by shooting himself in the thigh during a raid on the ship by Portuguese pyrates while sailing a well-used spice route. Luckily the pyrates had little need for much on the Falcon but they did take some tobacco, rhum, spare rope and sails. To the men's bewilderment, Captain Watkins managed to trade something with the pyrate captain who left without much trouble following a private talk in the small man's cabin. No-one ever found out how their captain had persuaded the notorious Portuguese pyrate captain to leave his ship taking no lives or prisoners. but Tripod made sure to claim the allotted compensation that was legally due to a sailor who suffered injury whilst serving on duty aboard Watkins' ship. Insisting that the surgeon saw off his injured limb lest it became gangrenous, Tripod made the most of his earnings at the first stew he came across in the next port of call.

Losing a leg did not seem to diminish Tripod's sexual appetite, in fact to the contrary, the wiry little horn-ball made fantastic use of the specially designed leg attachment that had a perfectly smooth phallus carved in place of a foot. When he visited his whorehouses, Tripod would remove his false limb and allow the girls to play with it as a dildo whilst they waited for the next girl to finish her ride. His reputation as the punter with the monster member preceded him in brothels world-wide and every whore wanted to try some Tripod meat wherever he ventured. Since he had been known to regularly trade his pistols and valuables for way under their true worth, Tripod's sexual addiction to women of the night had almost literally cost him an arm and a leg as his supplies ran low. Ironically, his name no longer described the unfortunate character's three limbs but no-one wanted to re-name the still popular seaman. Besides, his peg-leg had become extremely versatile and yet another quirky addition to his favourite pastime.

Gambling went on in the bilge of the Falcon for well over two hours that night and as usual, Tripod lost more than he had bargained for. Following a particularly bad start in the month when he had spent too much time in the Mexican gambling dens, the unfortunate one-legged man left with merely a few coins and a pouch of nails as his prize. Although Tripod had managed to win a few games, winnings taken from an Irish man whose country's currency was worth even less than his Scottish shipmate's were low. A handful of nails was worth more to an English sailor than the currency of Ireland and Scotland.

A rare lunar eclipse occurred on the evening when Shana had planned to carry out her vengeful attack on the despicable fiend who had raped and abused Simon for too many years. Moments after the moon appeared to be absorbed completely into inky blackened skies, an eerie red glow spread over its slowly re-emerging surface. Casting an atmospheric claret hue across the upper deck of the Falcon, the moon turned the bloodiest of red, high above the ship, as she battled before a strong westerly wind. Tripod suddenly regretted his earlier success at fear-mongering amongst an already superstitious crew. He had been preaching to the converted hours before the rare miracle that he had predicted earlier, albeit tongue in cheek, as a sure sign of doom. The fool was beginning to believe in his own bullshit. 'Keep 'er steady whilst she's betwixt two sheets!' his words were grabbed by the strong, rain enhanced blast of steady wind and ripped far from human ears. Normally one to take everything with a pinch of salt, but all too quick to torment others in their beliefs of foreboding prophecies, the worldly man's face showed a rare expression of concern and genuine fear. Tripod stood quaking at the wheel whilst orders and cries echoed around him... 'Starboard, larboard, the helm, amid ship!'

Carrying fresh slaves from the Guinea Coast of Africa in two newly adapted decks, some major alterations by the Falcon's carpenter enabled her to hold more than double the number of 'human livestock' than she was previously able. Panic reigned amongst usually even-tempered crewmembers in a situation that would not have been particularly challenging for such expert seamen under normal circumstances. This uncanny astrological event had certainly raised a few hackles and Captain Watkins was definitely amongst the most fearful. As Shana had predicted, the wicked little heathen barked orders from the helm and lost control as confusion reigned. Although Shana had been correct in her expectation of unruly management that fateful night, she could not have predicted the captain's next command. With mouth agape and a sudden dread filling her entire being, the poor girl's heart skipped a beat as she heard the Welsh accent just as she had years before when her Precious had stood beside her. 'Release the black vermin now!'

Closing her eyes tightly shut, she felt icy stabs pecking away at her skin as the raindrops turned into spiteful pebbles of hail. Knowing that she would be unable to do anything to help the doomed tribesmen and women whose valued trust she had gained in their benign communication, the young woman forced herself to block the blood-curdling screams and sounds of heavy metal chains that linked woman to man, man to man or woman to child, in a cruel chain of human cargo. Manning the pulleys to adjust the sails and help keep the heavy ship on track, Shana's heart wept in silent despair for the people whose lives were to be cruelly snuffed out all because of ignorance and fear of the unknown. Dragged along by chains that joined their shackles to each other, the helpless victims' bodies, inhumanly weighted with iron, crashed heavily into a hungry sea. Shana's wasted tears blended with the spray as her unheeded pleas grew louder but were drowned out by desperate screams of mercy from the people whom she had learned to understand well. Turning pity into relentless anger, Shana's eyes narrowed and she clenched her jaw, her teeth causing her immense pain as she ground them together. As she slowly turned her soaked body around to face the despicably inhumane events, Shana could see Captain Watkins clearly and decided that the man had already lived way too long. Fighting the urge to reach for the gutting knife that she had stored safely inside her fake horn penis, Shana focused on the manipulation of ropes that altered the position of sails in the Falcon's complex rigging system. Momentarily, she had no other choice than to postpone her long awaited attack on the beast who would soon be taking Simon's arse for its final and probably most eye-watering swiving yet!

Following the exhausting battle with the elements during which Captain Watkins coldly and efficiently documented, '3rd day of November, in the year of Our Lord 1559: 300 bodies cast into sea to reduce weight of cargo thus ensuring safe passage of the Falcon and its crew of twenty, all of whom survived the storm.' As far as his narrow little mind could see, the tyrant had simply stated how dragging out and hauling over-board three hundred fit and perfectly sane human beings had ensured the safely of his treasured vessel. They had been too weighty for the vital speed that he had deemed necessary to beat the winds. Sitting in the dry nightclothes that Simon had prepared for him, the captain did not move a muscle until every last detail of the lunar eclipse and events that night had been recorded. It was not until the logbook had been second-signed by the relevant officer that Captain Watkins finally felt he could relax and begin a private, self-gratifying celebration with his well trained cabin boy. Before he retired to his cabin, Watkins was peeved to learn that Tripod had lost an eye during the storm. What the captain did not know was that the desperate man had gouged it out himself in order to claim more compensation. The report written by the captain stated that a piece of mittenmast, broken due to heavy winds, had speared the sailor's eye.

As the compliant young lad had done on so many nights since Shana had introduced him to his uncertain world, Master Simon Stempton bent over the wooden writing desk and offered his bared rear to the nasty little man. Sweet smelling brandy that had been enhanced with honey was fresh on Watkins' stale, warm breath. In subconscious reaction, Shana's body tensed as she felt chubby, stumpy fingers trace light lines across the soft flesh of her muscular buttocks. Gulping in a large mouthful of air, Shana spluttered as her dry mouth failed to produce enough saliva to swallow. Feeling the familiar stump of semi-stiff flesh that formed the short, stubby penis that reflected its owner's physique and build, Shana waited until the member was about an inch inside the delicate rim of her anus. As Watkins' groaned with perverse relief and jiggled himself forward into the tightness, Shana acted. Reaching between her legs, she took firm hold of the panting captain's slippery sweat-covered bollocks with her left hand. Jolting with surprise at his tame submissive's out of character behaviour, the abusive captain became more aroused and pushed his entire length inside the woman who he had been led to believe was Simon.

Captain James Percival Watkins suddenly felt a sharp pain and gave out a shrill squeal that sounded to Shana rather like a stuck pig at the mercy of a butcher. Every little detail of the physical pain and emotional turmoil that Simon had endured at the mercy of the fiend flew spinning uncontrollably through Shana's enraged mind. Suddenly feeling himself become as limp as a raw sausage, the man who had subjected his cabin boy to uncountable sexual assaults felt the sharpened point of a fish-gutting knife. Slicing straight through the tightened skin at the top of the pouch holding his gonads, Shana's steady hand made an expert incision. Spinning around she expertly followed the cruel slash through with a high kick straight into his rapidly-paling face. Shana tore open her shirt baring a stunning pair of unbound, heavy but firm breasts. Unearthly screeching met the impressive display and Micken's cage swayed as his tiny, agile body leapt comically from perch to cage side, excitedly mimicking the captain's yelps and groans. Unnerving hatred seemed to ooze from the wee bird as he cackled with glee in his high-pitched mocking voice. Shana's memories took her back to childhood when she had delighted in watching a cackling little puppet pummelling away at his wife, Judy and their baby in a grotesquely violent binge.

Behaving in a calm, natural manner as if she had been carrying out routine daily chores as opposed to performing a primitive and gruesome performance of castration, Shana took a handful of dried exotic fruits and fed her loyal bird. Lying on his back, stumpy hands clutching in a vain attempt to suppress the bleeding from the most vulnerable part of his anatomy, Watkins stared in disbelief at the beautiful woman who had caused his hideous injury. Mouth agape and eyes bolting like a guppy fish, the ugly man looked in horror from the blood-pumping wound to the wench who had emasculated him. With a calm and almost aloof air about her, Miss Sushana Culley took the tumbler of brandy and raised it head-high in a toast to justice and revenge. Throwing back her head, while releasing her lovely long locks from the black ribbon that she had always worn when disguised as Simon, Shana swallowed the burning liqueur gratefully. Then she took another, longer gulp of the amber liquid in honour of Master Simon... and spat it down into Captain Watkins' pathetically pleading face.

Hands already soaked with blood, Shana picked up one of the Captain's plumes and dipped a neatly cut nib into the seeping dark red liquid that oozed steadily from the gaping wound between his open legs. A whimper of disbelief laced with agony escaped from the lips of the foul creature lying helplessly prostrate before his mistress. The one-time master stared wide-eyed with terror at her fantastic naked body. Trembling at her feet, the dying man twitched as he mumbled a silent prayer. Meanwhile Shana steadily scratched her feelings in perfect script upon a parchment.

Years of training within a thriving spice trade had taught the wordly-wise woman to always act in the fairest manner possible and she determined to begin her new career as she meant to continue. Penning the scroll that was to hang over the soon-to-be 'late' captain's bed, she helped herself to a little more of his sticky life-blood and completed her sentence neatly. Such wise words and what better to have hanging above a new Pyrate Captain's bed? Unable to take back what she had done, Shana inhaled a deep breath and sighed as stark realisation hit her. Fate had dealt her a hand and now, she had to take control of her life. Holding the parchment against the cabin wall, a now worldly-wise woman stabbed the blood-covered murder weapon through the parchment and deep into the wood. Climbing into the captain's bed, Shana decided to leave the candles burning so that her victim could witness his life blood slowly drain away. The last sight to meet Watkins' fading eyesight would be the words inscribed in his own blood...

Alea iacte est... The die is now cast...

Chapter 13

Metamorphosis!

Shana Culley had been surprised by the reaction from the crew of the Falcon when they learned of Captain Watkins' murder. Many of the men, with whom she had served on numerous hazardous journeys, had shown their utmost respect for the woman who had taken what most deemed as justified revenge on the rapist. Of course, Tripod had not been able to hide his 'pleasure-yardstick' when Shana had revealed her breasts to the men on the morning following Watkins' murder. Before falling asleep the previous night, Miss Culley had been busy. She carefully prepared the skin that she had flayed from the abuser who had raped her when she took on the guise of poor innocent Simon. As the men caught sight of the attractive wench emerging from the captain's cabin, their jaws dropped open. With fiendish delight they realised that she was wearing a trophy from her kill. The pale brown pouch of gunpowder that hung at her thigh had been expertly decorated with an exquisite design of Celtic knotwork. Cleverly, Shana had taken a needle and tattooed the complex pagan pattern into the hide that she had vowed not to be put to waste. Shana was desperate to display her trophy immediately but it would have to undergo the full tanning process at a later date. Made of what appeared to be soft pigskin leather, the pouch had caught the attention of more than one sailor and on further inspection, the gruesome truth was realised.

Dangerously beautiful, the statuesque woman wore a fine silken shirt unlaced to reveal her ample bosom and neat little naval. Numerous weapons tied to the end of several long silken scarves were secured at her belts and the powerful woman loomed impressively over her audience. Despite her menacing manner and majestic appearance, Shana still managed to appear innocent and pure amongst the group of sea-hardened men.

Not a single word needed to be spoken; Shana had simply nodded her head toward the captain's cabin, in open invitation to anyone who wished to view his body. Irish was the first to enter and had re-emerged looking sickened and pale, yet he felt admiration for the person who had finally taken revenge on the manipulative little lout who had abused too many for far too long. Slapping his newly revealed female friend firmly on the back, the huge man said nothing but continued with his duties. Soon after Irish had emerged from the murder scene Tripod limped inside to view the body of the well-loathed officer. Following the two old shipmates, a queue soon formed outside the small cabin. Until that memorable day, Shana had never witnessed so many puke attacks during her times spent at sea as a lowly cabin boy. Quietly and calmly, she observed some of the most hardened sailors throw up the soured contents of their guts as they viewed the cold corpse of David Watkins. All were humbly grateful to their shipmate who had rudely stripped the abusive captain of both commission and complete undercarriage! Once everyone who felt the need had satisfied their morbid curiosity, Shana stood on the main deck to address the men. Keeping her speech brief and to the point, the fine woman spoke with absolute confidence and brutal honesty. A trustworthy, loyal and brave crew knew that they were being addressed by a fiery, vengeful and natural-born leader. Regarding the strong-willed wench with absolute awe, admiration and occasional envy, they took in and believed her every word.

'I 'ave killed Cap'n Watkins an' plan ter sail the Falcon ter the Coast of Brazil. I invite e'ery man who chooses t' join me in a new life as a buccaneer. All men who choose pyracy must form a circle and sign together. Our signed document shall show our democracy as free men serving no-one but ourselves an' one other!'

Men wearing serious expressions on weather beaten, bearded faces stared at Shana in awe and respect as she continued, 'Any of ye not wishing ter live the life of a wanted man, prithee take yer leave at the next port of call. Ye shall be given yer fair share of pay from too many long, hard days of toil under a bastard commander! Now 'tis our turn ter elect a better in his place!'

Her final words had managed to hit a nerve and suddenly, a roar of cheers erupted from her shipmates in a splendid scene of camaraderie. Hats were thrown in the air and exhausted men embraced each other showing their support in brotherly union. For a few minutes, the gallant and brave men joined in triumphant celebration, displaying a rare masculine love that touched Shana's heart. No more words were needed and she had stood alone for only a spilt second, then her true friends embraced her as if she were their long-lost sister… all except Tripod, of course, who brazenly helped himself to a handful of breast as he buried his bony face between his friend's deep cleavage. Laughing heartily, the tall wench grabbed hold of the shorter man around his scrawny waist and lifted him head-height, planting a firm kiss on his dry, cracked lips. When his only foot reached firm, safe ground, he danced around like a jester, making everyone laugh as he kicked his fake limb high, performing a mock polka. Sailors helped themselves to rhum and some dropped to their knees, performing imaginary phalatio before Tripod's obscene penis-ended peg-leg. Grabbing Shana as he hobbled over the ship's wooden boards, the hilarious little sailor felt far happier than he had for too long a time.

Feeling a chill wind teasing her wavy, dark-blonde hair that hung loose below her waist, Shana stepped into the captain's foul-stinking cabin. Watkin's bloated body lay at her feet within the small, airless room. Flies had settled on the decomposing flesh and had already begun to lay their tiny opalescent eggs. The sailing master, John Clark entered the cramped quarters, ducking his head as he stepped through the low doorway. Shana was pleasantly surprised to have gained the support of such an important member of the crew. In silence, the pair began to prepare the parchment that already bore the words Shana had written using the previous commander's blood. Quickly agreeing on a simple statement for those who desired to live and serve as a pyrates from that day onwards, they cleared the walnut table of maps and navigation equipment to lay out the thick paper document. Taking the quill, Master Clark penned the oath whilst Shana summoned those who wanted to join in the official signing. Smiling to herself, Shana noticed that Irish had recruited loyal friends who jostled to gain a place around the highly polished walnut table.

No fewer than seventeen men signed the pledge together that day and showed their allegiance to the proud woman who had faced so many battles since she had been abducted and forced into a hard life at sea.

Shana Culley had been deeply moved by the impressive show of support from the men with whom she had served during some of the most difficult months of her life. Those who had chosen to continue in a lawful sailing trade took their share of profit from Captain Watkins' trading days and were free to go their own way once they had reached land. On closer inspection of the vile, uncompassionate man's cabin, Irish and Tripod found secret hiding places where the captain had tucked away copious amounts of valuables. For the conniving, inhumane man who had managed the Falcon and her crew abominably, it was finally time to leave the ship in the most fitting way. The late Captain Watkins' reeking cadaver was stripped of the clothes that he had been wearing on his final night and Shana insisted that his ankles and wrists be shackled. Stomachs heaved as they all tried their damnedest to pull the bloated, rotting limbs together to be bound by chains but it was no easy task. As pieces of decomposed flesh, finger and toenails came away from grotesquely swollen hands and feet, the men could eventually take no more. Pulling them roughly out of her way, Shana finished the unpleasant job herself. It was extremely important to her that Watkins' body suffered the most unimaginable degradation and humiliation. She had witnessed the captain order unwilling and terrified men to dispose of human beings; men, women and children who, despite their creed or colour, had not deserved to die. Over-ripe, shiny, puffed dead skin burst open as Shana manipulated soggy limbs into position. Matted hair and pieces of scalp began to come away from the skull. Despite the shit and piss that spilled from the cadaver onto her clothes and fresh young skin, Shana continued her task, devoid of emotion.

The wench was determined not to rush the final preparation of the body that had once been Simon's abuser and took a while to present it exactly how she wanted it to be found. Finally satisfied with her work, Shana stepped away from the dark skinned corpse. The men stood and stared in repulsion. The ship's surgeon suddenly let out a long and sorrowful sigh of sympathy and deep understanding as he realised what Shana's intention had been all along. Already he had expressed his concern about the corpse's lingering presence and strongly advised her that it should be disposed of immediately. Potential harm would probably come to the crew if the body remained on board as it went through the stages of decomposition. Now he looked down at the figure that had been forcibly curved into the foetal position, shackled and chained like one of the black slaves.

So many of the African people had lost their lives during transportation and the mass drowning had been the last straw for the compassionate woman. Everyone aboard knew how Shana had felt about the mistreatment of the men, women and children who had been abducted from their homelands. Forced below decks to live in appalling conditions, they were treated worse than animals. As word spread around, sailors and pyrates left the young woman alone with the body of the hateful beast. Hacking deeply, Shana filled her mouth with phlegm and spat it into the sunken eyes that stared unblinking in the sunlight. She picked up the remains of Watkins, leaving a sticky dark pool on the deck and flung it overboard without saying a word. Only she knew that with him, he carried a message... embedded deep in his anal cavity.

A brown vessel that had been given to Shana by an African woman went along with the remains of Captain Watkins. Whoever found the skeleton would also find his secrets wedged firmly between the pelvic bones. The dead abuser's victim had placed a message inside the 'effigy' bottle that had been crudely sculpted into the shape of a four legged supernatural entity. Shana had carefully rolled up a scroll on which she had listed every one of the cursed man's heinous crimes. Having placed the accusatory document within the bottle that was formed as a grotesque squatting figure, Shana had made sure that the devil-like craft was shoved as high up inside the late captain's arsehole as it could go. When the misshapen hind legs, ending in cloven hooves, disappeared up inside a once virginal orifice, Shana imagined the devil-like creature's grimace. In her mind's eye, she saw its eyes roll upwards as if looking towards its host's head... which was soon to be stripped of its remaining flesh by the creatures on the sea bed. Comfortable in the knowledge that someday the hideous truth would be known, Miss Culley did not care how or when that would happen.

Micken's tuneful whistle called her from the little room that had once been the sleeping quarters where Shana had been forced to endure so many nights of buggery. Whilst playing the passive role of natural victim, Simon Stempton, Shana had been shown so many different things and learned some harsh truths. Smiling triumphantly to herself, she thought of the young lad whom she had created for an important purpose during difficult times that now seemed so long ago. At long last, the hardened woman felt assured that Simon had not lived his abusive life in vain. Finally she was able to let him go in peace.

Having won back her own life, Miss Shana Culley breathed a heavy sigh of relief laced with triumphant revenge. Taking one last look at the gently lapping waves below, she idly toed the slippery black substance that had oozed from the carcass that was once Captain Watkins, merchant seaman and slave trader extraordinaire. Suddenly the rejuvenated and hopeful young female sailor burst into hysterical fits of tears that had been suppressed for too long. Her eerie, maniacal laughter rang through the bowels of the un-captained Falcon as the bows of the vessel sliced their way through darkening seas.

Huddled in the round Irish and the others, who had decided to join their colleague in a new venture, waited patiently under-cover for their friend to re-join them. Feeling totally useless, the men did not have a clue what to say or do to help the woman who had suffered, in their full knowledge, at the hands of a tyrant. The helpless men just stood listening to the haunting sounds of a human who had taken justice into her own hands. Shrimp's eyes filled with tears and he began to hum a tune, melodic and low. Fellow native of Scotland, Jock Mackenzie joined in with the tuneful Celtic lament whilst others stood and wept for Shana and the unfortunate souls who they had cast into the inky black depths. United in their grief and collective feelings of guilt, a group of once emotionally-hardened sailors bared their souls and unburdened feelings that had been stifled for so long. Their voices rose above the disturbing sounds of a woman whom they imagined to have been pushed over the boundaries of insanity.

The event was never mentioned again. The once united crew of the Falcon had jettisoned their human cargo during her last trip from the African continent.

Sadly this was not an unknown occurrence in the fast-growing trans-Atlantic slave trade. Money was all and a black, human life was worth less than a bag of salt. European traders' attitudes were that there were plenty of replacements available whenever the ships docked in an African port.

Strongly opposed to the whole idea of trafficking people for commerce, Shana Culley had managed to take her first step in a battle that she had chosen to fight. She was willing to lead the way in a cause against what she deemed as the sickening abuse of basic human rights. As an intelligent woman who had gained the respect and honour of men long used to a male dominated world at sea, Miss Culley determined to make the rest of her life worthwhile. Shana planned to plunder, pillage and ransack any vessel that she came across carrying human cargo that was to be sold into slavery. With a deep understanding of the consequences of pyracy, the innovative woman also vowed to despoil any ship manned by Privateers who stole bounty in the name of the queen of England or any other greed-obsessed nation. Shana's main aim was to take advantage of the times when the seas had become a popular way of transporting treasure in often slow and clumsy vessels.

Whilst Shana Culley was being elected as captain by the men with whom she had served aboard the Falcon, Queen Elizabeth was being urged by parliament to marry a suitable English nobleman as soon as possible. The House strongly advised her to marry so that she might bear a full-blooded English son as heir to the throne. Her sister Mary's widower, Philip of Spain was known to be an aggressively devout foe of Protestantism and he was pressuring the queen to marry him in order to keep a

Roman Catholic foothold in the country. In order for the Tudor Dynasty to survive, the succession must be ensured.

Elizabeth now reigned over a country in despair, weakened by war and religious strife. With her treasury almost bare, Spain and France waited in the wings ready to pounce. Both were powerful countries wanting to rule England's lands. With most English citizens calling for their young queen to marry a strong man who would guide her, Elizabeth had no choice but be firm in her response to the parliamentary delegation. In her official letter she stated her intentions quite clearly and wrote that she had 'no desire to make windows into men's souls' and that after careful consideration, she had chosen to remain a virgin for the rest of her life. Undoubtedly scarred by her father's abusive relationships, she had sensibly adopted an inherent mistrust of men. By remaining unmarried, Queen Elizabeth would be free to claim all entitlements as sole monarch and not have to sacrifice anything for a husband. Somewhere along the Guinea Coast of Africa, Shana felt great respect for the present queen of England in her decision to remain single and childless. The newly elected pyrate captain understood all too well the reasons why many women had come to mistrust men.

As a democratic union the men who had chosen pyracy as their newfound trade had elected to sail to Brazil. Their plan was to anchor their craft in the bay of Portobello and break company with those who had decided to choose a more righteous profession. With monies taken from Watkins' stash, their captain purchased materials to repair an abandoned Dutch schooner. Once her newly elected crew had decided rank and duties that each would perform on the altered vessel, they headed off to enjoy the wonders of Portobello. Shana and John Clark stayed near to the beach where the native tradesmen worked on their new vessel.

Supervising every addition, alteration and repair to the ship that the crew had collectively decided to call 'the Banshee', Shana and John ordered her hull to be pierced to enable her to carry extra guns. A successful pyrate vessel needed to be fast, small and light enough to enter shallow waters without fear of grounding. It was essential for her crew to be able to out-sail heavier, bulkier warships unable to follow her right onto land. She needed to be easy to maintain quickly so that they could be on their way before their location had even been realised. The Banshee's bulkheads were not necessary, so were immediately removed. Partitions were constructed below decks and space was cleared to enable the gunners to work her guns. She was soon made flush, her forecastle removed and quarterdecks lowered so the weather-deck continued from bow to stern, thus creating an obstacle-free fighting platform. Timbers were strengthened to absorb the stress of increased armaments as Captain Culley ordered that the Banshee be fitted with a dozen swivel guns mounted in gunwales.

Following two long months of intense and careful reconstruction, the impressive ship loomed before a happy woman on the tenth day of January in the year 1560. Weighing around a hundred tons, the vessel certainly appeared one to be reckoned with. She had been rebuilt to carry fifty men and housed twenty four cannons inside her small, streamlined belly. Expertly careened, her hulls had been scraped and rubbed completely smooth and barnacle-free. Spare sails and chains had been stored aboard and her single mast possessed an impressive large spread of sail. Shana had arranged for a personal flag to be made and was eager to fetch it before the crew gathered to celebrate the launch of the wonderful customised schooner. At the launching, the flag of the Banshee was revealed in a spectacular ceremony. Explosions and gunfire could be heard for miles around the coast as the pyrate crew celebrated initiation into their villainous career. The Banshee's flag would surely strike terror into the hearts of any sailor unlucky enough to meet with her on the open sea. Silently screaming, a hideous white profile stood out on the black silk banner. The Cross of St. George would be the colours flown up until the last minute before any surprise attack. Then Captain Sushana Culley's pyrate colours would be revealed… a black flag bearing a skull and crossbones beneath which swung one of her custom brown patterned pouches. A red slither of a moon shone above the skull representing the mutinous night when Shana became a pyrate.

Their project had not been easy and the two shipmates, Shana and John Clark had worked well together designing and supervising the construction of the seaworthy vessel proudly riding the sea before them. Finally, the pair felt able to relax a little. Their task was almost complete, only the food supplies and extra chandlery had to be loaded before she sailed on her maiden voyage. Shana insisted that John should take an evening off. At first, the man protested but Shana's stubborn character won him over and he joined his shipmates. Shana slept in her new cabin that night but before she retired, she stood on the upper deck and scanned the skies. A beautiful pink horizon met her gaze and stars surrounding a pale razor-thin moon blinked at random. Feeling a sudden chill, the new pyrate breathed a lungful of fresh sea air and stepped inside her little cabin. Soon after midnight, the pyrate captain was sound asleep inside the strengthened ribs of her new vessel, the Banshee.

Chapter 14

A Hard Lesson Learned

'Captain Culley the castrator' was the name that Shana earned as the tale of the horrific butchering conquest became the most talked about all over the New World and Olde England alike. The story of the brutal pyrate wench who had lived at sea amongst hardened sailors as a cabin boy soon spread, growing ever more grotesque as it passed from jabbering drunken mouth to eager ear. Her notoriety did most of the work for Captain Culley as slave ships were predominantly captained by men keen for their manhood to remain intact. The Banshee became a fantastic weapon in her captain's cause and the slave trade began to suffer at the hands of a fanatical human rights activist who had learned to value every human being's life. Determined not to be put off by the wealthy privateers who had full support of the crown, Captain Culley became quietly confident that the Banshee's acts of attrition would eventually have a positive outcome in the war against slavery. Many who had been freed by Shana in her lone battle against the barbaric trade were given the choice of freedom or the chance to serve with her in a worthy humanitarian cause.

The Banshee's crew gradually grew and changed until those who manned her consisted of a healthy mixture of nationalities, cultures, creed and religion. The strong African presence aboard Shana's ship soon became dominant. Any native African people who chose freedom over service were given the chance to return to Africa or to begin a new life in one of the many developing communities of the world. Whatever choice they made, each was given an allotted amount of currency taken from the ship from which they had been freed. In the case of emancipated slaves, the crew of the Banshee had set out strict rules that her Captain insisted must always be adhered to.

Continuing to journey across uncharted waters, Shana discovered places that it would probably take centuries for other explorers to discover. Sworn to secrecy, neither she nor any member of her band of pyrates would ever reveal the location of tribes that preferred to remain undiscovered and untouched by so-called western civilisation. Embarrassment and anger were the two major emotions felt by Queen Elizabeth of England when she was told of the treasonable antics of one of her female subjects. As far as the queen of England was concerned, she had enough to worry about dealing with the plotting of her cousin, Mary Queen of Scots, who was claiming the English throne. Public opinion had definitely swayed against the slave trade and the queen was treading on thin ice with her continued support of human trafficking. An undeclared feud began between Captain Culley and one of the queen's most loyal supporters. Captain John Hawkins, son of William Hawkins of Plymouth, a wealthy property owner and merchant, regularly crossed the seas with a cramped cargo of men, women and children from Africa. Although the enemies had not yet met, both Shana and John Hawkins had a good idea of how the other would react and their hatred towards one another boiled within each of their independent, stubborn souls.

Raids on vessels carrying riches of various kinds were carried out regularly by Captain Culley and her men. The impressive Banshee sliced through the waves almost as smoothly and silently as a hot knife through butter. Catching ship's crews unawares, the neat and compact vessel became renowned for sneaking up beside vulnerable heavier carriers. Her crew often managed to locate and gather together booty within minutes of boarding the unfortunate vessel and by the time any cutlass had been drawn in defence, all had been successfully transferred to the awaiting Banshee. A sighting of Miss Culley had recently become more important than the protection of valuable cargo that was all too often en route to a palace somewhere in Europe. Baring her ample and extremely beautiful breasts, Shana would often charm the men aboard by thanking them kindly for their valued co-operation whilst her men looted their bounty. As time passed by, the queen of the seas became more flamboyant in her choice of attire and the most popular pastime amongst mariners became trying to spot the most recent addition to Captain Culley's costumes and bodily adornments.

Ever since her first sea journey Shana had been fascinated by the wonderful ways many African tribes decorated their bodies. As a woman with strong respect for her Celtic roots, she had always wanted to outwardly honour her ancestral bloodline. On their journeys around an ever-increasing world of fascinating cultures, many of her sailing companions had symbols, names or ornate patterns tattooed into their skin. Tribal artists used a crude, spiteful-looking comb-like tool made of bone. Covered with ink or dye it would be tapped into the flesh creating intricate patterns. Shana decided that she would be proud to have her body decorated with signs and symbols to display her ancestral heritage and beliefs. Ever wonderfully individual in her dress and appearance, the picturesque pyrate captain adored jewellery. Each time she acquired a pretty new trinket, she had another hole pierced into her soft, tanned flesh to display her latest adornment. Standing like an Amazon princess, Shana looked every inch the pyrate queen that she had become. At last she had managed to turn her atrocious luck around and the legendary character that she had created was one not to be taken lightly. Her body had become a map of her life at sea, collections of marks and patterns from so many different cultures decorated her stunning figure. Everywhere that Shana travelled, artists added their skills and tribal markings of bravery, honour and protection. Whilst accepting multi-cultural traditions, the spiritual woman always respected and honoured her ancestors with intricate Celtic designs displaying her beliefs. Each time one of her crew lost their life, she would honour their loyalty by adding an appropriate permanent mark on her flesh. Her fingers and toes became a memorial site for those who had served with her and died for her noble cause.

As her bodily decorations spread, Shana's appearance had changed almost every time the Banshee dropped anchor. The crew of the infamous pyrate ship were very proud of their picturesque captain who influenced many in style, fashion and image. With an incredible array of the fascinating characters in her crew, the Banshee gained and lost some of the most skilled sailors, surgeons, gunners, cooks and cabin boys who died valiantly. Many signed up and served an allotted time under Captain Culley's command but there were some who pledged a lifetime of service with her. Thankfully few lives were lost in her service but when they were, each was given a burial at sea and never forgotten. Whenever possible, Shana would pay men with excellent combat skills to train her and the men in defence and attack. The crew were therefore highly trained in various martial arts ensuring that anyone who served with her was given the best chance of survival. Making regular trips to Cathay, Japan and the Far East, she remained good to her word, hiring only the best.

Many of the ever-changing team of sailors found a new niche in life but Shana's oldest and most solid friends stayed with her in a close-knit family. Irish remained in service as the Banshee's boatswain, Jock Macenzie as the master gunner, John Clark her sailing master and good old Tripod became the ship's cook... when he had bartered too many of his limbs and organs to be fit for any other job! Shrimp remained in service, delighting Shana with his wonderful company and collecting the most exotic creatures from each corner of the known world. His menagerie expanded as quickly as his waistband and Shana never once heard the tiny man complain, even when arthritis began to eat its way deep into his shortened bones. Ensuring that every person serving with her was rewarded with the finest of prizes, the fairest pyrate captain ever known became the most popular amongst her kind. There was never a time when Captain Culley had difficulty finding fresh crewmen and when she offered sailors the chance to serve with her or die with their captain, not once did she have to carry out the penalty. However, Captain Culley never allowed anything underhand to take place on the Banshee. Life had been hard for her learning all the ropes in a man's world at sea and if any crew's member slacked in duty or endangered another shipmate's life, he would always suffer the consequences. Many sailors came and left, yet Shana had to endure the bitter taste of betrayal only once.

A sailor nicknamed 'half-hanged Pete' joined the pyrate gang in January 1560 after they took over the slave ship on which he was serving. Shana recalled the first time she saw the very tall, lean and muscular man she had felt unusually unnerved and could not reason why. Choosing to ignore her gut feeling, Shana made the biggest mistake of her life and gave her total trust to the man. Half-hanged Pete had very dark skin and his neck was deformed due to an unfortunate accident with a hangman's noose... luckily for Pete, the accident was the hangman's. Shana knew that the murderer had endured a botched execution where the rope was too short. He had dangled for twenty agonising minutes before the crowd became frustrated and a riot threatened. The determined madman endured another ten minutes of choking before a surgeon insisted that the hangman cut him down.

Following his reprieve, Pete screamed hoarsely at the crowd and spat a curse over the townsfolk who had failed to take his life. Hailing from a well-known family in a city in northern England, Pete Shaw had murdered a young maid and tried to bury her body in nearby woods. Following a brutal, violent rape Pete had decided to cut the victim's throat to ensure that she would never be able to tell a soul what he had done to her. Rumour at the time of the hanging was that Pete's mother had helped him to kill the poor girl when he had made such a mess of her throat and neck that he was unable to finish it himself. His victim had managed to poke out one of his eyes during the barbaric rape which made him angrier still. Apparently there had been so much sticky blood from both victim and attacker, that Pete was not able to grasp the knife well enough to draw its blade across the unfortunate girl's larynx. If Pete's mother had not have stumbled in on the scene the moment she did, the struggling girl might have had to endure her son's torture even longer.

Half-hanged Pete was sent to the gallows for his diabolical crime that many believed not to be his first. The foul man had ruined his own mother's life as she had not been able to watch that poor wench suffer any longer at the hand of her own flesh and blood. Taking a fish gutting knife from the scullery, the devastated woman had put the girl out of her misery in a split second. Since the brutal slaying, Pete's mother had been struck with madness and was said to be living out her long, miserable days in an asylum, her screams of agony wracking the walls of the institute as she remembered the day of the crime. Pete gave no thought to his wretched mother and left for Scotland, taking his chance with the rebellious, fiercely patriotic clansfolk. With no choice but to leave the country, Pete offered his services as a Privateer and soon after encouraged mutiny amongst the fickle crew. Having no interest in captaining a group of sailors who could not be trusted, Half-hanged Pete offered his services to any successful captain who was willing to pay him well. Captain Culley happened to be drinking in a Scottish tavern with Irish and a few others one evening when Pete approached them. Both Shrimp and Smith had spent time serving with the character who stood tall and wore a black patch over his gaping eye socket. Trusting her two friends implicitly, Shana agreed to include Pete on their next voyage to the east.

On Saint Valentine's Day in the year 1560, Shana's men requested a night of roistering in the port town of Aberdeen. Having hired three new men to replace those who had chosen to stay in countries with sunnier climes, Shana allowed the hard-working sailors some well-earned free time. Half-hanged Pete was amongst the trio of newbies who were willing to keep watch and ready the Banshee for her onward journey. Shana settled in her cabin for a night of peace. Since her monthly bloods had only just stopped flowing, she was glad of some time to relax. Counting the spoils from the last four raids on slave ships around the English, Irish and Scottish coasts, she divided it equally between her men. Taking a fair amount for herself and some to stash somewhere safely for her anti-slavery cause, Shana tied the velvet pouches and began to disrobe. Privacy aboard a ship full of horny men was rare and women who dared live amongst the sea wolves had to be on guard and ready for attack at any time. Exhausted beyond belief, Shana loosened the heavily embroidered brocade corset and pulled off her camisole. Taking Micken from his cage, Shana let the tiny bird rub his body over her hands in a heart-touching display of pure love and affection. Kissing the soft down under his wings, the tired woman talked to her adorable pet as if he were a child. Putting him safely back into his cage, Shana lit more candles and took the heated water that Smith had prepared for his captain over to the china face bowl. Micken whistled happily as she washed, then a hideous occurrence made the parrot distraught. Sensing unusual signs of fear from his mistress, Micken screeched for help as he watched helplessly from behind thin metal bars.

The night when Half-hanged Pete burst his way through the small door of Shana's cramped cabin would be etched deep in her tortured mind forever. With foul, stinking breath, the man who Shana had felt uneasy about since their first meeting stumbled into her sleeping quarters with no warning whatsoever. Speedy reaction and well-placed blades and pistols were essential in a pyrate's dangerous trade. The canny pyrate leader had placed weaponry around her room as well as on her person. All were loaded or sharpened in case of emergency and Shana was able to take hold of each even when in the deepest sleep. Unable to understand how the intruder had gained entry without either she or Micken hearing anything, Shana yelped a helpless warning, 'Ye lay one finger on me and ye shall die fer it!' Her threat sounded lame and pathetic as she stood trembling. A sense of vulnerability overtook her whole mind and body. For a split second, she became Simon. Becoming the abused character once more cost her what she had come to dread most. Leaping head first toward his prey, Pete grabbed Shana around the neck with strong hands, knocking her off-balance. Falling sideways, the two crashed against the table, sending instruments flying. Bringing a knee up firmly between the tall man's legs Shana hit her target and felt a slight release of Pete's firm grip on her throat.

No sound came from her mouth as she stared at her attacker, wide-eyed with terror. Feeling beneath her for a hidden drawer, Shana felt weakness gradually take over her upper body as she struggled with the vile man. Dextrous fingers managed to pull the ring that opened the drawer and her hand felt the coldness of a blade stored inside. Realising her intention, Pete slammed his large boot against the drawer and Shana grimaced as she felt searing pain. She felt Pete's erection against her thigh and realised that their struggle was turning him on even more! With a final effort to escape from the iron grip of her molester, Shana lifted her forehead quickly upwards to hit him full on the nose. Head-butting had often helped

Shana when she had been in trouble but this time it did nothing but anger Pete more. Biting the side of her neck, Pete reached down between the pinned woman's legs and tore off her under garment. Untying his breeches, he released his penis and slammed it into her tight pussy. Unable to scream, Shana felt her skin tear as his huge member entered her. Tears welled in her swollen eyes as the grotesque rapist pumped his hot sperm deep inside her. Ripping off his eye patch, Pete made his worst mistake when he stared down at the woman who he had taken by force. To her surprise a poorly made, milky-coloured glass eye filled what Shana had imagined to have been a vacant socket. Pete's real eye widened as he realised that the vulnerable female who had been too weak to prevent his sexual assault no longer stared at him helplessly through terrified eyes. Her stunning blue eyes had narrowed into feline-like slits as he withdrew his semi-erect member from her tightened orifice. Beneath him now lay a vengeful and vicious pyrate who seemed to have gained an unexpected unearthly strength.

Drawing on every last morsel of hatred and loathing within her spirit and soul, Shana Culley reached for the drawer in the desk behind her once again. Agonising pain wracked her broken, bloodied hand as she tugged open the drawer and felt the cold metal blade. A sudden rush of adrenalin gave Shana the burst of energy she needed and she felt her confidence return as she gripped the ivory handle of the cruel-looking skinning knife. With mouth frothing and teeth clenched tightly together, the pyrate queen summoned the strength to overpower her foul rapist and free her other hand. Whether it was the shock of his victim's incredible metamorphosis or his orgasm that had caused the despicable beast to drop his guard shall never be known. All that mattered to the abused woman was revenge and her pretty facial features twisted into a terrifying frenzied grimace. Teeth bared, Shana managed to speak in a guttural, venomous voice that sounded as though she had been possessed by a demon from the pits of Hades. Bringing a long leg up and over her attacker's heavy limbs, Shana growled the most chilling of curses as her knee came into contact with Pete's ribs. A sickening crunch made Shana shiver with sadistic pleasure as she skilfully wrapped her free arm firmly around his deformed neck. Squeezing the gristly, elongated matter tightly in the bend of her elbow felt so good that she paused for a minute to lengthen her enjoyment of the sport. Amused by the astounded expression on her victim's face, Shana became bemused by her survival instinct and her weird ability to suddenly change temperament. Opening her pretty mouth wide like a snake preparing to devour its struggling prey, the warrior woman sank her shiny sharp teeth into her molester's ear. Tearing the whole organ away from the pardoned murderer's head, Shana spat out her first bite and readied herself for a second.

The scene had become gory as primal instinct overtook the damaged woman and she eyed her prey, toying with him like a lioness before the kill. Pete trembled and blubbered beneath the half-clad woman who he had unsuccessfully tried to dominate. A look of horror appeared on his face as he experienced the full extent of Shana's wrath. Before Shana drew the sharp blade between the top two vertebrae of Half-hanged Pete's spine, she placed a wide-mouthed kiss around the socket of his real eye and sucked with all the strength that she could muster. Popping out with incredible ease, her rapist's eye felt like firm jelly in her mouth and she rolled it around her tongue sensually, as if she were stimulating the juicy head of a lover's prick. Having released her grip on Pete's neck to enable him to beg for mercy, Shana rolled her own eyes up in triumphant glee as she bit firmly down onto the optical nerve. The metallic taste sent the wild pyrate wench into an uncontrollable frenzy as she heard the screams of her victim. Thrashing the knife down into the torso, she continued her attack long after Half-hanged Pete's well-deserved death.

Thankfully, Irish was the one who stumbled into the diabolical scene when he returned in the early hours to find the new watchmen asleep at their posts. Panic hit Shana's protective friend and he ran to her cabin where he found her straddled atop of a bloodied body. Guessing the reason why the new crew-member was in Shana's cabin, he acted quickly and prized the knife from his hysterical friend's injured hand. There was little left of the dark skinned, weather-beaten face of the repulsive criminal who had attacked his close friend. Blood pulsed from two gaping apertures and a grossly dislocated jaw gaped open wide in a macabre yet mocking pose. It was as if Pete's murderer had summoned the devil himself to make a sick display of his butchered corpse, however the savage scene was clearly the work of an abused woman.

Rocking like a child in Irish's protective arms with an insane look in her eyes, Shana hummed and wept to herself, clutching her latest trophy close to her heart. It seemed as if she already knew that the beast whose enlarged testicles she grasped tightly in her hand had impregnated her. Crying in despair Shana vowed to her friend that the baby, soon to begin its growth within her womb, would be the most cherished and loved child ever born. Calling for Tripod, Irish asked his drunken mate to prepare a mixture of rhum and opium which was greedily and hastily consumed by the captain. Gradually managing to calm his exhausted friend by listening to the foul account of the assault, Irish confirmed his loyalty, respect and undying love for his captain in his deep, soothing voice. Unable to sleep that night, Irish could no longer suppress the trauma and sadness that he felt for the vulnerable woman who he held safe in his strong arms. Bitterness was an alien feeling for Irish but that night he felt it a hundred fold. His hammock swayed gently as he wept himself to sleep. Distraught and devastated, Shana lay like a rag-doll in her drugged state and her whole life flashed before her in a dream. She and Irish had made a pact never to mention half-hanged Pete again.

Shana and her closest friend eagerly awaited the birth of her child and no other soul knew of her pregnancy. Loose flowing shirts covered the small bump that hardly distorted her lithe figure. Nine months later, aboard the Banshee, Shana Culley gave birth to a healthy baby boy who she named Patrick. No-one ever questioned the infant's sudden appearance and all were aware that their captain also had needs. Not one soul wondered or even cared who the father might be. Everyone knew that Shana desired no bonds or ties and was extremely happy in her free and adventurous world.

Travelling to and from Ireland, Shana decided to become acquainted with the notorious woman who she had heard all about from her old and well-missed friend, Eileen Conachy. Although Shana had revisited England's shores both with the Falcon and now the Banshee, she had yet to summon up the courage to enquire about her extended family back in Teignmouth. Frightened that she might learn bad news of her loved ones, the newly appointed pyrate queen vowed one day to return to visit Mary Maggy's. She wanted to ensure that her kin would never want for anything again. Until then, Shana asked the gods to watch over the orphanage and keep those who dwelled there safe and happy.

Sailing back and forth between England, the Netherlands and Ireland, the Banshee continued in her lucky spate and Shana's stand against the slavery trade held strong. Queen Elizabeth raised the price on Captain Culley's head and her capture was worth a small fortune. The penalty for aiding the feisty queen of the known seas was immediate execution but that did not deter any of Shana's growing supporters and fans. Incredibly and to her surprise, she had become a popular character and tales of her guile and notoriety spread all over Europe. Executioners at ports grew richer as people accused others of harbouring the infamous villain and quickly became expert at devising more gruesome punishments for felons.

The ever-growing popularity of public executions as entertainment meant that blood money could be spent on more elaborately engineered contraptions. Each executioner devised a unique trade-mark and the more that he made the condemned suffer, the more famous he became in his morbid trade. Shana had the nerve to disguise herself so that she and Irish were able to witness the occasional execution without her being recognised. On one occasion when they ventured ashore at Plymouth, they were disgusted to see a pregnant female pyrate hanged. It seemed as though England's days of mercy had gone and a pyrate's offspring was said to have been cursed at conception. Other women who had committed hangable offences were able to 'plead their bellies' and be pardoned, at least until the birth. Babies of pyrate wenches were now believed to be a seed of the devil himself in the eyes of ordinary folk. Shana held her belly with fear for her unborn child when she saw poor Molly Berkin hang after she had watched her own belly sliced open, her unborn child torn from her split womb and thrown to the crowd. Tiny pieces of the foetus could be seen as its little carcass was ripped to pieces, bit by bit. Shana shuddered with anger and disgust at the queen of England and her ignorant subjects who behaved like sheep under her cruel and greedy leadership. Fleeing from the barbaric scene, Shana ordered the crew of the Banshee to weigh anchor and make haste for the Emerald Isle. Anger boiled within her veins as she thought of the hypocritical Queen Elizabeth who was as much a pyrate as any.

When the Banshee docked in Dublin, Grace O'Malley was waiting ashore to meet Captain Culley. Both were keen to meet each other and join forces against the evil English queen. On hearing of Shana's displeasure with the monarch, Grace was even more enraged by England's false sense of divine superiority and vowed one day to wreak dreadful revenge. Patience was a good trait to possess and when the fates decided, Grace was determined to show the queen of England that an equally strong willed queen waited in Ireland, ready for the next battle. Far more powerful and dangerous than Queen Elizabeth could ever imagine her to be, Grace O'Malley would never allow her English counterpart to take over even one tiny piece of her beloved land.

Instant love was felt between the two pyrate queens and Grace immediately took Shana under her strong wing. Dressing like a man with her dark red hair cut close to her head, she had earned the nickname, Bald Grace. The older woman was beautiful in Shana's eyes. Like the mother that she had never known, the hard faced pyrate treated her as a daughter and apprentice, telling her everything about the history of Ireland. Feeling instantly at home, Shana relaxed under her new ward's tender care and enjoyed the wonderful Celtic hospitality. Grace O'Malley wanted to know every tiny detail of the times that her intriguing guest had enjoyed with her lover Eileen Conachy. Many days passed whilst the two kindred spirits reminisced together, drinking copious amounts of rhum and sharing the most intimate of stories.

As two very different pyrate queens swapped their most torrid and terrifying adventures, they created a bond that would never break. They roared with laughter, sang, drank and wept together and held each other in the utmost respect. Shana enjoyed many firelit nights deep inside one of Grace's stone fortress homes and their bond was sealed with the deepest love that either had ever known. Confiding in her wild new female friend, Shana explained how she had become pregnant and Grace felt savage loathing toward her attacker. Had he not been already cast into the depths of hell, Grace would have had the greatest pleasure torturing him over days of agonising pain, only ending his life when it was impossible to keep him alive any longer.

Heavily pregnant, yet her state still unbeknown to most of her crew, Captain Culley fought alongside her men when needed. Every morning Irish pulled a corset around her swollen belly, tying it tightly before Shana went above decks to address her men. When her baby boy was born on the 13th day of November in the early hours of the morning, in the year 1560, Shana did not utter a single cry of pain. Following three long hours of gruelling labour, Patrick Culley had to be cut from his mother's belly. The baby had become stuck within Shana's muscular cervix. Irish made a perfectly neat, expert cut along the pubic line, just as he had done to help birth the mares out on the moors years ago in Ireland. Insisting on sewing her own gaping wound, the stubborn pyrate wench took a bottle of rhum to her bed, pouring some on her baby's head and then on the bleeding wound on her baggy, shrinking stomach. Sleep came instantly to both mother and baby but to her disbelief, within an hour of his birth, Shana had to go to the aid of her men. Her most hated enemy, Captain Nut, an Algerian corsair enjoyed the rich pickings from the 'cinque ports' of Ireland and regularly raided her coasts, his favourite haunt being Youghal. Nut had finally lost patience and decided to attack the Banshee. Shana had no choice but join her crew and help them to fight Nut's raiding party. Through no fault of her own, Shana's careful plans to seek out the vengeful captain before he found the Banshee's whereabouts had gone totally amiss. The evil outlaw commander of three heavily armed ships was said to have buried some valuable hoards of treasure along the coast in that area. It was also reputed that a slave lay with the stash deep under windswept dunes.

Youghal was the perfect place for the fiendish lout, who Captain Culley had grown to despise, to lie in wait for her ship and carry out a surprise attack. The Banshee had made anchor at the thriving port of Youghal, a medieval walled town in Cork. Its strong colony had gradually been built up over centuries and the town had become extremely powerful and influential in Ireland

and Europe. Its port was one of the busiest in the British Isles. Sitting at the mouth of the Blackriver, the bustling town had gained invaluable trading privileges due to its convenient location.

Local belief was that Nut had grown bitter with jealousy towards his rival, Captain Culley. The pyrate captain felt deeply insulted that a woman, the inferior sex in his own culture, had become a serious contender in the battle to reign over the seas. Aware of Grace O'Malley's status and power in her homeland, Nut would never have dared pose a threat to her, so the thieving foreigner chose to bully another woman. Who better to choose than an English woman? The bigot was blissfully unaware that Shana had a close friendship with Grace's life-long friend and lover, Eileen Conachy. Rumour had it that, on hearing of Shana's disapproval of the thriving slave trade, Nut had begun a personal war against her. He was well known for capturing men and women during looting sprees on monasteries and towns and made a habit of using or selling his captives as slaves. To taunt Captain Culley he began to execute a slave after every raid then buried the body with the spoils. Nut waited patiently for the so-called pyrate queen to take his bait. When he sighted the Banshee lying at anchor close to his latest burial site, he gave the order to attack and board.

Although taken by surprise, Shana managed to slay the cruel captain within minutes of becoming aware of his unwelcome presence onboard her vessel. Weary from giving birth and masking intense abdominal pain, Captain Culley fought with as much ferocity as ever. Following a particularly hard struggle against determined outlaws who had pledged their oath to fight alongside an evil man, Shana kept control of her ship. Irritated by the blatant nerve and rather cowardly raid on her ship, Shana decided to make a mockery of the deceased captain. Having taken her customary trophies, she found to her surprise that Nut's were the smallest set of gonads that she had cut from a victim yet. Once prepared, they would make a fine gift for Grace. Nut's 'crown jewels' would be a fitting souvenir for one of Ireland's pagan queens. His rabble of a crew had killed some of Captain Culley's most trusted men and Shana was not going to forget them in a hurry. Ordering her surviving men to prepare to keel-haul Nut's only remaining crew member, Shana retired exhausted to her cabin.

Customary victory celebrations would soon begin aboard the Banshee and the captain was determined to join in as soon as she had tended to Patrick. It was by pure coincidence that the man who was about to die a gruesome death happened to be French. Following a victory as important as the defeat of such a beastly tyrant as Nut, Shana was going to ensure that her men were well rewarded.

After breast feeding her newborn baby and rocking him to sleep in her arms, she wrapped him warmly and laid him in the bottom drawer of her desk which had become a makeshift cradle. Swiftly she rejoined the party that was taking place above on decks still covered with blood. Grace's gift would have to wait to be decorated, as Shana had special plans for the design of her most prized trophy yet. Once she had closed the door to her cabin behind her, safe in the knowledge that Patrick lay snug and warm inside, the rejuvenated captain threw back her head in glee and leapt into Irish's arms. Joining in a wild dance to the lively Celtic music, the handsome pair swirled around to the melodic sounds of whistles, bodhrán, fiddle and squeezebox. Shana felt more alive than she had for ages and her pretty, flushed cheeks made her mischievous blue eyes twinkle with sensual delight. Irish had fancied his strong captain for a long while and his attraction toward the wild, free-spirited wench grew with each passing day. Well into the morning they danced and celebrated another victory whilst baby Patrick slept peacefully despite the din. Joyous music and drunken partying had become commonplace on the decks of the Banshee.

The day after the birth of her son, following a much needed sleep, Captain Culley rejoined her men on the main deck. She had bound her belly wound tightly and stood silently observing the man who had been spared only to suffer severe punishment. She planned a brutal end for the captive to show others how she would treat any who had the nerve to chance taking over the Banshee. Hideously black with dried blood and bruising from the pummelling that his killer had given him in his last minutes, Captain Nut's head was pierced by a spike from ear to ear and impaled on the foremast. Orders had been made clear that the late Captain Nut's head was to keep death-watch until the day that the Banshee reached Brazil. His headless body had been tied to the sole survivor of his gang as extra humiliation and punishment for the man who was bitterly regretting not taking his own life when he had the chance. He had hardly enough strength left to blink away the salty water that splashed against his chapped eyelids and his face appeared to be made of leather. Toughened facial skin had tightened around his skull during his torturous time tied to the bowsprit. Too many hot, harmful rays of sun had baked the prisoner's face into a cracked, ox blood red mask, making him look like a life-sized stuffed doll. Nut's headless corpse had remained tied to the condemned man but much of his remains had been eaten by seagulls that swooped down to peck off pieces of rotting meat.

For the first few days, the prisoner had hoped that Captain Culley would show him some mercy. At least he still had his testicles intact! As he sucked desperately at the wet sponge that was passed down to him every couple of hours, his hope soon dwindled. Finally he accepted that he had no chance of surviving even if his captors managed to keep him alive until he reached the location for his planned execution. His countrymen would have no pity for a pyrate, of that he was quite sure. Existing purely as an example to warn others of their fate if they dare attack the Banshee, the exhausted man could no longer feel anything in his numb, limp body. Only God knew how many days and nights had passed since he had been tied to the bowsprit of the Banshee. A smooth, blue-green sea and warm sunlight told him that they were in hotter climes but he had lost any concept of time along with his tortured mind. He was never aware of when the Banshee reached her destination, even as two of her strongest men climbed down to release him in readiness for his final punishment. Having almost completely lost his hearing from constant exposure to strong winds and torrential rain, the prisoner was dragged up onto deck and tied to the pulleys that would start the keel hauling process.

For those on land, in sight of the impressive battle-ready vessel flying the pyrate flag, the Banshee was surely a most magnificent sight to behold. Despite the vessel's menacing appearance and firing capabilities, she appeared solitary and almost vulnerable on the wide empty waters. Could such a single, tiny craft have wreaked such carnage alone?

Shana closed her heavily lashed eyelids and breathed the refreshing sea air deeply into her lungs as she prepared herself to order the inevitable torture. Although she knew that her captive deserved to die, a self-loathing always ate away at her heart and conscience each time she condemned a man to die. She had never forgotten the vile, agonising fate of her African friend who had been murdered so far away from his homeland. Waiting just long enough for word of her arrival to spread amongst the spectators, Shana fired a single shot from her pistol.

Worldwide, the appearance of the infamous pyrate queen's lone ship was a sure sign of Captain Culley's threatening, intimidating power. Her blatant nerve and daring had become well-known along the coasts that fringed the exquisitely lush tropical lands of Brazil. Somewhere along the São Paolo coast, a terrified man was trying in vain to prepare himself for a punishment that would undoubtedly end in a horrible death. Showing not a single ounce of mercy, Shana had denied the man any alcohol to numb his senses. Throughout the long trip to the Brazilian coast, the man had been allowed no food, only water to keep him alive. Shana had made an example of the most unfortunate man ever to cross her path and he was about to pay the price for her bitterness toward any who supported slavery. As she barked out orders for position and anchorage of the Banshee, Pierre Dupont prayed for a speedy death.

Sick to his stomach, Pierre shuddered in anticipation of unavoidable final agony. Seconds felt like minutes as the ropes that held the unfortunate pyrate tightened with a creak. The victim had been chosen for execution to set an example and deter anyone from attacking any vessel captained by the long reigning pyrate queen. The ropes that tied his wrists securely together strained as the pulleys were slowly turned. At each turn, they tightened to pull his lean, muscular body upwards. Suspended close to the yard arm, the terrified man showed incredible courage as heavy lead weights strapped to his ankles stretched his legs painfully. Spitting at Tripod and Irish as they lifted his shivering body over the side of the vessel, the French pyrate muttered helplessly in prayer. His final trip around the Banshee had begun and the sound of his body slapping the water below caused a stir on shore. Inaudible shouts and sounds of encouragement ensued as the offender was dragged slowly beneath the ship.

In full view of the French witnesses who inhabited São Vicente, Shana stood proudly on deck, her contented babe cooing in her arms. Patrick giggled loudly when he heard his mother's unruly crew erupt with frenzied, almost animalistic roars as they howled and taunted their prisoner who reappeared, spluttering and gasping for breath. Once again, he was hauled overboard and the crowd on land roared in delight at the spectacular show. Each time the bloodied shreds of the culprit reappeared, he had lost more of his flesh. Evilly sharp barnacles that were stuck firmly to the keel ripped into his damaged body. Every time he reappeared dangling from the lanyard he left a sticky trail of blood on the Banshee's decks. The sickly sweet stench of sweat, blood and the condemned man's puke mingled with the smell of gunpowder smoke as Tripod fired a shot each round that the condemned man survived. Stunned by the heavy blows every time his head struck the ship's bottom, the man gagged when Irish forced a rhum bottle between what was left of his lips and teeth. Unable to resist the temptation of alcohol, the slowly dying man regained consciousness. It was a piteous sight to witness the hardy soul gulping greedily at the alcohol in a vain attempt to ease his suffering. With a hopeful glimpse of salvation, the desperate man shot a pleading look Shana's way but she showed no sign of mercy on her vicious face. Eyes bolting in fear and loathing of his torturers the condemned man bit off his own tongue and spat it towards Captain Culley but it landed on Patrick's plump little face. Sudden hatred towards the fellow pyrate built up within the protective mother's heart and soul. Her captive and his loathsome gang had put her child's life at risk by attacking the Banshee and now he dared to insult her baby!

Drawing the short Arabic sword from its ornate sheath at her side, babe still clutched firmly under one arm, Shana leapt forward two steps and drove the blade into the insolent man's groin. Unable to resist the pain that seared through his body any longer, the bloody man screamed in agony. Hearing Micken's delighted cries from within her cabin, Shana venomously spat out an order of another circuit for the insolent victim. Adrenalin rushed around her body as she waited for the torn, shattered body of the drowned pyrate to be hauled back on board for the fifth time. Devoid of emotion, the cold-blooded captain held Patrick to her breast and allowed him to suckle hungrily as she surveyed the blood-thirsty spectators who had gathered to watch the gruesome spectacle. Surprised and delighted by the unexpected torture show, the audience cheered and sang loudly from across the clear turquoise stretch of water that separated them from the macabre spectacle. Having provided a show that would be talked about for months, Shana had managed to deliver yet another of the spectacularly shocking performances for which she was well renowned. Holding her newborn child naked above her head in an act of primitive and triumphant maternal pride, she let her huge swollen breasts hang bare, nipples hardened from Patrick's suckling. In an impressive display of power and blatant extroversion, the stunning warrior woman screamed her legendary bloodcurdling Banshee cry and disappeared below decks to prepare for disembarkation.

On land, three soldiers had been taken captive by French guards who had discovered the position of their military expedition led by their Brazilian Governor. Scheduled to be hanged, the prisoners waited, watching the gruesome keel-hauling. At least the event had bought them a little more time. As they looked around in hope for signs of a late rescue attempt, Shana and those remaining in her steadily dwindling crew boarded the cedarwood cockboats and rowed towards the shore. A school of flying fish leapt lightly into the air, skimming the smooth waters as they gracefully re-entered the calm sea. A light southerly wind aided the crew in their efforts to reach land as quickly as possible so that they could join in the celebrations and enjoy the entertainment of a good hanging. Quite suddenly, the sight of a bound and gagged woman standing on the wooden platform caught Shana's attention. Since their last visit, the Portuguese population had been forced out by the French. From what Shana had heard at various ports on the sailors' grapevine, it appeared that the new settlers had begun a witch hunt during their indoctrination of Christianity within a community of different cultures. Having no firm belief or interest in any Christian faith, Shana idly pondered whether they would make it to the shore in time to rescue the unfortunate wench. Allowing the fates to decide as she often did, Captain Culley began to hum a pretty tune to her suckling infant. Unsure whether it was mere instinct or something even more powerful at work, Shana suddenly had a gut feeling that she knew the condemned woman.

Noticing that several Portuguese galleons had dropped anchor near to the port, Shana was glad to see that the colony still gave priority to sea-borne trade. Previous occupiers' primary concern had been defence, relying on a predominately military presence, although soldiers' families often joined the men. It was always surprising how quickly new nationalities began to arrive soon after the retreat of former settlers. Like the English, the French enjoyed a good public hanging and an impressive gallows had been erected in a clearing between gently swaying palm trees. As the boat approached a suitable docking point, Shana strained her eyes, trying to make out more details of the unknown woman. With a desperate gasp of sudden dread and realisation, Shana confirmed what she had initially feared. The woman who stood proud and tall amongst smaller figures, also bound or shackled, looked all too familiar. Scanning the waters, Shana turned to Irish and roughly handed her lively bundle over into his long arms. Patrick was a strong baby and few were trusted to take care of him whilst his mother had other duties. Tripod and Shrimp sniggered openly when they heard Irish yell out, 'Yerr greedy young tyke! I have nay mammaries ferr ye ter suckle on!' Giggles erupted into healthy, full-bellied laughs as the men began to relax and enjoy their long awaited break from sailing duties.

'Sssssshhhhhhhhhhh!' Yon lan'lubbin' filth-riddled French bastards have Grace O'Malley!' hissed their angry captain. Stunned into shocked silence, Tripod quickened his rowing pace and Irish began to bang the side of the boat with the handle of his gutting knife to speed up the oarsmen. Whistling over to the other two boats, Irish made hand signals to explain the situation and passed Patrick back to his mother. Shana had to act fast and somehow free her Celtic friend before they could execute her. Whatever happened, she was not about to watch another one of her loved ones die in front of her.

That day, the usually delightful approach to the luscious shores of Brazil was ruined by the prospect of her soul sister's execution. As they neared the shore, Shana screamed an order to halt any execution until she was present. A single shot rang out and her heart filled with dread as she witnessed the first condemned prisoner drop through the hatch and perform a struggling dance of death. Her cries went unheard as the crowd roared with encouragement. Luckily for Shana, the unfortunate soldier had a sturdy strong neck and made an impressive attempt at resisting the tightening rope. Five whole minutes passed as the shit spilled from his rear and blood poured from his every orifice. Amazingly, the frantic fighter even managed to free his hands from the ropes and began to tug at the tightening noose that cut cruelly into his thick flesh. The crowd roared with bloodlust.

Diving into the sea, Irish decided to swim for it and do his best to delay the two other hangings before Grace took her turn. Shana watched helplessly, trying to calm Patrick who had sensed his mother's anguish and begun to cry. Tears ran down her own cheeks as she pleaded to the gods and goddesses to have mercy and come to her friend's aid. When the second prisoner stepped forward, the executioner placed a sack over his head. Watching in despair, Shana bit into her lip as the priest blessed the condemned soldier. The trapdoor snapped open and the man was far luckier than his comrade had been when his neck broke within a split second. Untying a thick woven square scarf from her hips, Shana placed it on her knees and folded it into a triangle, wrapping her wriggling baby inside the cloth. In her mind, she concentrated on positive thoughts, trying desperately to banish pessimism. She had not experienced such feelings of helplessness and vulnerability for a long time. With dexterity, she secured the makeshift sling around her neck and waist so that Patrick could ride securely on her back. Feeling her stomach turn over with dread, the brightly clad pyrate grabbed the side of the boat and leapt into the calm sea.

Walking was difficult in the thigh-high water but Shana carried Patrick faster than those unburdened men who followed her. A strong, whirling undercurrent tugged and teased her lower legs as she waded into more shallow waters. As the tide was going out, her thigh muscles ached as they battled nature's strongest force, the sea waters waging a natural resistance against her toil. On this visit, Brazil's beautiful landscape had no impact on Shana. Her usual feelings of awe and pleasure were absent as she fought her way to the shore on legs as heavy as lead. Mind firmly focused on how she was going to rescue the Irish pyrate queen, Shana held her pistols high to keep their powder dry. Her chosen weapons were impressive as she had originally aimed to captivate her audience. A cutlass sharpened and ready to shed blood, a selection of cruel knives and a sabre had been placed on her person to enable her to make numerous kills if need be.

The picturesque bay formed a huge semi-circle and to her left was a shallow white sandy beach with a backdrop of lush, dense tropical rainforest. Within these were wetlands above which pretty latticed canopies of tangled lianas, leaves and orchids grew. A huge spectrum of greens formed a natural aerial tapestry above the bare forest floor. Having visited those wondrous tropical labyrinths before, Shana's mind's eye was able to conjure a perfect image of the paradise that lay beyond the dreadful scene before her. As she emerged from the shallow waters onto the beach, approaching the crowds from the right which gave her the best view of the gallows, the crowd began to cheer. Noticing a few familiar friendly faces standing near to the forest opening, Shana whistled and shouted a greeting to the tribal men from the Tupi territory. Knowing that they paid random visits to the main port to trade with sailors and settlers, Shana was not surprised to see them at such a crowd-drawing event. Making a spur of the moment decision, she decided to change her original plan of attack and ran towards the grinning, black-toothed tribesmen. Usually strong legs buckled beneath her as the sodden cloth of her thick skirts weighed her down in the struggle to run through soft, deep sands.

Seeing the alarmed look on their trusted friend's face, the three Tupi tribesmen dropped their woven palm leaf baskets and headed straight towards the distraught pyrate queen. Carrying their long bows which were almost seven feet in length and reed arrows with brightly coloured flights, they blew a gourd trumpet as a warning to the Europeans present. Shana was well aware of how fast and accurate the Tupi warriors were with their arrows and so were the crowd. Menacing in appearance, the three warriors ran toward Shana with great speed and minimal effort. Having befriended them long before the French had arrived along the Brazilian coasts, Shana had gained their trust and great respect. Her own pagan beliefs and open-minded attitude towards all cultures had allowed her to accept the sacrificial and cannibalistic practices which had not shocked or frightened the worldly woman. When Shana had been given the rare privilege of attending a Tupinamba ritual, her reaction had been of honour and respect. Joining in with the chanting and howling, she had no problem with inhibitions and allowed the Shaman to cleanse her spirit and contact her dead ancestors. The Portuguese occupiers used to describe the whole Tupi culture as barbaric and believed the tribe to be devil worshippers.

The French citizens attending the executions turned terrified faces towards the three Tupi men running towards them. Shana felt sure that the French feared the natives as much as their predecessors had. Each tribesman displayed his kills by wearing necklaces threaded with teeth pulled from their victims. Unafraid of death, the men were ferocious in battle. An impressive array of scars and piercings formed a tally of dead enemies clearly upon their dark, lean and muscular bodies. Many small nomadic tribes had amalgamated to form what the Europeans collectively called 'Tupi Indians' yet not all of these were on friendly terms. Attacking at dawn, these skilled and violent warriors mainly fought amongst themselves.

Each tribe consisted of several villages made up of traditional long, oval cottages with grass covered roofs. Several families would live together in these long houses accommodating around three hundred people, each having an area allocated to them alone. The Tupi had established some thriving trading posts in their territory where they stored freshly cut Brazilwood that they traded with visiting sailors for a variety of goods and wares. Once shipped to Europe the sought after wood was used to manufacture dyes that had become extremely popular amongst cloth merchants.

Dropping to her knees in sheer exhaustion, the pyrate queen felt relieved to have found allies ashore. A unique sound gave her renewed energy as she felt a welcoming breeze from a lengthy arrow passing over her head. Another followed immediately after and then a volley of the brightly coloured reed arrows flew swiftly to land just short of the panicking crowd. Chaos ensued as people ran for cover, yelling for mercy. Only the Tupi warriors were skilled enough to be able to fire many consecutive shots so quickly and on perfect target. Gratitude to her friends and deep relief prompted Shana to reach behind her to stroke Patrick's delicate scalp before she drew her pistols. Lasting a split second, her reassurance gave the tiny baby an instinctive sense of safety. His mother's three allies joined her in line ready for further orders and Shana was relieved to see that Irish and his men had gathered at the opposite side of the gallows, weapons drawn awaiting her signal.

From the depths of her being, Captain Culley gave her trademark blood-curdling Banshee scream and thrust her unsheathed cutlass in the air as a signal to attack. Grace O'Malley stood tall, her ankles and wrists shackled and shaven head held high. As Shana had expected, her Irish sister in arms had taken advantage of the situation. She would no doubt explain later how she had managed to strike the bloodied executioner lying at her feet. Laughing like a madwoman, Captain Culley ran behind the tribesmen with Patrick's tiny fingers clinging onto her multi-plaited hair. Not a sound emerged from the bundle on her back and Shana knew from that moment that a future life of rebellion, excitement and danger would suit Patrick perfectly.

As night drew in, a stunning sunset framed the Banshee and an exhausted mother sat on a shallow beach feeding her babe in arms. A healthy fire glowed as its dancing flames licked at the fresh shrimp cooking slowly on long skewers. Once Irish had freed Grace O'Malley, they both set fire to the gallows and slaughtered any French fool who dared try to defend himself. It had not been necessary for Shana or her three friends to take any lives as the crowd had sensibly dispersed immediately. Monies, valuables and weapons were collected from the body of the executioner and the other victims. Shana looked down at her sleepy child and felt an immense surge of pure love. For this moment she had waited so long. Safely in her arms, she held the man child who would one day take over her reign of the seas. Grace embraced her friend like a long-lost sister. No words were necessary; their bond was strong enough to sense each others' love. Accepting the tiny bundle from Shana, Grace bowed her head in silent gratitude and the two women joined the Tupi men sitting on the sandy beach.

Offering Grace his pipe of sweet smelling tobacco, one of the men spoke in his native tongue, inviting Shana and her friends to stay in his village until it was time for them to leave. Drawing the pungent smoke in deeply, Grace passed it on to her neighbour whilst Shana accepted the invitation and went to find her men. It was time for them to return to the Banshee and relieve the others. They were all in for a long night of drunken debauchery. Shana knew full well that Tripod would be making the most of the local French stew hidden within the respectable bath house of the Christian community. Smiling to herself at the hypocrisy that she found wherever she travelled, she smoothed her warmed skirts and walked towards the source of lively music.

Grace O'Malley took to Shana's delightfully good natured yet feisty child as if he had spent nine months growing within her own belly. The three of them spent ten happy days living amongst the Tupi tribe and Grace even managed to pick up some of their complicated language. Shana learned of Grace's secret trips to Brazil in the guise of a male pyrate captain. Visiting the shipyards there, she was able to commission expert craftsmen to build purpose-built vessels to be used in defence of her beloved Ireland against the growing English fleets. As a well-respected queen and feared outlaw, Bald Grace was easily able to barter with the local shipbuilders. This enabled her to buy vessels of excellent quality for a meagre fee. Shana felt flattered to have been taken into her companion's confidence on such a top secret matter. Confident that she could rely on her new soul sister and trust her with her life, Shana vowed to help Grace O'Malley in the fight to keep the English from conquering Ireland.

Naturally gifted in learning languages, Shana became more fluent with each visit paid to the pagan tribe. In honour of their hosts, the two pyrate queens joined in the age-old cannibalistic sacrifice of enemies taken from other hostile tribes. A withered elderly chief invited them to visit the shaman to have the European demons cast out from their souls. He was concerned that the tall warrior women were in dire danger from the influence of the

'Tapuia' or 'people of strange tongue' as he called anyone who did not speak the Tupi language. Dressed in robes and brightly coloured ornaments and headdresses, Tupi men, women and children provided a spectacular sight even to flamboyant Captain Sushana Culley! Gifts of earrings, necklaces made of crescent-shaped fish bones and pearlescent white shells were given to the honoured pyrate guests.

The children of the Tupi tribe loved Patrick and Shana trusted them to paint his small body with scarlet urucum and black genipapo. Decorated with patterns and pictures of birds, the child giggled happily. Tupi men stood almost two heads shorter than Shana and Grace. Shaved almost hairless, including all pubic hair and eyebrows, the only hair left unshaven formed a circle around their crowns. Both Grace and Shana agreed that the unusual hair style was not as comical as that of the tonsured monks of Europe, for the bronze coloured skin of the small men made the neat black circle appear to be painted on. When in battle, the men wore nothing but red or black paint on their bodies and their primary motive was to take prisoners for ritual cannibalistic slaughter. Thus existed a vicious circle with barbaric cycles of vendettas, pitted against opposing tribes, constantly feeding the bitter feuds. Warriors proudly displayed tattooed stripes to represent lives taken and were eager to learn what Shana's tattoos signified.

Shrimp felt more comfortable with the Tupi people than he had ever felt before and was soon accepted into their tribe following a dramatic piercing ceremony. The tiny man was totally relaxed in a trance-like state whilst a tribal elder pushed a sharpened reed straight through his lower lip and both cheeks. Proudly wearing green, polished jadeite plugs through each new piercing, he took his new wife into an allotted lodge where they consummated their bonding. That special night, the tiny man and his child bride both lost their virginity.

Lying on a bed of palm leaves with her baby suckling contentedly from her full breast, Shana took in the interesting scene around her. Busy preparing children for a night's sleep, it was refreshing to see the Tupi women at total ease in their environment. Observing a routine that had probably changed little over hundreds of years, Shana pondered whether their primitive way of life was far more satisfying than that of her society. Giggling children gathered around for a story from a weather-withered elder whilst the men brought the animals inside or tended the communal fire. Women laughed together as they combed each other's hair with simple shell combs dipped in coconut oil to make their sleek, black locks glossy.

Everything was so comfortable and natural that it was easy for Shana to feel at home in such a therapeutic environment. The sweet smell of coconut oil made the smoke less acrid, smoothly quelling the caustic odour of burning wood. Nuzzled comfortably into the softness of his mother's breast, Patrick's eyelids flickered. Instinctively sucking for comfort alone, the tiny child slept soundly as Shana stroked his soft brow. Had she been given the choice that very minute, she would have quite happily stayed with the tribe for the rest of her life. Glancing over to find the source of an outburst of refreshing giggles, the contented mother watched Shrimp sitting with his tribeswoman. This unusual sight pleased Shana as she watched one of her favourite men interact with the attractive young girl. She could not have been much older than eleven or twelve and was plain to look at until she smiled. Within seconds her lips widened into an alluring beam that completely changed her face, transforming her from a rather boyish looking child into a captivating young woman. Shana could see clearly how her natural feminine wiles had totally captivated the Lilliputian sailor. The undersized man was bewitched by his new wife without any doubt. Shana seriously contemplated the situation but soon put herself at ease when she noticed the approving look on the chief's face. Satisfied that her employee had gained official approval of his marital prowess, the captain relaxed and continued her favourite hobby of people-watching.

Hours passed by as Shana observed the goings on around her in the communal home. At one point, she became very aroused as she watched a couple having sex only yards from where she lay. On all fours, the woman offered herself to her man, rubbing her tight, muscular arse up against his strong thighs as he knelt behind her. Flickering, golden light bathed the two firm, lithe, young bodies as they writhed seductively against each other in an arousing display. Used to sharing a home with so many, the act had become nothing to be ashamed of. In fact the couple's blatant lack of inhibitions made Shana feel extremely comfortable with her voyeurism. At one point, the woman who was being penetrated by her husband looked over at her and smiled with pleasure. Whispering to her man, she giggled and turned a little to show more of her body to her attractive, buxom voyeur. Shana reached her hand under the fine linen cloth covering her own shapely body and began to touch herself. Patrick was sound asleep beside her and did not stir as she brought herself to an ultimate climax. Just as she reached an incredible, pulsating orgasm, she looked over at the copulating couple who were both watching. The feeling was sensational as she imagined kissing the pretty girl's body whilst her man penetrated her. Muffled groans of pleasure could be heard as the pair joined their observer in rhythm and came together, then collapsed in a contented heap. Without any feelings of embarrassment, shame or guilt, the two whispered goodnight to Shana in their own language and she echoed her sleepy reply.

Although the men of the Banshee were sad to leave Shrimp behind, they knew that he would be happy with his new family and make a fantastic interpreter for these intriguing people. On the day that he waved farewell to his shipmates and a life at sea, Shrimp stood next to his minute wife. Joining in the dancing and sweet, hypnotic singing, the figure of the small man who had served his captain well gradually blurred as the Banshee gained speed. Shana held her baby close, finding comfort and an indescribable feeling of peace and wholeness in the scent of her own child as she watched her friends lining the shore in a farewell ceremony. Shrimp and his new family, the Tupi tribe gradually became a spellbinding streak of colour floating on the horizon. The sight made an enchanting scene that touched the hardened captain deeply. Smiling to herself in the realisation that a strong motherly instinct had brought a sentimental side of her multi-faceted personality to the surface, Captain Culley felt quite emotional. She was going to miss her little sailor friend. Very soon, the animated figures became tiny specks on the fading pastel landscape and the Banshee began her long journey back to Ireland.

Chapter 15

Homeward Voyage

It was strange for the crew of the Banshee to serve under the command of two captains but the female duo managed to work incredibly well as a team. Both women were keen to make the most of what was probably the only journey that they would ever take together. Determined to make the crossing of the vast seas on their return trip memorable and worthwhile, Shana and Grace agreed that their best option was to sail well-used trading routes. This offered the adventurous pair ample opportunity to ransack a good many ships of their choice. The heavily laden vessels were easy pickings for the cunning crew. The notoriety of the pyrate queens gave them advantage over trading vessels and sailors often surrendered without a struggle. A close encounter with such legendary characters would give any ordinary sailor the chance of becoming a hero on his return home. Recounting the exciting events of a raid carried out by none other than Captain Shana Culley, the most wanted pyrate queen who ever lived and Captain Grace O'Malley, would be enough to fuel a blazing fire of yarns... enough to provide a steady income of free ale for the rest of his days.

On the very first day of the return journey to the Emerald Isle, Captains Culley and O'Malley led their men in two consecutive raids on vessels carrying slaves. Plundering a generous amount of swag from each, the Banshee gained fresh African recruits and continued on her way. Grace was impressed by Shana's ability to converse with the African people in more than one of their many complicated languages and became keen to learn herself. She planned to take some of the liberated people to Ireland where she would set up a language school. There, they would be taught Gaelic and Grace hoped that they could then teach others their native language. Excited by this new venture, Shana translated for Grace. It delighted her to know that her friend was beginning to feel as passionate as she was about the freedom of these displaced people.

Micken was pleased to receive more attention since Grace had moved into Shana's cabin. He had been feeling neglected since Patrick had arrived. The comical little fellow enjoyed listening to the two women converse into the early hours and loved to perform acrobatics for them. Patrick was fascinated by his Mama's parrot and Shana allowed Micken out of his cage so that they could become used to each other. It was almost as though Micken knew that he had to be gentle with the child. He even began to take the odd peanut over to the little man and drop it near to his mouth. Shana was grateful for female companionship and although the two women were ridiculously attracted to each other, both respected Eileen. They often enjoyed passionate kisses but it always stopped there. Loyalty was important to both pyrate queens and they knew that they were never destined to be lovers. Grace loved to nurse Patrick and he soon became used to her. The sight of the dysfunctional family, made up of the most unlikely group of characters, was a touching one to behold. When Shana, Grace, Irish, Micken, Tripod and wee Patrick all ventured ashore, many found it amusing to see usually unsavoury characters doting on the cosseted baby. Officially and physically, Patrick had no father but Grace, Tripod and Irish all idolised the boy and he would never feel rejection.

As the days passed, the ship made its way along the planned route with little trouble. Plundering two Spanish vessels that were en route to Panama, one after the other, the Banshee pillaged their weighty chests full of gold. With her belly heavily laden with spoil, Grace and Shana decided to sail the vessel straight back to Ireland. Grace had five castles where she stashed her swag and invited Shana to store her booty at any of them at anytime.

Heading for Clew Bay in Clare Island where Grace's clan waited impatiently for her safe return, Shana knew that she would miss her new friend. The two adventure-craving women were kindred spirits who were making their mark in history. Only a select, trust-worthy few knew that Grace gallivanted off on secret adventures. She had a double who would regularly appear, disguised as Grace, so many never suspected her absence. It was imperative that all were led to think that Grace O'Malley never strayed too far from her homeland, lest they suffer attack. Ireland relied on her strong leaders and Grace O'Malley was one of the finest warriors in the land. Her mere presence proved to be a deterrent, especially to her most hated enemies, the English.

Faring well on the last few legs of her journey back to Irish water, the Banshee sailed leisurely as the men counted the knots in the line trailing in the wake to calculate her lethargic speed. Weeks passed by and the captains ordered that supplies be rationed for the final push. Deciding that it was safer to make their way home with no further stops, Grace and Shana managed the situation very well and at last, the Banshee reached friendly shores before hunger set in. Feeling relieved to be back in the land of her ancestral roots, Shana chose to spend a few weeks there with Patrick so that he could get a feeling for the culture of his mother's true homeland.

Weeks turned to months and time passed by too quickly whilst Shana and Patrick enjoyed being cared for by their generous hostess. Micken was not keen on the miserable, grey Irish climate and like many of the crew, caught an unpleasant head cold. Nevertheless everyone was happy with the abundant supply of alcohol and wild partying that lasted for days on end. Poor Irish missed the celebrations as he suffered from tertian fever, a reoccurrence of a bout of three day malaria that was rife in tropical climes. The hefty Irish man had no complaints when he came round to the sound of a Celtic melody being sung to him by one of the prettiest woman he had ever set eyes on. His faithful, old friend Tripod had been insistent that a virginal maiden be there when the boatswain awoke. Many a time Irish had given Tripod a sub when his pillcock ached for a whore's slackened cunnie and he never forgot a kindness. Shana was relieved when the young woman brought news of Irish's recovery and went immediately to him. Since he had fallen ill she had realised how much she loved the man who had always been there for her, no matter what. Despite his weakness, Irish was able to throw Patrick up in the air as the boy giggled with sheer glee. The baby loved the boatswain and his eyes would light up every time he saw him. For Shana it became quite painful to see her child with her favourite man as their bond grew stronger. She had always adored handsome Irish yet felt unusually apprehensive at the thought of any romance between them. Usually the vampish wench had the knack of attracting any man but Irish always seemed to act timidly whenever they were alone. Captain Culley had long accepted that she would never be able to enchant the man who she longed to be with. Rarely taking her loved ones for granted Shana was grateful for small mercies and happy that Irish loved her child. If she was not able to have him, then she would settle for him to be the man closest to being the father of her son. With a secret sigh, Shana lay down next to Irish and Patrick and felt extremely thankful that they were together.

A few of the African people who had been rescued chose to stay in Ireland with Grace but most were unable to cope with the bitterly cold winds and rain. Shana had befriended a Moorish pyrate who had been helped by Grace after falling ill with an infection that caused his whole arm to turn black. Her men had rescued the tall, emaciated man from the sea one stormy night. The whole story of how the stranger had managed to escape and make his way over to Ireland had been put together piece by piece, as the man had lost his memory since his apparent capture by the English. Contrary to popular belief that most pyrates had no heart at all, Grace had taken the survivor into her home. Severing the poisoned arm herself she had nursed him, day and night for two weeks until he regained consciousness. When he finally came round, he was confused and frightened but Grace patiently explained to him how and where he had been found. The men who had rescued him had given him the nickname 'Moses Mollusc'. Assuming him dead, they had spotted him lying face-down on a pebbled beach not very far from Grace's fortified home. The shackles on his legs had a broken chain attached and Grace and her clan guessed that he had been chained to a post. Pyracy was becoming more of a problem therefore crueller punishments had been devised and she had heard that the English were using more elaborate methods of execution.

Grace had even heard news that Queen Elizabeth was now offering pardons to prisoners under death sentence who agreed to take part in medical research. Surgeons keen to discover new ways of performing operations on internal organs would operate on the 'pardoned' subjects and then sew them back up so they could enjoy their freedom. Depending on the severity of their wounds, some might suffer months of agony from loss of an organ whilst others died of blood poisoning within days. Despite the enormous risk, many chose to suffer the barbaric trials in exchange for their liberty. Moses had no doubt thought better of it and opted to face the death penalty and die more quickly. Unfortunately for him, nothing could have been further from the truth.

There was no better way to entertain the crowds than to put on a good, drawn out execution. By the look of the Moses' scrawny body, his muscles had deteriorated over days without exercise or nourishment. Gaping sores on pallid skin and the loss of teeth in such a young, otherwise seemingly fit man, indicated that he had probably already been suffering from scurvy for a while. Many sailors whose poor diet lacked fresh fruit and vegetables suffered from this debilitating disease that caused progressive tiredness and a severe lack of energy. Unless their diet was improved, the poor buggers were certain to die a most unpleasant death. Grace's guess was that the unfortunate pyrate had been put ashore by his pyrate shipmates to allow him a fighting chance of survival. This had probably been prevented by his immediate capture.

The latest callous craze amongst the English executioners was apparently only being dealt out to condemned pyrates. Tied securely to a pole that had been erected on a beach at low tide, the prisoner was flogged. The mob was then invited to join in and pelted the battered victim with rocks and sponges soaked with vinegar. At the same time crabs would begin to feast on the bruised and softened flesh of the victim. Timed so the tide would come in following the first stage of punishment, the crowd would then withdraw to watch from a safe distance high on the rocky cliffs. Last rites would be given whilst the executioner prepared the villain for his 'final wash' as it had been named. Forcing the unfortunate soul to open his mouth wide, his tongue would be grabbed by a pair of pliers and pulled out as far as possible. To ensure that in the most unlikely event of survival the victim would be unable to speak again, the sensory organ was cut out and thrown into the lapping waves. Taking a thick, blunted needle, the executioner then proceeded to sew up the prisoner's lips and when he had bitten off the slack yarn, he would sew both upper eyelids onto the forehead to keep them open. This final touch ensured that the condemned was able to watch the approaching tide.

Moses Mollusc was a quiet man through no choice of his own and Shana enjoyed his company. Together they had devised a clever method of communication that involved signing with their hands. Ever since his discovery, Moses had been a hard working member of Grace's staff and loved to entertain the children with shadow puppetry. Whether he had been as gentle before his punishment no-one would ever know but since he had been in the company of Grace O'Malley and her clan, Moses had become a first class carer of her four children. Patrick also grew to love the gentle giant and was fascinated by the vertical row of pale scars that lined the dark man's lips. Lifting up his arms whenever he spotted Moses, the baby would make noises until he was picked up. Patiently Moses would allow the baby to finger the rough grooves that had once held cruel stitching that had sewn the kindly man's mouth shut. The silent man never once stopped the child from exploring his scarred face even though it felt very uncomfortable. It always touched Shana to see the big, villainous-looking pyrate holding her babe in his only arm as if he was gripping onto a pig's bladder football. She never felt any mistrust or apprehension where Moses was concerned and invited him to join her crew on their next venture. Overjoyed at the opportunity to serve alongside Captain Culley, the gentle giant was happy to accept his friend's offer and agreed to join her. He signed in the round with all of the pyrates placing his cross next to his new captain's signature. Feeling ready and eager to embark on another spate of emancipating missions, Shana ensured that the Banshee was in pristine shape and ready to set sail.

The great age of discovery had brought uncertain times to many in numerous different ways. Overseas travel had without doubt opened up the world, enabling opportunists the chance to live far more adventurous lives. On the other hand, slavery and exile had reared their hideous heads and created more problems. Many displaced people found themselves in an alien society not used to their culture and traditions. Shana had first hand experience of abduction as a youngster. One day she had been in a familiar place near to her home, the next she had found herself on a ship in the middle of an ocean. Luckily, the young woman was a natural born survivor and able to adapt to her new environment but many were not so adaptable.

Unique in her values and ideas Shana was soon able to influence others by her actions. She felt ready to act and was even more inspired by Grace O'Malley's unswerving loyalty to her country. Refusing to cede even one inch to English invaders, the wild warrior queen had refused to 'submit and re-grant' her lands as many of her fellow clan leaders had done. Piece by piece, Ireland was being taken over as Irish nobles relinquished their land without a fight. The English crown offered them an English title if they gave up their land but Grace and a few others revolted against these foreign dogs who dared to bully them into retreat. She loathed and detested their arrogance and swore to battle to keep Ireland independent until the day she died.

Determined to make a difference in a New World that she did not like, Captain Culley was ready to follow her admirable friend's example and do something to make her mark in history. Not caring whether her name would be remembered or be obliterated from all records by a disgruntled and jealous queen, Shana felt confident that her persistence would pay off in the end. Her followers and admirers were growing in number and she planned to begin to target ordinary, hard working citizens in her campaign to outlaw slavery. Foreseeing an eventual total ban on an already deteriorating slave trade, Shana felt sure that she could speed up the process by using her fame. Lately, she had heard that many peasants were becoming embittered by the shipping in of black slaves who were being given jobs that their white equivalents would never have been considered suitable for. Dressing black men, women and children in fancy costumes to stand around and provide interesting topics of conversation, the idle rich were all keen to own their token African slaves. Resentment was breeding within the poorer communities and Shana was determined to do something that would stir up the grievances of the people and encourage them to take action.

Having commissioned an artist to paint her likeness in miniature, Captain Culley began to circulate the images to declare her presence in England and fuel interest in her anti-slavery campaign. Once public opinion had been swayed in her favour against a greed-driven and extravagant queen, she planned to take advantage of her 'celebrity' status and stir the masses into revolt. Much of the pyrate queen's success had been due to help from ordinary folk willing to offer cover to the captain and her crew. She even had doppelgangers willing to give their lives in order to allow Captain Culley to continue in her rebellious cause. Their involvement was invaluable and Shana became renowned for rewarding her accomplices very well. Having many hide-outs, her well paid scouts often created a diversion allowing her to escape capture.

Back in Ireland, having returned Grace safely to her clan, the Banshee lay patiently in wait for a time when the queen of England and her fleets were busy on an important mission. Once Shana had discovered enough flaws and weaknesses in the royal defence, she planned to notify Grace so that she could choose the best time and place to attack. The Irish queen had been secretly expanding her fleet with vessels that she had commissioned overseas. Heavily armed and manned, they were anchored in France awaiting orders. Grace had gained full support from the French who were always keen to help towards the downfall of an empire that they had hated for many years. Ireland had no wish to conquer the English, so France was keen to take advantage of the situation. Sailing between England and Ireland became much easier for the Banshee as Shana's look-outs were always ahead of the queen's guards and warned the crew in plenty of time. Before deciding to spend some of the autumn with Grace and her clan in Ireland, Shana planned a raid that would fill Grace's chests with Spanish treasure. The Celtic queen would be able to use the loot to commission more ships overseas.

A heavy storm had hit the west coast of Ireland on the day the Banshee dropped anchor. Grace O'Malley had a strong hold on the west coast, having ownership of five castles and several islands in Clew Bay. O'Malley chieftains had held seats in Connaught for many years and had fortified homes at Belclare, Cathair-na-Mart, Carrowmore, Murrick and Clare Island.

As the Banshee approached O'Malley territory, Clew bay was surely a fair sight to behold, tucked neatly within a green and rocky landscape sprinkled with golden gorse bushes. Velvety green islands dotted the shallow turquoise waters. The crew were tired and all felt relieved to have reached their destination. Fresh horses were waiting ashore for Shana and her party and the isolated castle was a sight for sore eyes as they rode against the wind towards the small, arched wooden door. Patrick held tightly onto Irish as the black stallion cantered over the grassy moorland, skilfully avoiding jutting rocks and leaping over gorse bushes. The child felt safe and happy to be riding with the man who was like a father to him. Laughing as his mother passed them yelling a challenge to race her to Grace's fortified home, Patrick pressed his face close to Irish's back and squeezed his thighs together preparing for a sudden increase in speed. Without a word, Irish dug his heels into the strong horse's side, pulled the reins shorter and leant into his firm neck to gain more speed. Reaching the stream that ran alongside Rockfleet castle neck and neck, the three dismounted quickly and ran inside to change their sodden clothes and warm themselves by a welcome roaring fire.

Coughs and colds had affected Shana's newly formed crew and whilst some worked on the upkeep of the Banshee, others lay moping around the cold stone home of Grace O'Malley. Nights were full of laughter and merry-making and plenty of grog was eagerly consumed but daytime brought a remarkably different atmosphere as the depressive effects of the Irish weather took their toll.

Early one morning, a Kenyan man who had been amongst the last group of African people liberated by Shana's crew, sat tending a healthy fire. Still in awe of the environment in which he found himself living, Abedayo conversed with his friend Babatu in a deep, soothing yet confident voice. Patrick and Shana climbed down the rickety steps into the lower room and the boy joined the two picturesque, dark-skinned men by the fire. Giggling as he was thrown into the air by Babatu and caught safely by Abedayo, Patrick surprised and impressed them by shouting in their native tongue. Shana approached the playful trio and felt proud to explain to her new recruits how her son had an interest in foreign languages. She told them that ever since he was a baby he would listen intently to foreign people speaking and then mimic the sounds even though he had no understanding of their meaning. The men were impressed by the boy's respect for others' cultures which prompted them to discuss how they could help him to learn more of their language. A hot pot of coffee simmered over the fire making the cramped area feel cosy with its deliciously rich aroma. Shana took a roll of tree bark from a large wooden chest that she had brought as a gift for Grace. Pulling the bark apart carefully, she closed her eyes and savoured the delicious scent. Cinnamon was one of her favourite spices and she added a generous pinch to the strong brew. Replacing the precious spice roll, she then took out a large cone of sugar and broke off a generous piece from the tip. Taking the treat over to Patrick, she allowed him to dip the point of the sugar cone into the hot coffee. His beautiful blue eyes widened as the dark brown liquid crept higher and soaked into the sugar. Looking at his mother for permission to taste the delicacy, Patrick giggled as he bit into the bitter-sweet treat. Shana threw the rest of the sugar cone into the large pot and fetched some wooden tankards to hold the hot coffee. The smell in the main hall was good. A mixture of coffee, spices from the heavy chest and smoking turf on the large fire made a comforting mixture that everyone welcomed. A strong wind whistled through the cracks in the small door, draughts made the flames flicker and aromatic smoke curled upwards. High, cold, damp walls gave the impression of night time despite the thin beams of sunlight which shone through narrow slots in the upper rooms. Shadows danced across the grey stone appearing to be living, breathing imps performing before their guests. Taking in their surroundings the bonding group sat warming themselves by the fire and sipping hot coffee.

When the others joined Shana and the two men, they had prepared food to take with them on an afternoon outing that Grace O'Malley had planned for everyone's enjoyment.

Taking spare horses and plenty of supplies on the tour, Grace O'Malley was eager to show her guests more of her magical land. Travelling through the most lush green, wild and rocky territory, the party of pyrates appeared to be noblemen and women led by their royal Celtic host. Grace O'Malley's Irish name was Gráinne Uaile and her family was held in high respect by the citizens of the west. Her clan had been shipping merchants for as long as everyone could remember and her father had been a fearless mariner who knew his business well. Banned from trading in his local port of Galway, he had managed to gain a good reputation by trading regularly with Scotland, France, Portugal and Spain. Grace had maintained the trading relationships with these countries since she had inherited the leadership.

A stubborn realist, the Irish noblewoman had managed to keep hold of her part of Ireland and regularly ferried mercenaries from Scotland and Spain to help in the fight against England. Clare Island was tightly protected by a ring of O'Malley forces around Clew Bay and Grace owned a formidable fleet of galleys. Gaining an advantageous position as both pyrate queen and military commander, Grace had become feared and loathed by English noblemen who had moved into impressive homes on what she still deemed as Irish land. The noblewoman led her men and women on raids, cattle rustling and ravaging the countryside whilst an uneasy peace hung over much of Ireland. Gaelic lords who had accepted knighthoods to gain English titles quickly grew disgruntled by the demands of a notoriously penny-pinching English queen. Lords were reluctant to pay the heavy taxes to the tight-fisted queen who begrudged spending any of the crown's wealth on Ireland. Determined to resist Anglicisation of O'Malley territory, Grace continued in the lucrative and honourable pyracy trade and led a tightly-knit, brotherly clan. Refusing to lie back and watch as expanding English power took away Ireland's independence, Grace rifled, ransacked and pillaged towns that had given way to English rule.

Grace's party managed to cover a fair amount of ground in a few hours and it made a welcome change for Shana and her men to arrive at their destination without encountering any highwaymen. Organised gangs of thieves were commonplace in England and to make a trip without being attacked by highway robbers was a rarity. Always prepared for the worst, the travellers would have given anyone who dared attack their party a fight to the death. Patrick's eyes widened as the brightly coloured tent came into view and Irish winked at his mother as she watched her son's face brighten with excitement. Grace had heard of the travelling freak show long before she had left on her last voyage. Since she had been rescued by Shana she had planned to take Patrick to see the carnival of human oddities and weird exhibits.

Dismounting from, then tethering their horses, Grace and Shana waited for the others to join them. A smartly dressed elderly man came out of the tent and approached the two tall women, smiling happily and welcoming them with an overtly theatrical voice. 'I bid ye most welcome to the most fantastical show on this earth!' On seeing Patrick, the white haired, bearded man opened his arms wide. 'Young man, an it please ye, come hither! I am going to take ye into a world that is verily the most unbelievable, fantastical and perchance most horrific that thine eyes shall ever see!' Patrick stood close to Irish and looked up at him for reassurance and permission to go with the dramatic character. Shana and Grace were delighted by the boy's reaction to the surprise treat that they had planned for him.

There could have been no more fitting day to create such an eerie atmosphere. Breath turned into a milky vapour that crept away from their cold lips. A mist hung over the field but only waist high so their dramatic host appeared to be floating in front of them. Holding the heavy canvas flap of the large tent open for his honoured guests, Master Brandon Delyte, travelling director of the most incredible collection of human and animal oddities, bowed as the party entered. Patrick and Irish were the first to step into the musty-smelling darkness and they stood aside to allow the others inside. Seconds passed as Shana, Grace and Tripod joined the pair allowing their eyes to adjust to the inky blackness.

At first Patrick closed his eyes and absorbed the muffled sounds and unusual scents. The intelligent child always used his senses to the maximum and when unable to see a thing, he allowed his imagination to run wild. A quavering whimper came from the boy's left and a harsh rasping told him that something with substantial lungs was standing not too far in front of him. Whispers could be heard from the right, towards what Patrick guessed was the back of the tent. The mobile shelter was large and oblong in shape. The boy had never smelt such an odd mixture of sweaty smells even when amongst his sailor friends! Little nose twitching, the pyrate child sniffed in the wonderful amalgamation of odours from burning sandalwood, wood smoke and the bodily odours of unimaginable creatures.

Hearing a scuffle from outside, Shana exited the tent to find a comical caper in the misty field. Standing with a great beam on his face, the master of the freaks watched wide-eyed and bemused as Jock and John wrestled with the two new Kenyan recruits who thrashed around beneath them. Jock had a firm strangle hold on Babatu but John was struggling to hold Abedayo as his long, thin legs waved around in the fog. The scene was hilarious and Shana called Grace to come out to see. Laughing so hard that they could barely stand, the two women drew their pistols and each fired a single shot to distract the men. Red faced and embarrassed, Jock and John looked up at their captain with pleading expressions on determined faces. 'Yon yeller-bellied rrrascals dunny wantee view the frreaks!' yelled Jock in his Scottish drawl, rolling his r's in a particularly attractive manner. Giggling like two teenagers, Shana and Grace each took hold of a Kenyan man and yanked them up into a standing position. Babatu and Abedayo were clearly not faking their sheer terror and the pyrates struggled to keep hold of their slippery, wriggling bodies. Jock and John brushed themselves off as best they could, straightened their mud-covered clothes and grabbed hold of the tall men. Marching them straight into the tent, the pyrates laughed at the ridiculousness of the situation. Two hardened warriors, who had fought bravely against armed men before inevitable capture, had managed to survive a lengthy voyage in a cramped slave-ship and had helped fight their captors in order to gain freedom, were terrified to enter a dark tent!

Patrick stepped over to his mother and took Babatu's hand firmly in his. Then he reached over to Abedayo who took his other hand without hesitation. Shana's heart swelled with love and pride at her son's empathy and narrowed her eyes to see where he would lead them. She saw that Irish had gone ahead with Tripod who had undoubtedly spotted a woman of some shape or form amongst the freaks. As usual, her guess was spot on and the two were standing, gawping unashamedly at a dark-skinned tribeswoman with the largest arse that Shana had ever seen. The Hottentot woman was naked apart from two half coconuts that covered her breasts. Not entirely sure why the poor woman was hiding her modesty when her elongated labia swung freely for all to see, Grace and her friend looked at one another and burst out laughing. Patrick led his two Kenyan friends over to the Hottentot wonder who was dancing an erotic dance for her two spectators. Tripod's pillcock was standing to attention beneath the material of his trews encouraging the woman to flirt more with her audience. As Patrick approached the unusual erotic dancer with his two friends in tow, Shana was relieved to see the Kenyan men relax a little on seeing a familiar sight. Despite their different tribal origins, coming across a fellow African seemed to reassure the foreign men but Patrick wisely kept a firm grip of their hands. Tripod took it on himself to explain to the child all about the ins and outs of the female anatomy while the African woman gyrated before them. A crudely painted sign displayed the woman's stage name as 'The world's most exotic Hottentot dancer'. Grace and Shana left the men to their biology lesson and moved on to the next exhibit. The tent had been cleverly divided into sections with ropes and canvas drapes. Creating a maze-like tour of the most shocking display of human deformities imaginable, Master Brandon gave his paying visitors a sight of a collection of misfits that they would undoubtedly ever forget.

The experience was the most innovative form of entertainment even for the likes of Captains Culley and O'Malley. Their next encounter was called 'the incredible horse-woman' and they stood face to face with a human monstrosity. Horse-woman had an elongated face and small, slanted eyes that were wide apart on either side of an enormous nose. Hideously swollen lips moved silently too near the base of an impossibly elongated jaw and the creature's skin was covered with brown, velvety fur. Hoof-like hands lay motionless in her lap as she struggled to breathe, her heavy head dropped forward onto a shoulderless torso that was supported by thick, muscular legs. Grace sniggered at the sight before her but Shana felt immense pity for the equine wonder. Leaning forward, the compassionate woman gently touched the other woman's gnarled hand and the creature glanced sadly up at the first person who had ever actually touched her. Grace had moved onto the next exhibit but Shana stayed with the horse-woman until her son joined her and the disfigured showpiece. Patrick smiled and offered the grotesquely deformed woman his hand on his mother's introduction. Noticing the tears on the woman's furry cheeks Patrick asked her what was wrong, moving closer to her as he did so. Looking the horse-woman directly in the eyes, Shana's sensitive son showed a genuine empathy towards her. Taking hold of her face with both hands Patrick whispered softly, 'Dunna twy. Mama's found ye.' With bright blue elfin eyes the young boy looked up at his mother for confirmation of his statement but her eyes met his with a serious expression. Both of the women knew that someone so disfigured would never be able to live outside the freak show. It was unlikely that she would even make it past the local village without being stoned to death. Superstitious beliefs meant that anyone physically malformed was in danger of being accused of witchcraft or being called the spawn of the devil.

Shana left her young child with his new friend and walked around the canvas divider to the next exhibit where Grace was standing with Irish, Tripod and John Clark. A tiny man sat on a high wooden plinth clapping flipper-like hands together and honking like a seal. Dressed only in a black vest top the man perched before his awestruck audience was performing balancing tricks. Below his ribs there was nothing but two tiny malformed stumps. 'The human sea creature' as he had been appropriately named, manoeuvred his tiny stunted form around full circle whilst balancing a variety of objects on his long, narrow nose. Clapping loudly at the end of each trick, John Clark had grown rather excited about the whole concept of a freak show. Grace explained to Shana that the pyrate was very keen to begin collecting novelties for his own show. In his usual animated, over-exaggerated way of communicating Jolly John, as he had recently been nick-named, waved his hands about whilst explaining his plans. Suddenly noticing his captain's presence, the confident man shared his newfound dream of creating a 'freak ship' that he planned to captain and take around the New World. Jolly John asked Shana whether she would mind if he started collecting attractions for his exhibition as soon as possible. Laughing loudly at the sailing master's passion and eagerness to start his new venture, Shana agreed before she had time to think about the consequences. Such an ambitious project was bound to cause problems along the way but Shana felt that her skilled sailing master had earned the right to her help in beginning a venture that had great potential. Grace O'Malley roared with laughter at Jolly John's reaction when his captain agreed to his impulsive plan. Picking up the tiny seal-man, who yelped as he was thrown into the air, the sailing master caught him on his descent and planted a noisy wet kiss on the top of his forehead.

Two hours passed too quickly for Patrick as he met each human deformity within the confines of the portable shelter. It was clear to see that the boy felt concerned about the people who were exploited by their exposure to crowds from the outside world, a world that they could only glimpse as they were taken from one area to another. All but Tripod and the Hottentot woman had gathered outside in the fresh evening air. Shana pulled her mantel close around her body and gave Irish a knowing wink. Rolling smiling eyes skyward, the boatswain went back into the tent to find his insatiably horny friend. Five minutes later, a red-faced Tripod emerged followed by the large assed African woman who was grinning all over her face. Following an emotionally exhausting excursion Patrick struggled to keep his eyes open as he left the tent. Waving goodbye to everyone he had met at the show, the toddler rubbed his eyes and was lifted up onto Irish's horse to ride in front of the strong man back to the castle. A short but windy journey took everyone safely back to Grace's castle led by flaming torchlight. Even the two Kenyan men had finally enjoyed the strange experience and snores soon rose above the crackling sounds of a dying fire as they all fell asleep within the high, grey stone walls.

When the time came for Captain Culley to leave Clare Island, she felt unusually saddened. It had been years since she had spent a fair amount of time in one place and

Ireland had certainly become a land that she could call home. Freshly careened, the Banshee was free of any unwanted seaweed and marine life that might have slowed her down. Her crew bade a fond farewell to their Celtic friends and sailed away from the remote island. Within days of leaving Ireland Captain Culley ordered an attack on a slave ship bound for England. Jolly John was extremely happy to find that one of the emancipated African slaves was a tiny woman who had been thought to be a child and quickly introduced his first employee to her new quarters. Having wasted no time in preparing the small space below decks that Captain Culley had given him next to the chicken pens, the conscientious sailing master felt quite proud of the simple comforts that he had provided.

Setting sail for Spanish waters where Shana was always keen to lie in wait for returning vessels that may be laden with gold from far away shores, the crew prepared for more raids. Since many privateers preyed mostly on fleets docked in the Spanish Main of America, Captain Culley tried her luck at waiting for those that had escaped being plundered overseas. Gaining wealth beyond their greatest expectations in three consecutive raids, the crew made a joint decision to drop anchor in the busy port of Lisbon.

King Sebastian had ordered a new royal palace to be built within the original medieval St. George's castle which had suffered damage during an earthquake in 1531. The impressive royal residence that crowned the eastern hilltop overlooking the remarkable city created a spectacular view. Shana delighted in the medieval street patterns that formed the heart of the old quarter with its neat rows of red-roofed, whitewashed buildings. The artistic captain was keen to investigate the wonderful local architecture. She itched to take Patrick to explore the winding alleyways and hidden treasures that lay unseen within the heart of the intriguing city. Even from the decks of her anchored ship, the pyrate queen could sense excitement and adventure waiting on the lands that tumbled toward the Tagus River. A natural vantage point, the imposing castle and cathedral dominated the attractive city's skyline and offered a perfect place to begin exploring.

Having planned to stay for two weeks in the busy trading city, Shana and the men consumed gallons of the famous local wine. They made sure to buy enough barrels to keep them merry on their next voyage and to trade in another country. Tripod visited the local bawd house to 'tend to his pillicock' as he liked to say. Shana was concerned about her friend who had suddenly started to look old. Lately his face had appeared drawn and clearly showed the pain that he was in. One evening when the two old friends were enjoying drinking rhum by an open fire in a quiet corner of a small drinking den by the sea, Shana chose to confront Tripod. 'Tisna' like ye ter be drinkin' so mild! Pass me yer blackjack an' match yer cap'n's pace!' Laughing aloud, the concerned woman grabbed the leather drinking vessel that had been tarred on the inside to prevent leakage. Tripod smiled timidly and was uncommonly quiet for a while, totally out of character for the man who was usually the life and soul of a party… especially one when the drinks were on someone else! Wearing a melancholy expression on his wrinkled, wise-looking face Tripod began to explain his ailment.

Having always been fond of her randy shipmate Shana was shocked to learn that he was suffering from the pox.

She was even more amazed that he had managed to continue using his raw prick to screw tarts. The two close friends drank together until a beautiful sunrise lit up the morning skies. Insisting that Tripod visit an apothecary as soon as possible, the two drunken pyrates stumbled around the awakening city, pistols in hand, demanding to be taken to the local healer. Tripod was definitely worse for wear and weak from over-consumption of alcohol but the debilitating disease was also taking its toll on the parts of body that the colourful character had not yet had chance to trade. Suffering from obvious pain, the unfortunate man stumbled and puked his way along narrow cobbled streets with Shana's help.

Eventually, the intoxicated villains reached a small, wooden shack-like building on the outskirts of the medieval quarter where they had been told a healer lived. A small green door with paint peeling away from exposure to strong sunlight creaked open as the two friends stumbled in. Ducking under a low threshold, Shana heaved her semi-conscious companion into a small, dark room lit only by natural light from a window on the back wall. An exceptionally low ceiling forced the tall woman to duck her head uncomfortably whilst she waited for the healer. A fresh breeze disturbed some dirt that had blown into the tiny dwelling place and Shana took in the meagre resources in the sparsely furnished room. As a spice trader's daughter, she had expected to find at least one cabinet or chest that contained herbs and vessels to store salves or potions for a variety of common ailments. Idly watching the tiny whirlwind of dust particles that spiralled over the beaten earth floor, Shana pondered for a moment whether she should attempt treatment on her suffering companion herself. Suddenly noticing a crack appear in what she had originally accepted as a solid wall, the inebriated woman realised how vulnerable she had allowed herself to become. Asking the bent old hag in her native language for a drink of fresh water Shana lay Tripod on the warm earthen floor and waited.

Many Portuguese people had married their African slaves and this new acceptance of inter-racial bonding pleased Shana greatly. An entirely new race of people was emerging as the African presence was rapidly increasing whilst the white element was declining. Many white men had left and others were still leaving Portugal to become sailors, privateers or pyrates. The government encouraged their male citizens to marry native women and settle in the new colonies. Most African slaves brought to Portugal were adult males which further unbalanced the population. Portuguese women started to hire male black slaves and many began sexual relationships with them. In many cases these affairs eventually led to marriage. As Shana lost herself in thoughts of harmonious mixed-race families, she forgot that she had asked for water.

The tall, handsome black man standing before her smiled down at his guest as he held the pitcher in his rough, working hands. Taking the ladle from him, Shana dipped it into the crystal-clear liquid and sipped the cool, refreshing spring water. Fascinated by the man's pearly white teeth, Shana smiled gratefully back at him but was taken aback when the old woman pushed her way between them. Mumbling in pigeon English she explained that the Maasai warrior was her new husband and warned her stunningly beautiful guest to keep her hands off her man. Not wishing to offend the ancient-looking witch who she had been told could help her disease riddled friend, Shana managed to bite her tongue and not react.

As her eyes adjusted Shana noticed the African man was wearing a large necklace consisting of all of the potions and tools of a healer. Slowly realising that it was the African tribesman who was the healer and not the crone, Captain Culley drew her longest, most evil looking sword and held the point to the throat of the insolent woman. How dare she presume that Shana had her sights set on her husband! Screaming loudly, the hag left them alone to treat Tripod and Shana stripped the unconscious man so that he could be examined. A foul stench rose from the one legged man's crotch as his captain peeled pieces of sticky pus-covered cloth away from his large member. In his desperation the disease-riddled man had applied at least four pig's bladder sperm-catchers in hope that they would help to hold together the continuously rotting flesh of his yardstick. Unable to restrain her horror at the sight of the congealed bloody mass of rotten, stinking flesh that had once been perfect genitalia, Shana hurled a spray of vomit onto the compacted earthen floor. Thankfully Tripod was so intoxicated that he remained unconscious and undoubtedly numb from pain throughout the operation. Fortunately the skilled medicine man had a stronger stomach than Shana and continued to separate the reeking foreign matter from the meagre remainder of a human organ.

The two became better acquainted whilst nursing their patient and Shana learned some of the Maasai's healing ways. Koyati had been a warrior from East Africa and had lived a semi-nomadic life until he was kidnapped by another tribe. Since Maasai society stood against slavery they were avoided by slave traders so it was unusual to find a tribal member outside Maasai territory. Sadly Koyati had been captured together with his captors. Portugal had become Koyati's present home but he freely admitted that his nomadic nature meant that he would someday return to Africa. The man had quickly gained respect as a healer when he had treated a person with malaria on arrival in Portugal. By using traditional medicinal plants from his native Africa Koyati had been able to quell the Portuguese sailor's raging fever. Local traders had been unaware that the African plants that they had bought had powerful healing properties and Spanish apothecaries were eager to learn new treatments. Elzira was a Spanish settler and widow who took the handsome Maasai man on as a hand with the intention of learning his healing skills. Since both parties shared a passion for medicine and ways to cure illness they soon developed a close relationship. By offering the younger man a proposal of marriage, Elzira gave him a better opportunity to be accepted into the Portuguese community whilst she could look forward to security, companionship and a promising sex life from the union. Deciding that the arrangement would be suitable for both parties, the unlikely couple married, hence Koyati's presence in the tiny abode on the outskirts of a busy city.

Sweat poured from the two carers as they tried their best to cleanse and treat infected sores that had become hideous gaping wounds that had developed on Tripod's penis and testicles. As Shana applied salves and oils with soft lint cloths, Koyati fetched a coffin-like box with a hole at one end. The pair lifted Tripod, who was still under the effects of alcohol, into the large wooden box and closed the lid. A fire burned under the box to heat the mercury that Koyati had put inside so that the healing vapours would be absorbed by the ill man's body. Spanish apothecaries had been practicing this method of healing open wounds on pox sufferers for the past year and the Maasai healer had learned the technique well. Before Shana had helped the tall man lift the patient into the coffin-like box they had applied the liquid silver to the sores on his mouth and skin. Only the poor man's head jutted from a hole in the wooden box but Tripod was blissfully unaware of his predicament as he went through the gruelling treatment process. Kneeling cross-legged beside the contraption the two new friends chatted about Shana's life and how she had come to be a renowned pyrate queen. Had the honourable man not been married he was sure that he would have joined her crew. Time passed quickly by as the pair drank herbal teas and shared adventures until the time finally came to allow Tripod his freedom. On coming round he seemed to look much better and Shana felt both relieved and happy to be able to share a joke with her close friend. Tripod had been like a brother to her despite his sexual attraction to his sensual captain. 'Welcome back to the world my friend!' she whispered, then louder, 'From this day ye shall be able ter tell all that 'a night in the arms of Venus led to a lifetime on Mercury!' The sounds of laughter erupted from the small home and Tripod was released but Shana vowed that she would nurse her horny shipmate by applying the miracle mercury to his wounds for the rest of his days. Before they left the company of their new friend, he called his elderly wife to join them in a toast to another successful healing and she reluctantly brought in some delicious port wine. Elzira looked at Shana's glowing face and her own thin lips tightened as if she was sucking a lemon.

Back aboard the Banshee, Patrick had been in the care of Jolly John and the pair had been plotting their new venture together. They had made a plaque to display before the tiny woman and had aptly named her 'Taddie, the tiny tribeswoman' and had become better acquainted with their first acquisition. Before leaving the port Shana and her men stocked up with supplies and extra equipment. Tripod and Irish made sure that there were plenty of barrels of fine port aboard too. A calm sea welcomed the sturdy ship and fresh winds carried her speedily around to the coast of Spain where the pyrates boarded and looted several wealthy trade vessels.

Continuing on the next leg of their voyage the crew of the Banshee docked in Algiers. There Shana met an old friend Gerardo Remendo who she had known and trusted back in her childhood many years before. Remendo means 'patch' in Portuguese and the well known pyrate wore a black eye-patch over the empty socket where his left eye used to be. As a child the pyrate queen recalled speaking pigeon Portuguese with the dark skinned, shaven-headed man who had always made time for her between his regular black-market deliveries. He would use the well-known and safest entrance via Mary Maggy's to carry his tax-free merchandise into Teignmouth. As a small child, Shana had been fascinated by the man who she thought to be a smuggler like the other men who carried illicit wares through Culley clan land. Fluent in Spanish and Portuguese, Remendo became very fond of the little girl who was always keen to learn more of his languages. Born in Portugal, the healthy only child of a beautiful dancer and her Spanish pyrate lover, Gerardo Franco Gonçalves Furtado was adored by both parents. When his mother died soon after

Gerardo's second birthday, his heart-broken father returned to Portugal to attend his wife's burial and claim his firstborn child. Following a particularly nasty argument, Remando's father had shot his father-in-law dead when he had tried to prevent him from taking his grandson. During the struggle the poor boy had been stabbed in the eye which later became infected and had to be removed. Fleeing immediately, father and son escaped and rejoined the pyrate crew on the 'Vingança do Diablo', the pyrate vessel where the one-eyed boy spent the rest of his childhood days. Remendo had been aboard that very same ship when Shana first set eyes on him as a young girl back in her home town of Teignmouth.

Shana was not at all surprised to come across the stocky, muscular man drinking in a tavern in the well protected city along the Barbary Coast. Situated on the shores of a deep bay along the northern coast of Africa, Algiers had become a popular pyrate den. Warning her crew that the company her old friend kept was particularly unsavoury, Captain Culley approached him with caution, pistols cocked ready to fire. Remendo was drinking with Filthy Jack Meek, a notoriously cruel pyrate captain and bastard son of a Cathayan concubine and Portuguese prince. Against all odds, their illegitimate child had survived after being cast into the sea by his desperate mother. He was spotted by a female Cathayan pyrate captain who named him Jack Yin. The childless woman had ordered her men to hook the baby in and she took him on as her own son. Having been raised by a fearsome pyrate leader, Jack became hard and cruel and his evil temperament was well-known from a very early age. Unbelievably the toddler Jack Yin enjoyed disembowelling men who had survived attacks by his adoptive mother's merciless gang. Captain Death-Lily Yin, as she was known in the pyrate world, took pride in the inherently barbaric actions of her cold-hearted son and had her smith make him his own disembowelling weapon before he had reached the tender age of four. Filthy Jack was not a man to trust and Shana was determined to persuade Remendo to part from his company and join her clan. She was more than willing to offer the tough felon the coveted position of quartermaster aboard her ship.

Since being elected as captain Shana had never officially recruited anyone for the rank of quartermaster. Her boatswain and trusted friend Irish had always carried out the extra duties unofficially. As Captain Culley had always run a tight and orderly ship the crew had so far trusted her choice of second in command. Irish had unquestionable authority over crew management and no-one ever complained or argued against his decisions. As his captain's equal, Irish had always had the power to punish anyone who committed a minor offence, although serious crimes were different. In these circumstances the offender would always be given a fair trial by jury that consisted of unbiased members chosen from the crew. Having made an impulsive decision that she would offer her old friend Remendo the position of quartermaster, Captain Culley approached the group of villainous looking rebels.

Unlike Shana, Captain 'Filthy Jack' Meek commanded his men by striking fear into their hearts. The incompetent bully was well-known for his evil temper and he was quick to punish members of his crew for the slightest misdeed. Marooning was his favourite punishment and he would not even provide the culprit with a pistol and single shot... which was an unspoken rule for anyone who suffered this fate. Disillusioned by their leader's unfathomable greed and lust for blood whether spilled from his enemies or his own men, Meek's crew was never a loyal bunch. Shana was determined to take advantage of this weak spot and approach Remando directly inviting him to join her straight away.

Irish, Tripod and Jolly John Clark were with their captain when she approached one of the most dishonourable pyrate captains that ever sailed the seas. Dressed like a Portuguese nobleman, the bloodthirsty brute treated his new audience to a taste of his brutality before they even had chance to take a seat. Filthy Jack Meek had spotted the infamous Captain Culley as soon as she had entered the dark room. He had gained his atrocious reputation as the most brutal pyrate captain by preying on women and children. Treating these defenceless souls abhorrently before selling them into prostitution, the cunning sea dog knew about Captain Shana Culley's strict moral codes. Seated next to Filthy Jack was a beautiful woman wearing a cord that held a thick piece of cork tied around her neck. She deliberately made eye contact with Irish. When her master noticed the tall, handsome man looking her way he lifted his elbow and brought it swiftly back against her mouth, causing fresh, red blood to spurt from her full, sensuous lips. Irish's eyes narrowed and he grimaced as the small woman yelped like a young animal terrified of its keeper. Her delicate features made the captive slave look young but she was probably in her early twenties. Small breasts with erect nipples pressed against the finest silk fabric of her revealing dress. Slit to the tops of her muscular but slender thighs her skirt showed the golden skin of her inner thigh as she leant forward to bow her head in shame.

Filled with rage, Irish squeezed the handle of his sheathed cutlass wishing that his captain would hurry up with whatever plan she had in mind. Sliding quickly into the wooden seat next to Filthy Jack, Shana shouted for the proprietor to fetch more rhum. In response to her hospitality Jack parted thin, dark brown lips to reveal dirty, shark-like teeth. The notorious pyrate leader had filed each tooth to a cruel point so that a bite from Filthy Jack Meek caused as much injury and infection as possible. Shana could hear the clink of his gold jewellery rattle as his bulky body shook with mocking laughter. A sudden flick of his thick wrist alarmed Shana's men as Filthy Jack produced what looked like a fish-gutting knife. In a flash he had driven the thin, lethally sharp blade into the back of his slave-girl's hand that she had raised to wipe the blood from her lips. With an expertly fluid movement the knife that had pierced her hand was driven down deep into the table. The poor girl's eyes stared in disbelief and pain as she looked at her hand pinned to the table in front of her. Flinching as her master grabbed the large piece of cork on her makeshift necklace the slave opened her swollen mouth almost automatically so that he could ram it inside. 'Cork zem up!' shouted the abusive man and his mucus- filled chest rattled as he wheezed out another drunken chuckle, 'Zen zey keep fresh longer!'

Shana was quite shocked to see movement under the table and noticed two sets of deep-set, wide eyes staring up at her pathetically. When Filthy Jack was sure that the pair had been seen by his new guest he took hold of the youngest one's hair, untied the laces of his red leggings and pushed the child's head into his crotch. Soon the child's head moved back and forth in regular rhythm as he performed his unpleasant duty. Shana was disgusted but held her temper. As Jack sat back enjoying fellatio his wide, rough hands fondled and squeezed his small Asian slave-girl's breasts as she sat with her gag firmly in place. Until now, Shana had never witnessed such blatant sadism... in a public place at least! Surprised to see that Remendo did not react at all to his captain's abusive behaviour, Shana assumed that he had been influenced by the huge man's bullying ways for longer than she had originally suspected. Lifting her empty tankard to signal Jolly John to pour out the rhum that had been delivered to the table Shana addressed Remendo, totally ignoring the foul man by her side. This angered Filthy Jack who became more aggressive with his pitiful slaves. Having obtained no reaction to the gruesome show of sadistic power that he held over his three servants, he became even more determined to shock. Pushing the table away from him to reveal the two children, Jack stopped the one who had continued his sexual duty that kept his master's thick pillcock stiff. He twisted around grabbing his corked slave-girl around the waist with both hands and whilst staying seated, hauled her slight form over onto his ample lap. Straddling the big man the unfortunate woman breathed in sharply as he pushed her hips down onto his hard shaft. Knowing that Filthy Jack's crew had become aroused by their captain's show, Shana felt uneasy about the whole situation. His men were double hers in number and as seasoned pyrates they were armed to the hilt with several weapons that she was sure would be loaded. As the tiny woman rode her master Captain Culley said what she wanted to say to Remendo who sat staring at her in shock, amazed that she was behaving so brazenly in the presence of his notorious tyrant leader.

It was as though a light had suddenly been switched on in her old friend's mind as his hands reached slowly for his pistols. Cocking his weapons Remendo pointed one at his captain and the other at the man sitting beside him whom he knew to be the best fighter amongst the gang. As if the whole thing had been planned, Irish and the lads responded immediately as Shana drew her cutlass and sliced a back-handed thrust into Filthy Jack's tough side. All hell broke loose as an ugly fight broke out. Jack had sliced the slave-boy's head clean off and his tiny body still moved mechanically back and forth for a few seconds before falling over. Before they even realised that Shana had killed Filthy Jack the evil captain's men had suffered losses. Three of the dead tyrant's men were still standing and none of Culley's men had fallen. Numbers had at least evened out and Jack's pyrates were worse for wear following a heavy drinking session. Stray shots had already killed two men who had not been involved in the skirmish. Sparks flew as metal clashed with metal and pistols were fired. The smoke-filled room had become an instant battleground, the ground was sodden with alcohol that poured freely from shot barrels. Having used his last shot Tripod unsheathed his sabre and slashed an enemy throat. Finally the chaos came to a halt and left Shana and her men triumphant. Sadly the two children who had been under the table lay where they had fallen, their little bodies stamped into the ground.

Irish scanned the smoky room looking for the young woman who had been treated so cruelly only minutes before. Cowering in the corner with the cork still in her bloody mouth was the slave-girl. Signalling at once to

Shana for help with the injured and distressed girl, Irish felt relieved that she had lived. Tearing a large piece of material from her brightly coloured skirts Shana approached the frightened woman and wrapped the makeshift blanket around her delicate frame. Releasing her sore hands from the rope that looked as if it had bound her wrists for a while, the kindly pyrate queen pulled the victim's head to her chest. Rocking the shocked woman as if she were a child, Shana reached down to remove the cork. A sudden bang made the girl jump and she clawed at Captain Culley's clothes, trying desperately to get closer to her protector, like a hunted animal.

Pushing the tavern door open with his foot, the messenger boy peered gingerly into the smoky darkness of the dimly lit room. He was surprised to see the legendary Captain Filthy Jack Meek lying dead on the ground whilst Captain Culley and her men lay scattered around draining dregs of booze from upturned bottles. A large barrel of rhum shot full of holes leaked dark fluid from its innards as Tripod lay beneath with his mouth open wide. A woman's deep voice commanded the boy to introduce himself asking what he needed from there. Slowly and carefully he pulled his shoulder-bag over his head and placed it on the floor in front of him. Hands above his head the nervous boy backed away and explained that he had brought a letter for Captain Sushana Culley. Tripod hauled himself up clumsily and limped unsteadily over to the sack, put his wooden leg into the loop of strap and flicked it over to his captain. Taking the small satchel Shana untied the top and pulled out a thick parchment scroll bearing Grace O'Malley's trademark green wax seal and tied with a bright green ribbon. Shana smiled to herself at her friend's patriotic pride and guile... the green seal and ribbon stood for the Irish cause. Bald Grace had sent Queen Elizabeth several similarly marked and bound manuscripts declaring her intentions to fight to keep Ireland under Irish rule forever. The two pyrate queens kept in touch via letter taken by trade ships with trustworthy captains and then by courier over land. Forced to use cunning and care when communicating, the suspicious women were always careful to destroy each parchment once they had read their ally's news. They took great care to never use the same courier twice.

Wiping blood-stained hands on her skirts Shana unrolled the manuscript making sure to put the ribbon and seal in one of her pouches for safe keeping. Sentimentality was in Shana's make-up and she was careful not to lose anything that she deemed precious. Letters from loved ones were stored in a special chest with a few other treasures, the most precious of these being a lock of Patrick's baby hair. As she read Grace's neatly penned message Shana felt a sense of triumph and renewed determination to fight for Ireland's freedom and preserve O'Malley territory. Grace O'Malley's fleet had made numerous successful attacks on Elizabeth's ships. Hearing from her soul sister always made Shana happy.

Careful to keep the news of triumph against the English queen to herself, she read aloud a funny story about a recent visit that Bald Grace had paid to one of her new neighbours. Shana's gritty soul sister wrote in such an amusing way that her recounted tale soon had everyone in stitches laughing with joy at her Irish kindred spirit's nerve. Her newest neighbour turned out to be a pretentious nobleman who was totally ignorant of Gaelic hospitality rules. When Grace O'Malley called on the lord of the manor that had once belonged to her old Celtic friend Paddy Sheehan, the English manservant explained snottily that the gentleman was already at table. Flatly refusing to invite the Irish noblewoman to join his master the butler took his orders too far. Grace was furious, absolutely livid and felt more insulted than she had ever been in her colourful life! Drawing her pistols she fired two shots into the bell that hung by the front door. Grace yelled a menacing threat to the overdressed party sitting ridiculously stiff and upright in what used to be her old friend's dining room. The lady of the manor was aghast and began to cry hysterically screaming at her husband that her mother had warned her not to enter such savage territory. That did it! Grace knocked the uppity butler unconscious and pushed past his crumpled body to enter the refurbished home. In faux awe the Irish queen mocked the English nobles describing their elaborate décor as she smashed it to pieces. On entering the grand dining room, Grace picked up a leg of roast chicken and bit into it greedily, throwing the rest onto the floor. In a deep, menacing voice using her beautiful Gaelic language she turned to her reluctant host and laid a curse upon his family. Terrified and disgusted by the woman's behaviour the English nobleman retorted yet already knew that he had gone too far. Storming out of the property Grace went through the grounds back to her boat that was moored on the river. As she ranted and raved she noticed a small boy eating grapes in the shade of a weeping willow. Grabbing the child, kicking and screaming as he struggled for freedom, the angry woman hurled his tiny body into her boat and rowed off.

Lord and Lady Carter of Sussex apologised profusely to the Irish noblewoman later that day pleading dire ignorance of Gaelic rules of hospitality. They visited her castle in person bringing extravagant gifts and begged her to have mercy on their only child. The boy had been gagged and left bawling his piggy little eyes out in a convenient nook within the high walls of Grace's castle. Having ordered two of her most vengeful men, who had both lost their entire families by the English sword, to brick the boy up Grace wallowed in the parents' despair. The tables had turned and Captain Grace O'Malley enjoyed the piteous begging and pleading for a good hour before releasing the miserable boy... on condition that the Carter family and any of their offspring remain in Ireland for the rest of their days. Forcing the Carters to take an oath to become the first Englishfolk to take Irish citizenship and swear allegiance to Gráinne Uaile's cause, she demanded that a place always be laid at their table in case of a visit from one of her clan. Shana had no difficulty in conjuring up a wonderful image of her proud Irish soul sister standing tall and triumphant over a snivelling, utterly deflated English 'nobleman' stooped and grovelling in total submission before her. A renewed thirst for rhum overcame Shana as she reached a natural break in her friend's news.

Dismissing the courier after paying him generously and warning him that he would be dancing the gibbet gig if he ever told a soul of the two pyrate queens' correspondence, Shana and her men helped themselves to grog and lit a fire to warm the room. It was beginning to feel cold as night closed in. Tripod made it easier to strip the dead men of their valuables by lighting oil lamps around what was once a quite comfortable establishment... at least until Captain Culley had walked inside! After corpses had been stripped of everything of use or value, everyone gathered around the fire to listen to the remainder of the letter from Ireland. Pulling up a seat next to Irish, who had taken over care of the shell-shocked slave-girl, Shana took up where she had left off. Grace wrote of desperate times over much of Ireland yet the determined warrior woman still managed to keep control over western lands and sea. Reading between the lines Shana could sense her friend's desperation and mentally urged her not to lose heart. She knew only too well how difficult it became when surrounded by extreme danger. Like Shana, Grace was clever to hide her fears from others in the personal battle not to lose hope.

Grace had wanted to give the English a taste of their own bitter medicine and her run-in with the pompous nobleman had given her a good opportunity. In Ireland heretics were being dragged from their homes and publicly tortured by English invaders trying to force them to convert to Anglican Protestantism. Many of Grace's friends and clan had been murdered by the English who continuously ravaged her homeland and terrorised the Celtic people. Many had refused to convert from their Roman Catholic faith and suffered death for their steadfast beliefs.

Colonisation of Irish lands continued and still sparked off rebellions but no Irish leader had yet been able to prevent the torture and murder of their rebellious civilians. There were horrific accounts of proud old women who refused to leave their homes where they and generations before them had been born. Many were evicted by gangs of men acting by order of Queen Elizabeth, anyone resisting her authority was forcibly removed and executed. Countless brave rebels had already died and more were choosing to die for Grace O'Malley's patriotic cause.

According to Grace O'Malley's letter the most favoured method of torture, by English executioners in Ireland, was to break victims on the wheel. Callous brutality was believed to act as a deterrent but the growing number of victims suggested quite the opposite. Torturers and even audiences preferred their victims to be Irish women! A row of female victims pleased the English settlers more as they made a grotesquely sadistic display. First the victim was tied spread-eagled to a cartwheel then their arms and legs smashed with mallets and hammers. Where fully functioning limbs had once been, four tentacle-like strips of blubbery flesh encased agonisingly broken and smashed bones. Limp, shattered limbs were then woven in and out of large wheel spokes. This despicable process was called 'braiding'. When the victim had been suitably secured to the cartwheel, the executioner's handy-work would be propped on the ground for viewing. Before the wheel was hoisted up by pulleys and ropes to the top of a pole, the unfortunate victims were at the mercy of anyone in the crowd. For a small fee, anyone was able to buy time with them and do anything that they pleased. Many men paid to fuck helpless women whose torsos were still in perfect condition. It was so easy and comfortable for the men to penetrate the gaping cunnies or mouths of the 'wheel-whores' as one particularly evil executioner, Olaf Hickford preferred to call his victims. The final scene had been described by one witness as being akin to a macabre human puppet show with its puppet-like performers writhing in agony, streams of blood dripping from them onto the spectators below.

Sometimes days and even weeks passed by until the unfortunate souls eventually starved to death. Meanwhile, as if the wretched victims had not endured enough agony, hungry crows pecked at their wounds, ripping away pieces of flesh and often gouging out unprotected eyes to take back to their young. Death would finally be welcomed after what was probably the longest and most atrocious agony that their torturers could possibly inflict. If an Irish person dared to complain about the barbaric treatment of the prisoners they were flogged and dragged onto a wheel to suffer the same punishment. Passers by would gain pleasure from giving the pole a spin and watch the helpless blubber-like monstrosity above them suffer even more in a gruesome aerial ride. Wagers were often made to see if their spin was good enough to make the victim vomit!

When Captain Culley had finished reading Grace's letter she re-rolled the scroll of parchment and threw it into the dying fire. Stoking charred wood vigorously with an iron poker, Shana watched the calfskin glow a wonderful bright orange as hungry flames devoured the dry kindling. Pouring more spirits the crew settled in for a night amongst their dead enemies and decided to discuss suitable methods of torture for others who dared to attack their ferocious crew. Jolly John piped up with a fantastic idea of torturing foes so they became hideously deformed then saving them for the sole purpose of living out their days in his freak show. Everyone roared with laughter at his prospective venture and Shana and Tripod were keen to help their friend by carrying out the torture! Tripod managed to sicken Shana when he told of his favourite method of torture which involved a tool with four claws that was heated over a fire until it became red hot. It would then be clamped around a woman's breast and pulled slowly away ripping deeply into soft mammary tissue. The process would be repeated on the woman's other breast leaving her with a formless bloodied mass where two attractive organs had once been. Not satisfied by disgusting his listeners with details of the effect this particular method of female torture had on an ordinary woman, the intoxicated sailor continued to revolt his audience even more. According to the connoisseur of everything female, Tripod relayed the fact that lactating women's breasts made an incredible mess when torn apart by the scalding claws. Milk had been known to spurt up to a distance of five yards if the torturer was skilled enough to pierce the breast in the right place. Countless women had been subjected to this gruesome punishment after being accused of heresy, blasphemy or other lascivious acts. An outbreak of mass hysteria had erupted in Tripod's hometown when he was a child. A young, pregnant and unmarried woman had been dragged from her bed and accused of witchcraft by her lover's jealous wife. An investigating tribunal was held following ten hours of torture during which the poor girl confessed to being a worshipper of Satan. Adultery was a serious crime punishable by 'a hot bite from the iron claw on each of the sinner's breasts thus ensuring that the devil would be unable to suckle from the witch's teat.' This form of torture was becoming even more commonplace in communities all over Europe including England, France and Germany. The condemned adulteress was tied spread-eagled to vertical posts and if she was pregnant the child would be removed from her womb. Often, abortion tools were crude iron pokers or metal hooks, anything that would do the job of tearing the unborn foetus from

its mother. Often still alive when removed, the tiny form would writhe on the ground before its devastated mother, covered in her blood. A baptism would then take place before the tiny baby was stamped into the ground by a priest. Once he was satisfied that the devil's spawn was no more, the woman would receive her bites and then a fire would be lit beneath her. The 'witch' would choke to death if she was lucky but in many cases the fire was managed so that the victim slowly burned to death. Her soul had been saved by the righteous townsfolk. Tripod ended his account of this foul method of torture on a lighter note. He believed that punishments were designed according to the extent of public outrage and there were none more feared or loathed than suspected witches...
'...or pyrates!' added Captain Culley and the subject was quickly changed to everyone's relief. After a brief silent spell the group fell about with laughter and found a place to sleep off the alcohol.

Many months passed by as Shana took the Banshee all over the known world leading her men on many a successful raid. Whilst his captain freed slaves Jolly John Clark began to collect a variety of curiosities for his future 'Show Ship of Freaks' as he had chosen to call the floating amusement vessel. Every time that anyone encountered an oddity they sent for the sailing master to assess the possibility that he, she or it might become a popular attraction. Shana allocated an area in the Banshee that became known as 'Jolly John's den' where he and his valuable assets slept and practised various performances and introductions.

Patrick loved the company of the disfigured people and animals. The pyrate boy interacted happily with all of them and spent much of his time with his new friends.

Sadly most people did not have such an empathic attitude toward those who had been rejected by most of the world. Amongst Jolly John's attractions lived a boy from Peru who was covered from head to toe with hair. The Turkish trader who had sold him to John had already named him 'Wolf boy' so he kept that name. A 'lion man' from India who had an incredibly large head and facial disfigurements joined the troupe in Ceylon. His unfortunate appearance had been the reason why the villagers had beaten him with long sticks every day of his miserable life. Even his parents had loathed their child as they thought that they had been cursed. Having what was deemed as perfectly normal brothers and sisters, poor Leo as Jolly John called him, had become so timid and scared of rejection that he barely made a sound. A pair of the most gorgeous Cathayan female twins, Yin and Min who were joined at the hip, managed to perform wonderful acrobatics. A tribeswoman with an elongated neck that was supported by no less than twenty two rings provided a visual delight for those who harboured a morbid curiosity for body-modification. Shana was reminded of one of her murder victims when an unfortunate person with a penis, cunnie and what everyone agreed were the most perfect pair of breasts that they had ever seen joined the growing freak-ship show. She had hailed from bonnie Scotland and John was enamoured by her delightful sing-song accent. Jolly John had also managed to acquire Maureen, a woman with four legs, her extra pair being tiny and malformed. Dressed in miniature stockings and slippers to match her normal-sized legs, the extra-small limbs jutted awkwardly out from below her skirts at odd angles. Maureen had a little movement in the knee joints of the smaller legs but was able to perform an excellent seated rendition of a polka. Jolly John was thrilled by her efforts and managed to talk 'Herhim' into joining Maureen halfway through to dance around wearing no underwear. Each of Herhim's high-kicks treated spectators to a peek at a double helping of genitalia that they had not expected, considering the feminine way the supple dancer was dressed. Squeezed into a tight bodice to accentuate ample cleavage, Herhim looked every bit the woman until she displayed her extra hidden talents! Tripod in particular became extremely fascinated by this particular person... to no-one's surprise.

Jolly John's 'Animal Collection' so far consisted of a dwarf pig with two heads, a huge three-legged chicken and the cutest albino chimp called Boo-Boo. Two Indian pyrates were kind enough to part with the latter exhibit when they joined Shana's crew. The twin brothers from India, Sala and Sulabh believed that it was fate that they had found employment with the infamous pyrate captain and were only too happy to help out one of her loyal crew.

It was a sad day when Jolly John decided that he had collected enough exhibits to make a decent freak show. Dropping anchor at the beautiful island of Malta, the crew of the Banshee were sad to leave another valued sailor on foreign shores. During his time serving with Shana the jovial, comical and independent man had earned enough money to buy a good-sized ship and be able to pay a crew to man her whilst he ran his innovative and amazing new business. Captain Cully breathed in deeply and whispered a pagan blessing into the wind for her jovial friend. She was going to miss Jolly John Clark.

Chapter 16

A Warrant and the Plague

Long months at sea blended into years as Captain Culley inspired many a menacing tale to embellish her already infamous reputation as a pyrate leader and freedom fighter. Leading her band of men in her mission to ransack many heavily burdened slave ships, she managed to inflict more than a few fair sized wounds into the once thriving slave trade. The year 1562 soon arrived and the queen of England was diagnosed with smallpox by a German doctor. Word was that the great Queen Elizabeth had become gravely ill with the pox and red spots had begun to appear upon her soft, delicate white hands. On hearing the serious news, Captain Culley had taken to her cups and remembered when the Turnbull twins had suffered a similar ailment during an unnerving period back in England. In a drunken toast to the lady-in-waiting who had volunteered to nurse her queen, Captain Culley and her crew commended the bravery of the loyal woman willing to suffer or indeed die for her queen.

From her sickbed, the queen of England ordered ships to be sent out to the countries of the Baltic where she knew there was an abundant source of materials that could be used to build more ships. Queen Elizabeth was determined that her country did not miss the opportunity to send more vessels for exploration and map out new trade routes. The seas became busier than ever and competition between countries grew ever fiercer. Privateers were able to earn a good percentage from their spoils and rulers grew richer with every vessel that they 'sponsored'. The Banshee covered many miles and her Captain took advantage of every money-making opportunity possible. Shana became a brilliant business woman and was able to pay her crew well, keep them happy and take care of all other needs.

As western nations battled to dominate the oceans, each desperate to become the most successful and dominant trader, hemp became an essential resource. Sails and rigging needed to be as strong as possible in order to withstand long and arduous journeys to the Orient. Shana was wise and only too aware of the dangers of shipwreck. She made sure to carry hempseed on every journey in case they were stranded on a remote island. If ever such a disaster occurred, Captain Culley and her crew would be able to grow crops of hemp. When harvested the hemp could be used both for nutrition and to provide the material to weave into strong sails. In fact, the crop became so invaluable that Queen Elizabeth ordered landowners to set aside at least sixty acres of their land solely for hemp cultivation.

Shana's native isle was under constant threat of invasion and a strong naval presence was absolutely essential. Queen Elizabeth insisted that all English farmers produce a percentage of hemp for the British Navy's needs. Demand became so great that she had no choice but to hit landowners with a hefty fine if they refused to grow the all-important crop. Once harvested, the precious hemp was usually taken to correction houses where the prisoners pounded the stalks with heavy wooden mallets to separate its fibres. The strongest of the long fibres were set aside for making ropes and sail canvas and many an outlaw could have had a hand in the process of making the hangman's rope that they could possibly dangle from one day in front of a jeering, frenzied crowd.

Patrick Culley turned two in November aboard the hardy, sturdy Banshee and he and Shana enjoyed a relationship like no other. The small boy adored his mother and was rarely away from her side. The pyrate ship that his mother captained in a fierce but fair manner had become the young lad's home. The boy was a natural born traveller and Shana firmly believed that the nomadic lifestyle was in the Culley clan's blood. In utter awe of his mother, her only child made her the happiest she had ever been and the two were inseparable. Micken had become smitten by the charms of his mistress's child and the comical duo had more energy than anyone could have deemed possible. Growing as mischievous and quick to learn as his pet parrot, Patrick could soon mimic all that he heard. His knowledge of language gradually expanded both in his own tongue and the tongues of foreign lands.

1562 was also the year when several wealthy English gentlemen contributed large sums of money to fund an enterprise to be led by John Hawkins, an English navigator. Taking three purpose-built ships and a hundred men, Hawkins sailed to the Coast of Guinea and captured no fewer than three hundred of the diminishing so-called 'negro' population of Africa. Then in Sierra Leone he captured a vessel laden with ivory, wax and five hundred African people. Sailing with his bounty, he made for the port of Monte Christi where he sold a hundred and twenty five of them as plantation slaves at one hundred ducats each. The remainder of the cargo were sold on to Spanish slave traders in Hispaniola. The Spaniards were known to treat their slaves abominably. Hawkins returned to England with his spoils which included caskets of pearls, expensive sugar and ginger amongst the booty.

Disgusted by the abhorrent and barbarous trafficking that had apparently been carried out in the knowledge of the queen of England, the nation became restless. To avoid rebellion, Queen Elizabeth was said to have called Hawkins to her court where she had demanded an explanation. She told him that if any of the Africans had been carried away without consent 'that it would be detestable and call down the vengeance of Heaven upon the undertakers.' A reply from a deceitful John Hawkins settled the queen's conscience. He reassured her that the Africans' souls were sure to be saved on account of their introduction to Christianity and civilisation. Satisfied with his answer, Queen Elizabeth gave her consent to future ventures, allowing him to continue trafficking whilst making sure that she received a substantial share of his profits.

Maddened by the queen's decision to allow such a diabolical breach of human rights to continue, Shana decided that she would take her fight for the freedom of the African people a step further. Making her intentions quite clear, Captain Culley penned a letter to Her Royal Majesty, Queen Elizabeth stating that she would fight against queen and country in a battle for what she believed to be a just cause. On receipt of her letter, Queen Elizabeth drew up a warrant for Miss Sushana Culley's immediate arrest and Shana's name became well-known as 'England's most wanted criminal, the dangerous and merciless pyrate queen'. The bounty for her arrest, which would lead her to the gallows, was higher than any set before and began Shana's vengeful reign of the seas... the seas that had offered safe passage to horrifically inhumane slave ships for far too long. A new war had begun in Shana's colourful life.

Instead of opting for the more obvious choice of attack, Captain Culley kept the Banshee close to England's coastline for a few months. Not wishing to draw unwanted attention to her presence, Shana made sure that the Banshee steered clear of the main ports and was ready for a speedy getaway at the least sign of any threat. Sidling up to lesser used quays, the Banshee was able to offload her booty to keen merchants willing to fence treasure and goods at the risk of dancing a jig on the end of a hangman's rope. As Queen Elizabeth would most likely expect the insolent woman who had challenged her so vehemently to sail as far away from England, Shana decided to call her bluff and pillage Privateers as they returned to their virginal monarch's shores. Whilst she planned the daring raids of vessels that had committed what she deemed as pyracy in the name of the Crown, her crew did her proud and carried out attacks with confidence, great haste and extreme nerve.

The Banshee's crew operated under cover of darkness, working expertly in unpredictable seas that had overturned many prospective invaders' vessels, dragging them down into their gloomy grey depths. Staging numerous successful attacks on returning slave ships, the Banshee seized blood money that Privateers had made from selling the African captives. Laden with bountiful booty the Banshee fled back to the safety of Ireland. Each attack also brought fresh supplies of tobacco, cotton, extra sails, ropes, weaponry and ammunition. Following every raid, Shana would bare her ample breasts and offer every man aboard the chance to join her crew or fight for their lives. She had become quite a performer over her years as a notorious nautical brigand and never once failed to mesmerize her audience. Although she never intended to accept all of the men who decided to serve as pyrates, the sense of power that she enjoyed would rush over her like an orgasm. Her banshee scream struck terror into the heart of every person who had refused her generous offer and the skirmish that followed was never long but always spectacularly violent. Covered from head to toe in the blood of those men whom she despised most deeply, Shana would hack off her trophies and leave the vessel without feeling the slightest bit of remorse. The stench of cowardice would sometimes stay with her for days and the sight of the quivering louts who dared call themselves captains sickened her beyond description. Hacking and stabbing them with a purposefully forged short blade that she reserved for her most loathed enemies, Shana made sure that the men who helped the slave industry to prosper suffered an agonising death at her hands. When she had taken her final prize, the blood-soaked woman ensured that her victim felt every last slice of her knife. Before passing out, the last thing that he would see was his own dismembered testicles being squeezed and rolled around in her dextrous hand. Leaving the dying to suffer the final moments of their sorry lives, Shana would always be the last one to leave the ship.

When all of her crew were back safely aboard the Banshee, she would soak the boards of the defeated vessel with spirits and set light to her as she wailed her banshee cry and leapt for safety. Her only child waited for his mother safely aboard the Banshee, his specially made short sword in his strong hand. Irish had fashioned a fine, perfectly weighted, double-edged weapon from a single piece of steel as his first gift to the boy. Watching the struggle from afar, Patrick would emulate his mother's slashes and thrusts energetically, and cheer every time his mother made a kill.

Ireland fast became a second home for Shana as the Banshee made regular trips to and from the pagan isle which soon became the perfect haven for England's most wanted pyrate. The notorious Captain Culley was admired by many for her rebellion against England and her power-obsessed queen. The feisty seafarer was welcomed to her ancestral homeland as an honourable guest amongst the clans and the Gaelic people trusted and respected her as one of their own. Shana felt more at home in the wild and mystical lands than she had ever felt before and some of her happiest times were spent on Irish soil.

Life was good and invigorating for Captain Culley. One Saint Patrick's day, she sat in her cabin decorating her latest trophy with the most intricate pattern of Celtic knot work. Her collection of tattooed pouches had expanded extremely quickly consisting of a pretty assortment of beautifully crafted leather-work, each a different shade, ranging from palest cream to dark brown. Shana had become a very talented tattooist, even though the skin that she worked on was always dead.

As safe from discovery as possible, Shana docked in Dublin with permission of the king of the Sweeney clan. She was taken by surprise at the sound of a shot which was the usual warning sign from one of Grace O'Malley's trusty watches. Shana was aware that sporadic inter-clan warfare could erupt at any moment. She had managed to gain the support of most chieftains as she had proved her strength by standing up to Queen Elizabeth. They also respected her close friendship with Grace O'Malley. A relatively calm sea gently bounced the Banshee on playful waves. Putting aside her craftwork, she took hold of a pistol. Her keen hearing recognised the sounds of an approaching cockboat and she readied herself for a second warning shot which would mean certain threat. With baited breath, Shana stood in the tiny room, poised for attack. Her blood suddenly raced with adrenalin and she braced herself for battle. A male voice with a soft Irish accent called from below, stern side and Shana relaxed when she heard the clatter of wooden slats against the side as a rope ladder was thrown over. When she heard laughing, she instantly took a seat and laid down her weapons. The late night boatman had no doubt brought a female visitor for Tripod to spend his dwindling earnings, fucking the living daylights out of her for the next six hours. The man weighed less these days due to his limb and organ compensation trading spree, yet he still had the stamina of a horse when it came to pleasures of the flesh. Shana smiled contently to herself and thanked the gods that her friend no longer had to rely on dismemberment to pay for his insatiable sexual appetite.

Suddenly the handsome woman caught her breath and a weird feeling enveloped her very soul. Perched comfortably on his mistress' shoulder, Micken played happily, gently toying with her dark golden locks. Patrick played at her feet with hand whittled pyrates that Irish had made for him. A perfect set of miniature cannons had recently been added to his growing toy collection. Reaching up to stroke his mother's leg, the child sensed a change in her. Micken had also felt her tension and froze, cocking his head questioningly and cooing comically in apprehension of the possible outcome. Shivering with excitement, Shana Culley sensed a presence, an aura that made her heart fill with love, emotion and sexual tension.

It was Richie, she knew it! Her heart pounded and she sat bolt upright, voluptuous breasts thrust forward, their large, hardened nipples tingling with anticipation. Only fanatical lovers could feel the way that the pyrate captain felt at that moment and seconds seemed to last forever as she waited with both glee and apprehension. Her mind spinning, Shana wondered how Richie would feel about her after all of this time. Floods of different emotions filled her confused, damaged mind as she recalled the foul abuse that she had endured since her abduction.

For a split second, Shana's life played before her in a series of flashbacks, some hideously grotesque, others blissfully happy. Her final vision was of herself as a pretty young woman, her whole life ahead of her, sitting in a barn with Richie as he fondled her breasts. She was aroused beyond belief and had reached her hand down between her legs to feel the tingling wetness as her vaginal muscles contracted in orgasmic delight. The last thing that she remembered was his firm and needy touch... then tiny white flecks of light began to dance around an approaching blackness and her hearing suddenly failed. Micken flew wildly around the cabin and smacked into the wall beak-first, flapping his wings helplessly as he lost control and dropped clumsily to the boards. Irish scooped the alarmed bird carefully up with his strong but gentle hands and returned him safely to his cage. Regaining his wits and shivering his feathers back into place, the parrot blinked at the sight of his mistress lying unconscious beneath him.

Muffled sounds gradually became clearer as Shana opened her wide, blue eyes to see the man for whom she had fallen many years ago. His gentle, Irish accent soothed her pain and confusion as she lay in Richie's lap, gazing up into his eyes. After all these years, she had allowed vulnerability to emerge; the shock of an encounter with a beau from her past had proved way too much for her. Thankfully only Irish and Richie had witnessed Shana's fainting attack. Irish knew all too well that a moment of weakness could prove to be fatal for his captain.

Calmly reassuring Patrick, Irish made sure that Shana was happy to be left alone with the newcomer then took his little friend away for a rare treat of working with the crew. Since Shana's life had changed so much, she had grown all too used to being powerful, dominant and dangerous in a man's world. When she came around to see one of the people from a life that she had been forcibly torn away from, she had totally lost control of long suppressed emotions. Her pain had become almost unbearable, especially since over the past few days life on the Banshee had been unusually relaxed and redundant from duty. She had spent long hours reminiscing whilst her crew partied in the most hospitable land in the whole of the New World.

A surging, intense passion rose up from Shana's inner being and she lifted her head, closed her sore eyes and joined lips with the first and only real lover that she had ever known. As their kiss intensified, Richie's beard felt so soft against her cheek and Shana longed to feel his face between her legs once again. Just then, tiny fingers touched her nipple and a sudden, hard squeeze made Shana yelp. Her body had been wracked with so much pain from abusive sexual torment that what would once have been a harmless pinch of her nipple, now caused her to scream and leap. Her violent reaction terrified the tiny ape who had tweaked her to gain attention.

'What did the fiends do to ye m'lady!' Richie's question was rhetorical. Over the arduous, often agonising years spent fighting for survival, treasured memories of fun times spent with the impish ape had kept her going but she was not yet ready to cope with his teasing ways. As the drama played out before him, Micken screeched a warning to the wide-eyed creature and rattled the bars of his cage door violently with his strong hooked beak. Scampering like a bolt of lightening into a dark corner, Flint screeched a high-pitched squeal as he leapt for cover. When Richie looked deeply into Shana's terrified eyes his expression showed empathy, sorrow and dread at the thought of what his lover had been through since she had vanished from his life. Having held Shana in his melancholy heart over the past few years, Eileen Conachy's only son breathed in the scent of the woman who he had adored since the day he had set eyes on her in the grounds of her home. Memories of the ecstatic times that Richie had shared with the adorable young woman had helped him through some hard times. Relishing the moment, Richie pulled the confused and terrified woman to his chest holding her tightly, safe in his arms. They stayed huddled together for what seemed like a lifetime within their private heaven. No words were needed between the bonded souls and Shana felt secure, needed and loved beyond any doubt.

Cowering in the corner, a little crumpled form shivered with sorrow at the thought of Shana not recognising him. Flint's mind was focussed on the devastated woman who had been scared of him. Confused beyond belief, the tiny ape's comically bulbous eyes were mesmerised as the couple before him held each other close, rocking together slowly in a hypnotic rhythm. Primitive instinct told Flint to stay under cover yet the little male wanted so badly to make the female laugh again and look into his eyes as she had always done before. Time meant nothing to the animal and as he picked at the crumbs beneath the cupboard where he had hidden, instinct soon took over and he began to look around for food. Collecting some seeds and dried fruit that Micken had discarded, he nibbled away grumpily, chattering to himself. Micken cocked his head to one side, then another watching with one eye at a time as the furry intruder picked at his rubbish. Trying out a high-pitched whistle, Micken was surprised to find that Shana carried on canoodling with the stranger, ignoring him completely. Sulking on a perch, the little bird tried a few lines to distract his mistress. Nothing seemed to work!

Shana and Richie's bodies thrashed together with pure lust and need as they pulled at each others' clothing, desperate to feel the other's bare skin. Micken whistled with delight at the erotically charged scene that was playing out in front of him. Keeping his eye on the couple before him and the strange being that was desperate for Shana's attention, the parrot began to sing to his heart's delight. Flint stayed huddled in the corner still wearing a confused expression on his crumpled old man's face. As the two humans in front of him began to copulate, the miniscule primate relaxed as he caught a sudden whiff of sexual juices. Reaching his miniature hand down to his erection, Flint enjoyed the view of his master and the beautiful creature. He was determined to make her adore him as she had before.

Richie's head was spinning with an amazing array of feelings. Lust filled his whole being as he thrust himself deeper into the woman who had been in his passionate dreams for so long. Each movement brought them closer in lust, spirit and love as they pleasured one another beyond belief. Shana's body responded to every thrust as Richie's thick shaft entered her tight vulva. Shivering in orgasmic delight, the lusty wench writhed beneath her Irish lover. Grinding her hips in perfect rhythm against her partner's, Shana's mind and very soul savoured every quiver of ecstasy that her body experienced. Hours passed as the horny pair ravaged each other's body. Faces flushed in sheer delight at the perfection of their sensual union. Even Flint had given up his voyeuristic peep show and in between grabbing morsels to eat, had decided to postpone his efforts to gain Shana's attention.

Still horny, Micken wriggled his hips against a small bell that Tripod had fashioned out of a lead shot for him to mount. Quite naturally, Tripod was always concerned about every living creature's sexual well-being! Flint's penis had given up hours before when the show had gone on far longer than expected! Glassy, wide brown eyes scanned the room looking for possible ways to cause mischief and end the couple's primitive behaviour. Flint's face was a picture! Used to entertaining and shocking folk with his masturbatory antics, he just did not know how to react when the tables were turned. With one spindly leg crossed over another, lying on his tummy only inches away from the woman who he was desperate to embrace, he rested his furry chin on the heel of his hand. Neither of the lovers had broken eye contact with one another and what had started as a wonderful fantasy for the horny ape had turned into an absolute nightmare. Micken studied

Flint with interest and concern as if he was a silent accomplice. Suddenly, Flint's half-closed eyes widened with hope on spotting the navigation instruments on the mapping table. With an agile leap, he sprang into the air, landing right in the centre of the valuable equipment used to calculate the ship's position. Grabbing each valuable piece in turn, Flint licked, sniffed and eyed them until he had chosen the most suitable for his needs.

Grinning wildly at the copulating couple below him, the mischievous little creature made an impressive vertical jump and landed in the small of Richie's strong back. Lifting the sharp instrument above his head, Flint made ready for a speedy escape once he had done the deed. In a flash, the naughty monkey stabbed the muscular left cheek of his Celtic friend's arse and leapt for freedom. Micken squawked wildly, flapping his wings with excitement. Yelling in shock and pain, Richie withdrew himself from his long-lost lover and jumped up, spinning around wildly. 'Where are ye, yer wee fecker!?' he yelled loudly. Shana had leapt up and stood with Richie, weapon ready until they heard the ape's panicked screeches. The tiny secret door that Flint had discovered on his earlier examination of the cabin was locked. His terrified yelps made the surprised lovers burst into raucous laughter as it dawned on them how selfishly they had behaved in their besotted state. The mere sight of Flint with his wiry little legs banging desperately on the small door, hands pulling at the handle, was all that the horny couple could bear. Micken laughed a cheeky chuckle and wolf-whistled the embarrassed monkey. Shana began to giggle and Richie soon joined her, vigorously rubbing his nether regions. When Flint heard their roars of laughter, he somersaulted in a display of utter relief and jubilation at his final success in gaining their attention.

Reunited at last, the three collapsed in an exhausted heap on the creaky wooden boards of the cabin floor and held each other tight. Sleep soon took them away into a world of blissful dreams. Richie was certain that he had found his soul mate yet his Mama's foresight had told another story that he did not want to accept. As he fell into a deep and satisfied slumber, he relished the moment and vowed to himself that he would take each day as it came. Concerned about the welfare of his mistress, Micken stayed awake all night, watching the wild man and miniature beast who had rudely interrupted peaceful cabin life. His cage swaying therapeutically, he had to battle to stay awake and busied himself untangling his colourful assortment of ropes. Eating regularly, he managed his first all-night guard and puffed his brightly coloured plumage proudly.

Dawn arrived all too soon for the blissfully reunited trio. Sounds of the crew making important daily checks on the craft and her apparatus woke Captain Culley as always. Nestled firmly between her two perfect, warm orbs lay a totally contented Flint. His soft thin, little pink lips curved, satisfied in a blissful smile as his body snuggled into Shana's bosom which formed a perfect pair of alternative pillows. Reaching over to kiss Richie on the forehead, Shana felt an incredible surge of emotion. Her mind was momentarily transported back to days spent at her home surrounded by the clan whom she loved dearly. A knock at the cabin door alerted the natural mother to her son's presence. The youngster burst in with tales of an exciting night spent in the company of his favourite mates. Having satisfied himself that his mother was safe and happy, Patrick's thick little legs carried him off up the wooden steps and out onto the deck. Waking in the warmth and comfort of his true love's body, Richie held Shana close wanting the moment to last forever. Tears flowed freely and the pyrate queen felt immense relief as her lover held her close. Flint slowly edged his warm, sleepy little form up onto his true mistress' shoulder so that he could lick away her salty tears. As the lovers lay close together Shana gradually unburdened her tortured mind, weeping openly as never before. Micken tucked his leg up to benefit from the comfort of his cosy belly down and his delicate eyelids closed contentedly. The parrot could no longer fight sleep. Feeling totally satisfied that the alien visitors meant his mistress no harm, his primitive instinct had accepted the new arrivals into his world. Purring like Eddie the Banshee's most favoured lucky cat, Micken gave Flint a final glance and the ape winked cheekily back at the beautiful bird.

Irish had become immediately smitten with the ship's new pet, Flint the Tamarin monkey. He had heard of the Satare Maues tribe whose people lived deep in the Amazon jungle and a few of his sailor friends had reported sightings of gremlins. Few believed that the tiny creatures that caused havoc along the jungle trails were actually mammals. Hacking their way through the wilderness, their trek would all too often end abruptly due to loss of equipment or a barrage of missiles aimed by unseen attackers. Seemingly no-one was hiding within the matrix of branches that formed a wonderful canopy high above their heads. Superstition always got the better of the usually ambitious and determined explorers eager to find new cultures and land to conquer.

Irish became fascinated by the wonderful creature, Flint and his immense intelligence.

Carrying a leather-bound book with him everywhere since the new character had invaded the Banshee, Irish began to make the most accurately detailed drawings of Flint. The artist's work was exquisite and provided all aboard with much entertainment when he showed them his latest piece of artwork. Flint had become Irish's muse and was very proud of his inspirational talents. Posing in the most comical fashion, Flint led his new companion around the vessel, perching atop of masts and posing with fellow crewmembers. The gifted pair gradually provided Captain Culley with a perfect pictorial journal. Irish documented many interesting encounters on his travels and added leaves to the priceless book wherever he journeyed. Writing inscriptions along with the drawings, Irish's quirky sense of humour helped to make the unique work a masterpiece. Page after page was filled with caricatures of people with whom he had served, fought, killed and befriended. No-one was spared and even Flint's hobby of keeping those aboard the Banshee lice-free did not escape the pencil! A favourite image of Shana's was a picture of the comical Tripod busy with two wenches. Playing with both whores at once, Tripod ignored Flint who balanced atop of his head, picking lice and popping them into his mouth. Shana howled when she had set eyes on the cartoon and begged for a copy to hang in her cabin. Humble Irish had been very flattered by his captain's praise, so in future Flint would take his master's latest creation to Shana. Irish and Flint became inseparable when Shana was busy and the man firmly believed in the Satare Maues belief that Tamarin monkeys were reincarnations of their dead children.

Richie was all too glad that Flint had managed to befriend another as it meant he was able to spend more uninterrupted time with his lover. As time passed by, the two grew ever more infatuated with one another and the day came when he felt that she was able to take the devastating news from her old home. Too many days had passed by and neither Shana nor Richie had wanted to speak about the people back in England. Shana was terrified that she might hear tales of more disaster and she also had to face her fears and tell her lover how she had become withchild. Despite knowing that Richie would be devastated by her news, Shana felt she had to tell him of the rape. Then only he and Irish would know the diabolical truth. As far as everyone else was concerned, Shana had fallen pregnant by choice. Since she was committed to a life as a pyrate captain, she had no need to be tied to a husband. Since the day that Richie and Shana had been reunited, he had realised how desperately his woman needed to know how her extended clan were faring.

When he felt that Shana was able to accept his news, Richie planned a night alone and arranged for Patrick and Micken to sleep down with Irish and the rest of the crew. Flint was always game for a night spent out beneath the stars, so it could be arranged for him to keep Tripod company on watch. Literally having to prize the two newfound friends apart, the hardened pyrates took the captain's precious pets, trying to ignore the atrocious din that they were making. Since Flint had gained Micken's trust, a surreal bond had developed between the two. It was an uncanny bonding but a touching sight to witness. Flint's name was soon added to Micken's limited vocabulary and the spindle-legged ape would drop anything that he was doing whenever he heard his feathered buddy call his name.

When Richie and Shana were finally alone, he explained everything that had happened since she had left. Neither one had looked forward to this moment of truth but both knew that it had to happen someday. Richie began by telling Shana how worried everyone had been when Shana had disappeared. Everyone in the Culley estate had imagined that the poor girl had lost her mind through grief when poor Albert died. Refusing to accept that his lover had left her clan without a word, Richie knew deep in his heart that Shana was alive. So did his wise mother. Eileen Conachy had been devastated by the death of her soul mate and Shana's surrogate father, Albert. No-one had been able to comfort her since she had lost him and Richie had been beside himself with unnecessary feelings of guilt. He was the only one who believed that he was responsible for his mother's fiancé's death. Eileen had not once blamed her adored son and it drove her mad to see him torture himself for something that he could never have prevented.

Inwardly dying of a broken heart, the poor gypsy woman eventually lost her mind and began to wander away from the safety of Mary Maggy's. Since she read Tarot cards, the locals soon began to take advantage of her and ask for their fortunes to be read for free. Trusting and good-natured, Eileen was happy to tell the future of those seeking knowledge. Soon, the community became uneasy and began to fear the Celtic sooth-sayer as her accurate predictions began to come true. One cold, frosty night, a hysterical, angry mob came with lanterns onto Shana's land and demanded that Eileen be brought out. Richie went into the field to see what the local hooligans wanted with his mother and was knocked unconscious. The poor man's body was wracked with pain as he told his lover how he came around to see his mother's naked, battered body swinging from a rope in the tree above him. Battered beyond recognition, Eileen looked as though she had been savaged by a mad animal. A crude cross had been cut deeply into her pale flesh, across her breasts and down from her throat to her vagina. Thankfully, Richie had never learned the sickening truth that his mother had still been alive when the noose was pulled tight around her neck. The few witnesses from the Turnbull family who had been pinned down and forced to watch his mother die slowly and in absolute agony, never told him the complete story. Richie never learned how long poor Eileen had struggled for her breath, ripping the nails from her fingers as she pulled at the rough, specially made hemp rope. Trying in vain to release her neck from an ever-tightening death squeeze, Eileen mouthed the Lord's Prayer as she was senselessly murdered by a group of ignorant men. The drunken mob had acted on impulse through sheer, unreasoned fear of the unknown.

Lying closely together, the two lovers brought each other up to date on events since their unexpected parting. Ma Turnbull was as healthy and bubbly as ever but poor Benjamin, her husband, had died of consumption two years before Richie had left to search for Shana. Both twins had married farm hands and fallen pregnant at the same time, each giving birth to a healthy baby girl. Abi, Shana's closest childhood friend had named her newborn Sushana after her soul sister who had suddenly and inexplicably disappeared. When Shana heard of this honour, she felt so homesick that she vowed someday day to return to her old home and introduce Patrick to his extended clan. News of Gift and his family's safe arrival at Mary Maggy's made Shana feel so thankful and relieved that Precious' horrific death had not been in vain. Had the intrepid character not been abducted on that night long ago, when her bladder could hold no more booze, who knows what would have happened to her African friends? Feeling a comforting confirmation of fatalistic trust, Shana told Richie all about her kidnapping and every perilous adventure that had followed. Mesmerised by the accounts of his lover's adventures, Richie listened as she poured out her heart.

Growing closer with every tear shed, Richie and Shana vowed to love each other until the end of their days. Richie gave Shana the rabbit's foot and lucky silver coin that Bess had placed in her cot so long ago. He had mounted the foot on a silver brooch. The lucky talisman was the most precious gift that she had received since Albert had given her the compass that he had once given to her mother on her wedding day. When she told Richie about the compass he produced one of Albert's kerchiefs and unwrapped the treasured item, returning it at last to its rightful owner. Next to the invaluable piece lay Bess, the peg doll that its namesake had lovingly made many years earlier. Tears welled in Shana's aqua eyes and Richie would never forget her words in that intimate moment: 'I will love ye forever, my Richie. Verily, ye have made me so happy with thy love and I shall ne'er be able to repay thy kindness.' Shana's words were whispered but clear and her eyes showed her Celtic lover nothing but sincerity, honour and a deep, undying love. Richie held his woman close to his large chest and promised that he would stay by her side until death.

From that night onward, Richie became a pyrate and began a new life aboard the Banshee, serving bravely beside the love of his life. Patrick and he soon became close friends and Irish welcomed Shana's new lover as a brother although secretly he felt envious of the lucky man who had captured the captain's heart. The boatswain had been in love with her since she had revealed herself as a wench after she had killed the ruthless Watkins. Not wanting to rush the abused and, he guessed, damaged woman into a sexual relationship, Irish felt apprehensive in his approach to declare his intentions. Loving Shana as he had never loved any woman, the handsome man was determined to marry her some day.

Richie taught Patrick how to play the bodhrán and gave his own drum to the boy when he had learned a few techniques well. Overjoyed with his new instrument, Patrick often joined the other musicians on board, practising his skills and becoming faster and faster with his rhythm. On pleasant evenings when the crew were out on deck drinking rhum, the band would play under moonlit skies whilst Patrick accompanied them and his Mama danced. The wild beauty was able to turn her heel to any tune and her audience delighted in seeing her curvaceous body sway seductively in a mesmerising gypsy-like dance. Swirling and clapping, her skirts rising high as the rhythm grew faster, the ravishing belladonna always became the life and soul of any party. Her very presence conjured an electrifying atmosphere as every man fell under her hypnotic spell. Richie had a permanent erection whilst in Shana's company and whenever the couple had chance, they would sneak off to copulate.

Tripod found the role reversal amusing when he would happen upon the lovers, engrossed in each other.

One day he limped down to the brazier to refill the sand box and tend the fire that always had to be kept alight. The lovers' muffled groans gave them away and the disabled seaman found the libidinous captain squatting before Richie as she gave him oral pleasure. Clearing his throat loudly, Tripod squeezed himself past the busy pair and carried on with his duties. It soon became a running joke that wherever you went aboard the Banshee, you would most probably bump into the carnal captain and 'Richie the rabbit' as he became fondly known. Swiving like a pair of over-sexed teenagers at every given opportunity, the lovers could not get enough of each other. They were certainly doing their level best to catch up on the years that they had missed!

Whilst Shana Culley and her friends honoured their ancestors and celebrated Eileen Conachy's journey to the Otherworld, the Bubonic plague prowled the squalled, filthy streets of London. The 'Black Death', as it became known, spread like a hideous curse inflicting its victims with the most horrific boils and unbearable pain. In 1563 Queen Elizabeth decided to move her court to Windsor Castle for fear of her life. Self-protection became paramount and when she was safely inside her haven, she ordered a gallows to be erected outside the fortified building. Warnings were clear; anyone from London who was unfortunate enough to come near to Windsor would be hanged in front of the queen's sanctuary. Their bodies were displayed in hanging cages as a deterrent to any citizen of England who dared to endanger the life of their monarch. On hearing word of the Bubonic plague that was thought to have arrived in London via the docks, Shana also made plans to ensure the safety of her child. She, Irish and Richie decided that it would be best to take Patrick as far away from danger as possible.

Goodbyes were more like farewells when Shana and Richie left Ireland for they both knew that they would return someday. Grace O'Malley provided her newfound soul sister with a new craft, a carrack that she had captured from a Spanish privateer. The Banshee had served her captain well but was in need of renovation. She would make a decent addition to Grace's fleet when work had been carried out. Renaming the ship 'The Slayer' Grace ensured that she was packed with ample supplies and offered places aboard to some of her best men. Setting sail for Cathay, Captain Culley felt sad to leave Ireland and her friends. At long last she felt that she had finally found the place where she belonged.

Chapter 17

The Long Voyage to Cathay

Tackling the tumbling waves with ease, the majestic Slayer covered many knots at an impressive speed. Shana delighted in her new vessel and pushed her to the limit. Having purposely chosen a challenging route as a worthy test-run Shana was pleased with her new vessel's performance. The carrack's nickname, 'The beast of burden', aptly described her as the most competent transport ship of her time. Offering ample space for Shana's crew of seventy two men, cargo, provisions and thirty eight guns on a single deck, the craft would be virtually impervious to attack from small crafts. Shana planned to make the lengthy journey to the Cathay seas with as few stops as possible. Patrick was sure to like Cathay, the largest country in Asia.

The Slayer was the first vessel that Shana had captained that was capable of such long voyages. The roomy carrack was able to sail the most efficient and shortest route across to Asia with ease but Shana had decided that her hard-working crew deserved two breaks en route. Battling two violent rainstorms on the outward journey, Shana's hardy ship suffered minimal damage and the first leg of the trip took them safely across a turbulent ocean with relative ease. With a combination of four sails which allowed a good deal of flexibility, the Slayer maintained a good sailing speed. Shana was extremely impressed by the vessel's performance and found it easy to understand why many ex-privateers were choosing Carracks in the newest money-making scheme of pyrate hunting. Fire power was immense which enabled her to attack a full fleet of ships if the need arose. Although maintenance was far easier on the smaller vessels, the Slayer was in her element on lengthy hauls and proved to be perfect for the pyrate crew. Once back in Ireland, Shana planned to return the robust ship to Grace and take a sloop or brigantine... both far more suitable for her notorious filch and flee raids.

Taking after his sea-faring mother, Patrick was a born traveller. His mother's nomadic lifestyle suited the adventurous spirited toddler perfectly and he soon became an invisible presence amongst the team of experienced sailors. Rarely a nuisance, Patrick always kept away from sailors performing their duties. Listening to and obeying orders with no fuss, the energetic child rushed around the decks with natural agility, his keen senses helping him to avoid danger. Patrick had been blessed with an uncanny amount of common sense and showed early signs of intelligence, way above average. He particularly enjoyed helping Jock, John and the others man the sails and he and Flint loved to climb the rigging, often acting out faux duels high above the working men on deck. Proving to be as eager to learn as his mother had been when she found herself aboard the Falcon, the clever toddler amazed his self-elected ward, Irish. The boatswain knew that any offspring of Shana Culley would be hardy, fearless and bright as a button, nevertheless Patrick outshone even the most enthusiastic of ship apprentices he had ever known. No task was too menial for the boy and he mucked in with the other lads despite his inherent 'rank' as captain's son. Always fair and helpful, the small boy was liked by all aboard the

Slayer and Irish began to think of him as his own son. When off duty, the two were inseparable and Irish's sketchbooks illustrated the daily life of Patrick Culley, Micken and Flint. Of course, the kindly sailor had to include the wee monkey in his illustrations to avoid any feelings of rejection. After all, Flint had been his first model and for that, Irish would be eternally grateful. Growing more skilled with every pen stroke, each week Irish presented Shana with a neatly bound set of immaculate, wonderfully detailed drawings with amusing captions. She always looked forward to these storyboards which gave her an insight into the life aboard the Slayer that she never witnessed. Mischievous characters jumped out at her from the thick parchment pages and their antics took her into the secret world of the ordinary sailor. Although most images featured her son and his pets, the rest of the crew could be seen in the background getting up to all sorts of capers. Unbeknown to them, their captain was aware of their behaviour and not in the slightest bit bothered.

In her cabin Shana had a weighty oak chest, carved with a splendid scene that featured her dressed in her finery standing in front of the stately Banshee. Elaborate costumes were the main contents of the coffer but a false base held Shana's most treasured items. Unlike other pyrates, the child-woman's precious objects were simple and inexpensive yet to her, absolutely invaluable. A lock of Patrick's baby hair, a rabbit's foot brooch, a silver coin, a tarnished compass, her childhood doll, a single Tarot card and Irish's picture books were Shana's only irreplaceable possessions. When overcome with sorrow, the insular captain would retire to the privacy of her cabin and take out her treasures just to feel close to those she had loved and lost. She never quite knew why she had taken the Lovers tarot card from Eileen's pack following the reading long ago but it had been something that she had needed to do. It had been the only thing that she had on her person at the time of her abduction apart from the clothes that she wore. When things had become almost too much to bear, Shana would take out the crumpled card and stare at the entwined figures that had been painted on so delicately.

The vast, square sails of the Slayer were easily reduced during stormy weather whilst the smaller sails at the bow and stern allowed her to be manoeuvered expertly by her skilful crew. Her lateen sails enabled the impressive craft to sail across wind and her stable, roomy deck made an excellent gun platform. Grace O'Malley had customized the majestic ship in readiness for battle and had ensured that she was well equipped with ample gun power and ammunition. Patrick, Flint and Micken would run around the gun stations in a wild chase, reenacting the last fight that they had witnessed. The little boy always played the part of captain and Flint would make everyone roar with laughter as he limped behind Patrick imitating Tripod. With complete trust, the monkey sometimes even allowed Patrick to tie a small wooden stick to one of his legs so that he could impersonate his favourite character! Irish had made a wonderfully accurate ink sketch of the little ape acting as Tripod and Patrick had been smitten by the likeness and pasted it above his hammock. The boy idolized the good-looking man and the feeling was mutual. Every spare minute that Irish had, he would find 'his little man' as he fondly called him. They would take parchment, inks and brushes and immerse themselves in drawing. Many of Patrick's pictures decorated the boatswain's sleeping area and the men had long since accepted their superior as the boy's unofficial father. The two looked uncannily similar; both were stocky in build yet not fat with broad shoulders and long legs, each had dark blonde hair lightened considerably by the sun. Their bone-structure was finely chiseled with high cheekbones and their slanted blue-green eyes were framed with long, black eyelashes. Wide, generous mouths with full lips and straight, white teeth made their smiles both attractive and cheeky. Irish and Patrick were totally unaware of their fantastic good looks which made them even more attractive. Self-conscious and nervous around women, Irish hoped that his mini dopple-ganger would have more self-confidence with the female species. Vowing never to settle with any woman but his true soul mate, Irish had strict principles when it came to love and taught the manchild these values. Shana would often watch the two interact and it touched her how the older man had taken on Patrick as his own. Her heart ached for Irish but she believed that he felt only friendship towards her. Besides, her fantastic lover Richie gave her more than enough love and she felt content with their relationship for the time being... although deep down, she remembered Eileen's premonition. After years of misfortune with one tragedy following another, Shana had become well accustomed to accepting her fate. The best advice she could give to any she came across was to leave yesterday behind, live for look after today and tomorrow will look after itself.

Looking forward to introducing her son and Richie to the native people in the area, Shana stood at the side of her ship scanning the beautiful shores of West Africa, their first port-of-call. Leaning into a fresh, warm breeze and stretching her arms above her head, she grinned naughtily as she recalled the night before when her adventurous lover had managed to sneak up behind her without her noticing. Each of Richie's previous attempts at surprising her had failed and he had ended up with her sword poised at his throat or pistol aimed at his head. Last night, he had finally been successful and startled her as she was mending Micken's cage. It was so unlike her not to notice an intruder's approach but Richie had been determined to catch her unawares. To her alarm, Shana had suddenly felt a large hand clamp firmly over her mouth and another around her waist. Her lover's familiar musky smell soon put her at ease as his hand slid down and over her shapely hips. Feeling hot breath on the base of her neck she felt her body tingle as Richie planted firm kisses over her smooth skin. Passion overtook him and he reached down, pulling up heavy skirts to run his hand up, down and inside the aroused woman's warm legs. Keeping hold of her head, hand still over her lips, Richie reached around to feel the soft, delicate skin of his lover's stomach. Her breath quickened and her heart raced as she craved for his fingers to touch her cunnie. Aching for him to be inside her, Shana's legs began to quiver in anticipation as his hands explored her responsive, needy body. Reaching behind her to take hold of Richie's thick, hard member beneath the course cloth of his breeches, Shana moaned with pure lust as her hands massaged him slowly and firmly. Each knew exactly how to please the other and their love-making was never selfish, both keen to satisfy. Suddenly feeling the urge to enter his lover, Richie released his penis and thrust it deep inside…

As usual, Shana had risen early that morning and left Richie sleeping soundly where they had eventually fallen. Every day and night since their reunion, the lovers had been greedy for sex. It was the best either had ever experienced and without a doubt, would ever know again with anyone else. The chemistry between them was amazing, not only could those in close vicinity feel the lust but they could almost see, smell and hear it! Tripod was certainly envious as he had never managed to find his match but everyone felt happy for the enamoured couple.

Shana was determined to make the most of these happy times and the satisfied captain smiled as she heard Patrick's unmistakable footsteps. Then came the familiar sound as he dragged one of the smaller barrels over so that he could climb up next to his mother and take in the view. Her son's simple greeting melted her tender heart. 'Dud mornin' Mama, I wuv ye soooo muts!.' On waking, Patrick had sensed that the ship was approaching land long before the order of anchorage was given. Before joining his mother out on deck, he had scraped his teeth with the beech twig dipped in coarse salt, swilled his mouth with a tankard full of clean water. Following his usual routine, he had then gone below decks to help the apprentices feed the livestock.

Having a wonderful rapport with all creatures, Patrick could calm them in most situations including stormy weather. Without the need to be summoned for help, the young boy would simply be wherever he was needed when it involved animal care. Many a time he had helped Irish with birthing, and one morning the boy had surprised all aboard when he appeared from below deck, without warning, clutching a bloodied lamb to his chest. Unable to produce milk, the ewe had rejected the tiny creature and Patrick immediately took it into his care. Adopting the lamb, he named it 'Chop' and carried it with him everywhere in a sling. Tripod showed him how to feed Chop goat's milk through a teat made with a finger from a leather glove pulled over a bottle's neck. Tucked inside Patrick's waistcoat, Chop lived to become a fine ewe that followed her saviour around everywhere. Irish made an exception to rules by allowing Chop to wander around on the main deck until one day she caused Tripod to have a nasty accident and as a result, Chop ended up in an Irish stew, prepared by the injured party and Smith, the ship's cook. Unbelievably, Patrick proposed a toast to his late pet that cool evening and was soon tucking into the hearty meal with a clear conscience.

Dropping anchor in West Africa, Captain Culley left Irish in command on board whilst she took ten men ashore. A sleepy but elated Richie joined Patrick, Flint, Micken and the rest of the landing party that day which, unbeknown to the wee lad, was the thirteenth of November in the year of our Lord 1563; his third birthday. Perched atop of his shoulder, Micken mimicked Patrick's mispronounced words and the weary sailors were in good spirits as the Slayer approached the port of Edina along the cape coast of West Africa. With its abundant source of gold, pepper and ivory, the bustling trading centre's population was growing steadily. Unfortunately, the trade in human lives was also rearing its ugly head hence Shana's reason for making regular visits a priority. St. George's whitewashed walls glared brightly in the sunlight making a fine coastal landmark. It was wonderful to watch the fishermen skilfully manoeuvre their small, colourful canoes in and out of the fishing port. Relying on fish as a main source of food, the people of Medina's whole way of life was centred around their fishing skills. Portuguese settlers had long been exchanging gold extracted from the rich mines for copper, brass and European cloth with visiting voyagers. Unwilling to continue the back-breaking job of mining gold themselves, the colony began to use African slaves to do the dirty work for them. Acting swiftly, many were willing to begin shipping in strong African people for manual labour and fulfil demand.

Relishing the refreshingly cool breeze that gently caressed her face, Shana spoke softly to her inquisitive child and explained the customs of the tribes-people whose hospitality they would be receiving over the next few days. Always making sure that her son understood and therefore respected the culture of everyone that he met, Shana described the beliefs of the people of the Medina. Patiently she answered all of Patrick's questions as they gazed at the beautiful beaches that lay beyond the bluest lagoon that Shana had ever seen. Enjoying the sight of many different species of migratory birds that flocked to this peaceful haven, mother and son appreciated the tranquil location in different ways. Both avid lovers of nature, Shana and Patrick longed to walk the virgin sands fringed with coconut palms. The natives of Medina prepared fresh salted fish that was ideal to store for long journeys. On the first Tuesday of every July, long before the Europeans had discovered Medina, the natives celebrated the start of the fishing season with the Bakutue festival. Roughly translated Bakutue means, 'the opening of the Benya Lagoon into the sea.'

Shana was looking forward to buying more spices from Medina. Grains of paradise were her main priority but she had to be careful to hide this potent aphrodisiac from Flint! She smiled at fond memories of days past when the randy monkey could never get enough of the stimulating pepper. Whenever possible, she would add to her collection of the most exotic spices available. The mere thought of discovering new herbs or spices filled her with indescribable delight. Certain scents conjured faint memories from long ago, some happy but others brought excruciating emotional pain. The spice world still had a strong magnetic pull on Shana Culley and she had no desire to break away. Exquisite perfumes and delightful aromas filled her cabin. At every opportunity possible, the spice expert would add a new ingredient to the delicious amalgamation of exotic scents collected from all over the world. Her cabin always smelt divine and the captain would alter the mix to obtain the desired effect. Whatever her mood, Shana was able to enhance, stimulate, reduce or even totally change it by using powerful, potent aromas. Occasionally a breeze passing through cracks in the wood of the tiny living space lifted the scent of exotic spices and oils and wafted their vapours throughout the ship. Using her ability to mix essential oils, the cunning woman was able to create her desired effects on the crew. This enabled her to alter their moods according to the situation. No-one but Patrick was aware of the potency and power of the oils and spices as she had ensured that her child learn his inherent family skills. The intelligent lad was quick to learn under his mother's supervision and was soon able to create sensory ambiences ranging from soporific to stimulating. Occasionally crew-members were invited individually into the captain's cabin to enable Shana to teach Patrick a new aroma's affect on an unsuspecting subject. Always brutal in her honesty, Shana explained to her student that people were being persecuted and even murdered by the Christian church for practicing this age-old healing tradition. Their ability to use herbs in medical treatment had been passed down through generations but was now seen as a reason to be hanged. Refusing to be deterred by such evil malice, Shana taught her son to practice what he believed, no matter what the penalty might be.

Ensuring that Patrick grew up with a healthily open mind and deep respect of different cultures and practices, Shana never hid anything from her son. From an early age the boy had witnessed cannibalistic rituals of African tribes and was never discouraged to join in if he felt comfortable. Nothing seemed to deter the unconventional child and Shana felt a deep maternal pride. Shana and her son shared a passionate love of nature and anyone who chose to travel with them simply had to accept it. Eager to learn about all living things, Captain Culley's enthusiasm for the animal and plant world never waned. Despite her extremely volatile nature, she had incredible patience with all living creatures... with the exception of any human who angered her. As Patrick grew older, the Culley clan's menagerie expanded and the crew never knew what kind of critter the child would bring aboard every time he ventured onto land. The men always made a habit of checking their clothes before dressing after Smith found a lizard inside his boot one morning.

Accompanying Patrick everywhere he went, Flint became a valuable guardian for the growing child who was often over-enthusiastic, hyperactive and inquisitive. Afraid of no beast or creature, no matter how big or fierce, Patrick soon became the bane of the poor monkey's life. Due to his notoriety as a trouble-magnet, Flint was always the one to be blamed whenever the impish child met trouble. If Patrick was in danger, panicked, high-pitched screams were heard from the hyper-active ape, accompanied by scuttling noises or any signs of warning that the unfortunate animal could muster. Ignoring his Mama's pet's commotion, the mischievous boy would giggle to himself and blatantly ignore his minder.

The landing party arrived ashore safely and began the short walk to the settlement where the tribe prepared for the popular Bakutue festival. To celebrate Patrick's birthday Shana and Irish had planned to ask the Chief to invite Patrick to join their tribe as an honourary member. A colourful regatta of freshly painted canoes bobbed gently on the waters as the visitors passed by the enchanting lagoon. The sound of distant drums beating in a pulse-like rhythm made Patrick's heart quicken as he ran confidently ahead of the group. Scuttling alongside him, Flint looked nervous as his eyes darted from left to right, looking out for any prospective danger.

As they neared the village, a welcome party met the captain and took her and the others into their small community. In a private introductory meeting, Shana and her group were taken into a shelter where the Chief was waiting. Patrick was in awe of the tribe leader who looked spectacular in his fine, multi-coloured kente cloth robes and splendid gold jewellery. His mother spoke to the Chief in his native tongue and translated his words for the others. Patrick was delighted when he was invited to join the tribe of Medina and his mother gave him a heavy silver torc necklace and matching bracelet for a birthday gift. Overwhelmed by the whole experience, Patrick was overtly grateful as he was presented with a variety of gifts from the crew and his new tribal family.

It was a day that he would never forget and everyone enjoyed seeing the good-natured boy enjoying himself. When they were joined by other Chieftains from neighbouring tribes, the local dignitaries all mounted elaborately decorated palanquins and were carried in a parade through the town. To Shana's surprise, the chief allowed Patrick to ride with him in the covered litter and all were amused to see Flint sitting on top trying to peek through the silk blinds. Huge parasols provided shade for the royal subjects and Patrick sat in comfort next to the chief whilst everyone else walked behind them in the strong sunlight. On reaching the Benya lagoon, a solemn ceremony began when fishermen cast their nets to symbolize the beginning of a new fishing season. Everyone was entertained with dancing, singing and drumming, then saluted with a rally of musket fire. When the nets were gathered in, the catch was offered to the deities to ensure that the people would be blessed with prosperity and unity. Richie joined in with the drummers and they were in awe when they heard his skills. Shana felt happy as she watched her lover enjoying himself; the man was loved wherever he went. He had a wonderful knack of being able to make people happy and she loved him for it. Time almost stood still for Shana that day as she relaxed in the spiritual atmosphere and watched her son interact with African children as if he had been born in their land. Drifting off into a world of her own, she joined the women who were preparing a banquet of delicious smelling fish dishes. Occasionally it felt good to belong and right then, Shana felt very comfortable in her environment.

Apart from a brief territorial argument between Flint and a larger monkey over a coconut, the visit to West Africa went very smoothly. A defeated Flint made a great fuss of a slight tear in his left ear but everyone knew that it was his pride that hurt most of all. Returning to the ship wrapped up like a babe in a soft leopard-skin headdress that the chief had given Patrick as a leaving gift, the tiny ape whimpered like a lame puppy. Patrick nursed his little friend until sleep overcame him. Careful not to disturb the sleeping patient, he gently placed the newly-claimed fur bed under Micken's cage and joined the crew in preparation for the onward journey. Blessed with a good trade wind, the heavily-laden vessel made its way to Cathay making its final stop along the North African coast where Shana delivered goods from the west for her friends.

A healthy diet of salted fish, peanuts, bananas, fresh milk and coconut kept everyone strong and fit for the months at sea en route to southern Cathay. Following a pleasantly easy journey, the Slayer finally arrived in the seaport of Hoi An lying on the banks of the Thu Bon River. Asian traders had recently set up residence and the sleepy town was beginning to develop into a promising commercial district. Organizations were keen to do business with Vietnamese traders bringing fine silk and porcelain from their country. Captain Culley had unwittingly chosen the perfect time to visit as the Emperor had lifted the ban on foreign trade, allowing trade with Southeast Asian ports however Japanese ships were still denied entry. The year was 1565 and the Cathayan year of the wood ox when Patrick Culley turned four.

Chapter 18

Hoi An Brings Unexpected Love

Hoi An town was becoming a popular location for western traders but Shana and company enjoyed Cathayan culture and hospitality, choosing to stay away from the new settlers. Low wooden houses with red tiled roofs stretched along a lengthy narrow street. These delightful small homes were decorated with lacquer panels that had been intricately engraved with Cathayan characters. Ornamental pillars with beautiful carvings framed wooden balconies that looked out onto the bustling daily life of this fast-growing port. Shops with elaborately carved wooden facades backed onto the river, coloured silk and paper lanterns lighting their wares with a golden glow in the still of the night. Shana had never witnessed such a romantic sight as the rows of illuminated, jewel-coloured orbs that swayed gently in a silent breeze. Incense burned in front of golden figures, grinning or posing dramatically before sweet smelling, fresh floral offerings and food on large leaves set out on ancestral alters. Patrick was excited to see the statues wearing garlands of tiny flowers that added exquisite perfumes to the warm air. Dotted with elaborate temples and shrines, the riverside town offered an ambient atmosphere and felt welcoming and peaceful to the foreign visitors.

A nearby beach became a favourite place for Shana and Patrick to spend time. Waters as smooth as glass and powdery white sands welcomed the pair early each morning. Sunrise was the most stunning time of day as the golden orb glowed a beautiful deep orange. Local visitors collected coconuts and spoke gently in hushed whispers as if they were scared of disturbing the peaceful silence. In the early evening, a blood-red sun glowed in a dark azure sky and mother and son watched silently as it disappeared below the horizon, the inky shadowed waters gently shivering as if missing its warmth. Lighting a fire on the beach, Shana and Patrick made a habit of cooking their evening meal of fish over dancing flames. Coconut added a creamy flavour to the meal and Shana added her spice mix to the barbequed fish. Patrick's catch was improving and he had mastered the art of skewering the lightening quick fish with a spear given to him by Cathayan fishermen. It had not taken the boy long to learn and he made sure to sharpen and look after the valued weapon. A wood carver's daughter, Li-Ying meaning 'beautiful flower' began to join the pyrate and her son on their daily beach visits. Patrick was growing very tall like his mother and the tiny girl appeared doll-like as she stood next to the strong, heavily-set boy. The two children became very close and Patrick felt deep new feelings for his little friend.

Early one morning, Richie offered to take Patrick and his pretty little friend out for a swim. Shana always put her trust in Richie… he and Irish were the only two people who she would allow to be alone with her child. The sea was wonderfully calm and there was a light westerly breeze that day. Shana bought some food from a woman who prepared the most delicious seafood mixtures and sold them in a half coconut shell. Crabmeat, prawns and fish were some of the ingredients that made up the delicious recipe and Shana could detect a pinch of ginger and black pepper amid the subtly spicy flavours. Having relaxed for most of the day on the soft, pale sands Shana began to worry when the bright red sun began to descend beyond the hazy horizon. Richie had left very early with the two children and they had gone out on a fishing boat to visit a cove where there was said to be a shipwreck. Excited at the prospect of finding treasure the two children, who spoke little of each other's language, left full of energy and wearing huge smiles on their faces. Richie was a very strong swimmer and Patrick was also good despite his age and size. Li-Ying's parents were happy to allow the child to go swimming with the wealthy white man and seemed not to worry what time she returned. With a family of only girls, her father was keen for Li-Ying to marry a foreigner who would not expect a hefty dowry with his daughter's hand.

Hours passed while Shana sunbathed and relaxed on the beach until her instincts told her that the time had come to take a boat out to search for the party. She went to find Tripod and Irish. As usual, Tripod was in the nearest whorehouse and having sex with a tiny Cathayan girl. To Shana's surprise, the miniature woman seemed to be enjoying the rough pounding and raised opium-glazed eyes to gaze seductively at the tall western woman who had entered the tiny room. Tripod did not alter his rhythm when he heard his captain's call but shouted that he would join her as soon as he had 'shot his load.' Trying to stem her panic, Shana ran out of the opium den into the street. Seeing Irish standing with Jolly John who was bartering for opium with an old Cathayan merchant at a rickety mobile stall, she ran over to explain the emergency. Mothering instinct had completely taken over the warrior woman and she begged Irish to do something to help find her loved ones. As soon as the realization hit home, the two men acted immediately and Irish grabbed hold of the woman he adored. Looking deep into her tear-filled eyes the man who Shana had loved for so long calmed her spirit and she knew that she was no longer alone. Jolly John went to gather a search party whilst Irish and Shana returned to the beach where Richie had taken the children out in the boat.

The search party approached the beach of white sand fringed by a sun-kissed border of palm trees stretching along the shores of the vast blue ocean. What was usually a delightful scene appeared stark and barren that day. Shana dreaded the possibility that her child's and lover's body might soon be washed up on that very beach. Feeling the heat through the leather soles of her booted feet, Shana felt as though she was jogging in slow motion towards the group of fishermen who had gathered around something on the shore. Panic erupted within her as she approached the men. Dropping to her knees beside the body of her child, Shana screamed in sheer despair. Foreign words jumbled confused in her mind as she battled to translate the fishermen's language. Holding Patrick's head close to her chest, she rocked him like a baby. The pyrate queen pleaded piteously with anyone to help her son. Irish's voice became clear amongst the garbled foreign sounds and he was able to gently prize Patrick away from his terrified mother. Instinctively, Shana's hand reached for her pistol and the fishermen dispersed, running to safety. Blurred vision caused by the intense sunshine confused her even more as she tried to take in the stark reality of the situation.

If she lost her child, her life would be over... Irish pushed in steady rhythm on Patrick's tanned chest...

Nothing mattered to Shana anymore... a crack as the child's ribs snapped under pressure... screams as a single shot was fired... Irish's whispered prayers so loud... the next shot would be to her own temple... Wandering in circles around her friend as he fought to revive her child, the pyrate queen was beginning to lose control. Spinning around wildly as she was tackled from behind by an unseen assailant, Shana dropped one of her pistols after firing a second stray shot. Jolly John had seen the hysterical mother and acted on pure impulse, pulling her down onto the soft sand before disarming her. Whilst wrestling his captain into a safer position, the sailing master had taken a nasty slash from the dagger that Shana had managed to unsheathe.

As if he had sensed his mother's anguish, Patrick let out a horrible rasping breath and spewed seawater and dark brown bile onto Irish's shirt. Groaning from pain and exhaustion the child opened his blue eyes wide in fear as he scanned the faces staring down at him. Shouting for Richie and Li-Ying, the young boy tried to get up onto his feet but Irish held him securely. Patrick's struggling form was a piteous sight and Shana kneed the sailing master in the groin to be with her son. Poor Jolly John rolled around in shock and confusion but then laughed with relief as he heard the boy's cries for his Mama. Exhausted and terrified, Patrick slowly explained how he, Richie and Li-Ying had been swimming happily until the little girl had begun to panic, thrashing around in the water. Distressed and concerned about his missing friends, Patrick's desperation overcame him. Shock had set in, his skin paled and his body was wracked with uncontrollable waves of shivering. Despite the heat the boy's skin was covered in goose-pimples and his mother held him tightly in her arms. Patrick was taken to the safety of the house where they were staying in Hoi An. Only paper-thin walls separated the crew from their captain's room. The house-owner kindly allowed the crew to have a room next to Shana's in case she needed help with the child. Irish slept in the room where Richie and Shana had been staying. He kept watch over the sleeping mother and child until early morning sunlight streaked the wooden floor of the small space where they lay. An empty vial of opium lay close to the ornately carved screen that separated the rooms of the wealthy spice trader's home.

Shana had known of Ming Zhan's business within the spice trade from her early childhood but had not met the shrewd old man until this visit to his beautiful country. Having an extremely wide and in-depth knowledge of spices and aromatic oils, the woman had impressed the wise merchant. Ming had known of both Thomas and Elijah Culley and enjoyed years of mutually beneficial and successful trading with them. Respect rated high in Cathay culture and trust was essential within any business deal. Both Culleys had built up an excellent relationship with the Cathayan man and he felt bound to treat any member of the family with respect. Traditionally, occupations were passed from father to son in Cathay but Ming had been an exception to the rule. Unlike many Cathayan citizens living in the Ming period, he had been able to work in just one trade. Others had no choice but to work the land in the fertile season, finding a second occupation when times were lean. This variation of skills had developed naturally as suburban farmland blended into urban cities. It was not uncommon to find farms within city walls and Hoi An was one such city.

Irish scanned the pretty but functional room in their wealthy host's home and imagined how it would have been if he had summoned enough courage to tell Shana his feelings. Tears welled in the boatswain's eyes as he regretted his unnecessary caution. When he had seen his best friend and captain's beautiful eyes light up at the sight of Richie his heart had sunk under with a terrible weight of despair. He had failed to see that Shana was desperate for love... the right kind of love... Irish knew all too well that he would have been able to satisfy her in every way. Since she had met Richie, Shana had become a different woman. Free and unashamedly lustful, sensual beyond measure; the woman was simply perfect in Irish's eyes. No jealousy had warped the man's mind and he had felt happy that Shana was in love with Richie, but now he sat and pondered an impossible problem. He had always liked Richie and was glad that a fellow Irish man had been the one to capture Captain Culley's heart, but what had happened to him? Irish felt sad that Shana had taken opium again. Richie had helped her kick the habit since they had been reunited and it had not been easy. A disaster such as this was the worst imaginable event and Irish knew that Shana was unable to survive it alone. After satisfying himself that Patrick was sound asleep and safe in his mother's arms, Irish left the room.

Outside the temperature was still warm but the atmosphere close and oppressive. Streets bustled with life as people enjoyed their night-time activities. Makeshift stalls offered paper lanterns in all sizes, shapes and colours. They lit a long line of trading pitches in a seemingly never-ending street market. Sailors from overseas loomed tall above the small Cathayan people, their heads bobbing up and down in groups within the stream of market-goers. Wealthy merchants proudly paraded their miniature, doll-like wives with exotic tiny feet that had been squeezed into elaborately-embroidered shoes. Irish noted that a token wife had no more control over her body than she had over her own destiny. Tottering unsteadily along, taking little footsteps and balancing themselves with lace parasols, finely dressed merchants' wives lived only to please their husbands. Cruel foot-binding of young female children kept their feet incredibly small. In Cathayan culture this epitomised feminine beauty, virtue, and social status. Lost in deep thought the troubled pyrate noticed a double-door guarded by two huge eunuchs, arms crossed and clad in gloriously embroidered silk costumes. Without a second thought, Irish entered Madame Ying's well-known establishment and felt the cool air from hand held fans wafting his way.

Two delightfully pretty young girls approached him taking his large hands in theirs. Leading him along an ornately decorated entrance hall to a small room where two other girls were waiting, kneeling on identical purple silk cushions. The first two prostitutes passed him a card then tottered out of the room. Prostitution flourished as wealthy officials regularly visited their mistresses and quite openly kept concubines. The Ming government encouraged registered brothels like Madame Ying's, taking a tidy percentage of the courtesans' earnings in taxes. Cathay's prostitution ring enjoyed a steady income from their own citizens but also provided their foreign visitors with an excellent service, creating a flourishing and valued trade.

As Irish lost himself in an opium-induced dream world he lay back on the soft cushions and allowed the drugs to unburden his busy mind. Drawing the welcome substance deep into his lungs, stress fell away and emotional pain was quickly replaced by a sense of warmth and contentment. As the small women's high but soothingly mellow voices faded, Irish felt his penis harden as his senses became more sensitive to touch. Drifting in a whirlwind of sensory delight the tall, handsome man let the two women pleasure his tanned, muscular body in ways that he had never allowed before. Thinking only of Shana, Irish fantasized about being with his perfect woman, feeling ultimate ecstasy as both girls took turns riding their gorgeous client. Whilst one served the pyrate the other stroked and pleasured her colleague as he fondled her small, perfect breasts. Irish suddenly erupted deep inside one of the prostitutes as she bounced her tiny frame on top of him, fast and hard. Groaning in ecstasy, the woman's slanted brown eyes narrowed mischievously as she giggled with her pretty playmate. Climbing off to allow the other girl to take her turn to mount the still erect but sticky organ, the elegant woman straddled Irish's face. His tongue slipped inside the silky soft lips of her cunnie. Facing one another the two Asian beauties delighted in touching each other's bodies as they reached climax together over and over again. A wonderfully free feeling of lust, love and total, guilt-free pleasure filled Irish as he played voyeur to the delightfully seductive women who were intent on pleasuring each other as well as the client. The smaller of the two girls shivered as the strong muscles of her vagina squeezed in orgasmic pulsation. Looking down into Irish's kind eyes, her pupils widened as she continued to grind her firm young body against his pelvis.

All of Irish's problems and inhibitions had been put aside and he enjoyed twenty four hours of pure bliss.

After he left the 'welcoming parlour', he was led from room to room, where highly-skilled sex workers waited offering a new experience every time. Relaxed and satisfied, a totally different man emerged from the steam-room... the up-tight and worried person who had entered the establishment the previous day was no more. One particularly erotic beauty with impossibly miniscule feet, encased in purple silk slippers embroidered with lotus blossom, stood politely waiting for her valued guest. Following strict Cathayan custom, she bowed before the rejuvenated man and then tottered daintily forward towards a pair of exquisite silk curtains. She parted them to reveal the largest room of the house.

Inside, the house's famous 'piece de resistance' was in full swing with an orgy of oil-covered bodies writhing together in perfect sensual rhythm as if their movements had been choreographed. A misty cloud of opium smoke formed constantly changing patterns above the mass of people who were engaging in wild, sexual acts. Men, women, young girls and boys enjoyed each other's bodies in a scene that Irish could no longer resist. He approached a pretty girl who was being serviced on all fours by a blond man. She had caught his eye and the two shared a drug-induced connection as their eyes met. Parting her small, full lips to reveal her wet tongue, she traced it over the upper lip in invitation. Someone passed Irish an opium pipe and he took a long, deep drag as he walked forward. Dropping to his knees, he put his mouth against the pretty girl's. After blowing the potent mouthful of smoke into her mouth, he stood up and took hold of her long, silky black hair guiding her gently to give him fellatio. Whilst watching her skilful lips moving in pleasure, he felt hands begin to touch and fondle his muscular body. After ejaculating, Irish collapsed onto a bed of comfortable cushions and closed his eyes.

Later back aboard the Slayer following a satisfying visit to the most famous brothel in Cathay, Jolly John began to rant about how disgusting the rich Cathayan men were in their sexual practices. Boy love was accepted and viewed as something that men should indulge in to prove a man's elite status. Young male catamites were able to make more money than female concubines. Poor Irish found himself in the middle of a full-blown argument between Tripod and the sailing master but had no recollection of how he had come to be back aboard ship.

Blissfully unaware of Irish's visit to Madame Ying's, Shana lay on the mat holding her traumatised child in her arms. The worldly-wise captain fingered the Tarot card and wondered why she had kept it for so long. Her inherent superstitious nature meant that she was still unable to destroy the card that Eileen had turned over so long ago. Folding it carefully and replacing it in the silk kerchief, Shana tucked the package safely inside her stays... she reached for another vial of opium... stifling a desperate need to cry she put out her tongue and welcomed the bitter opiate taste. She hoped that the drug would dull her pain and eliminate the image of Li-Ying's parents when they had learned of her disappearance. The girl's mother had been sick with worry, terrified that one of her daughter's might be dead but her cold-hearted husband had merely asked to be compensated for the loss of his child. Shana longed to forget the dreadful screams of the mother as her husband dragged her home.

From Hoi An Shana took the Slayer to explore possible places where she and Patrick could settle. Hiring new men to man the ship alongside the few special friends who had decided to take a break from pyracy, she planned to wait a while in Cathay in the hope that her lover would return. Amagoa Island seemed the perfect choice to settle for a while. The picturesque paradise isle provided the strange little pyrate gang with a peaceful home environment but also offered the choice of a busier atmosphere in the traders' markets. The experience of slow-paced island life made everyone feel lucky just to be alive. Even though trade was good, the settlers who included Portuguese traders and native Cathayan people alike, appreciated a quieter existence away from busier trading communities in mainland Cathay. Amongst the wares traded from Amagoa Island were silk, timber, sandalwood, eaglewood, gold, ceramics, ivory, cinnamon, sugar, pepper, dried areca nuts, tortoise shells, fish and sea-swallows' nests. Shana began a prosperous trade in arms and Patrick learned all there was to know about weaponry and guns. Building a happy new life together on the island paradise, Shana and her extended clan settled for a year in the vain hope of Richie's return. It never happened. When Patrick turned five on the thirteenth of November, Shana and her surrogate family made a joint decision to leave the island and return to a perilous life at sea.

The night of Patrick's party was great fun and everyone had a wonderful time. His mother had arranged for a Buddhist storyteller to entertain the guests on the local beach around a fire. A full moon lit smiling faces as they listened to an ancient tale told by the gentle, wrinkle-faced man. His calming voice almost sang the enchanting words. Following tradition the long, exciting yarn had been divided into four chapters that each took half an hour to tell. Listeners were encouraged to drink whilst the storyteller created a wonder-filled ambience of fantasy, keeping his audience eager to hear the next chapter. A small boy with a collection bag wandered around the audience taking donations during every break whilst local women brought all kinds of delicious foods for the guests.

As dusk set in with its gift of a delightful sky, dimly lit with exquisite shades of burnt amber and deepest blood red, the dying sun dropped beneath the sea line. Guests went home contented and happy leaving Shana, Patrick and their few closest friends sitting around a night fire. Well known for her unpredictable and often impulsive nature, Captain Culley stood to address her make-shift family. Proposing a toast to her lover and sadly missed friend, Richie Conachy, Shana told her men that her next plan was to sail to port Keelung in Dongfan. There, a barbaric Cathayan pyrate captain, Lin Dao-cian was committing atrocities amongst the indigenous population. Word was that he had a trio of junks that kept close to the coastline, sneaking from village to village raiding, looting and slaughtering men, women and children. The tyrant had managed to make Keelung a pyrate base and Shana planned to return to her reign over the seas with an unexpected attack on fiends that preyed on innocent civilians.

Having hired a crew of Cathayan and Portuguese sailors to man the Slayer, Irish, John, Moses and Tripod had everything ready for their impulsive leader. Rowing out to meet Jock who, as master gunner had preferred to stay with the majestic vessel, the sailing master helped prepare her for battle. The Slayer was soon to undergo a huge test of strength and her power of defense. Her captain and crew were keen to take the challenge. Little Patrick was eager to try out his favourite birthday gift, a custom-made pair of pistols, their wooden handles inlaid with mother of pearl... the time had come for the Slayer to fight again.

Reaching Lin Dao-cian's hideout in the early hours of a still, warm day, Captain Culley and her men fired a rally of cannon fire at the junks that lay unmanned in a cove close to the pyrates' camp. Shana had already sent a raiding party ashore whilst Lin's men slept. Blood flowed onto the silver sands as throats were cut while the pyrates lay in drunken slumber. When Jock was sure that the junks had been damaged beyond hope of providing the means of escape for the murderous cowards, he signalled to shore. Most of Lin's pyrates had been slain during the initial assault as they had been taken unawares and unprepared for attack. Unfortunately their leader, and undoubtedly many of his men, were no where to be found. Shana and her men split into three groups and began the hunt. Deciding to stay close to the camp with Irish, Tripod and Jolly John, Shana waited with pistols loaded ready for attack. Patrick stood next to Irish, the top of his head barely reaching the tall man's thigh. The boy was tall for his years but a miniature figure in the shadow of the man who he admired most. With his weapons tied securely onto various parts of his elaborate costume, Patrick looked every bit the heir to the coveted pyrate throne.

Shana could not help but smile at Flint as he sat sulking at Patrick's feet. Chastised earlier for climbing a palm tree without permission, the tiny ape was not impressed. Luckily, Patrick had discovered him sitting, hidden amongst the large leaves that formed a wonderful natural canopy over the hard-shelled coconut fruits, keeping a lookout for enemies. One of Flint's favourite pastimes was to sit on a branch awaiting an unsuspecting passer-by. Armed with a heavy coconut, Flint would drop the missile onto his target's head then keep totally still, perfectly camouflaged against the pale brown mottled bark. He had yet to be discovered as the culprit and only a few knew of his antics. The ape had no idea how dangerous it would have been had he bombarded this enemy with coconuts! Hearing a sudden hail of shots Irish grabbed the little ape and, to his amazement, threw him back up into the palm tree. The little fiend quickly scuttled out of sight chattering his disapproval before disappearing. Patrick would have to wait and see if Flint was going to help in the fight.

No sooner had Shana's group taken their defensive positions than their enemies appeared, storming out of the tropical bushes and lunging toward their prey. Captain Culley and her men were prepared for the onslaught and stood in a circle, cutlasses drawn and trigger fingers ready. Patrick was experiencing the first skirmish that he had ever been permitted to join and fight in. He felt no fear, only excitement as he awaited his mother's orders. Standing together, whilst Lin's men attacked them with ferocity, each member of the small group managed to pick off an aggressor as they hurled their clumsy bulk at the well-organised ring of defense. Adrenalin pumped around Patrick's little body as he shot at and hit a hefty pyrate in the forehead. On impact, the lead made a sickening sound as it broke through bone.

The din was dreadful as the attackers yelled and screamed in panic until all were dead. Flint made a great job of his missile drops and managed to split open two enemy heads. One weakened a man but the other killed a short skinny pyrate stone dead! Managing to stay focused and concentrate on an accurate aim, the little monkey screamed triumphantly at each successful hit. When Patrick took a blow to his temple poor Flint's protective instinct finally kicked in and he began to scream hysterically. Realising that his mistress's boy was in terrible danger he left the safety of his hiding place and scampered down to Patrick's rescue. On reaching solid ground, he put his tiny hands over his eyes and peeped through them gingerly, shaking his head violently. Shooting panicked glances at Shana and back towards the group of aggressors, the nimble ape acted without further thought. Jumping lightly onto his shoulder, he held Patrick's dimpled hand and comforted his disquieted master. Thankfully, Micken had stayed aboard with Smith and Jock otherwise all hell would have broken loose! The ape and parrot had become very close and were overtly sensitive to each other's emotions. Flint's fear was obvious and Micken would have reacted in utter panic.

The ugly fight that took place on the paradise beach between Captain Lin Dao-cian's men and Captain Shana Culley's gang went on for over half an hour. When Lin was the last of Shana's enemies standing, she broke away from the ring and attacked the tyrant with such vicious anger that she took the trophies from her victim before leaving him for dead. Lin lay bollockless and dying beside one of his men who Shana kicked onto his back so that she could untie his trews. The last thing that the feisty pyrate queen expected to find beneath her boning knife was a neat little pussy!

In mock anger laced with secret respect Captain Culley slapped the Cathayan pyrate wench around the face making the young girl as angry as hell fire. Sheer hatred filled her narrow, brown eyes. Screaming at the woman straddled over her small but muscular body, the Cathayan girl only appeared to be about thirteen years of age. With intense rage, the pretty young woman spat and jabbered curses at her elder through gritted teeth. Shana was laughing so hard that she failed to notice the strong girl twist her slim, supple legs around hers in a vice-like grip. Before she knew it, Shana was flipped over with surprising speed and strength. Lying winded beneath the smug-looking child-woman, Shana regained composure and nodded at her opponent with respect and honour. In her mind, she felt glad that it had taken another woman to finally defeat her. Waiting for the sensation of cold metal to slice through her pretty throat, Shana's final thought was of her Patrick. The boy shouted loudly as he leapt onto the small woman's back and bit into the back of her head. Driving his blade into her ribs as he spat out a mouthful of scalp and black hair, Patrick wrapped his muscular little legs tightly around the Cathayan warrior's hips. Screaming a threatening cry, the injured woman lost her grip on the pyrate queen and rolled over to tackle the boy. Pulling out his knife, Patrick steadied himself to prepare for another strike. Shana's strong hand reached up to grab her son's wrist and the Cathayan girl stood back. Her eyes wide in shock, the young warrior bowed in front of Shana in a gesture of respect and surrender.

Untying the bandana from around her forehead, the young woman retied it firmly around her bleeding wound and retrieved her weapons. She had fought hard and skilfully but had lost to a western child. Her pride and honour had been marred beyond repair. Drawing her short sword, the slight woman dropped to her knees. Shana stood up quickly and pulled Patrick close to her.

Together, they watched the child-woman plunge the blade deep into her stomach. Falling forward, the beautiful girl's eyes looked at Patrick for a split second that was to haunt him forever. Mouthing silent words that neither witness would have been able to understand, even if they had been spoken clearly, the dying woman slumped forward onto the wide blade driving it even deeper into her body. As the bloodied tip emerged from the brave woman's back, Shana jumped up and took hold of her long silky black hair. Drawing her dagger, she traced the sharp blade from ear to ear, ending any prolonged agony for the gallant young woman.

Dropping to her knees next to the small lifeless body, Shana disarmed the female pyrate. Captain Culley would ensure that her strongest and bravest opponent would be remembered with honour by the display of her weapons. This wonderful warrior woman's death would not be forgotten, at least in the lifetime of Shana or Patrick. Two appropriate Latin words entered her mind as she looked at her own reflection in the gleaming blade that had been used in a most honourable ancient Cathayan ritual... 'Cedo nulli'... 'I yield to no-one.'

Chapter 19

Tripod's Torment

The mountainous island of Bali was the Slayer's next port-of-call. This isle of seemingly perpetual happiness did not disappoint the tired crew. They were met by small native women who looked like dolls, their delicate features painted with the prettiest colours imaginable. The costumes they wore to welcome foreign visitors were grass skirts decorated with shells. Rows of pearls hung loosely around their necks drawing attention to their soft, bare breasts. As dancers swayed their beautiful, child-like bodies, sailors watched with mouths agape.

Hot rays of sun streamed through the jungle canopy creating a spectacular lightshow around the undulating forms. It felt like a dream to Tripod as he was helped ashore by two of his shipmates. Beads of sweat formed on his pale face but soon streamed down onto his chest in the intense, unforgiving heat of a midday sun. Wafting palm leaf fans, local children gave their visitors occasional comfort from the close, stifling heat that they were unused to. Flint wore an impossibly wide grin, baring his sharp white teeth for the women whose breasts and brown nipples made his little prick stand to attention. Contrary to his normal reaction, Tripod behaved totally out of character showing not even the slightest sign of arousal. Shana was very concerned about her weary friend and decided to propose that they stay a while in the heavenly tropical location. Flint and

Micken had already made their presence known and were enjoying attention from the young dancing girls.

Crickets trilled their calls from the cooler forest land that appeared so inviting. Rustling noises came from within the deep, lush tropical shrubs and greenery and, having gained his mother's approval, Patrick scuttled off into the depths of the forest wonderland. Flint quickly shadowed his human friend and Irish was not far behind the agile ape. Micken made a good effort at flying, flapping his bright green wings twice as many times than necessary. After much effort and panic the comical parrot made a successful landing on Shana's shoulder. Cawing with relief and also disapproval that Patrick and Flint had decided to desert him, Micken sulked in his mistress's company.

The night soon drew in and everyone was grateful to feel a quenching sea breeze. A large fire burned on the fine silver sands and a contented group of pyrates enjoyed hospitality and entertainment from their hosts. Shana had sent for the local healer in the afternoon and the woman arrived whilst everyone was eating fish around the fire. Shana and Irish carried the very sick man into a beachside hut and the woman began her work. The elderly healer had a small pipe that she lit and offered to her patient. So many sores had encrusted Tripod's dry lips that he found it difficult to open them and allow the thin stem to enter his ulcerated mouth. Wide blood-shot eyes showed the agony that the pyrate was in as he sucked in the heady smoke. Mere minutes passed before the man relaxed and laid back his scab-riddled head looking around him as if he was seeing everything for the first time. Shana sat back and crossed her legs awaiting the healer's next move. The older woman nodded at the pyrate captain and mimicked her actions. Singing softly, the healer held the enhanced pipe to Tripod's lips and allowed him to inhale its substance greedily. Very soon, all three people inside the small hut were stoned out of their heads but the wise woman showed no sign of halting the treatment. Shana was more than happy to stay with her whilst she tended to her friend and allowed her mind and body to fall into a wonderfully therapeutic, drug-induced state.

Irish stood watching Shana sleeping soundly next to Tripod who seemed to have gained a little more colour in his complexion. Irish was as concerned as Shana about the state of his lustful friend's health. The usually able sailor, Tripod had never made any fuss since Irish had known him and was not one to complain. They had worked alongside each other at sea for many years and Irish silently prayed that they both had many more adventures before them. Stirring slightly, Shana rolled over revealing a sand-covered cheek. Stifling a laugh Irish used his cotton shirt sleeve and carefully flicked the rough grains from her smooth skin. Tripod snorted loudly, eyelids flickering in his sleep. Irish lowered his face to Shana's and felt her warm breath on his lips. He had never felt such a depth of love for another being. Lingering for a while, the enamoured man allowed his senses to take over his entire body. A surge of mixed emotions swept over him and he felt immense pleasure in the presence of this wildly sensual woman, but sadness overwhelmed his delight.

If only he had possessed the courage! Inwardly cursing himself he allowed a whimper to escape his lips. Tripod suddenly sat bolt upright and looked straight at him. Completely taken by surprise Irish rolled quickly away from his captain. The sick man smiled knowingly, his cracked lips splitting from the sudden tension. Without saying a word the two men shared a melancholic moment. Irish stood inside the small hut looking down at his two friends who meant more to him than any blood relative. As if she had somehow sensed the intense misery felt by her two friends, Shana awoke and sat bolt upright, pistols at the ready. Relaxing her trigger finger when she was sure that no danger lurked, she rubbed her eyes and looked over at her patient. Her face lit up when she saw a great improvement in Tripod and the three burst out laughing at his morning glory that pointed skyward beneath the cloth of his trews.

Taking the Slayer out on regular local raids of passing trade vessels, Captain Culley and her crew gained a reputation amongst the Balinese people as local heroes. The African people who were rescued from the cruel bonds of slavery enjoyed the hospitality on the small island and a few of the men decided to settle there and take wives. Culturally, the two peoples differed immensely but their laid-back nature was uncannily similar. African-Balinese love matches seemed to work and soon Shana was delighted to see beautiful offspring from the mixed-race union. Other emancipated slaves decided to move on or return to their homeland, but none ever forgot the pyrate clan who had helped them regain their freedom. Captain Culley became a folk hero and was loved by the populous in that part of the world. Revered for her incredible resolve and bravery in the fight against white imperial power, Captain Culley continued the battle on behalf of the oppressed black and oriental races. In her arrogance and lust for power Queen Elizabeth continued to encourage privateers to use the

African people as a commodity. Even English citizens had become more accepting of slavery and had, of late, suspended their disapproval. The Queen of England had won over the masses and her bribes of extra holidays and propaganda had been effective yet again.

Between plunders, Shana and her gang enjoyed the family life, entertaining and being entertained by Patrick and his growing menagerie. Flint had met a female ape on one of his jungle forays. Everyone soon noticed that she had started to walk in a particularly odd way. Her small back legs bowed outwards as though she was carrying something between them. Tripod joked that his little friend had been observing him during his sexual exploits and the poor girl had experienced hours of non-stop intercourse. Shana became more worried and decided to check the female ape's nether regions in case of infection. 'Sparky' as the men had named her did not look at all well. It turned out that she had indeed been suffering from a nasty tear in her vagina. Incredibly, she allowed Patrick to apply a soothing salve, that his mother had mixed, to the infected area. Within a few days the wound had healed and Patrick and Sparky had become best of friends. Flint was also grateful to the lad for his help in his mate's recovery and made a habit of taking him thank you gifts. Afraid of hurting the sensitive monkey's feelings, Patrick stashed the offerings in a small chest that he kept in the cabin aboard the Slayer. Micken became over-protective of his little ape friends and started to keep guard when they needed some private time together.

Patrick and Irish disappeared on regular treks into the lush tropical rainforests. With quills, inks and parchment in their leather bags and numerous weapons hanging by elaborate ribbons and ropes tied to their belts, the pair of unlikely artists made quite an impression on the local people. Children and adults alike enjoyed being shown the results of the artists' work and on their return, many began to ask if they could keep the beautiful pictures of their island. Images of the sacred volcanoes proved most popular and began to appear alongside other sacred offerings on shrines around the captivating island. Irish's immaculate drawings of ancient temples were exquisite. Shana was always mesmerized by her close friend's artistic skills as his pictures had such an alluring quality. Everyone who saw them felt the need to look deep into the compositions, relishing the smallest detail. By recreating scenes that featured farmers working in lush, green paddy fields or an exotic beauty performing traditional dances, the skilled artist was able to capture the very essence of the charming island. His little apprentice worked happily alongside him making a brave rendition of his idol's works and the local people loved to watch the boy draw. During the day, the creative pair would wander off into the wilderness for hours, to return each evening exhausted yet buzzing with news of their daily discoveries. Once Patrick came running back to report that one among the cluster of volcanoes in the middle of the island was bubbling angrily. According to the local people the dragon god who lived inside had not shown his displeasure for a long time. Many of the villagers expected the volcano to erupt soon but assured their concerned visitors that their holy images would subdue his unrest for the meantime. Many would gather around a huge fire on the beach awaiting the artists' return. Irish and Patrick would then display their work on the sand for all to see. Natives enjoyed sharing their knowledge and history of their island home and the pyrates were keen to learn everything about this newfound paradise. Tripod enjoyed the company of several dancers and seemed to have perked up a bit... literally... so Jock kept telling him!

Irish, Jock and Patrick ventured inland to experience more of the island paradise and they were glad that they had been inquisitive. Following their young guide, who had spent the previous week harvesting rice crops from the terraced paddy fields, the visitors enjoyed the scenery. They were eager to learn about traditional Balinese rural life and the sculpted rice fields that had been fashioned into the contours of the landscape. They laughed as the guide explained how, as he worked barefoot harvesting the rice, tiny food-fish in the water nibbled at his toes. In the evening, he would feel a slight sense of revenge as he mixed the same fish into his bowl of rice. Almost immediately after leaving the lush green paddy fields the exploration party found themselves back in the luscious Sangeh rainforest, which was sacred to the people of Bali. It was forbidden to fell or even chip bark from the trees that grew there. As apes lived within the sanctuary, they too were deemed to be sacred and could not be harmed. An overhead canopy of healthy vegetation created the perfect shelter from a blazing sun, as the enthusiastic group continued on their trek. Monkeys could be seen in the foliage of trees, leaping from branches high above them.

Within an hour, the group stopped to eat at the heart of the tiny island where plantations grew crops that flourished in the cool mountain air. Coffee, bananas, coconuts and rice were the most prevalent. The pyrates' guide was proud to explain the irrigation system that he had helped construct by diverting small streams that flowed from the mountains. As they continued along the ancient route, their journey took them through isolated villages and past spectacular temples. In every temple the guide pointed out intricately carved and brightly painted statues of a turtle and two dragons which symbolised the creation of the world. Patrick's favourite temple was the Puser Jagat temple which had been built under the shade of a huge Banyan tree. Two more temples stood in the heart of the forest and another at the edge. One of these temples had been built inside a cave and thousands of bats fluttered restlessly around their heads. Finally, with perfect timing, the guide led his group back onto the peaceful beach where their friends awaited their return.

A stunning sunset lit the dusk skies and the wonderful Pura Luhur Uluwatu temple, set on a huge rock of black coral, created the most awe-inspiring silhouette. The spectacular view brought tears to Shana's eyes as she stood with her son and some of her closest friends. It was as though the sky had been set alight with amazing colours offering a masterpiece of its own, paying homage to the guardian spirits of the sea. In total contrast, the sea seemed to be accepting the offering by complementing the delectable reflection with her aqua and turquoise calm waters. The Slayer even appeared to be content within the scene as Patrick and Irish began a joint painting to record the memorable moment. The palm-lined beach curved gently out of sight and night gradually crept in. Another blissful day had passed by on the tranquil shores of Bali. Shana, Irish and Patrick built a sand stone temple on the beach in the firelight and the exhausted child slept soundly in his mother's arms.

It was a sad day when the pyrates decided to leave Bali and Shana took gifts of paintings, intricate carvings, woven goods and basketry back to the Slayer. Patrick had been given more gifts than he could manage and the men helped him to load every one into the small rowing boat. The child's favourite gift was a miniature traditional Balinese shrine that housed five tiny effigies carved from ivory. Patrick and Irish had made sure to leave offerings at some of the many shrines dotted all over the island. Their gifts would remain long after the well-loved visitors had left. Shana and her friends hoped to return some day but something told her that she would never again set foot on Bali's soft, white sands. Determinedly, she ignored the eerie feeling in her bones.

The miniature shrine occupied pride of place high on a purpose-built plinth in the Culley's cabin aboard the Slayer. Patrick continued to respect the gods that the small figures were meant to represent. When at play, Flint and Sparky took the part of the gods whilst Patrick and Micken solemnly presented them with offerings of food and trinkets. Unfortunately, the power began to go to the male monkey's head so Patrick put a stop to that type of role-play. Micken often received a back-handed swipe until one day he had taken enough and embarrassed the egotistical monkey by tweaking his penis in front of his mate! To everyone's relief, the pair never fought again.

A refreshed looking Tripod worked the rigging on the main deck as the distant sound of rumbling thunder echoed in the air. A cool breeze came before the rain and the skies darkened above the ship as it was tossed by strong waves. Heading for South African shores with plans to make a short stop at Madagascar, Shana and her able crew prepared to battle a heavy storm. As a strong wind took the ship away from the island that would be missed by everyone aboard, Patrick obeyed Irish's orders. He performed the duties expected of him well, but could not help try to visualise how lemurs looked with their vertical ramrod tails that Irish had vividly described.

Chapter 20

Patrick Claims his First Trophy

Deep in concentration, Patrick's tongue traced his upper lip as his fingers guided the slim nib of his mother's quill to form the letters of his name. Extremely dextrous like his mother, he had learned to write simple words in the most exquisite script. Dipping the nib into the purple ink pot with great care, the able child hummed a tune accompanied by Micken's tuneful whistle. Shana often left Patrick alone in the cabin for an hour or two when she was needed above deck. Flint, Sparky, Micken and the wise boy would while away the hours contentedly in each others' company.

Following a very brief stop spent collecting fresh fruit and fish, the Slayer left Madagascar at noon and was heading towards West Africa at full sail. Disappointed at not having spotted a single lemur, Patrick attempted drawings of the creatures that Irish had described. At the rate of knots they were travelling, Irish expected to reach the Cape Coast before the next full moon. The heat of the midday sun scorched down on the lone ship that was travelling at full speed. Shana had heard that a slave ship was nearby and she planned to head them off along the Cape Coast, board the ship, grant the slaves their freedom, then sink the floating prison. The final leg of their journey would take them back to Ireland via Portugal where Shana planned to sell her majestic ship in exchange for a briganteen. She already knew that she would have no trouble finding a buyer for the popular transport vessel.

The unexpected attack came as a shock to Captain Culley but Irish had felt that their fortune had been far too good to be true. Surely the pyrate band was due for a catastrophe. A Spanish ship had appeared from nowhere and the Slayer shook from the impact of so many cannonballs. Bright sunlight had temporarily blinded the lad on watch that hot midday and the lighter Spaniard's craft had approached the Slayer at great speed, almost without a sound. As the sea was relatively calm, many of the crew were relaxing below decks in the cool shade. A sudden jolt startled Patrick and feathers flew as Micken fell off his perch. Flint instinctively leapt onto the boy's shoulder and held on tight as he ran out on deck, grabbing his sword as he went. Seeing Irish fighting two smaller men at the same time, Patrick calmly scanned the area looking for his mother. Cannons fired simultaneously as the Spanish vessel sailed alongside her target.

The hardy Slayer ploughed steadily through the waves as her crew fought off the assailants one by one. Blood spilled onto the decks as they cut the enemy down. Flint hid his eyes and jumped up and down at the sight of John Smith duelling with a bearded Spaniard. Suddenly producing a flintlock from behind his back, he aimed low and fired a shot straight into his opponent's fat belly. No sooner had he grabbed another pistol, then another Spaniard jumped on him from behind. The blow knocked John forward into a stack of barrels, one of which he grabbed and hurled at the other man. Splitting his head wide open, John followed through with his sword, stabbing the man under the ribs. A fire had been started near the main mast so Patrick grabbed a leather bucket of sand and ran towards the flickering flames. In an instant, Patrick had reached the fire and thrown on the sand, quenching the flames. As the nimble boy took flight, a cannonball whistled through the air towards the middle of the foremast, hitting its target perfectly. Diving past another skirmish between Jock and a tall sailor, Patrick managed to hack the enemy's Achilles tendon, causing him to stumble. Glancing quickly backwards just in time to see his Scottish friend drive a short axe through the injured man's head, Patrick took cover beneath the cockboat. Squeals of anguish caught his attention and he glanced back toward the main mast in search of Flint. Leaping over the heads and backs of friend and foe, the little ape darted in a haphazard zigzag toward his friend, eyes bolting from their sockets. What happened next appeared in slow motion to the excited child as he recognised the familiar voice. Irish's warning yell made Patrick turn just in time. Responding immediately to the alert, he just managed to jump clear of the small boat before it was smashed beneath the weighty sail. There was a deafening crash as the felled mast crashed into the cockboat where the boy had taken cover. Adrenalin pumped around his veins as his head buzzed with excitement and renewed energy then suddenly he remembered Flint. To his relief, he saw a little furry body hurtling through the air above him as the frantic creature sprang from rope to rope. Patrick's hearing had dulled and an eerie, echoing amalgamation of sound filled his ears as his mind took in the chaotic scene. Had he not been distracted by Irish's warning cry, Patrick would have been crushed beneath the weighty sails.

A nervous laugh escaped his lips as he watched Flint pass straight by him and run towards Irish. Unable to take in the whole complex incident at once, the boy's attention skipped from one place to another in a surreal moment of suspended time. Stark realisation hit him like a sudden death blow, Patrick let out a blood-curdling howl as he saw his guardian lower his defence. If only Irish had not stopped to warn him of the falling mast, he would not have turned away from his aggressor. Flint's high-pitched scream was somehow piercing enough to restore Patrick's hearing and the scene returned to normal speed. It had all happened so quickly that the boy felt as if he had suddenly woken from a dreadful nightmare... if only that had been true... The Spanish sailor plunged his dagger into the side of Irish's neck, severing his carotid artery. Falling back onto the gun-deck the brave man fired his pistol, the shot taking a good part of his enemy's ear. Flint landed in perfect time on top of the dying man's leg and scuttled up to his handsome face. Panic-stricken and devastated, the tiny creature clasped his hands to his head in despair as he looked down at Irish. Patrick ran as fast as he could and landed on his knees next to the man who he had known as a father.

Irish's eyes slowly closed and rolled back into their sockets and it was a tragic sight to see the child holding his dying friend. Unable to accept that he was going to die, Patrick gently pulled his eyelids open as he had when his companion feigned sleep. Looking deeply into Irish's glazed eyes, desperate for him to become alert once more, Patrick spoke softly, 'Tum on 'Eye-wiss'! We donna till 'em!'. Gaining no response Patrick suddenly feared the worst and took the big man's face in his hands shaking his head roughly. When he failed to wake the muscular man who had been like a father to him, his face reddened with hatred and anger.

In a moment the vengeful boy had leapt to his feet and climbed the rigging until he was positioned right above the pyrate who had slain Irish. Gritting his teeth together and roaring like a maniacal beast, Patrick drew his short sword and flung himself into the air. Landing on top of the unsuspecting man, the wild child bit into the side of his thick neck and managed to tear away a substantial piece of tough flesh. Only just missing the jugular vein, Patrick head-butted the man on the temple, sending him into a giddy spin. The huge man cursed loudly and blindly jabbed his sabre above his head, trying to dislodge Patrick. Feeling no fear whatsoever, Shana's son kept a strong hold of his target who was battling to rid himself of his burden. Riding his victim like a wild horse, Patrick's little body thrashed as he kicked and squeezed with all his might. No amount of effort would bring the furious man down. Blood seeped over Patrick's clothes as the pyrate finally succeeded in throwing his aggressor to the deck. To the boy, no-one else existed but the enemy in front of him and he felt no fear, only loathing for the man who had taken Irish from him. Summoning all the strength he could muster from deep within, the small child lunged himself forward with a final burst of energy. Whether it was by sheer fluke or skilful aim no-one will ever know. The sharp point of Patrick's sword that had been lovingly forged and hammered by his deceased friend penetrated his opponent's thigh. His face was a picture as the shocked man realised that he had been stabbed in the femoral artery by a babe!

Immediately withdrawing his weapon, Patrick thrust the double-edged sword into his victim over and over again. Then, absolutely saturated with blood, the child stood on top of the dead man and jumped on his ribcage. The sickening crack of breaking bones went unheard amidst the chaotic din. As the breathless child's leaps gradually slowed, his legs buckled beneath him and he fell astride the man who he had just killed. Physically exhausted but with his heart and mind still fierce with burning hatred, Patrick burst into floods of tears. His mother's screams did not register in his busy mind as he tore a hole into the dead man's breeches. Echoing sounds of gunfire and muffled yells were all that the devastated boy could hear as he grabbed hold of the testicular organs. 'Patrick Culley! Unhand those bollocks this instant!' Shana's disappointment was obvious by the tone of her trembling voice as she bounded over to her son. Time and time again she had warned Patrick never to mutilate any corpse unless it was his own kill. Then and only then would he be allowed to take a trophy from his victim.

The youngster had always shown a morbid curiosity in battle and was allowed to watch fights from a suitably safe place when aboard his mother's ship. Shana was strict with 'ship rules' and her men were under strict orders to protect Patrick with their lives. If anyone refused, they would simply not be welcome to serve with Captain Culley. Despite her protective motherly instinct, Shana made sure that her unruly son was given the freedom that she had enjoyed as a child. Independence and stubbornness were the strongest amongst the many complex traits in the Culley clan and Patrick had inherited his fair share of both. Quick to learn self defence and keen to learn the art of swordsmanship, the boy took everything in his stride and never once became frightened when witnessing combat. On the contrary, the lad longed for the day when he could join his peers who fought bravely and violently for his mother's just cause.

Just as his sharp sword sliced through his victim's flesh to cut away his first trophy, Shana grabbed her shocked son by the shoulders and shook his sore body until his crying ceased. Patrick felt numb and did not react at all when his mother slapped his muscular bottom hard. With each smack, Shana accentuated her grudge with words broken into syllables. 'Ye-ee-vil-tyke-I-told-ye-ter-stay-clear-of-scur-mish-es!' As if his senses had suddenly returned, Patrick winced at his mother's final blow and he released his bloody sword. Finally the shocked captain had vented her frustrations and was sure that her child had understood her message. As Patrick's protruding lower lip began to quiver, Shana broke down and cried with him. Having taken his rightful claim, Patrick timidly offered the trophy to his mother who ignored the prize and shot him a scornful glare. On hearing the unmistakable sound of Tripod's footsteps approaching from behind, Shana span round still clutching her child by the scruff of his neck. He shot a pleading look at his one-legged ally and regained his composure, waiting for the chance to break free from Shana's firm hold. With a determined look on his red, tear-stained face, Patrick Culley looked every bit the offspring of his fearless, daring and stubborn mother.

Yelling over the groans of the dead and dying, Tripod tried to defend the child, ''Tis not as it seems ma'am! Thy young 'un slayed yon lily-livered whoreson who finished Irish!' Wriggling free of his mother's grasp, Patrick took advantage of the moment and made his escape. Still gripping the bloodied ball-sack of the man who had murdered his best friend, Patrick scurried off towards where Irish had fallen. Shana's eyes bolted wide as she took in Tripod's tragic news and looked over to where he was pointing. Making out the bloodied body of her closest friend, Shana felt an all too familiar dread.

Catching up with her fleeing child, she swept him swiftly up into her arms and ran towards the stern. Her heart sank as she dropped to her knees beside Irish's corpse. Still holding his most cherished sword, Patrick jumped onto Irish's lifeless body, wrapping chubby little arms around his neck. Shana allowed her son to remain lying with his head resting on the chest of their mutually beloved friend. Prizing his little fist open to take the testicles, Shana walked away from her irreplaceable friend and soul brother with a heavy heart.

Alone in her cabin lit by a single dim oil lamp, the captain of the Slayer felt the weight of the world on her shoulders. The beautiful woman's eyes looked tired lately as she felt the effects of her hazardous life wearing her down. Having chosen a career that offered adventure, excitement and danger, she experienced turmoil and grief every time one of her trusted 'family' lost a life. Irish had given his life to save her child and she felt responsible yet unfathomably grateful for his valiant act of bravery. Eternally indebted to her friend, Shana wept bitterly as she prepared her son's first trophy. Pride filled her heart as she imagined how Irish would feel had he known that Patrick had gained his first kill. The design that she would help her brave little warrior mark permanently into the skin of his first victim was clear in her mind. Taking the very same quill used to write the Falcon's rules with the blood of her dying captain years ago, Shana wrote her companion's name on parchment. Above the word 'Irish', she wrote 'father' and under that, her son's own name. Taking a deep breath, Shana folded the parchment and began to prepare the skin so that Patrick could begin the decoration as soon as possible.

Out on the main deck, Patrick lay with his head on Irish's motionless chest. His small arms stretched around the tall man's neck, he slept peacefully. John Clark had covered them with fur pelts that he had collected from Iceland. Their value no longer seemed important. As a bright full moon lit the ink-black skies Shana sat awake in her cabin, worrying about her son. Risks had to be taken as a pyrate but she had always felt that she and Irish were invincible. The cold truth had suddenly dawned on her that it was time to allow Patrick to gain independence. It would be difficult for them both but it had to be done. That cool night following the worst attack that Shana had ever experienced since she had become a pyrate captain, the exhausted woman changed inside. Vowing never to allow another man full access to her heart, she pledged her love to the dead man who she now understood had been the one and only man for her. Micken's cage shook as he tried to undo the door but Shana hardly noticed his anguish. It was too late to tell Irish that she adored him. Shana sobbed uncontrollably as she reached for the tiny vial of liquid opium. At that moment she felt that she could take no more and tipped the bitter, potent fluid onto her tongue.

Tiny nails dug painfully into the back of Shana's neck and a high pitched squawk made her wince. Her senses had been dulled by the previous evening's fix and she found it difficult to focus her mind on what was happening. Reaching clumsily for the nearest weapon, Shana swung a stray fist at Flint who had begun to tug viciously at her hair. Drowsiness overtook her and her head dropped heavily onto the table that she had been slumped over all night. Cold water thrown by Flint finally brought Shana to full consciousness and she leapt up, a look of sheer panic on her flushed face. As realisation dawned on her that a calamity was taking place out on deck, Shana Culley's maternal instinct suddenly kicked in. Immediately taking flight, the panic-stricken woman grabbed her tiny companion by the scruff of his delicate neck and flung him against the wall without a care. Armed and ready for combat, the protective pyrate queen ran out to investigate.

It came as a shock to see her only child standing with legs apart in a defensive position. With treasured double-edged sword in his hands, he stood guarding over Irish's stiffened body. Rigor mortis had set in and Tripod and the men were trying to persuade Patrick to allow them to cover his corpse. 'Teep away! Ye best nay dare tuts my 'Eye-wiss'!' demanded the enraged child, his face turning blood-red with bitter anger. Eyes wide and wild as they darted from face to face, Patrick was behaving like a predator cornered by hunters and refusing to concede. Shana watched in silence not knowing quite how to respond. The poor child was beside himself with grief and torment. Desperate to be understood, the young boy begged his mother to join him and shouted more threats to the bewildered crew. 'Tum any terlowser an I sal till yer all!' Had the situation not been so harrowing, the child's mispronunciation of words would have been amusing. This instance was not at all funny. Shana dropped her weapon and fell to her knees, sobs of anguish and torture wracking her body. She wanted to walk forward confidently and take her tormented child into her arms and tell him that everything was going to be alright... she could not do that... feeling weak and distraught, Shana dragged herself to her feet and stood motionless, looking deep into her son's eyes. At that instant, mother and child's bonded souls appeared to connect and Patrick called out, his tension dissipating; 'Mama! Tuddle, tuddle, tuddle!' Running towards his mother, still holding his sword tightly, the devastated child showed the first sign of vulnerability. Shana felt a wave of relief wash over her. She had really thought that she could take no more. Still not having shed a single tear, Patrick jumped into his mother's arms and held her protectively. Taking her chin firmly in both hands, he lifted her face so that he was able to look deep into his mother's elf-like eyes. With a serious expression, the small child addressed Shana, 'Mama, peez wet me teep Eye-wiss for a mickle bit.' Taking his hand in hers, the distraught woman led Patrick across the deck and stepped down into their cabin.

Micken's welcoming whistle broke the silence and the crew began to prepare Irish's body while they had the chance. Inside the cabin, Shana tried to explain the concept of death to her confused son who did not respond. Suppressing his emotions, Patrick cuddled his grieving mother. Focusing his mind only on her, the young boy decided that he had to start looking after her immediately. Shana held her child close, ''Tis 'bout time I took ye t' visit England, honey.' Kissing the top of his warm head, Captain Culley called for Jock Mackenzie to tell him her change of plan.

CHAPTER 21

Sworn Enemies Finally Meet

Shana never got over Irish's death and true to his promise, Patrick had watched over his mother ever since that dreadful day. Realising her vulnerability, the boy grew up with a heavy responsibility and duty of care toward his mother. Despite her apparent strength and confidence, inside Captain Sushana Culley there hid a desperately frightened child. Maybe this was part of the reason why many felt such a magnetic attraction towards this incredible woman. Patrick was still too young to understand but he was intuitive and regularly noticed how men would stare at his mother with carnal lust. People could not help but feel drawn to the sensual woman yet they also felt a great need to protect her at the same time. The unexplainable allure of this unique child-woman appeared so powerful and Shana took advantage of the attribute. Captain Shana Culley possessed both the power and independence of a strong and able leader yet also displayed the traits of a young girl in dire need of protection. She had the uncanny ability to attract and sometimes lure admirers from both sexes. Although many women felt bitter jealousy toward Shana, they still held a strange respect towards her and even liked her in an odd kind of way. Whilst most men wanted to fuck the sexual vixen's brains out, at the same time they felt a closeness akin to that of a best male friend. No matter what their feelings, most just wanted to hold their idol safe and close, vowing to look after and adore her for the rest of their days.

Shana had it all and what made her even more attractive was the fact that she had no idea just how beautiful she really was. Inside the stunningly beautiful temptress there lurked an insecure, self-loathing and abused woman who was desperate to find true love. Attracted to both men and women, Shana never really knew who she wanted to be. In her erotic fantasies, she craved for the touch of a women yet the thought of a man's phallus turned her on immensely. Occasionally when captain and crew spent time on land, Shana had experimented with other women. Her natural ability to take another woman to the heights of ecstasy was amazing and she loved the feeling of being able to break boundaries. Sending a pretty woman over the top in a frenzy of pure, unabashed sexual pleasure made the sensual captain so aroused that she would often experience orgasm without even being touched. With male lovers, she was always unselfish and if she saw another wench who took her fancy, she was keen to share. Delighting in making others tremble and explode with passionate bliss, Shana Culley had to beware of whom she allowed into her life. Having an insatiable sexual appetite was difficult when she had no permanent lover. Since Richie had disappeared, the frustrated captain had little choice than make do with pleasuring herself and the occasional clandestine tryst.

She and Richie had been the perfect match and managed to take each other beyond the boundaries of ecstasy into an indescribable world of sheer euphoria… Jokingly they had named their new experience 'exphoria' which had become their secret word to let one another know they wanted to fuck. Not that they ever wanted much else when they were together! Shana missed her ultimate lover more every day and as time passed, she began to feel that their whole relationship had been a fantasy. If only the fates had been kinder to them. With her infamous reputation and the colossal bounty on her head, it was vital that Shana was careful who she trusted. Unfortunately that fact alone only added more excitement to her risqué sexual ventures. Dressing as a man once again, Shana hit the seedy streets and brothels whenever she visited a port.

Finally accepting that she would have to make do with the occasional intimate encounter when heavily disguised, Shana would often remind herself of the motto that she had adopted when she became a pyrate; 'Alea iacte est.' Her eight year old son had learned the Latin words early in his life and had been brought up to believe that fate held the key to everything in existence. Following Irish's death, the return trip to England had been sombre as the crew all grieved over the loss of the popular boatswain. Irish was given a burial at sea. As a deep sign of respect, his body was wrapped in Captain Culley's infamous flag; the flag which had flown on the ships that Irish had helped her command over a good many years. Patrick and Micken attended the service that was held one peaceful evening under a blood-red sky. Flint refused to come out of Shana's cabin no matter how hard Patrick tried to persuade him. Taking the incident worse than anyone, the over-dramatic little monkey wailed all through the ceremony. He had good reason to mourn though and his grief was undoubtedly genuine. Flint and Irish had shared an unusual bond and everyone felt for the tiny creature who had seemed to have diminished in size even more since his traumatic loss. Standing proudly next to his mother with face set in serious contemplation, Patrick played his bodhrán as the corpse was tipped overboard. When Captain Shana Culley's pyrate flag went with Irish into the depths, no-one said a word. Crew dispersed and an eerie silence fell over the ship for the rest of the night. It was as if a cruel spell had been cast on the Slayer and superstition was becoming rife amongst a normally fatalistic clan. Jock had been busy making rosaries for his shipmates and Shana had noticed one in Patrick's hammock. A cold wind cut through her as she stared at the miserably grey clouds that moved swiftly westward over a turbulent sea. A bedraggled Flint finally emerged from the Captain's cabin at the call of sighted land, shivered and scurried back inside. On a harsh winter's morning in the 1567th year of our Lord a lone fisherman spotted the Slayer on the horizon. Checking his lobster nets for a fresh catch, the old man was surprised to see such a large vessel approaching the coastal town of Teignmouth. With a shudder and a sigh, Shana felt the tiny hairs stand up on the back of her neck in stark realisation that she had finally made it back home.

As expected, Captain Culley was able to sell the Slayer for a fair price. Paying a well-trusted courier to take word to Grace of her return to England, Shana briefed her men and dismissed them. Most of the pyrates joined other crews immediately, soon setting sail for sunnier climes. A loyal few promised to stay in Teignmouth and await their captain's return; a couple more had decided to join Shana later that day after they had wet their whistles. Tripod and Remendo insisted on joining Shana at Mary Maggy's after they had painted Teignmouth town red which, according to Tripod's history could well be in over a month's time! Having said their drunken farewells and wished their captain, her son and the ship's pets a safe trip for the umpteenth time, the loveable pair of friends went off to find the local whores' hang-out.

Shana's plans were simple. First she would pluck up the courage to visit the Turnbulls and her African friends at Mary Maggy's. She realised how heartbreaking it was going to be returning to the place that held such painful memories yet she also knew that it had to be done. Part of her had always longed to go back home and visit her extended family but another dreaded facing the place where her Albert had burned to death. The memory of that tragic night haunted Shana, sometimes she imagined that she could still smell the incinerating flesh and hear Richie's inconsolable cries... And now she had lost Richie too...

Teignmouth harbour had changed little over the years during her absence. Old women wearing black bonnets, heavy linen skirts and woollen shawls still sat patiently along the quayside selling seafood. Their neat wicker baskets were full to the brim with fresh cockles and mussels. Gnarled fingers worked steadily with hooks catching yarn that had been twisted around swollen joints. It had always amazed Shana how quickly they were able to create weighty woollen items with such deformed hands. Shuddering again as she began to feel the dampness enter the pores of her cold skin, the pyrate queen felt thankful that she had been taken away from the miserably cold isle where she had been born. Gazing along the harbour Shana Culley watched her son playing happily with Flint and Micken as a crowd of inquisitive locals gathered around the appealing trio. With no fear,

Patrick stood addressing the audience while the two creatures huddled nervously behind him. Jock was not far away from the boy but kept enough distance not to cramp his style, remembering only too well how it felt to be on the brink of adulthood. Allowing Patrick as much freedom as she possibly could within the hazardous world that they lived in, Shana also made sure that her successor was as safe as he could possibly be from abduction. Infamous and wealthy as she had become, it was essential that Patrick had bodyguards at all times. Irish had always been the boy's guardian but ever since his death the independent boy would allow no-one else anywhere near him. Other than spending time with his mother, Flint and Micken, the insular boy preferred to be alone.

Despite his introvert nature, everyone who met Patrick liked him and most children wanted to befriend him. Both Shana and Patrick were temperamental and impulsive, they were very skilled artistically and creativity was one of their strongest talents. When experiencing highs, mother and son were buzzing and needed little sleep, always active and feeling on top of the world. Down times were spent leading a solitary existence and understood only by each other. Indeed many thought that Shana and Patrick Culley were more like brother and sister than mother and son.

Smiling to herself when she observed Micken squawking and flapping around like a brightly-coloured, crazed chicken, Shana pulled the dark green hood of her thick velvet cloak around her face to shelter her eyes from the wind. A chill had already set in her bones, so she walked down to the water's edge to call Jock. It was time to take a stage coach to Mary Maggy's.

It was as though time had stood still as the creaking wooden wheels of the stage coach came to a halt outside the large gates at the entrance to Shana Culley's land. She felt as though she had never been away. Patrick bounced up and down on the narrow leather seats as he noticed the horses grazing in the fields. 'Mummy, will ye peez teach me to ride?' Shana smiled an unspoken confirmation and felt relieved that Patrick would feel happy for the duration of their stay. Flint did not look so happy, sitting on Patrick's lap dressed in a small thick, linen shirt and felt hat, feeling bitterly cold. Micken had settled on Shana's shoulder and dug his sharp curled claws deeply into the material of her dress. He did not feel at all safe in England but then, as Patrick always reminded his mother, Micken never felt safe anywhere. 'Micken is a coward and a freak!' Patrick would joke, knowing that Shana was particularly protective of the little bird. Although there was love between her son and favourite pet, there was still rivalry and the two taunted each other at every opportunity.

Before the coachman had pulled the reins to halt his two handsome horses, Patrick Culley had jumped down from the carriage without using the steps. By the time Shana had exited the cramped coach, her son had run over to the largest stallion in the field. Flint was panicking and held tiny hands over his eyes as he always did when worried. Peering between scissoring fingers, the little ape jumped up and down as Micken flapped frantically inside his cage. Between them, the pair created chaos wherever they ventured! Yelling a warning that her rapscallion of a son would no doubt ignore, Shana sighed and waited for Jock to jump down from the coachman's seat. In amazement she watched as her son confidently cupped one hand under the large horse's nose. Standing on tiptoes, the child nuzzled his face into the muscular animal's body and with his free hand Patrick stroked the thick, coarse mane that fringed the palomino stallion's elegant neck. By snorting, shaking his head gently and whinnying Ted signalled to the herd that he felt at ease with the child. As dominant male, the handsome horse neighed and flounced around his new friend whilst the other horses gathered around. A sound from the building caught their attention and all but Ted trotted toward its source. Shana bit her lip as tears welled in her clear blue eyes at the sight of her childhood friend. To Shana's surprise, Abi Turnbull had dropped the weighty sacks of apples and oats and ran indoors when she spotted the stage coach. Shana felt deeply disappointed that her old friend had reacted so badly to her return after all these years but she also understood completely. The young woman, who had walked away from her friends and home on a night long ago, had returned as the infamous and most wanted pyrate queen. 'Captain Culley the Castrator's' likeness was displayed on wanted posters all over England and suddenly this villainous wench was here at the estate that the Turnbulls had been running. Then sudden realisation hit Shana Culley. The woman she had spotted in the distance was not Abi Turnbull at all but her daughter. At that very moment, Abi and Flo came flying out of the house and bounded over the fields yelling and laughing just as they had as children. Breathing in a deep breath of fresh country air, Shana lifted her heavy skirts and ran towards the twins.

Jock Mackenzie had travelled ahead of the rest of the crew who had chosen to serve their captain in the next stage of her career. By the time the intriguing bunch of characters had reached Mary Maggy's, Patrick, Shana and Jock had already enjoyed a hearty meal of roasted boar and warm manchet loaves with fresh butter. When Shana's pyrates walked in on the homecoming celebrations, they were met by a drunken party who had consumed two bottles of hypocras; a very expensive, deliciously sweet eastern Mediterranean liqueur that Shana had bought for her extended family. The Turnbull women burst into raucous laughter at the sight of the mud-spattered men who had ridden for the first time over the muddy, hilly terrain of Devon. Cold, wet and filthy, the men were glad to pull off their boots, warm themselves by the fire and be served a hot, scrumptious meal in their temporary home.

Patrick had chosen to spend time out in the paddock with the horses but now sheepishly joined the new arrivals. Feeling extremely shy around the company of pretty girls, Shana's son sat quietly blushing at their blatant advances. The boy was handsome and never short of female attention, gaining admirers wherever he went. Patrick had also inherited his mother's modest nature which made him even more attractive to the opposite sex. Shana felt safe and happy back in the company of the Turnbull family and was overwhelmed by their welcome. As if she had never been away, Shana and her oldest friends chatted away happily for hours until everyone felt sure that their returning heroine was ready for her big surprise. Faking a drum-roll Flo banged her hands on the table and everyone fell silent. In the threshold of the kitchen door appeared a pretty brown face with the most glorious open smile.

When Shana saw Princess she burst into tears of absolute joy. Behind the African woman who Shana had helped escape from the slave vessel stood her sister, Kia. Rushing forward to embrace the woman who they had learned much about since reaching the safety of Mary Maggy's, the two free women felt happy to finally be able to thank her properly. Gift appeared where Princess and Kia had stood, a small boy holding onto his hand shyly. Realising that the child had to be Taru, Shana beckoned for him to come closer. Spotting Flint in the corner of the room with Micken rubbing his fluffy little body over his ape companion, Taru ran over and joined in the petting. The boy looked so much like his father! Shana bit down on her lower lip as she pictured the horrific scene of Precious' foul murder. Taru seemed to sense the woman's distress and a small, dimpled hand silently reached for hers, unconsciously fingering the sparkling jewels that stood proud of heavy gold rings. Taking the smallest from her little finger, she placed it on the toddler's thumb and his wide brown eyes lit up with gratitude. 'A legacy from your father.' whispered the saddened woman as she made eye contact with the son of the bravest warrior she had known. Tottering over to his young mother, the boy glanced back at the pyrate queen with inherent curiosity. Shana was sure that Taru would be a fine man someday, just as his father had been.

During the time spent at Mary Maggy's Patrick learned to ride and became a competent horseman within weeks. An orphan who had been given a home and chance to lead a decent life had decided to stay on at the institution and give the Turnbull family something back. Josh was a tall, skinny lad who had an amazing rapport with horses. Having spent most of his time with the stallion and mares whilst in residency at the orphanage, he was loath to leave when the time came. Ma Turnbull and her daughters helped those who had come of age to find work as apprentices with local tradesmen. Since Mary Maggy's had opened, it had gained an excellent reputation as an organisation that offered a basic but comfortable family environment to orphaned children. These children were taught simple skills and etiquette and many ended up working as blacksmiths, bakers, butchers, tanners and candle-makers. A letter of introduction from Ma Turnbull always managed to seal the deal as she was well-known as a fair and good judge of character. She would never recommend anyone's service if they were not trustworthy and hard working.

Josh and Patrick became good friends despite their age difference. Patrick had grown up amongst adults and Josh loved to hear the boy's thrilling tales of pyracy. Eager to learn about different countries and cultures, Josh was always up at the crack of dawn, waiting for his enthusiastic student to saddle up and join him on an exhilarating ride. Soon Patrick grew more daring and the wild and competitive pair would dare each other to tackle dangerous jumps. After returning from an exhausting jaunt, Patrick would help Josh to unsaddle the horses before running to find his mother to tell her all about his adventure.

Patrick was a private person who led a rather solitary life and Shana was delighted that he had found friendship in Josh. Ma Turnbull loved Patrick and Abi and Flo's daughters both fancied the pyrate boy, holding him in such reverence that he felt embarrassed. It was quite comical to watch Patrick trying his damnedest to avoid the girls who would pounce on him at every chance. Sushana's namesake was much shyer than her cousin, Trudy and Patrick felt secretly attracted to the pretty wench.

The twins' daughters soon became besotted by the pyrate boy and miraculously, Patrick felt closer to them as time passed by. Harmless but definitely much too excitable whenever the young lad was around, the youngsters became close friends in the short time that they had known each other.

Within a few weeks, Shana felt the urge to return to her old life at sea. Purchasing a briganteen in pristine condition she invited Patrick to help paint the mermaid figurehead. Shana was amused when she spotted the siren who gazed out over the ocean wearing a seductive half-smile. Like the captain who was soon to command her ship, she had the most beautiful sculpted breasts that had undoubtedly been carved by a connoisseur! Patrick named the vessel The Mermaid's 'Venge and joined his mother on her first voyage. Captain Culley was soon taking a newly hired crew on regular trips between London and Dublin where ever-expanding fleets of English ships patrolled the waters. Continuing to raid the massive vessels that delivered African people to sell to wealthy gentry, Captain Culley was surprised that unsuspecting crews still offered little or no resistance. Shana took advantage of the captains' unexpectedly passive nature and began to give parchments to those in charge of the ever-expanding slave-ships. Ordering the bewildered officers to deliver the anti-slavery propaganda to Queen Elizabeth herself, Shana enjoyed the power that she held over the cruel monarch who showed little regard for African people. She had appointed a printer to engrave one of Irish's clever caricatures of an over-fed captain poking left-over scraps through the bars that separated him from a starving slave cargo beneath decks. She also paid him to produce batches of an illustration-only version of the message to be nailed to trees in villages so that everyone would be able to understand the stark truth.

Patrick always insisted on sailing with his mother and they enjoyed many voyages back and forth to Mary Maggy's until the traumatic day Abi's husband died. Riding one of the horses that had been unusually frisky one summer day, the skilled horseman managed to stay on the gelding until he reached a cliff. Unable to steer the crazed horse away from inevitable danger, the brave man held on until the last minute when he knew that he could not save the animal. Throwing himself clear of the flailing hooves of the poor doomed beast, Abi's husband fell onto a grassy verge. As he fell from his terrified mount his head hit a hidden rock and his neck snapped on impact killing him instantly. A travelling minstrel found his body only a few hours later, hauled him up onto his ass's back and took him into the nearest town. When poor Abi viewed the corpse of her true love she broke down, took to her bed and was inconsolable for months.

The shock of seeing her dead husband turned her mousey-coloured hair pure white overnight. Her new appearance gave her an almost ethereal beauty, her pearly locks a stark contrast against her golden, sun-kissed skin. Devastated by the news, the whole family fell apart. News of Abi's withdrawal hit Patrick much harder than anyone could have predicted. He was definitely his mother's son, so sensitive and loving, always thinking of others. Concerned about his new family, the child decided not to accompany his mother on her next few voyages. Patrick's patience and knack of listening to Abi's sobs and incomprehensible ravings without reacting eventually paid off. Hours of sitting by her bed and allowing the woman freedom to bawl and curse without interruption allowed the poor grieving soul to gradually heal. He felt no desire or need to stop Abi's angry ravings at the God who she believed had punished her and her soul mate unfairly. Gradually, Patrick's benign presence helped ease her agony. His mother was so proud that her son had helped Abi and her mourning family with their grief by choosing to stay with them whilst she carried on with business. One day, when Patrick was telling Abi about some of the adventures he had shared with his brave mother, Abi decided she wanted to try a sailing trip herself. Leaving her only daughter at Mary Maggy's with her aunt and Grandmother, Abi joined Shana's crew and headed off to Spain. Abi had always had a strong desire to dress as a boy, so now she cut her hair and became 'Adam'. Fitting into her new gender role with ease, Adam soon became a permanent member of the crew and signed in the round, pledging to live a new, democratic life of pyracy under Captain Culley's command. Her life-long friend and peer was proud of her new recruit and felt inwardly happy that she had been able to provide an escape route for her mourning friend. It was inevitable that the two women soon rekindled a steamy affair and Shana was able to enjoy the newfound sexual satisfaction of a constant lover.

A fake letter of introduction, supposedly written by Sir Francis Drake, introduced Shana as Lady Elspeth Culley, Explorer under commission of Queen Elizabeth of England. Shana was often invited to board privateer vessels. Standing six feet tall with her curvy build, long dark blonde hair and blue eyes, the striking pyrate queen was a vision to be remembered by her victims. Her blatant nerve and guile enabled her and her crew to plunder several privateer ships returning from the Americas laden with tobacco, silver and grog. One of their most successful plunders was that of John Hawkins' ship in 1567.

On the day of the attack the two captains had a massive argument aboard his ship when Hawkins challenged Captain Culley's authority. Forgetting herself, the quick-tempered, feisty wench soon lost her temper at his insolence. Holding a knife to the surprised officer's groin, she made sure to leave him with a deep incision before leaving with a generous amount of tobacco, a chest full of doubloons and several fine emeralds. Particularly disgruntled that the bitch had stolen gifts that he had intended to take back to England as a gift for the virgin queen, Hawkins was determined to seek revenge. Before boarding his ship, Shana had showed him her letter of introduction and the accomplished, experienced captain was disgusted with himself that he had allowed such a blatant thief to pull such a low trick. Desperate to find out who his beautiful attacker was, the besotted captain asked patrol boats to keep a lookout for the woman with whom he had fallen helplessly in love. Shana's feelings for Hawkins could not have been further from his for her, in fact they were quite the opposite. Captain Culley despised the privateer with a passion. How dare he challenge her authority! Neither would quickly forget their fiery encounter and it would not be their last!

Sailing into the small harbour of Lynmouth on the north coast of Devon, Shana had decided to offload her latest bounty at the Rising Sun Inn, a renowned smuggler's den. The sleepy little village was a delightfully welcome sight that calmed the captain down considerably. Well-known for her hot temper, although she seldom lost it, Shana was given plenty of space when the crew knew that her blood was boiling… and Hawkins had certainly managed to irk her. As the men and Abi (Shana had difficulty calling her lover by her adopted male name, Adam) loaded the cockboat with spoils to trade at the inn, Shana stripped off her skirts and donned a tight pair of breeches. Only a thin, loose white shirt made of fine Irish linen covered her huge, heavy breasts. As she climbed the rigging Shana felt herself relax but her mind was still firmly fixed on the tall, handsome lout who had dared to challenge her. His audacity impressed her now she had time to think of it. Had he not been so damned attractive he would have had his bollocks hanging around her Abi's pretty neck by now! 'Fucking pillcock!' Shana shouted into a brisk wind and inhaling a lungful of blissfully refreshing sea air, she dived into the turquoise waters. Surfacing below the jutting stern of her magnificent ship, the pyrate queen heard whistles and wild whoops as Abi stripped naked. Blowing salty water out through her nose, Shana looked up admiringly at her belle. Feeling the gentle undercurrent tease her inner thighs, the aroused woman reached a hand down between her legs. Moving dextrous fingers over the tiny, hardened mound she soon brought herself to orgasmic satisfaction. When Abi saw her lover's flushed face, she giggled and swam over to caress her wonderful curves. Abi had a beautiful, fit body but her perfectly formed breasts were smaller than the captain's ample portions. Lining the decks, the men cheered at the sight of the two women kissing passionately. The randy pair played to their audience who egged them on more. Ordering the men to get on with their work, Shana held Abi close, coiling her long legs around her woman's body and was ecstatic as she felt her lover's long tongue flick over her hard nipples.

Sheer cliffs covered with a carpet of lush greenery were caressed by a light breeze that made millions of leaves ripple in a cascade down to the shore. Ancient trees twisted back almost flattened against the steep, lichen covered rock-face. Dry, gnarled, bone-like branches reached skyward as if rejoicing countless years of battle against harsh winds. Silent woodlands, watching over the sleepy fishing village, created a breathtaking landscape. Had Abi been able to conjure her own version of paradise, she would never have been able to create such blissful perfection. As the breeze tantalised the women's responsive bodies, Patrick played freely aboard the Mermaid's 'Venge and Micken's raucous whistles and screams could be heard from the shores. His mother and her lover pleasured each other for an hour before climbing back aboard. When they ventured ashore and ran up to the inn, Shana felt proud to be able to treat Abi to an overnight stay in the pretty thatched building where she had traded for years.

Smugglers made regular drop-offs at the popular drinking den and contraband merchandise fetched a pretty penny. Jeff, the owner of the black-market establishment, ensured that no-one ever interrupted his shady business deals by lining the purses of every local punter. Alcohol to suit every palette was made available for all who supported and protected the scam and so far it was very successful indeed. Tobacco and opium were available at a very reasonable price and Jeff ensured that prices did not fluctuate too much. Shana had supplied her friend with tobacco and grog for a good many months and he was always pleased to see her. Jeff was a young man who had spent much of his life in the Americas. His parents were amongst the early Scottish settlers and had planned to raise their children in the New World. Sadly Jeff's family had all been killed by Native Americans and he had been lucky to have survived the attack. Somehow he had been brought back to England and settled in Lynmouth where he had landed on his return.

Abi pulled the bed-strings tight and retied a strong knot. Micken whistled loudly, making a real fuss about the scrabbling above them. Mice had nested in the thatch and Flint was hanging out of the window, pulling and poking at the straw of the roof. Patrick giggled loudly at the naughty pets and Shana scolded the troublesome ape. Back-handing Flint with a warning slap she pulled the window shut and went over to cuddle her child who lay on a mattress next to Micken's cage. Within minutes, the exhausted child fell asleep and his creatures soon joined him in slumber. The trio had spent hours exploring the higgledy-piggledy maze of narrow corridors, seeking secret hiding places for contraband that Jeff tucked away under the rickety stairs, behind false wooden panels and under loose floorboards. The Rising Sun Inn was the perfect place for a child at play and Patrick was, without doubt, a lucky boy to have had the opportunity to do so.

Blowing out the oil lamp Shana climbed in beside her waiting lover's soft, warm body and kissed her passionately. Ducking her head under the sheepskins and furs, Shana slowly traced hands and lips over the other woman's silky skin, feeling goose pimples rise over every inch of the trail. Kissing and licking the delicate folds of her lover's cunnie, Shana worked her tongue around in circles and then pushed it slowly inside. Shivering in delighted and uncontrollable response to her expert lover's oral stimulation, Abi thrust her hips up and pressed harder onto Shana's lips. Touching her own nipples that had risen as her breasts brushed over the thighs of her responsive partner, Shana reached a powerful orgasm as she teased Abi with her busy tongue. Slowly wriggling her long, lean muscular body over Abi's until their heads were level, Shana caressed her lover's breasts and pressed her own firmly against them. The two women pleasured each other until the early morning hours when they both fell asleep in each other's arms. Satisfied, the couple slept soundly through until midmorn when the three boys woke them. Breakfast was served downstairs and the straw-covered floor smelled of fresh rhum together with the stench of stale cider. Sweeping out the old to replace it with new, Jeff hailed his special guest to join him outside.

Hog-backed cliffs, with grey peaks partly obscured by thin veils of mist, loomed above. Lobster pots full to the brim and a fresh crate of herrings lay before the pair as they chatted. Slippery, silver scales sparkled now and then as the sun's weak rays shone through sparse clouds. Gulls screeched above waiting for the discarded innards that spilled out of the fish as Jeff sat patiently gutting. Jeff and Shana struck future deals and confirmed orders as the morning passed peacefully by. A fresh westerly wind whipped the locks of her loose hair onto her skin, creating a pleasurable tingling sensation. When she smelled rain in the breeze, the captain decided that it was the perfect time to move the Mermaid's 'Venge to her next port of call. Farewells were exchanged and a strong, firm handshake sealed an unspoken oath. Shana parted company with Jeff and took a walk down to the sea. She sat alone on a smooth rock that lay dominant amongst millions of tiny pebbles and enjoyed the sensation as the ebbing tide lapped at her golden-brown legs. It felt as though the frothy white waves were drawing out every last bit of stress from Shana's very soul. Content to sit and be one with nature, Captain Culley took the time to pay respects to the many loved-ones she had lost since her traumatic birth. Watching groups of tiny bubbles form and inch their way over dry pebbles, leaving glossy kisses behind them, the captain stretched. Before gathering her clan she took one last look at the heavily laden fishing boats that had returned with an excellent morning's catch. Fishermen were busy unloading their colourfully painted vessels as they bobbed on the harbour's hushed waters. A distant call made Shana start and her lulled mind managed to shrug off the hypnotic enchantment of the sea.

Chapter 22

A Premonition and a Pyrate Lair

Tripod looked ill. A fresh crop of seeping open sores had appeared on his face. Shana had kept up regular treatments and patiently applied mercury to new infected areas but the disease seemed to have returned with a vengeance of late. Sailing did the horny character plenty of good and helped take his mind off his agony. Every night, Tripod joined Shana, Abi and Patrick in their cabin where Shana treated his wounds behind a temporary screen. She was reluctant to use more pig's bladder to replace the rotting flesh of his penis but there was no other choice. Against all odds, the virile sailor still managed to produce a mighty fine erection.

It was a cold, wet and windy night when the Mermaid's 'Venge dropped anchor a safe distance from Lundy Island. Tripod had decided to refuse his three m's as he had nicknamed the painful clinical procedure, 'murderous mercury melts.' Although Shana was upset about her friend's decision, she empathised deeply and knew that their battle against the foul sexual disease was over. Joining her in the cabin, when he had completed his duties, the pyrate toasted his captain wishing her continued success. Abi and Jock had taken Patrick, Micken, Sparky and Flint out on deck so that the master gunner could point out the numerous wrecks around the jagged, fatal shores. A ships' graveyard displaying bleached carcasses jutting broken and useless from the bluest sea, the dangerous coastline provided a wonderful, natural defence. None but the cunning pyrates who had made the convenient island their lair knew about the deadly trap that awaited them.

Tripod and Shana drank late into the night whilst Jock took the others ashore into the anarchic world of murderous thieves. Jock had been amongst the first to discover the natural fortress that had proved to be the perfect place to lure trade vessels. The ship on which the Scotsman served had been under the command of Captain Todd Freeman, a murderous, greed-riddled villain. The vessel had run aground during a terrible storm and Jock was one of the few survivors to make it to the shore.

Managing to live on the meagre supplies that they had salvaged from the wreck, the pyrates took shelter in the many caves scattered around the small isle. Living off what they could catch and vegetation from the luscious plant-life, Jock and his companions had plenty of time to explore Lundy Island. Lund-ey is Norse for puffin so-called by the original Nordic settlers who were no doubt delighted to find an abundance of these comical birds populating the small isle. Everyone had agreed that the island, with its many hiding places, was the perfect place to store bounty.

Jock decided to take a boat over to the mainland and find out more about the surrounding area. On arrival he was met by two imbecilic men who were undoubtedly brothers, they looked alike and were deformed and lame. Dressed in animal skins, the filthy men had long, matted hair and beards. Grunting and signalling for Jock to follow, the brothers led him into a dark cave where they attacked him. Producing a pistol, the master gunner shot one of them in the foot during a violent struggle. Managing to overpower the other sibling who had gone crazy with worry, Jock had felt sickening pity and decided to spare their miserable lives. With child-like respect and gratitude the brothers then made their visitor welcome. They behaved like wild animals and taking a proper look around the cave, Jock realised their cannibalistic tendencies. Appalled and disgusted, he pieced together the loathsome truth. The couple had doubtless been luring ships to their doom for many years and their victims' bones lay scattered on the rocky floor.

Headland point was the perfect place to watch out for approaching ships. Waving their lanterns slowly so that sailors would think that they had spotted a static lamp-light on land, the brothers would wait until the ships came too close to the treacherous approach and ran aground. Jagged rocks that jutted out of the waters like shark's teeth bit into the keel of the doomed vessel. Trapped and vulnerable inside their damaged ship, sailors would battle for their lives as heavy waves crashed on surrounding rocks.

When their evil trap succeeded and the wrecked ship lay broken on the boulders below, they would scuttle down an impossibly steep cliff-face and bludgeon the poor survivors to death. In an insane, blood-hungry frenzy the lunatics then began to feast on human flesh. Depending on the length of time the brothers had gone without food, the doomed sailors would either be consumed where they lay or chopped up into smaller portions for storage. In some horrific cases, the victims had only been beaten unconscious! The foul truth was that many a time a sailor had regained consciousness to find his bones being stripped of flesh by a fellow man! Desperate cries and pleas for mercy went unheard as they were mockingly echoed by the excitable maniacs who continued to gnaw greedily on a piece of the shocked sailor's thighbone. When the crazed duo had eaten their fill, they would gather together valuables to be hoarded in one of their many caves. Jock was shown the many caves that had provided the barking mad siblings with shelter and storage space. Quickly scuttling away from the scene, the cannibals always left the shell of a wreck stripped clean at the mercy of the sea. Some pyrates knew about the fiends who frequented Headland point and made regular visits over from Lundy Island to take advantage of the ignorant creatures. Trading measly amounts of tobacco and mead in exchange for valuable hauls, the pyrates made a tidy profit.

Jock told his captivated listeners the story of the two men who were believed to originate from Clovelly, a fisherman's village that had been recorded in the Doomsday book. The two brothers, who had settled somewhere along the lush, green rolling hills dotted with sheep, were thought to have been driven from the quiet village when they were babies. According to Jock, an old woman had given birth to the boys at the incredible age of forty four, with no knowledge of how or when the pregnancy had happened. She swore that she was a virgin and had never lain with man or beast.

An old fisherman had told Jock the story of a soothsayer who had visited the isolated village that consisted of a couple of fisherman's cottages and a quay. Arriving on a German ship, the wise-man had insisted that the captain drop anchor and have the sage row ashore to the quay at the bottom of the quaint village. A reader of runes, the strange visitor believed that he had been led to the sleepy settlement for an important reason. Amazed to discover that someone had managed to construct sturdy, well-built homes on such steep, rocky terrain, the soothsayer stayed overnight to learn more about the intriguing, picturesque place. He never left and made his living telling the fortunes of the fast growing number of visitors who wanted to experience the unique charm of Clovelly.

The two resident fishermen had created a thriving business, charging for the use of their harbour and quay. Using the profit wisely they had built more homes and created a unique, picturesque oasis where visitors could relax and enjoy the fresh seafood, cooked by their wives. Making the most of the perfect gem of a fishing location, the expanding families decided to offer room and board to visitors who loved the peaceful atmosphere at Clovelly.

Jock understood full well how the German visitor had become attached to the pretty village as it still remained the most enchanting place that he had ever seen. Donkeys laden with baskets full of seafood climbed the extreme incline so that the fishermen could broaden their market. Everything that came into the village had to be brought down the path by donkey and the same applied for anything that left. All seemed blissfully perfect in Clovelly until the day that the two children who had been born to the unmarried woman were banished.

One full moon, the German seer predicted that disaster would strike the community if the bastard children remained in the village. Terrified, the villagers turned on the single woman and demanded she put her two boys into a small boat and push them out to sea. The woman could not bear to send her sons to their death and tried to escape with her children. The fishermen dragged the woman back down the rocky track using two chains with large hooks on the end which they forced deep into her flesh, one under each ribcage. Yelling and cursing as they dragged her kicking and struggling all the way to the water's edge the poor women still refused to let go of her babies. Tearing the cruel hooks out of the woman the men stuck each into a baby's jaw, hauled them over their shoulder and threw them into the small boat. When the men had dealt with her babies, they walled the distraught woman up in her own home. No-one in Clovelly ever spoke of the dark secret.

Ending his gruesome tale in the same way that it had been told to him by the pyrate who claimed to have actually survived an attack by the fiendish freaks, Jock lowered his voice to a dramatic, over-exaggerated whisper, '...Folks say that ye can hear the brothers 'owl across the sea whene'er the moon is full'.

Back in the captain's cabin Tripod had begged Shana to make him a promise that she had dreaded him asking of her. The thing that he had always feared most was to lose his mind. Knowing only too well how the sexually transmitted disease that was slowly rotting his body would eventually destroy his mind, Tripod wanted to die before he went insane. In their drunken state, the two old friends wept together and celebrated a swashbuckling life that many would not even have dared to dream of. By the time that Jock returned with his party of tourists the companions were both sound asleep.

That night, the pyrate queen had a horrific nightmare and awoke in the morning with a sickening feeling. When she confided in Abi they made plans together to hide Shana's legacy. Pensive and confused whether she had foreseen Tripod's death or her own, she felt strongly that the warning had been most urgent and decided that she had been shown her own end. Seeing the large collection of pouches made from the skin that she had collected from her victims over years, the successful pyrate queen decided that the time had probably come for the tables to turn. It seemed inevitable that her luck would run out one day and she had never been afraid of death. Her only concern was for Patrick to be secure and able to live a life of his choice never wanting for anything. Grace O'Malley would ensure that he always had support and family and the two women had immeasurable stashes of treasure hidden.

Desperate to ensure that her son and no-one else received her most prized bounty, Shana took the two most valuable yellow diamonds ever discovered in the world and hid them inside a monkey's skull. The precious stones had been amongst the spoils from an Indian trade ship bound for the Persian Gulf with a precious cargo for her wealthy prince. With a predominantly Indian crew Shana's lighter craft sped up beside the trade ship and attacked the heavily laden vessel. Many of the sailors abandoned ship and some joined Shana's pyrates but some brave men lost their lives defending the tremendous jewels. On discovery of a huge treasure chest well-hidden amongst ship supplies, Captain Culley had felt triumphant and overwhelmed. Never before had she encountered such an elaborate, expertly made piece of engineering as the casket that they had discovered. A hidden mechanism opened the sturdy and seemingly impregnable container so Tripod and Richie had hauled it back to their own vessel to investigate further. Their captain was determined not to damage the wonderful piece. It took the pair almost three whole weeks to solve the masterpiece of a puzzle but their determination finally paid off. The opening drew a crowd, all eager to feast their eyes on the contents of the armoured box and two men paid the highest price for their curiosity. When huge hinges had slowly creaked open as the men lifted the heavy lid two angry king cobras, poised ready for attack, flew at their neck and face. Dripping fangs full of poison that had built up during their confinement sank deeply into flesh and injected the lethal dose before they were sliced in two. Shana could still hear the screams of agony as her men thrashed around the floor in their frenzied death squirm. That day had proved to be an important learning curve for everyone. Following the shocking event Shana had made sure that everyone who served with her knew to always be ready for anything. One day they too might face a similar incident as if conjured from a surreal nightmare.

Within a few days Shana and her current lover had prepared Patrick's inheritance, tucking it safely inside a monkey skull which they placed inside a tiny metal-lined wooden casket. They knew that people would be afraid to open a child's coffin; even the most hardened grave-robbers were known to leave a child's final resting place undisturbed. Claiming a substantial area of land in the middle of Lundy Island, Captain Culley and her crew built sturdy shelters using the Island's light-coloured granite. Everyone chose at least one name each for certain prominent or important points. Staking an unchallenged claim to over a third of the pyrates' haven, Shana and her men had finally found a permanent base to call home. Devil's Slide, the Pyramid, Devil's Chimney and the Battery were amongst the chosen names for key landmarks. The most comical name of 'Cow's Point' had been chosen by Tripod and was an area about halfway along the west coast. Its name had been inspired by an experiment that he and Jock had tried one drunken night. On the day in question, the two had been unloading a wrecked vessel of booty when they discovered a cow in the animal quarters, which was the best find as far as they were concerned. In their intoxicated state the pair later concocted a crazy plan to kill the beast so that they could surprise the rest of the crew with a midnight feast. Tripod and Jock somehow managed to get hold of a pulley which they used to lift the incredibly co-operative cow which continued to chew the cud as she was hauled up the cliff-side in stages. Below her the two plastered sea-dogs debated how high she would have to be lifted before they let go of the rope. During the stunt, Tripod had become quite fond of the placid cow and although he was keen to enjoy a fine piece of steak, he wanted the death to be as humane as possible. When the cow finally lay dead on the rocks beside the crazy sailors, morning had broken and they had sobered up. Exhausted from their nightly slaughter, Tripod and Jock took their ropes and pulley and wandered off to catch up on sleep. By midday, the cow was discovered by their friends who could not believe that a cow had fallen so conveniently from the cliffs. A clever, makeshift spit had been assembled over a pit containing freshly-cut firewood, all stacked and ready to ignite. The two embarrassed sailors never confessed to their mad over-night antics but joined their gang for the steak party the following night when Shana had named the area Cows Point. Each time Shana visited the area her mouth would water remembering the deliciously tender meat that was roasted that day. Shana's men had built two walls that very same day to mark and isolate Culley territory. They were aptly known as quarter and three quarter wall. Shana and Abi buried her secret treasure somewhere within the boundaries of her land and Shana determined to make a note of the exact place.

Alone in her cabin Shana expertly engraved a complete, detailed miniature map of Lundy Island on the face of a cob, a Spanish coin used mostly in the New World. The two women decided that this was the best choice of currency to use to hide the crucial clues. As the island was unknown to most, the map appeared to represent an elongated pattern. Drilling a minute hole to mark the spot where the booty lay, Shana ensured that the naked eye could not see the mark. The casket would lie there until Patrick claimed his prize.

As soon as he had been able to understand his mother's words, Shana had taught her son rhymes. Old Albert used to teach his girl ditties and traditional tales that she could chant off by heart. She and Irish, the man who had captured her heart in a sad and most unfortunate experience of unrequited love, had enjoyed creating treasure trails for Patrick aboard the ship. They would give the boy a riddle to solve that led him to his next clue. Occasionally, the clever boy would ask Tripod to help him but most of the time he was able to fathom out the correct answer alone. Unbeknown to him, every game that Patrick played had been devised to teach him invaluable skills. Reciting the riddle that revealed the crucial clue as to where her son could find the coin, Shana smiled proudly as she thought of her child solving it with no problem:

> 'Season the bald one's gift wi' great care,
>
> It may ignite so pri'thee beware!
>
> Peel gently back and do not tear,
>
> Then ye may take it if ye dare!'

The night that Shana had chosen to perform the most delicate operation imaginable, she had retired to her quarters where Abi waited with Flint and Micken. To enable the two of them to carry out the intricate exercise, the two women had decided to give the two pets a treat that would hopefully both distract and stupefy them. In order to conceal the coin safely and securely in the secret place she had chosen, Shana would need total concentration and a very steady hand. Sensitive Captain Culley secretly hoped that it would not be too long before Patrick found the clue that would lead him to his hidden inheritance. Plying Flint with three consecutive doses of neat rhum served in a thimble and bribing Micken with two whole chilli peppers Abi petted the mischievous pets while her lover made final preparations. Still finding it difficult to shake her unnerving sense of impending doom, Shana made sure that she had smoothed every sharp edge down and formed the coin into a suitable shape before she placed it safely inside the unique and extremely novel hiding place. Thankfully everything had gone as planned. Her task almost complete, the pyrate queen and loving mother could finally relax. She need never worry about her son's legacy again. Now all that remained was to ensure that Patrick had learned the riddle back to front and the job would be done.

Singing happily to himself as he practiced firing shots at a dead rabbit that Tripod had tied onto the end of a branch, Patrick felt content and happy in his new home. Shana and the crew had built some good shelters where they slept, ate and gambled during times they were not at sea. Steep, rocky cliffs, seemingly unfathomable canyons and enchanting secret caves had become ideal playgrounds for the wild, free-spirited pyrate child.

Through play, Patrick had discovered and learned so much about Puffin Island. Irish had taught him to draw and so he made detailed studies of the island that he planned to always call home. Cleverly, the boy charted a map of the section of Lundy Island that his mother owned. He would mark each new discovery that he made on the map and his mother helped him write what they were. One day he decided to make three separate maps, each featuring different subjects. He and his mother displayed the detailed artwork in the captain's cabin and everyone who saw them became fascinated by them. One showed different species of plant-life, another animals and seashore life which included birds of prey, seals, sika deer, breeding puffins, cormorants, sea gulls, crabs and many more. The final map showed moors, buildings, waterfalls, hills, wells, coves, islets, springs, ponds, cliffs, beaches, canyons, standing stones, quarries, walls, caves, marshes, woodland, streams, tracks and even a castle! To a child, the location was an adventure land full of every wonder that anyone could ever hope to conjure from the most exciting dream. All of the inhabitants of Lundy Island made use of the old Castle on Castle Hill and Patrick made regular trips south to visit the other pyrates and trade with them. A popular boy, he was well-respected and never once found trouble with any of the villainous bunch. His mother had taught him to defend himself and he feared no-one yet he had a strange fear of the unknown. The idea of ghosts troubled him greatly and Shana never understood why that was.

Patrick loved living on the island and learned to tame and ride the wild ponies bareback. He knew the caves, trails and lie of the land as if he had been born on the isle. The earthquake cracks intrigued him and he would often disappear on a new venture to learn more about his habitat. Shana and Abi slowly roasted lobster, fish and crab on a spit over a fire every day. Abi soon learned from her lover which spices to add and the seafood was always done to a turn. Some extremely happy days were spent on Quarry beach not far from Quarter wall cottages where Shana and her crew lived. Island life was wonderful for the outlaws and their new territory allowed them their ideal anarchic existence. Passing trade ships were a common sight and easy pickings for the predatory pyrates. Amongst the other pyrate clans who had settled on Lundy Island, Shana was delighted to meet a long-time friend of hers who had set up a permanent base where he managed to make a very good living tattooing. Many pyrates on the island proudly displayed Coemgen Shercliff's immaculate ink work. Captain Culley already had some of her talented friend's work on her skin but she had something extremely special in mind. When the two old friends reunited it seemed as though they had never been apart. Laughing and joking for hours of sharing amusing stories and consuming a ridiculous amount of rhum, the pair planned designs that Shana wanted to be tattooed into her skin. Within a few days, the pyrate queen's body was adorned with new tattoos that meant more to her than mere decoration. On her left hand, Coem tattooed Patrick's initials in leafy vines that represented mother and son's love of nature. Next to it was a fine triquetra, a three-cornered endless knot that symbolised the circle of life. Shana firmly believed that this early sacred symbol of Venus also represented the female genitalia making the triquetra a perfectly appropriate symbol for female celebration. She also considered the triquetra to represent the triplicate of mind, body and soul and had deliberately chosen the powerful symbol to wear permanently on her body to honour the three domains of earth, sea, and sky. Although each piece of ink-work held an important personal meaning to the pyrate queen, her favourite was on her left wrist. Patrick had wanted the same words tattooed onto his own wrist and she allowed him to have his first tattoo at the same time as his mother. 'Alea iacta est'... 'The die is cast'... Shana's famous pyrate motto had been permanently marked into both mother and son's skin in a special bonding ceremony in honour of their mutual love and respect.

Shana's most intimate tattoo came as quite a surprise to Abi when she discovered it the night that Shana returned after spending the day with her close male friend. An elegant pattern of flowers had been impregnated into the most delicate and sensual area of her lover's body. On discovering the new tattoo, Abi felt deeply touched and loved as she applied soothing camomile balm to her lover's swollen outer pussy lips. As she studied the pretty tattoo of a crescent moon entwined with ivy leaves, Shana explained the meaning of the pagan symbols that symbolised the two women's lesbian love. When she had finished Abi shed tears for her woman and passion quickly ensued. Knowing that their reunion was fated to be short-lived, the two women made sure to savour every available moment that they had. Craving each other's bodies, the unselfish lovers gave each other pleasure as often as possible, never taking the other for granted and making the best of borrowed time.

CHAPTER 23

An Unusual Abduction

Standing amongst the fish merchants who were bartering for the best price for the catch of the day, two cousins were catching up on news. At Plymouth docks Francis Drake and John Hawkins gazed out at a rough, grey sea. Heavy rain fell from dark looming clouds as the men discussed latest events. Francis Drake had immediately guessed that his cousin's attacker had been Captain Shana Culley. In confidence, John had told Francis that he had fallen for the wild, strong yet strangely vulnerable pyrate wench who had barged her way into his life, stripping his ship of her cargo and quelling his male ego. John was still in total shock that this incredible woman who had invaded a proud man's world had managed to make such an impact on him that he could barely function. John asked Francis not to reveal his new infatuation to the queen as he knew that she detested the mysterious woman who he had fallen for. There would be nothing more satisfying for Elizabeth than to see the notorious pyrate queen dancing before her on the gibbet. With no further ado, Hawkins set sail on a mission to find the woman who he could not rid from his love-stricken mind. As he had given up slave dealing sometime before, John felt confident that he would eventually be able to convince the wonderful woman that he was no longer the man who she had hated so venomously. John Hawkins had even managed to obtain a miniature of the woman with whom he had fallen head over heels in love. He was not sure how or why but he knew that he needed Captain Shana Culley in his life and was determined to be with her somehow. Owning a thriving shipbuilding yard in Plymouth, John knew that he could at least prove to be of some use to Grace O'Malley's notorious supporter. Whatever it took, the determined man would make sure that the notorious pyrate queen fell in love with him. Taking one of his newest vessels, John set sail for Ireland where he guessed might be one of the places to find the elusive Mermaid's 'Venge.

Weeks of sailing around Ireland finally paid off for John Hawkins and Captain Culley's vessel was eventually sighted just off the west coast in waters surrounding O'Malley territory. Attacking the speedy vessel, Hawkins men were under strict orders to take Shana alive and not to harm her in any way. The chase took hours and carried on well into the night. Eventually Hawkin's well-equipped and unburdened vessel was able to gain enough speed to run alongside the agile Mermaid's 'Venge and hook up to her. Grappling irons were thrown over to bite into the wood and cannons were fired in attack and defence. A ferocious Captain Culley stood on the main deck, cutlass and pistol in hand, hitting every one of her targets. Men fell before her like wheat in the path of a scythe and she provided an awe-inspiring sight for John Hawkins who wanted this woman more than he had ever wanted anyone before. Fighting gallantly at her side, shooting and reloading expertly, Patrick killed almost as many of John's men as his mother. The besotted leader did not care how many gave their life for him. All he was able to focus on was the lust, incredible passion and love that he felt for this statuesque woman. A furious, untouchable goddess of battle stood before him and all that he could focus on was her preservation. Standing as if frozen by Medusa's multi-eyed glare John felt the heat of flames around him but was unable to react. A stale-mate had been reached and for the first time in his gallant life, John felt apprehensive. His next move was essential as his men were now few. A retreat had become necessary to allow them to regroup and prepare for another attack. The delicate situation demanded more care than the usual attacks and John's men had served him extremely well, taking as few lives as possible, even at the risk of their own.

When they had first met, Shana had held no respect for the man who she had heard was amongst the most famous of sea dogs. Yet this time she felt quite differently and she was not about to let the famous Captain Hawkins off his revenge attack lightly. Securing her bloody and smoking weapons, Shana made a sudden chance move. Leaping over the Mermaid's 'Venge's clear decks she leapt up and grabbed a rope, swinging her agile body across to land beside John Hawkins. Unsheathing her deadly sharp weapon Captain Culley jabbed her cutlass into her victim's side and a ferocious skirmish began. As the two duelled the pyrate woman ridiculed John in front of his crew. Unbelievably, her taunting jibes made her admirer even more smitten with her dominant behaviour. Patrick's cries could be heard clearly over the din of battle ordering the privateer to flee or die a horrible death by his mother's hand. The Spanish had called him 'master thief of the unknown world' and Shana told him breathlessly between gritted teeth how disappointed she had felt when she had finally met such a coward. Firing a perfect final shot that hit the foremast of the once pristine vessel, Shana gave her challenger an insanely erotic smile before she leapt nimbly onto a boarding ramp and back over to the Mermaid's 'Venge. Recalling his crew at once, John lay bloody and injured on his damaged ship. Dropping his head back onto the boards he looked up into the pouring rain and smiled. She was as incredible as he had first believed and this encounter had sealed the undying love and respect that he felt for this woman. Feeling a renewed confidence that he had made a lasting impression, John pulled himself up and prepared for a busy night ahead.

Strong winds hit the western coast of Ireland that night but those remaining of Hawkins' determined crew made alterations and repairs to their vessel. Inside his cabin, John lay on the small wooden bunk looking into the eyes of Shana Culley's portrait. He was aroused beyond belief and full of lust for the woman who had captured his heart. Torrential rain beat against the pebble-glass porthole as John fantasised about the desirable pyrate queen. He dared not touch himself lest he ejaculate and spoil his plans for the rest of the night. She was beyond beautiful and Captain John Hawkins knew that he could make her the happiest she had ever been. A man of his word, he made a promise to himself that he would love, cherish and nurture his feisty equal until death took him from this world.

The storm hit them harder than Shana had expected and the rocky bay where they usually managed to drop anchor had become more dangerous than ever before. A landing party had gone ashore to warn Grace's militia of impending danger and Shana had sent a reluctant Patrick ashore. An ailing Tripod limped onto land answering questions from a high and buzzing Patrick as he struggled to stay conscious. Two of the crew noticed the sick man's voice tremor as he stumbled on slippery rocks and quickly came to his aid. Patrick became concerned and ran ahead for help. As he pushed hard against the cruel wind and rain the echoing shouts behind him blended with the sound of violent waves crashing against the rocks. Afraid to look back at the state of the Mermaid's 'Venge, Patrick gritted his teeth and pushed himself hard fighting against unforgiving, angry elements. A flickering light urged the boy on and he managed to quicken his pace on the challenging climb. Pure grit and determination pushed the exhausted boy's body to its limit and he managed to make himself heard, delivering his breathless message that his mother was in danger. Taking a wary look below him down the unforgiving steep cliffs, Patrick closed his eyes and begged the gods to save his mother and the crew.

Broken pieces of wood that had been part of an immaculate piece of engineering were being tossed around uselessly by the consuming torrents. Splintered and smashed beyond salvage or repair, timber masts and boards had become temporary floats for the survivors. Squinting in the hope of spotting his mother, Patrick began to pant, urgently trying to regain energy to enable him to return to the cove below. As he felt the weight of a warm sheepskin on his back the boy was lifted up just in time. Patrick's legs felt very hot and jelly-like and he let them dangle freely. No longer resisting, the worried child gave way to his rescuer and closed his eyes. He accepted that he could do nothing but wait.

Luckily for Shana and her men, Captain Hawkins returned that night and saw Shana's ship was in trouble. Launching two cockboats, John and his crew managed to save many of Shana's crew. John refused to give up searching for Shana who had been knocked unconscious and washed inside a smuggler's cave. Had it not been for John's infatuation, she would have surely died alone in the small, dark cavern.

Survivors were dropped safely onto the large rocks at the base of the steep hill climbing up to grassy gorse-lands of the Emerald Isle. After ensuring that the fittest amongst Shana's crew were enough to carry the injured to safety, John's men returned to their ship that still battled the heavy storm. Far enough away from land, the ship was only just managing to withstand the erratic waves and when the working crew had helped their captain carry the limp body of Shana aboard, they pulled anchor and rode the rough waves away from dangerous land. Captain Hawkins's crew had managed a perfect rescue mission and John was proud and extremely pleased. Carrying the unconscious pyrate captain into the shelter of his cabin, John could not resist stealing a kiss. Freezing but soft lips twitched under the full, moistness of his own and he felt his heart leap. A heady, almost drug-induced feeling overcame his very being as his heartbeat quickened and blood rushed to his loins. He could not wait to touch Shana's naked skin. Her captivating beauty was indescribable. The woman simply looked delectable as her cool, wet skin glistened in the dim lamplight of the cosy cabin. Standing speechless and motionless for a few minutes, John could hardly believe that the woman who he desired so deeply was lying defenceless before him. Taking total advantage of the unique and miraculous situation, John quickly began to unlace the tight corset that held Shana's substantial breasts together in such an aesthetically pleasing erotic manner. How could anyone have possibly resisted such temptation? Telling himself that he was merely disrobing the woman for her own good, he took a heavy breast in each hand and pressed his lips between their soft, damp curves. Smelling her divine, arousing scent and tasting the sweet sweat that had mixed with salty sea water worked John up to an ecstatic state of arousal. His breath quickened and the pressure of his erection against the wildest woman he had ever encountered almost brought him to orgasm there and then. He quietly withdrew from the small bunk where Shana still lay motionless in a seemingly peaceful slumber.

Out on deck, the team of professional sailors worked efficiently and quickly as they fought to manoeuvre the large vessel on a turbulent and unpredictable sea. From land the ship appeared to have reached a relatively safer position where she had a fair chance of weathering the unexpected storm. Grace O'Malley thought the worst of the tempest to be over and managed to calm Patrick who had been made fully aware of the situation. Although she had managed to convince Shana's only child that his mother would be safe with John Hawkins, he had still attacked one of Hawkin's crew who had been saved by Grace's men and brought up for questioning. Like a small demon possessed, Patrick had literally flown at the bewildered man, dagger drawn and grimacing menacingly, screaming an unearthly battle cry. Sinking sharp teeth into the side of his target's neck Patrick clung onto the sailor as if his life depended on it. Piercing cloth and skin, he jabbed the point of his sharp blade randomly into the shocked man's body. Shana's over-protective son swore that he would make his prisoner suffer if his mother did not return unharmed. Hours passed in the small castle whilst Patrick guarded his prisoner by a roaring fire. Wind howled around the solid structure and whistled through gaps in the small, wooden door. Staring at his captive, Patrick never once let his eyelids fall shut although his whole body was wracked with exhaustion and pain from the day's adventures. Grace had allowed the child a place to sleep in her room where she slept soundly but lightly as a woman in her position had to. A thick rope was secured to her bed post and occasionally it was pulled taut by the pyrate captain's favourite ship that she always kept tethered to the other end. The wily woman had to be sure that she would be warned if anyone dared steal the vessel. Patrick's face had set like stone and remained so until the early hours. Pissing out of the slot in the stone structure the boy never once lowered his defence whilst guarding the sailor. When dawn threw weak rays of the rising sun onto the cold stone floor, Grace took over guard and made her ward lie in her vacant bed for some well-earned sleep.

Aboard John Hawkin's ship many of the exhausted crew had retired to catch a few winks sleep. A skeleton crew kept the vessel steady and ready to act if a secondary storm broke out. Temporary repairs had been carried out and all seemed well. Below deck in the captain's cabin an hour had passed quickly by as John Hawkins took advantage of his fascinating unwitting guest. Tracing his fingers along the contours of Shana's perfect body, he carefully stroked her inner thighs and parted her long, tanned legs. Lying beside the most beautiful, sensual woman he had ever known, John pressed his warm body against hers. Resting his head in the nook of her arm, he nuzzled his face into a plump, round breast, drawing the large, stiffened nipple into his mouth. Groaning with pleasure, the aroused woman arched her back up from the feather-filled mattress. Shana's limp hand moved to rest on the back of John's neck but stayed there once it had found comfort. Every nerve-ending in his body felt alive and stimulated and his prick was rock hard. Keeping his breathing slow and steady, John kept his movements minimal and tried to stay quiet for as long as he possibly could. Shana's body responded wonderfully to every touch and caress. Wanting to give the desirable woman pleasure whilst pleasing himself, the attentive man stroked and teased every inch of her into semi-conscious arousal. Shana had the most inviting cunnie that he had ever seen. Breathing a sigh of sheer delight, he looked closely at the intricate tattoos along her large outer lips. Firmly but gently, he stroked the pretty floral patterns and traced a fingernail lightly along the lines until he had covered every part of the leafy design. Unusually large pink inner lips protruded from their decorated protection. Slowly lowering his bearded face, John swallowed before he began to kiss the incredibly soft, hairfree skin of Shana's silky cunnie. A contented moan told him all he needed to know as Shana came over and over whilst receiving John's tender attention. When she finally gained full consciousness, she grabbed the man who she had hated so passionately and drew herself up onto her knees. Straddling him whilst they shared a deep, desperate kiss, she sighed with pleasure and pushed down onto his hardness. Taking in his full length, the pyrate queen fucked John Hawkins hard and fast. They looked deep into each others' eyes as they reached an explosive climax. Fate had taken over and they both accepted that their love was meant to be. No words were exchanged... both sensitive souls knew from the depth of their hearts that they were madly in lust and love. What a perfect combination!

When mother and son were reunited and John Hawkins introduced into his new Celtic clan everyone felt slightly unnerved about the situation. Aware of Shana's impulsive nature, her family and friends watched her newest lover like hawks. Abi was surprisingly accepting of John and the two women shared him well. Patrick grew to trust his mother's new man and within a few months everything had settled nicely. John promised to help however he could with Grace's battle and openly admitted that he would do almost anything that Shana asked of him. The love that he felt for Shana was beyond any that he had experienced before and he intended, some day, to be with the defiant revolutionary.

The queen's favourite privateer had one more mission to accomplish for the fickle martinet before he would offer the beautiful pyrate a proposal that he hoped to God that she would accept. Before Captain John Hawkins and his cousin, Francis Drake set sail on the first attempt of a round the world voyage, John trusted Shana with the details of their ambitious mission. He was only too aware of her active opposition to slavery and although it infuriated her, she promised that she would not intervene and would allow him safe passage. In order to secure the queen's faith in him, John Hawkins had no choice but to complete his final mission as a privateer. It truly grieved Shana to think that she would be unable to free the slaves and seize valuable bounty for her own cause: She knew that this was the only way to confound any suspicion that John Hawkins and Captain Culley were linked. Despite her trust of the man who had saved her life, Shana decided to shadow her handsome admirer on his final contracted mission with the crown. It was an exciting prospect for her to follow two famous, respected privateers and unbeknown to them, witness the experienced sea-farers at work. Shana planned to have some fun with the wealthy mariner who had fallen head over heels in love with her. She was interested to find out just how besotted Captain John Hawkins really was.

Chapter 24

Tables turned

In the autumn of 1567 Queen Elizabeth had agreed to loan two of her vessels to John Hawkins for his voyage to America. The loan was to be in exchange for a generous share of profits earned from the ambitious world voyage. True to character, the tight-fisted monarch had sent him a pair of large, out-dated ships that had sailed on too many voyages over their recommended half dozen. Long voyages soon took their toll on many a vessel. Shipworms weakened the wooden structure and damage occurred regularly during lengthy journeys across dangerous seas. Unpredicted squalls and hurricanes forced navigators to change their route and many shipwrecks lay broken and useless on the sea bed.

On the 2nd October Hawkins set sail from Plymouth with a fleet of six ships. He captained the Jesus of Lubeck whilst his cousin, Drake commanded her sister ship, the Judith. The Jesus of Lubeck was one of the largest English vessels in the small fleet of six that left England's shores. Despite her impressive carrying capacity of up to seven hundred tons, the men-o-war and the Judith were over thirty years old and needed constant attention and repair. Despite this major flaw, the ships were fully armed and carrying good cannons that would hopefully deter any attack.

Shana hired a small crew and bought a ship that Hawkins would doubtfully recognise. Following two weeks after the privateer's fleet, Captain Culley made a speedy journey over to Africa to witness this intriguing man at work. Having obtained many African people from their own land he boosted his slave cargo to four hundred by seizing a Portuguese slave ship, the Madre de Dios. Shana was impressed by the capture that was carried out both efficiently and with speed and respect for the slaves... whether John had actually changed or was acting humanely for fear of word getting back to his love-interest, she could not be sure. Either way, Shana was pleased that the necessary mission was causing as little harm as possible to those people who did not deserve to be traded like lowly cattle. Unbeknown to anyone but her son and loyal crew, the freedom-fighter had plans to help the slaves to be freed after John had sold them.

Whilst Hawkins' flotilla was at anchor before setting out on the ambitious voyage, several Spanish ships had approached Plymouth harbour rather too closely, in Hawkins' opinion. Acting on impulse, he ordered his men to open fire and the Spaniards later protested that the English officer had violently over-reacted to their benign presence.

The Spaniards of the New World were easily persuaded to make illicit deals with Hawkins and Drake who managed to sell most of the slaves for almost 30,000 gold pesos. Shana and her men had dropped anchor near to the flotilla's docking point and kept watch from a comfortable distance. Hawkins soon continued his voyage and the wind speed increased dramatically. From the decks of her lighter vessel, Captain Culley watched the crew of the Jesus of Lubeck reduce her sails. Shana and her men managed to run ahead of the wind and Hawkins ordered his men to do the same. As she witnessed one of Hawkins' fleet, a barque called the William and John, disappear from sight, she feared the worst for the man who she respected more every minute. Hawkins needed all of his ships for a successful mission. Forced northward by storm force winds that had caused substantial damage to the Jesus of Lubeck, Hawkins ordered men to plug her leaks. Tossed and pounded by unforgiving waves the ship managed to survive four gruelling days of battle against the unrelenting storms. Driven further southwest into seas that no other English ship had claimed to have sailed, the Jesus of Lubeck was eventually spotted by a Spanish vessel. The captain told the exhausted mariners that the only refuge on that coast was in the harbour of San Juan de Ulúa, the sole official port of Nueva España.

In the autumn of 1568 the surviving ships of Hawkins' fleet regrouped and approached the port of San Juan de Ulúa where they planned to sell the last of the slaves and repair the vessels. All too aware of the dangers posed by docking at this enemy port, Hawkins promised that his presence would be short-lived whilst his men restored the battered ships and replenished water and food supplies. Hot on Hawkins' trail Shana made her presence known, taking fresh supplies and materials to her keen admirer. Shocked but delighted to see the feisty woman who he had painfully missed since leaving her only a few months before, Hawkins swallowed his pride and accepted her much-needed help.

Spending a wonderful night of pure passion with her lover aboard one of Queen Elizabeth's own ships, the pyrate queen felt a well-deserved sense of one-upmanship. Unable to resist intervening on behalf of the African people who were still chained helplessly below decks,

Shana made plans to give them their freedom. Taking full advantage of her aroused and vulnerable lover, she seduced him over and over again. When the cheeky pyrate temptress sat perched on top of John, who lay beneath her in a blissful post-orgasmic state, she persuaded him to allow the last few slaves their freedom. Holding a dagger to his throat, she told him that he had no choice in the matter but wanted to hear him give his consent. Undercover of twilight the shell-shocked slaves were successfully transported onto Shana's ship where they were fed and their wounds tended by her willing crew.

The following day a strong Spanish fleet sailed into San Juan de Ulua harbour. Shana was still aboard the Jesus of Lubeck when she counted thirteen Spanish ships from John's Hawkins' cabin. Two of the vessels were warships which was bad news for Hawkins. Shana had a terrible feeling about the whole situation and urged John to attack. Despite having enough cannon-power to prevent the enemy fleet from entering the harbour, Hawkins was aware that this would only incite war and they would stand no chance of survival. Don Martín Enríquez, newly appointed governor of Nueva España was on board the Merchant fleet. On arrival, he agreed to negotiate with Hawkins but the Spaniard was pedantic and the proceedings lasted for three days.

Finally a pact was agreed between the two men and Hawkins' men would be allowed ashore only to buy supplies and material to repair their storm-ravaged ships. The viceroy insisted that the Spanish fleet anchor close to the English vessels to ensure total compliance. When John returned to his ship he was surprised to find Shana livid and ready to 'attack the arrogant bastard who dared doubt a fellow ca'tain's 'an'rable word!' John and his temperamental lover argued loudly and during the heated quarrel Shana punched him square on the jaw. Losing control of his temper John told his attacker that she was the most impossibly violent woman he had ever met and that his wife would surely shrink in her presence... After a few seconds silence, the two burst into fits of laughter and Captain Watkins ordered his men to make ready their cannons. While the battle-hungry pair shared their most passionate kiss ever, the Spanish had already opened fire on the English vessels. After playing for time, the viceroy had sent for soldiers from Veracruz whilst lulling the unsuspecting English captain into a false sense of security. In a sudden fit of ferocious rage Shana ran below decks to take charge of John's crew manning the cannons. A fierce cannonade began and two of the Spanish ships were sunk. John leapt out onto the decks and drew his pistols firing his first shot right between the eyes of a Spanish sailor. Safe in the knowledge that her crew was nearby and undoubtedly ready for a surprise attack, Shana encouraged the men to fight harder than they had ever fought before.

During the treacherous ambush, most of Hawkins' fleet was completely annihilated by the Spanish traitors. The Jesus of Lubeck's foremast had gone and her mainmast crippled. With ropes still attached to the dock, the queen's vessel sank and the Swallow and the Angel soon joined her. In the fierce battle only two small ships managed to escape the onslaught. Hawkins and Culley managed to make it to the Minion and Drake boarded the Judith. Five hundred men and boys perished that day because of a cowardly act of betrayal and only two surviving, over-burdened ships were able to retreat. Had it not been for Shana's pyrate ship firing on the Spanish from her advantageous position, Hawkins's whole fleet would have been destroyed.

In his later book, Hawkins' failed to document that almost all of the gains from the voyage had been transferred to a nameless ship... or that the African people aboard that very ship were able to start a new life in Nueva España with a fair share of Spanish gold. It was merely reported that all but two of the small ships were lost, together with their spoils. Drake had led the way out of the harbour but the two ships became separated during the night. It was however sadly true that the overburdened vessels had to abandon many of their crew on the North American coast. There were not enough provisions for all of the survivors and conditions aboard were miserable. Forced to eat leather, vermin and the flesh of dead crewmembers, the starving men endured agonizing days without water. Many men volunteered to take their chances ashore rather than face such degradation and Hawkins sailed those 'most desirous to go homewardes' back to England.

Only a few reached home and told horrific stories of the men and boys who were left behind. Unbeknown to most, Hawkins never forgave himself for his bad decision and despite Shana's reassurance that he could not have foreseen such disastrous events, he still anguished over the fate of his men. Some survivors walked for months, their party steadily diminishing as they lost hope of returning to friendly shores. Others had been captured and suffered terrible torture and imprisonment in the Spanish galleys. Three survivors were reported to have been burned to death. Most of the men left in New Spain suffered atrocious cruelty under the laws of the Inquisition. A few were accused of heresy and burned at the stake whilst others were hanged. Some died of injuries inflicted during horrific torture and others were made to work the oars on Spanish galleys or left to rot in dark, damp prison cells. Mercifully any boys were spared and sent to monasteries.

On their return to England in 1570, Hawkins felt unfathomable bitterness towards his monarch. Elizabeth showed more dismay for the loss of her privateer's bounty than the lives of the gallant men who had served with him on the disastrous and useless venture. Secretly he decided to join Captain Culley in a life of pyracy and allow his cousin, Francis to take his place as daring seafarer and explorer. Hawkins wanted no glory for being amongst the first to successfully circumnavigate the globe. Drake was welcome to the role. By choosing to be with the notorious pyrate queen, the privateer had turned his back on England's official monarch. Having lost all faith and respect for Elizabeth, Hawkins had chosen a new queen to whom he intended to devote his services and heart. In future he would have to tread very carefully, ensuring not to ignite more hatred from the palace. He would rather die than lose the woman of his dreams and the egotistical Elizabeth was going to have to accept that brutal fact. Francis Drake agreed to manage his shipyard company in his long-term absence and John asked him to commission a worthy new ship to be built especially for his new lover. On hearing his rebellious cousin's decision to live as a pyrate, Francis feared for his safety whilst in the company of Captain Culley. He knew of the queen's hatred of this dangerous woman and vowed to do everything he possibly could to protect the lovers. Francis left immediately for Hampton Court and paid Queen Elizabeth a visit. Gossip had already reached the monarch's ear and she demanded to know the identity of the mysterious female captain who had come to the aid of her privateers. By showering Ann Boleyn's hardened daughter with the most precious jewels from the Spanish bounty, Drake managed to distract her bitter mind from the thought of the saviour being the infamous pyrate queen.

Before returning to his comfortable home, Francis visited the shipyard and hired enough craftsmen to ensure completion of the majestic galleon that John had ordered. He would personally ensure that the Emaleeza would be a fine vessel, worthy of its owner... a vessel capable of carrying a crew of a hundred, hold twenty cannons and still have ample room for storage and livestock. Most important of all, the figurehead had to be carved and painted in the exact likeness of her beautiful captain. Looking down at the miniature painting of Captain Shana Culley that Francis held in his hand, he smiled to himself and understood perfectly why the queen of England loathed the woman who had managed to capture a nation's heart.

Chapter 25

An Extravagant Gift for a Perfect Lover

The launch of the Emaleeza coincided with Patrick Culley's tenth birthday. The child had been let into the secret of the purpose-built ship that would hopefully serve her captain well for many years to come. Patrick had impressed John Hawkin's beyond expectation and also captured the heart of the man who had fallen in love with his mother. Having built up a trust in Shana's lover, Patrick chose to spend much of his time in the ship merchant's company. The growing boy was adult in his ways and a strapping lad. Tall, muscular and handsome like his mother, Patrick shared her need for adventure and excitement. Anyone seeing the pyrate boy, who looked much older than his age, noticed the uncanny resemblance to his mother. Patrick's tanned skin enhanced his mischievous bright blue eyes, broad shoulders and proud, upright stance that gave an impression of power and confidence.

Nombre de Dios was the destination of choice where the new family hoped to begin a happy life together. John and Shana made short term plans not knowing how long they would be able to enjoy much needed privacy. Captains Hawkins and Culley made sure to hire men who had no respect for the English monarch and set sail for Brazil as soon as possible. Apart from Moses and Remando, the crew were all newly-hired pyrates happy to serve under the two strong characters. Patrick and Abi loved the new ship that John had commissioned for his pyrate queen and whilst aboard, they enjoyed modern luxuries that they had never experienced before. In the mild winter of 1571, Shana and her new clan settled in Nombre de Dios. Despite their unusual relationship Shana, John and Abi got on very well together and there was no jealousy. Captain Culley kept both of her lovers satisfied and never showed favouritism. Although Shana had aged since her first affair with Abi, her firm body had changed little but had only become more curvaceous. Attractive lines had formed at the corner of her eyes and she wore the look of an experienced, satisfied woman. People would feel excited in her presence and there was an inexplicable aura surrounding the free-spirited soul. Natives of Nombre de Dios warmed to the pyrate queen and her company, especially Patrick. He quickly picked up the local language and was able to help Moses and Abi understand the ways of the indigenous people.

John quickly became accustomed to pyrate life and enjoyed planning raids with his lover. Shana and Abi preferred to stick together on forays whilst John captained his own vessel. Between them, the team managed to continue Shana's war against slavery and operate a successful system re-locating willing African people to uninhabited islands. Having accumulated a large amount of wealth between them, the two captains were able to live very comfortably in their new home on the coast of Brazil. When a letter arrived from Drake informing them that he had managed to convince Queen Elizabeth that John was very active in his shipbuilding business and unable to attend court for a while, John felt more settled. Francis had been successful in reassuring

Elizabeth of John's continuing support for his queen and therefore making more money for her. The conniving captain had managed to persuade the materialistic monarch to grant newly promoted Admiral Hawkins a seat in Parliament and more importantly, make him her naval treasurer. This would enable Drake to act by proxy and continue making profits for the sovereign. He was showering affection upon the conceited monarch and fast replacing his absent cousin as the queen's new favourite. These diversions should allow John and Shana some freedom... for a while at least. By a complete stroke of luck Hawkins had already begun to gain his queen's confidence by demonstrating loyalty just a month before he had met Shana. To his queen's delight, John had acted as a double-agent when the Spanish were plotting to depose her. His fidelity and devotion pleased Elizabeth greatly, especially when he had been successful in foiling the mission. John and Shana were more relaxed in the knowledge that Drake felt sure that the queen was confident that Hawkins would never betray her... however they never dropped their guard as the self-obsessed woman was as temperamental as her father had been.

Patrick was very happy in the new home that his mother had designed to house her ever-expanding family. Originally built as a single story structure, Shana's home had been extended. Patrick called the rickety construction 'Prop House' when the addition of an upper floor started to overhang the lower floor. It was comical to see the wooden props, gradually added to keep the heavy construction from falling sideways. Prop House was a very happy home despite its strange appearance. John and Shana loved the eccentricity of the crooked house. Flint loved to climb and swing around the props whilst Micken sat perched above him, one skinny leg tucked beneath him.

It was a memorable day when Juan-Pedro Primondramendos came into Patrick's life. The little, fat sailor had always longed to become a pyrate. He went by the name of 'Whoo' since foreigners had always found great difficulty pronouncing his full name. From an extremely religious Roman Catholic family, Whoo was a God-fearing man who had never managed to find the right woman to marry. One of thirteen boys, Juan Pedro was the black sheep of the family. Back in his Spanish hometown, whenever anything had gone wrong, Juan-Pedro had been involved in some way. No-one had ever disliked the mischievous character but all were aware that he was trouble. With his sing-song voice and happy-go-lucky manner, the crafty rogue had an uncanny ability of getting away with everything. He played the vihuela excruciatingly badly plucking away at the strings with stumpy, sausage-like fingers whilst singing like a tomcat whose testicles were caught in a mangle. Patrick loved the animated little man and Juan-Pedro returned the feeling.

Shana met Whoo, which he pronounced with a long, drawn-out hack as if clearing mucus from the back of the throat, due to a bar brawl. She had taken her ailing friend, Tripod out alone one night to help drown his sorrow. Her friend was now fading fast and could not have weighed much more than her healthy son. When Tripod had made advances to a sailor's wife thinking that she was a whore, her husband had over-reacted. In his intoxicated state the pyrate had been knocked senseless by a strong young man who should have known better than hit a harmless drunk. Whoo had punched Tripod's attacker in the mouth but the man had immediately counterpunched with a perfect left-hook splitting the shorter man's eyebrow open. Blood poured from the gash and Whoo was unable to see the cut-throat razor sweep in front of his eyes slicing most of his nose from his face. Had Shana not been near enough to thrust her disembowelling weapon into the intestines of the offender, then Whoo would have taken a fatal gash to the throat. Screaming as she saw her son leap towards Tripod's assailant just as the long razor blade sliced through the air in a wide arc, Shana froze. As the commotion settled a spray of blood shot up from the floor and she feared the worst. Blood was flowing everywhere and Captain Culley was unable to see the extent of the wounds that her child had suffered. Terrified that Patrick had taken a fatal cut from the evily sharp razor, she pleaded desperately for help, unable to control her despairing cries. Patrick lay still, covered with thick, red blood. Dreadful fear gripped Shana's heart and she felt it squeezing the beating muscle. Searing pain wracked her body as she felt the grief and dread build to a crescendo within her trembling body. Sounds became muffled and a strong stench filled her nose. The man who she had cut through lay at her feet and she saw that he had sliced open his own throat rather than die in prolonged agony.

Dropping to her knees beside her child, Shana began to wipe the blood from his beautiful face, frantically checking for wounds. Nothing... Patrick was alright... Instantly sober Shana picked up her son and carried him outside for fresh air. Smacking him firmly on the back, she felt relieved when he spluttered and coughed himself into consciousness. Tripod and Whoo joined mother and son and all went back to prop house where Abi, Moses and John had spent the evening mapping out new voyage routes. Patrick had settled down for the night outside where he often enjoyed sleeping under a moonlit sky. Flint and Sparky, who was showing signs of pregnancy, lay snuggled together on the woven grass mat next to the boy.

Having an inherent natural gift with animals Patrick had taken on it on himself to care for the female monkey during the period of gestation. His concern for the wild creature was well-founded as the two monkey mates were of a different species. Curious and eager to see the offspring that the unusual ape union would produce, Patrick made sure that Sparky ate the best fruit available and Flint was keen to fuss over his partner. Sparky's kind were usually much larger than tiny Flint and the two primates looked remarkably different. It was clear to see that the attraction was largely due to appearance as the male Tamarin monkey paid so much attention to his mate's large protruding nipples and white-blonde hair. Sparky was an albino ape and had to stay in the shade most of the day as her pale blue eyes caused her pain when exposed to sunlight. She was much smaller than any of the other female apes in Nombre de Dios but still much bigger than her new mate. Almost obsessively Flint would groom and fondle Sparky's unusual silver fur and permanently erect nipples. He had even started to suckle milk from the swollen conical-shaped mammary glands! Still allowing Flint to mate with her, the patient mother-to-be seemed to enjoy all the attention.

Within her original troop, Sparky had barely had any contact with the others and was treated as an outcast. Sadly, this happened once again in the lush forests of

Nombre de Dios. There had been a drop in the male population of local apes over the past two years. The day a particularly horny little Tamarin playboy arrived with his mate, Sparky caused a great deal of jealousy amongst the female ape community. Patrick was sure that Sparky's platinum-blonde coat had attracted his little companion's attention and her remarkably long nipples had reminded him of delicious cinnamon sticks. No longer able to resist temptation, Flint had leapt over to the branch along which Sparky was parading seductively. Flint had been ignited again by the pregnant female's spark and she was clearly inviting her mate to mount her. Sparky lifted her pretty, coiling tail upright to display her moist, pink nether regions more clearly. Grimacing as he mated with the brazen female, Flint mounted his mate amidst the flowers and leaves, high on the branch of a sacred Brazilian tree. The sweet smelling wood of this tree could only be used in sacred buildings. Local people believed the mating between Flint and the pregnant white ape to be a good sign for the people of Nombre de Dios. Ever since Flint and Sparky's sexual encounter the lofty tree had become the most sacred in the land. Shrines were placed at the roots and amongst the flourishing branches. By worshipping and preserving the tree, the people paid homage to the spirits that they were sure dwelled within. Women and children dressed the trunk of the sacred tree with symbolic silk. Patrick painted Shana's favourite picture, a surrealistic version of the sacred branches that held the loving apes with twig fingers, shading Patrick, his mother and Micken beneath its outstretched branches. On first glimpse it could not be seen, but on closer inspection Shana noticed Irish's strong, broad shoulders and long, flowing hair. Her son had drawn his guardian as if he were a spirit within the trunk of the sacred tree. Feeling deep sadness, Captain Culley had asked her son for what she deemed his finest piece of art yet and placed it in a frame that she hung in her cabin.

When Shana told Tripod that Flint was going to be a father, he felt proud of the miniature primate's conquest. Although the disease that riddled the pyrate's body had caused his mind to stray into bouts of full-blown mania, he occasionally had a lucid moment. Shana made sure to make the most of these and paid a local widow to care for her dying friend. The woman had also been paid to tend to his sexual needs. Shana knew that sex was one of the few pleasures that he could enjoy during his last days and besides, the widow was glad of the money.

Patrick had lit a small fire outside and was busy sewing parchment together when his mother shouted for him to fetch some fresh spring water. Moses did not utter a word but gently touched the boy's shoulder signalling him to stay and continue with his work on the bindings. He hauled his large body up from the floor and lumbered off towards the spring carrying a large bucket. The widow was riding Tripod inside prop house whilst Shana, John and Abi tended to Whoo's injuries. The Spanish man's face was a mess. Not being blessed with the best of looks, Whoo had lost all of his teeth and was in the habit of wearing a terribly carved set of wooden ones. Lisping as he pleaded with Shana to take care of his 'clackers' as he referred to them, the Spanish pyrate held a filthy blood-covered hand firmly over the middle of his face. John Hawkins stood over the bleeding man who was flatly refusing to allow anyone near his nose. When Moses entered the room with fresh water, he sat on the chubby little man's legs whilst John pinned his arms down onto the table. Shana took hold of the glob of grisly flesh that had flapped back onto a shattered cheekbone in the struggle to pin the patient down. He was lucky that a piece of skin was still attached to the shapeless mess that was only just recognisable as the poor man's nose.

With a steady hand, the dextrous captain pushed the nose back into place, the razor had sliced so deeply that bare bone was visible. Trying her best to place the nostril holes in line with the open part of Whoo's skull, Shana managed to stitch the sensory organ onto his face. When the operation was over, Whoo leapt up, ran over to grab a pitcher of wine and threw back his head, guzzling the welcome nectar. He would always be hideously scarred but with a little luck at least he would be able to breathe more easily. By some miracle, he might even regain some of his sense of smell.

The grateful Spaniard never finished his thank you speech as everyone disappeared outside at the sound of Flint's blood-curdling screams. Knocking into Patrick, who was on the way in to fetch his mother at Tripod's request, John managed to save himself from tripping over the frantic little monkey. Teeth bared and eyes wide with terror, the frenzied animal was wringing his hands in stress and fear. Leaping onto John's shoulder, Flint pulled at the tall man's collar and signalled in the direction of the temple where the sacred tree stood. Knowing that the situation had to be urgent, John started to run fast with the ape clutching his neck tightly. It only took a few minutes for them to reach the horrific scene but the damage had already been done.

Baring long, sharp, pointed teeth as their evil-looking mouths opened wide in threatening snarls, four male apes stood over the torn and bloodied mound of white fur that had once been Flint's mate. Drawing his pistols, John fired two shots at the maniacal monsters who had murdered poor Sparky. Glazed eyes of the palest opaque blue stared unblinking into the peaceful branches of the sacred tree above as if expecting to be rescued by its delicate branches. Flint jumped down as the apes scattered at the sound of the shots. Fleeing in different directions they disappeared into the lush undergrowth leaving a devastated Flint tearing frantically around the body of his pregnant mate.

All poor John could do was stand and groan, unable to comprehend the whole situation. Hearing Patrick's call, John warned the child to stay away but he still came into the clearing. Birds had stopped singing and the forest appeared to be holding its breath in disbelief at what had happened that afternoon. Flint held Sparky's head in his hands and placed his lips against her forehead, flashing pleading looks between Patrick and Jock. The noises that the bereaved monkey was making were so disturbing that neither knew what to do. As Patrick approached his tiny friend he started to cry whilst trying to calm the confused and devastated animal. Flint was desperately trying to push his dead mate's arm back into her shoulder socket. Uncontrolled, high-pitched squealing echoed through the forest and Patrick watched his pet in utter despair.

Shana had gone immediately to Tripod's room where she found him lying alone on his favourite silk cushions. Before he asked his best friend to mix the concoction that they had agreed would be administered should he begin to lose his mind, he gave her a small box to give to Patrick. Without a word Shana left her friend and sent a boy to fetch the widow. By the time she returned to his room with the drink that she had made using a combination of poisonous substances to create an extremely potent brew, Tripod was enjoying the pleasures of the flesh for his final time. He was not terribly lucid but showed signs of enjoyment as the widow massaged his erect penis using the healing and stimulating salves. Shana had spent many a night learning as much as she possibly could about natural sexual stimulants since she had learned that Tripod was suffering from a terminal disease. Painstakingly mixing a variety of lotions, salves and tonics, Captain Culley was determined to try everything to help her hypersexual friend retain his renowned sexual prowess. As she had stood measuring and mixing together the poisons that she had calculated would give her friend the quickest, most painless death possible, Shana did not shed a single tear. Abi sat silently not knowing how to help her lover, but she knew that nothing could possibly ease the difficulty of the task that Shana was about to carry out. Passing a leather-bound volume to the pyrate queen, she kissed her gently on the cheek and left her to her unavoidable duty.

Shana had managed to acquire a copy of 'The Book of Venoms', written by Magister Santes de Ardoynis back in 1424. This particular volume was still valued amongst modern apothecaries as the most valuable piece of reference material of the time. Having read the manuscript from cover to cover and learned about the properties of every poison listed, Shana had concocted the most effective toxic mixture to carry out Tripod's euthanasia. If the wise spice trader's calculations were correct, the heavy helping of ginseng would enhance and maintain her horny friend's libido. She hoped and prayed that she would be able to quite literally, send her randy friend off to the Otherworld with an explosive bang. Finally satisfied with the fruit of her labour, a walnut-sized pill containing a dose of aconite, more commonly known as wolf's bane or thung; the Anglo-Saxon word for this very poisonous plant, a little taxus baccata; a lethal poison extracted from conifer trees, a snippet of fool's parsley or deadly hemlock root, not forgetting a generous helping of belladonna, or 'pretty woman', as the Italians called the most apt poison, added to help induce Tripod's final orgasm. As a precaution the shrewd alchemist threw in a smidgen of arsenic and bitter almonds to guarantee death. Lavender took away the bitter taste and also added its valuable therapeutic, calming properties and finally Shana stirred in a drop of honey, a sprinkling of coffee and the pyrate's favourite 'poison' rhum, to make a long drink.

Taking the fatal beverage into Tripod she made no fuss but handed it to him as she would on a normal day. The only difference that evening was the toast that she proposed to her special friend: 'Aude aliquid dignum', were the powerful words that she chose… 'Dare something worthy' and as she left the man who she would miss dreadfully, enjoying his final romp with an attractive woman, Captain Culley whispered more Latin words as she bid farewell to a remarkable man: 'Cosi vivo piacer conduce a morte'… 'Such intense pleasure leads to death.'

Chapter 26

Jumping the Broom

São Vicente had been one of Tripod's favourite haunts and the crew missed hearing the gregarious pyrate's witty comments as they went through the routine landing process. Both John and Shana realised that morale had plummeted to an unusual low as the crippled seaman had without doubt, been the life and soul of any ship on which he served. The Emaleeza had been no exception and, as the rigging was tightened and the huge, weighty sails gathered in to allow her to rest on the soothingly gentle lapping of an ebbing tide, Shana shed a tear for her old friend. Whoo was the new comedian aboard the vessel yet despite his optimistic nature even he found it difficult to lift the eerily morose atmosphere.

Patrick had been awake all night with Flint clinging to him like a baby whilst the boy did his best to care for the miniature premature ape that had been cut from its dead mother's womb. Even Micken had tried to feed the vulnerable animal and regularly dropped a sweetcorn kernel into its creased little lap. Barely the size of Patrick's thumb, the minute creature squirmed slowly in the warm palm of his nurturer's hand and accepted drops of goat's milk. Living in one of his mother's handy multi-purpose pouches, tiny Tripod managed to thrive under the tender loving care of Patrick Culley.

Within months, the little fellow had managed to cheer his father up although he still found it difficult to hold his son. Sadly, poor Flint had completely lost his lust for life and loving and was terrified of harming his defenceless baby. Wherever Patrick roamed, the two monkeys would be concealed somewhere on his person and many a time Flint would appear, seemingly out of nowhere, to surprise a passer-by.

Once John and Shana had found somewhere private and relatively quiet to settle for a while, Whoo became the family and ship's cook. Providing delicious Spanish dishes for those who had decided to stay with Shana until her next venture, the stocky little man felt that it was the least that he could do to repay his debt to the pyrate captain.

During 1572 and 1573 São Vicente was the place that Captain Culley and her clan called home for a stable yet melancholy year. One of Irish's finely detailed drawings of Shana hung on the wall of her small, simply furnished new home and the words that he had written with his quill beneath her likeness read, 'Dum spiro spero...' their translation, 'As long as I breath I hope'. In the year of our Lord 1572, religious unrest had reignited bad feeling amongst Protestants and Roman Catholics. John Hawkins received a letter from his cousin, Francis Drake telling him that Sir Walter Raleigh had witnessed angry Protestants massacre Roman Catholics in Paris. This shocking and appalling event had caused civil unrest all over France and had sparked off similar atrocities all over the country.

Roman Catholics in England had become worried that the same situation would develop there. News from his cousin always spurred John Hawkins into action and the dreadful events prompted the man into making an important decision. During the month when his cousin had captured a substantial shipment of silver that had been destined for Spain, Captain John Hawkins asked his pyrate lover for her hand in marriage. Although Queen Elizabeth had encouraged the word to be spread of a huge haul of riches being brought back to England by the patriotic and noble Sir Francis Drake, the hoard had been remarkably less than most of Captain Culley's hauls. Propaganda had become an essential weapon being used by the intelligent and cunning English monarch to help lull the fears of her uneasy subjects.

Agreeing to make their union a little more secure, Shana told John Hawkins that she would accept his offer of commitment if he would unite with her in the old Celtic pagan way. Patrick was consulted before Shana would agree to a Handfasting ceremony and accept a Claddagh ring to represent their love. A gold and ruby necklace that had been fashioned into a flame-like star was John's gift to his new bride. Shana's lover, Abi turned out to be the most refreshingly feminine flower maiden and Patrick tied together the wrists of his mother and her new husband, sealing their union. The couple promised to remain together for a year and a day whilst two monkeys clung onto their permanent host, Patrick for dear life. Moses bawled like a baby for the first time ever and his joyous tears continued to flow when the two pyrate captains jumped the broom together. Shots rang out and could be heard for miles as the pyrate party went on well into the early hours. Music and celebrations changed the mood of the Culley pyrate clan and Remendo kissed Abi in an impulsive moment of tenderness. The lingering kiss sparked off an unforeseen romance and Abi was surprised to find her heterosexual tendencies return as her new lover managed to take her to the heights of sexual arousal. Spending a long and hot night together in the opium fields amongst the heady poppies, the amorous pair found a new emotional high in their union.

As the only natural port of São Vicente, Port Grande was the best place for Shana and John to build their language college. Their plan was to fund a project to educate local native Indians. Since the main income for the area was from cattle produce and sugar cane plantations, a small college would hopefully encourage and empower local people, giving them an opportunity to begin new ventures in their community. Shana and Abi enjoyed working there and Patrick quickly improved his language skills. Living in São Vicente was wonderful in the sunny season but proved far more testing during the rainy season. Tropical forests provided plentiful supplies and John and Shana led their own raids on a variety of trade and slave ships, but made sure to take advantage of their ideal position. Plundering many heavily-burdened privateer vessels bound for Spain, they brought wealth to São Vicente. Married life, albeit unconventional, suited Shana well. It also allowed the pyrate captain and her female lover the freedom to enjoy each other as they pleased. John was good to Patrick who was fast growing into a fine pyrate. It pleased him greatly that his mother was proud of him. Without wanting to tempt fate, Shana felt that finally she and her son could look forward to happier times.

Chapter 27

The Gloom of 1574

1574 turned out to be a dreadful year and began with a heart-breaking event. A dreadful, searing pain in her groin woke Shana one hot and oppressive morning. The Alberto College in São Vicente had gained an excellent reputation and wealthy merchants had begun to give substantial donations to the principal of the successful establishment. Abi had taken over running the educational institute and more than fifty students were on her records. Absence was a rarity and the tutors managed to keep the students' attention and even entertained the young people with stories of pyrate heists and adventures.

The small village where the Culley clan had built their simple wooden home remained peaceful and quiet. Surrounded by coconut, corn and sugarcane plantations, it nestled on the outskirts of a rather sparse forest in comparison to the lush tropical woodlands back in Nombre de Dios. John had risen early as usual and had gone out with Patrick to buy fresh fish from the fishermen who brought in their first catch at sunrise. The warm, sticky blood between Shana's legs smelt sweet... at least in comparison with the gallons of blood that had sprayed from the wounds of her enemies. This time, the strong metallic stench was not present and as the distraught woman stared in horror and disbelief at the red sodden cotton sheets beneath her. She dreaded the thought of touching between her legs. It felt as though a small, soft ball had been inserted inside her, but Shana was only too aware of what was stuck inside the tight muscular vaginal wall. Squeezing her muscles as hard as she could, she felt so frightened. The poor woman wanted nothing more that to give Patrick a baby brother or sister.

Teardrops splashed onto the wooden blood-spattered floorboards as the desperate mother shuffled toward the seat of easement that her husband had constructed for his pregnant wife's comfort. Groaning in absolute agony, Shana ground her teeth furiously as she waddled unsteadily toward the plank where she could urinate. Placing a hand very gently under the jelly-like protrusion, the expectant mother dared not feel too much detail of the tiny, lifeless foetus that her womb had rejected. Refusing to allow her body to expel her second child, Shana began to shout loudly. 'Fie upon thee should this chile' fall dead from my body!' Cursing the sanctimonious Christian God who she had grown to detest since the birth of Protestantism, the weakening pyrate queen fought to stay conscious. Sweat streamed from every pore of her skin as she collapsed onto the holed plank of wood. Trapped painfully under the weight of her body, her hand still held the small being that felt colder every second. In utter desperation Shana tried to grasp the sludgy mass and push it back up inside her womb... in hope of some miracle that would enable her spawn to survive the fatal miscarriage. As the room began to spin around her, she hurled a spray of projectile vomit before finally losing consciousness.

Weeping uncontrollably, John Hawkins held his wife's limp body and rocked her gently in his arms. The tiny baby girl who lay on the floor in front of its mother looked so painfully beautiful. Shana's watery vomit had washed away most of the blood that had covered the perfectly formed foetus. Baby Bess had the prettiest soft dark hair and tiny black eyelashes just like her big brother's. Since her eyes remained closed, John never knew what colour they had been but her mother had taken a look before she allowed John to take their baby to prepare her for burial. The most beautiful pair of almond-shaped blue eyes stared unseeing at Shana as she wept for her stillborn child. Patrick did not say a word but held his mother close and kissed his tiny sister's pale and delicate forehead before leaving the room to shed his tears alone. John stayed strong as men were supposed to but inside his grief was like none felt before.

On the day of Patrick's baby sister's burial, the tiny corpse was baptised before she was laid to rest in the local churchyard. Bess Sushana Hawkins-Culley looked so peaceful and perfect as the tiny coffin lid was fixed in place. On the evening of the quiet family wake, Abi was surprised to receive a letter from her home back in England. Terrified to read her sister's words in case they told her something bad, Shana took the parchment and unrolled it on Abi's behalf. As her lover read the words aloud, Abi broke down in tears ... Ma Turnbull had been taken ill with the sweating sickness and although Flo was nursing her, she feared the worst. Patrick tried in vain to console the hysterical woman but Abi would not calm down. Unable to react and prevent her friend from leaving, Shana told her concerned son to fetch some food for her long journey back to Mary Maggy's. Whilst Patrick prepared a bag of spare clothes, nourishment and money for the twin, Remando told Shana that he was very concerned about Abi. The kindly cook insisted that he would go with her to Mary Maggy's and the two left immediately for the docks. They made it just in time and boarded one of John's trade ships bound for England.

Remando and Abi grew closer as he comforted her in the confines of the small cabin that the captain had lent to the couple for the duration of the journey. Abi felt safe in the kindly man's arms and was able to voice suppressed feelings of guilt and concern for the family she had left behind. Admitting that she had been selfish in running away with her pyrate lover, Abi sobbed as Remando listened silently. She could not stress her regret enough and was grateful when she saw the tiny vial of opium that her comforter produced. She smiled as she appreciated her thoughtful lover's unselfish nature as Shana had passed the potent drug to Remando. Even in her grief, she had been thinking of Abi's welfare. Within an hour Abi was sound asleep, her pain numbed for a short while.

When the whole ship suddenly jolted with a mighty crash Remando struggled to keep hold of the unconscious woman. The small cabin shuddered with the aftershock of the collision and the Spanish cook checked for Abi's vital signs. Despite a huge gash over the sleeping woman's brow she was still breathing normally but Remando had to move fast. He could hear the yells of protest out on the decks and had experienced too many pyrate attacks not to recognise the panicked sounds. The devoted man stood as upright as he possibly could, given the awkward angle that Abi had fallen across him. He tried in vain to lift the young woman... she could not be moved.

When he noticed that the captain's weighty oak desk had fallen onto Abi's ankle, Remando let out frustrated cry and was relieved to see the captain of the ship appear at the open cabin door. Yelling for his help, Remando's face fell in despair as he saw a bright red spot of blood expand into a large, dark mass on the pure white linen shirt. The captain slowly sank to the floor and died. With a last attempt the desperate man heaved Abi's floppy, weighty bulk out of the trap and dragged her from the confines of the cabin. Remando's hearing suddenly failed and eerie muffled echoes accompanied the brutal scenes that were taking place around him. Seeing that there was no hope for either of them if he did not act quickly, the stocky man laid Abi down and drew his pistol. Even the sound of the gunpowder firing the gun sounded muted yet the gun-wielder later swore that he had actually witnessed the shot spin out from the barrel in slow-motion. As Remando took the blow to his head from a heavy club, the last thing he would remember was seeing his precious Abi being molested by a tall, dark pyrate.

No-one asked Remando how he had managed to make it back to São Vicente and even if they had it was doubtful that he could have told them. Shana refused to believe that her Abi was dead. She just could not bear the thought of losing another loved one. At night, the pyrate queen lay awake listening to Remando's disturbed cries and remembered the dreaded day when Richie had vanished without a trace.

Every day Remando took a boat out to search for his lover and every night he returned alone. Months passed until one morning a fisherman called at the house with news of a young boy's body that had been washed up on the shore. As if sensing Captain Culley's dread, Remando appeared fully dressed and ready to go with the fisherman to identity the body. Shana told Patrick to stay in the house whilst they went to see if the unfortunate victim was Abi. A strange numb feeling filled her mind. It was as if she had reprogrammed herself to expect the worst rather than hope for the best. She had witnessed so many deaths of loved ones lately. Although Shana's mind was prepared for the traumatic experience, her heart beat quickly. As usual the beach was deserted at the time when most were busy with daily chores. On seeing the fishing boats tethered side by side Remando's pace quickened and he began to jog through the powdery sand. A young boy stood with a large stick occasionally knocking off the crabs that scuttled from the clear, blue sea. As their large pincers snapped, successfully grabbing a piece of wet, rotten white flesh, they went hurtling through the air from the force of a direct blow from the guard's branch. Stamping on the fleeing sea creatures who dared to mutilate his friend's dead body, Remando yelled loudly in his native tongue '¡Puede dios castigar los bastardos que mataron mi ángel hermoso!' Shana had confirmed her worst fears. As she looked down at the seaweed-covered body of her lover and closest childhood friend she froze in panic.

Just as she had feared, Abi's closely cropped platinum hair had misled the man who had discovered her broken body into believing that she was a boy. Her facial skin was pure white and bloated and the hideous scars had vanished. Tiny flies walked over sightless eyes as they stared skyward. The clothes that she had been wearing when poor Remando last saw her had been ripped to shreds and were unrecognisable, stained with dark blotches which were no doubt blood. As the waves nudged Abi's lifeless form, then withdrew in perfect time with Shana's breathing, she willed the ocean to bring her lover back to life. Bounding up behind his wife, John grabbed her and turned her face to his. Without a word he pulled her close to him and held her as she trembled.

Years of pent-up anger, agony and despair boiled inside Captain Culley's soul and the little girl that lurked just under the surface of a strong pyrate queen's façade suddenly appeared. Taking her tear-stained face in his hands, John Hawkins looked into the deepest, most magnetic eyes that he had ever seen and willed her to stay strong. She collapsed onto the sand next to her dead lover, while back at home, Patrick squeezed his own eyes tightly together as he heard his mother's hauntingly melancholy howl. The pyrate queen's desperate screams made even the most hardened rogue shudder uneasily. Eventually, Moses was able to take Abi's limp, lifeless body away from Shana's clutch.

Moses and Remando buried Abi Turnbull on the brow of a beautiful hill overlooking the sea. Patrick was devastated and John tried his best to comfort the child but he withdrew into himself, choosing to speak to no-one but his mother. Moses kept watch over the boy day and night and kept a fire alight outside the room where he slept. The huge mute had taken over Irish's role as the boy's bodyguard and Shana was eternally grateful to him. Since Abi's death she had grown so very tired of the sadness that seemed to lurk at every turn along her difficult fated path. Strong in her pagan beliefs, Captain Culley refused to lose hope as she remembered one of Irish's favourite sayings. Her long-dead soul-mate would repeat it every time they got drunk together and reminisced about harder times. As she rocked herself to sleep every night, her eyes sore from hours of crying, Shana could hear the soft, calming voice of her Irish as he spoke the wise words, 'Dura usu molliora' …'Difficult things become easier with practice.' Oh how she longed for easier times!

Chapter 28

'Cum Larvis non luctandum'

Shana had been utterly devastated by Abi's death. No-one ever found out how she had died but the dark, bloody bruises and cuts between her legs told a sickening story. Sometimes sporadic bouts of news were overheard that pyrates had attacked the ship on which she and Remando were travelling but no evidence was ever found. The whole incident was a mystery but Shana could not help feeling that the bitterly jealous bitch of an English queen had been involved in some way. John and her friends were very concerned that Shana was growing more paranoid than ever since the terrible incident. A whole year passed by and Patrick became increasingly worried for his mother's safety. He refused to leave her side and even started sleeping at the foot of her marital bed in fear of her being attacked. Despite his mother's popularity he had learned only too well that one jealous enemy could be more dangerous than an army.

On the last night of 1575 celebrations amongst the small party of forlorn pyrates were much quieter than their usual New Year merrymaking. The first few months of 1576 were spent sailing the Emaleeza back to England. Patrick had collected many gifts for the Turnbulls. He had bought trinkets and crafts from the foreign lands that he and Abi had visited together. During the long voyage the thoughtful boy spent time meticulously documenting each adventure that they had experienced. He planned to give the bound parchments to Abi's daughter so that she could at least have some connection with her deceased mother. Sewing the pages together, he studied each of the drawings that he had added of Abi and remembered how happy she had made his mother. Chasing his most dreaded fear of losing his own mother from his mind, Patrick kept himself busy planning the best way to approach the Turnbull girl who he knew to be fond of him. Moses smiled reassuringly as if he had heard his thoughts and the large man nodded as if understanding the boy's dilemma. Patrick felt safe with his older friend. Looking down at a sleeping Flint, who had been very low since Abi had gone, he stroked his soft fur and watched the little ape twitch as he dreamed. His tiny son slept in Micken's cage and the parrot stood on one leg, perched on a branch above him. The pretty parrot's delicate, silk-like eyelids opened regularly to check that his friends were still close. As the ship's boards creaked, Shana rocked Patrick to sleep as they sailed steadily onward over good-tempered waves.

Moses' head was full of turmoil. He felt scared for Shana having to return to the most dangerous country for her at this time yet felt proud that she had entrusted him with her only child. Whatever happened, the man who was indebted to the beautiful pyrate had silently vowed to Allah that he would protect the boy with his life. Patrick Culley was destined for bigger things. Of this, Moses felt sure. He had seen in a vision that the Culley reign of the seas would not end with Shana's death and that he had a big part to play in the long battle that Patrick would have to fight to live up to his mother's reputation. Roles had been reversed and Moses had been shown that it was going to be even more difficult for a male to prove himself as a worthy pyrate king.

Anchoring near Lundy Island, which was more crowded of late as more sea-dogs had heard of the ideal pyrate's lair, Shana and her crew made for Coemgen Shercliff's tattoo place for cover. Coem and Shana went back a long way. The talented artist had spent years tattooing sailors. He had travelled all over the known world, doing much of his work aboard ships. His archery skills were exceptional so he became a valued member of every crew on his travels. Coem would often spend time in Spain where he had a place on the south coast but Lundy Island had become his favourite haunt since pyrates had settled there.

Micken and Flint stayed aboard, the ape unable to face the world in his terrible grief. Coem had been concerned about his faithful friend's welfare and as always, welcomed Shana with a huge hug. 'By my beard, thy tits 'ave grown bigger Sharn!' The tall, popular artist could never resist a dig at his old friend. Squeezing one of his nipples as she laughed at Coem's cheek, Shana felt glad to receive a warm welcome from one of her closest friends. She loved the big softy like a brother and he always cheered her spirits. 'By my beard, yer carryin' a bit more timber aint yer, wench?' It was always custom for the pair to exchange insults when they were together.

Patrick giggled behind his mother and Coem's face lit up when he realised the boy was with her. 'A'reet lad?' Ow's thy tatt bin?' Patrick pulled up a wooden stool and showed Coem the perfectly healed lettering on the underside of his wrist. Coem was a born leader and even the most wanted murderers held a high respect for him. Whatever kind of help Shana needed Coem would sort it for her. His contacts were innumerable and invaluable.

As always, the tattoo artist was busy working ink into the flesh of customers. Since Shana's last visit, the clever man had built up a successful business in the middle of Lundy Island. A gypsy called Stig who had known Eileen Conachy well, sat busily knocking a comb-like tool into a fat pyrate's back with a small mallet. Coem was a brilliant engineer, designing and making tools to tattoo customers more quickly and easily so that he could add the finest detail into the ink work. Stig was tattooing an intricate pattern of Celtic knot-work into his customer's skin. Pagan symbols surrounded the complex, interwoven design that formed the shape of two lovers entwined. When finished, the back-piece would be stunning. As he worked, he chatted about his pagan beliefs... how bad it was that Christians were dragging defenceless people from their homes, torturing and hanging them for practicing the ancient sacred art of herbal healing. Coem regularly interrupted Stig's spiel, telling him to stop harping on about something that no-one could do anything about. Adding to Stig's rightful concerns, Shana expressed her anger with the hierarchy of the churches whose leaders wanted to replace all of the Celtic pagan circles with crosses.

Stig had been amongst those brave few who had fought for the right to preserve the citizens of England's original religious beliefs. Unwilling to back down totally, the Church had reluctantly agreed to compromise to avoid an uprising. Stonemasons were now being commissioned to carve new stone crosses with a circle of Celtic knot-work that looked almost like a halo, incorporated into the design. Like Shana, Stig was overtly passionate about his beliefs that were being threatened by Christianity and when the two met they would always preach their strong views. 'Silence ye pagan, mad-bred 'eathens!' Coem piped up in his Middle-England accent as he worked on a portrait that looked uncannily life-like.

Paul was another tattooist who had joined Coem to help tattoo the many pyrates who wanted immaculate ink-work and refused to settle for anything but the best skin art. Coem was very fussy about who he worked with as he had built up a reputation second to none. He had promised to teach Shana some day but whenever she reminded him he would retort with a jibe, 'ye're ne'er feckin' in one place long 'nuff for me ter show ye the art! 'Tis nay an easy skill ter learn, Sharn... an ye can stop flashin' yer tits! 'Tisnay gonny work on me, wench!' Everyone burst out laughing at Coem and he pulled up his ink-stained shirt to reveal his belly. As he gave it a good, hard scratch he lifted his arse up off his chair and released a long, loud and particularly smelly fart without even cracking a smile. Patrick giggled away as his mother threw one of her oldest and most faithful friends a glance of mock disapproval.

'Awright Shana?' Paul asked as he always did. 'How's things wi' ye matey?' Without losing concentration the bald man with tattoos completely covering his scalp, continued tattooing a tiny toothless man who looked quite comical seated next to Stig's larger customer. As he worked, a stunning Cathayan dragon slowly emerged from the minute dots of blood and ink that he added roughly to the little man's pink flesh. The small wooden establishment felt almost comforting to Patrick as he listened to the therapeutic tap and enjoyed the strong smell of neat Poitín. Coem distilled and sold his own version of the strongest alcohol known to man. Using potatoes that Shana had shipped over to him from the

New World the wise tattooist had made the wonderful discovery when he had found no other use for the tasteless vegetable. Whenever Coem came across anything that could not be cooked, he made it into some form of grog, making a tidy profit selling the lethally potent concoctions to his customers, the spirits took their mind off the pain of being tattooed. If their stomachs were too weak to keep the potion down, he simply soaked the area of skin to be tattooed with the spirits. Within mere seconds there was no feeling whatsoever.

'Brought any o' them spuds back wi' yer this time bab?' Coem asked louder than needed whilst continuing with his work. Shana promised her friend that she would have some potatoes shipped over for him. She pulled up a chair, grabbed her blackjack and helped herself to a generous helping of potent spirit. Settling comfortably for a night of nostalgia and hilarity spent with some of her kind, she felt so happy to watch Patrick interact with the men whose company she enjoyed. The child's laughter was music to his mother's ears and she felt contentment in her heart.

Coem arranged for a few of his friends to escort Shana's party on their journey to Teignmouth. They went by boat, then horseback and arrived at Mary Maggy's in no time. When Flo heard the horses approaching the orphanage she put down the leather bucket used to draw water from the well and strained her eyes to see who had entered the grounds. When she recognised the lead rider as Shana her heart leapt with joy and the happy twin ran to meet her. As she felt the icy wind rush through her hair, Flo suddenly felt depression hit her and she slowed her pace. Her face took on a sickly pallor and when Shana reached Abi's beautiful, unscarred twin the woman had passed out on the grass. Dismounting the black stallion Shana lifted Flo up onto the saddle and jumped up behind her limp body. As she screamed into the wind Shana rode the horse to the courtyard where some children were playing happily. Flo's and Abi's daughters were amongst them and Shana's heart sank when she watched the girls take hold of Flo and gently lift her down from the mount.

It took a while for Flo to come round but she seemed to have lost all sense of time. Staring up in confusion at the concerned faces peering down at her, Flo suddenly started to panic as muscles in the left side of her face began to spasm. A terrible sharp pain shot down the left side of her body and she felt a stabbing feeling behind her eyes. Tremendous heat spread over her entire body and numbness replaced pain. No matter how hard she concentrated, Flo could not make her mouth and tongue work properly to form any coherent words. With bloodshot eyes bolting from their sockets Flo looked pleadingly from one person to another. Her pretty face had become hideously contorted.

Flo's husband, Robert rushed into the room having heard the disturbance. He could not believe what he was witnessing when he saw his daughters struggling to hold his wife's contorted body as it thrashed uncontrollably. The convulsions were sporadic and quite violent but after a while they ceased leaving poor Flo limp and exhausted in her husband's arms. As he stared in utter disbelief at the usually fit and healthy mother of his strong children, Robert wiped the drool away from her chin. He kissed her gently and tried to calm her. Totally petrified, Abi's twin sister lay on the cold stone floor unable to move. Desperate to make herself understood by her concerned family, Flo could not believe that every word that she tried to say came out in an incomprehensible drawl. Try as she might, her tongue and mouth would not do what her mind instructed. Shana's concerned face came into view, surrounded by an animated kaleidoscope of multicoloured patterns. As the traumatised pyrate captain looked into the beautiful but haunted eyes of her dead lover's helpless double, she felt unable to handle any more sorrow. Woe filled her heart as she lifted Flo's slack body and carried her up to her mother's room.

As Shana carried Flo Turnbull carefully along the corridor separating Mary Maggy's residential area from the main dwelling, concerned and distressed children joined the mini procession. Unused to seeing Mary Maggy's strong and confident principle so vulnerable, they whispered reassuring words as she was carried past. Little hands reached up to stroke their surrogate mother's face and many began to shed tears of fear for the woman who had shown them so much love and kindness. Flo and Abi's daughters tried to distract the children by getting out a selection of wooden toys and hoops. Patrick and Josh took the orphans out into the fields to organise games whilst the adults tended to Flo and Ma Turnbull.

During the week when her only living daughter suffered a stroke caused by a bleed in her brain, Ma Turnbull lost the will to live. Almost totally paralysed, poor Flo was left with severe difficulties with speech, eating, drinking and perception. Unable to recognise simple everyday objects, the debilitated woman could not even tell the time. Luckily her daughters, husband and poor, simple Josh took over the running of the orphanage whilst Abi's only daughter cared solely for Flo and Ma Turnbull. The older woman had decided that she was nothing more than extra work for her granddaughter.

Uncannily, pock marks suddenly appeared on the only remaining twin's face… it looked exactly like the scarred area of skin that had formed following her sister's childhood illness. Everyone knew that Ma Turnbull had died of a broken heart within days of learning the dreadful plight of her daughters. Shana had had little choice but tell the poor woman the truth about Abi's death. On hearing the news of her sister's death, a single tear ran from the corner of Flo's eye and down her cheek. Looking at her lover's twin with sympathy and despair the hardened pyrate queen broke down and wept.

John Hawkins and the religious Remando kindly took charge of funeral arrangements and to say that Ma Turnbull was sent off in style would be an understatement. Remando ensured that Shana's clan member had the most elaborate funerary procession that had ever graced the winding, cobbled streets of Teignmouth town. Everyone lining the streets on that misty, gloomy morn showed their great respect for the upstanding, charitable member of their community. Tears were shed for the family who had recently suffered tragedy after tragedy. Covered with a silk flag made by the children of Mary Maggy's, Ma's coffin was taken to the Church in a glass-sided carriage pulled by four black mares wearing ostrich feather headdresses courtesy of Patrick Culley. He and Ma's grandchildren had made the spectacular decorations with some of the gifts that he had brought back on Abi's behalf. They had dyed the huge feathers purple and threaded beads made from real jet sewn onto black leather harnesses. An expensive walnut coffin was carried to the grave by six black-clad pallbearers. The long procession of mourners followed in silence wearing black hooded cloaks.

Shana had arranged for Ma Turnbull's body to be buried inside the church. A doleful single bell rang out as the coffin was placed in a vault within the walls of St. Michael's Church, the oldest church in East Teignmouth. A hefty fee had ensured that an engraved plaque marked where the remarkable woman lay behind a heavy polished black marble slab. Following the funeral, mourners went to Mary Maggy's where a huge feast had been prepared. During the wake, money was collected for the upkeep of the orphanage. Most of the three hundred inhabitants of East Teignmouth attended the wake at some time during the three day vigil. Many citizens of the western parish attended to offer their last respects to a fine and well-loved woman. The Turnbull family would have no shortage of offers of support which comforted Shana. Many widows and pretty unmarried maidens fussed around Robert Reed but he still only had eyes for his poor wife sitting next to him in a bath chair. Abi's daughter, Shana glared at every vulture-like female who dared to flutter her eyelashes at her uncle whilst her aunt Flo sat helplessly watching them flirt with her devoted husband.

After the wake, everyone pulled together and helped tidy Mary Maggy's. Taking advantage of some private time, Shana drew up her final will and testament leaving everything she owned to Patrick. Mary Maggy's was to be left to Flo, Robert and Josh, the young man who had been so kind to Patrick. The infamous pyrate queen had a sickening feeling that she had brought bad luck to Mary Maggy's. She also felt that this was to be her last time spent in the happy orphanage that she had founded as a child. Shana Culley said her final goodbyes and left with her pyrates, taking a stagecoach back to Teignmouth docks where the Emaleeza was anchored.

The journey was short but the passengers were armed to the hilt. After they were attacked by a gang of highwaymen who were no contest for the ferocious pyrates, Shana questioned the only survivor of the raid. Patrick and Remando were busy disarming the dead attackers and John was stripping them of their valuables when their captain discovered that her prisoner was wearing a gold signet ring that bore the Royal Crest. On discovery of the valuable trinket that the queen only ever awarded to her most favoured subjects, Shana began to pull off every fingernail until her victim squealed that he had been paid by the queen to assassinate Hawkins. Cutting off the would-be assassin's ringed finger and tossing it over to Remando to bag, Shana penned a letter to Elizabeth using the man's blood that flowed from the bleeding stump.

Somehow John Hawkins' estranged wife had found out that he had returned to England and was visiting Teignmouth. She felt betrayed on learning that he travelled with a lady and informed the queen of his guile. Luckily for Shana, the scorned woman had been misinformed. Far too conceited to believe that someone of her husband's rank and breeding would entertain the idea of leaving her for a vagabond harlot pyrate, John Hawkins' wife believed his mistress to be a baroness at least!

Elizabeth had hired a small band of men for the relatively simple job of dismembering her disloyal servant and sending his woman away in shame. Little did either scorned woman know that the infamous pyrate queen was his companion. After extracting the information from the blubbering coward who only lost four nails before giving in, Shana head-butted him to the ground and stamped his face into the soft, muddy track. Hastily the angry woman leapt up beside the terrified coachman who sat clutching his unfired blunderbuss, took the reins and made for the port at great speed. Inside the coach John sat with Patrick and they spoke of a mother's wrath whenever her child was threatened... no-one present had ever witnessed such insane fury as Shana's when anyone threatened Patrick's life.

When the Emaleeza returned to the port of São Vicente, a letter awaited Captain Culley. Grace O'Malley's neatly scribed words ate into Shana's soul like venomous parasites, as she read that Queen Elizabeth had given strict orders to 'hang Irish harpers wherever found'. In her desire to extinguish all aspects of Irish culture, the monarch had sunk lower than anyone had ever expected by executing harmless musicians! Grace O'Malley had decided that it was time for her Fianna Fail, or Soldiers of Destiny, to make their military presence known to the cruel English queen. Ireland's ruling party leader's patience had finally been pushed too far. Grace was not prepared to wait any longer. When Shana had finished reading the Irish noblewoman's letter to John and Patrick, she closed her eyes. She begged the pagan gods and goddesses to bless Grace with enough strength and power to force the English from blessed Eire.

Meanwhile Martin Frobisher, an English merchant, had set sail on a voyage in search of a northwest passage as a trade-route to India and Cathay. He had been trying to fund the project for fifteen years and had finally managed to convince the Muscovy Company, an English merchant co-operation, to license his expedition. Three barques and a pinnace weighed anchor at Blackwall and following a personal blessing from Queen Elizabeth, set sail via the Shetland Isles. Shana had unofficially made that voyage many times, and the ridiculous amount of fuss being made about an unknown privateer retracing an already well-established pyrates' route amused her greatly. Along the 'important new discovery route' the pinnace was lost and one of the barques abandoned. On the 28th July 1576, the Coast of Labrador was sighted and soon after, they reached and named Frobisher Bay. On the 18th August Frobisher's two ships arrived at Butcher's Island where they were met by local natives, the Inuit tribe. Having no understanding, respect or indeed desire to befriend the Inuit people, hostility ensued and five of Frobisher's men were taken hostage.

Frobisher had captured one of the Inuit men but his own men were never recovered. He sailed back to England where he presented a sod of black earth which assayers thought not to be gold-bearing. Despite this opinion, the Muscovy Company hired another expert to assess the properties of the earth. Incredibly, he believed there to be a fraction of gold present so the company used this assessment to lobby for funding for another voyage. The following year an important expedition was organised and the queen lent Frobisher a royal navy ship, she also gave him a substantial amount towards expedition expenses. The Company of Cathay was founded with a charter from the crown and was allowed sole right of sailing in every direction but east. Elizabeth appointed Frobisher high admiral of all lands and waters that he might discover.

Patrick Culley celebrated his sixteenth birthday that leap-year and his mother and friends made sure that the special event was celebrated in style. They organised a firework display and an archery competition that Patrick won. Since a young child, the boy had been gifted with a perfect aim and had trained well for years. Tudor times encouraged archery as a sport and made it compulsive for young men to practice regularly after Sunday worship. A law had even been passed that every fit man over the age of twenty four must be able to hit a target from 220 yards away. Patrick was delighted when the archery tournament was followed by a falconry display. The falconer allowed him to fly the bird and showed him how to use the glove to handle the bird of prey correctly. Flint took baby Tripod and joined the parrot in his cage whilst the deadly bird of prey flew free. Huddled together in a corner, they all shivered with fear each time the bird swooped over. Poor Flint had become almost as nervous as his little feathered friend since Sparky had been savaged to death.

Drinking, feasting and merrymaking went on well into the early hours, when the town crier announced that Queen Elizabeth had declined an offer to rule over the Netherlands. England's relationship with Spain had worsened so it seemed a sensible time for Grace O'Malley to make her move. Having gained much support from the Spanish navy the Irish warrior woman had a good chance of a victorious battle but she knew that it would not be an easy one.

CHAPTER 29

Immaculate Deception

In the year of our Lord 1577, Grace O'Malley attacked and pillaged southern lands in Munster. Finally, the brave warrior woman had been over ambitious and was defeated and arrested by Fitten, an English nobleman. He ordered his men to take her to Dublin Castle where she was imprisoned. There Grace learned that her brother and children had been kidnapped by the English to force her to give up her fight. From her prison Grace wrote to Shana back in Nombre de Dios to explain the situation. Although Grace wanted her soul sister to know what was going on, she forbade her to try any rescue attempts.

The Irish warrior queen had a strong feeling that her arrest had been planned by Queen Elizabeth to lure Captain Culley as it was inevitable that she would come to her rescue. If Shana took the bait, the virgin queen would finally catch the determined agitator and put an end to the humiliation of the crown. Grace had learned of Elizabeth's anger and murderous jealousy when she had heard of Shana's affair with Hawkins. The spoiled queen wanted her favourite seafarer to return to England and renew his pledge of undying love to the aging monarch. On receiving word from Grace, Shana left for Ireland despite her friend's stark warning. Terrified that her execution might be ordered by the vengeful queen of England, Grace had asked Shana to ensure that her children inherited her vast lands and numerous properties. On reaching Ireland, Shana lay low in Rockfleet Castle awaiting her friend's return.

In the meantime Queen Elizabeth visited Grace O'Malley in person. The Irish noblewoman refused to courtesy, demanding that the English queen showed her mutual respect because of her equal status in Ireland. Grace stood tall and spoke to her captor in Gaelic. Amused by Grace O'Malley's nerve and bravery, the queen began to laugh and the two women agreed that Grace be set free on condition of good behaviour. Unbeknown to Grace, Queen Elizabeth planned to re-arrest her and secretly take her to England where she hoped Captain Culley would fall for the bait.

Meanwhile, her majesty's new favourite, Francis Drake was planning to set sail on a voyage to circumnavigate the world in his ship, the Pelican. When Shana heard of his venture, she took to her cups. Referring to the master sailor as a 'pelican's pillcock', the pyrate queen felt saddened that her lover's cousin had become such a creep towards his monarch. All over England, huge celebrations were underway and the fickle, ordinary English people reacted like puppets under control of their greed-riddled queen. A day off from hard graft never failed to please the poor population and their manipulative queen took advantage of that.

Elizabeth had a wonderful arrangement with her Privateers who were fighting her cause at their own risk and cost. Things appeared to be improving for the English monarch and an alliance was struck between England and the Netherlands. Drake became Ambassador of the Cimarrones, a group of rebellious African people who had escaped from the binds of slavery by running from their cruel Spanish owners.

Their name derived from the Spanish word for 'runaway slaves' and they had fled from captivity in the New World to settle in places like Brazil and Panama. Drake and his men encouraged the hatred of Catholicism amongst the Cimarrone people who were the leading New World enemies of Spain. The Spanish feared that the African settlers might join forces with the Indians and sent a strong force of armed volunteers from Panama. Their task was to invade Cimarrone homes and fields of crops, burning them to the ground. Angered by Drake's hypocrisy and misuse of the trust given to him by emancipated slaves who had suffered appalling mistreatment under Spanish ownership, Shana planned to help liberate these black pawns in the cruel game of chess being played between two rival nations. The main issue was not that the slaves were being mistreated by their Spanish owners but that African people should never have been enslaved in the first place!

Admiral Sir John Hawkins had been given control of the Royal Navy and was determined that England had the best ships in the world and the most skilled sailors to man them. He managed to persuade Queen Elizabeth to raise his seamen's wages, encouraging the men to be better motivated and pledge undying loyalty to queen and country. Although the admiral was a strong and able leader of English Naval forces, he also had a rebellious streak and had plotted to betray his queen to the Spanish. It was well known that the admiral gave money to his cousin to help fund his missions. Shana was willing to do anything that would help reveal the hypocrisy of the queen of England's self-obsessed 'humane' privateers.

Chapter 30

Ensnarement

When Shana set sail for England, her sole plan was to rescue Grace O'Malley. Remando accompanied her and she hired new crew for the short journey. On reaching Plymouth a fleet of awaiting galleons fired on the Emaleeza and the vessel took a serious hit. As she always did in such a dire situation, Captain Culley ensured the safety of her crew and ordered them to escape in rowing boats. Her men would probably be picked off one by one, shot or captured to be sent to the gallows but she wanted at least to give them a fighting chance of survival. They had all served her well... Shana told Remando to make sure that Patrick recited their special rhyme. Remando was reluctant to leave his friend but determined to return to Patrick and deliver his mother's message. Shana was taken by surprise when the hardened pyrate thanked her for helping him change his ways before he kissed her lightly on the lips and plunged into the cold, grey English sea. Aware that she had finally been trapped by Queen Elizabeth, Shana planned to go down with her ship. Her final thought was of her son who was safely back at São Vicente with her husband and the over-protective Moses. She knew that her child was safe and that knowledge made her strong and ready to die.

Shivering with cold and soaked to the skin, Shana awoke lying on the cold, damp stone floor of a dark cell. Gradually falling in and out of consciousness she could hear the jeering and screaming crowd shouting her name. A small boy who had somehow managed to sneak up to the thick bars of her gaol pressed his grubby little face against the iron. Hurriedly he told her that she was to be executed the following day by order of the queen. Gritting her teeth together angrily, Shana guessed that the wise monarch had declared the day to be a holiday in hope of pacifying the mass of Shana's admirers. This would have been the only way that Elizabeth could have possibly promoted even the smallest amount of good feeling towards their monarch, for she had been the one to demand the execution of their pyrate queen and heroine. Yelping as a large stone hit him on the back of his head, the poor urchin scarpered off. Feeling a sudden sick faintness wash over her body from lack of nourishment, Shana heard a key turn in the lock of her cell door and passed out on the cold, soiled stone floor.

Final Chapter

She Who Laughs Last..........

It came as a total shock, yet the Master Executioner's gut feeling had been right. Spiteful shards of glass hit him full in the eye as he squeezed the softness of her breast with an iron grip. He yelped like an injured, terrified cur as Shana spat the cruel, sharp splinters that she had cleverly prepared and concealed beneath her tongue. Shana could have not wished for a better revenge. Carefully, she had removed glass from the spectacles that her kindly lawyer had left following his final and particularly satisfying conjugal visit the previous night. Master David Hall had tried to persuade his lover to comply with his escape plan but his mistress steadfastly refused his help and he left in despair. Master Hall adored his mistress but would not chance insulting such an independent, strong willed and wily wench by begging her to avoid her fate!

Later that night Shana had received a most unwelcome visitor. The grotesque and repulsive Olaf came to claim what he regarded as his right. The degradation of her beautiful body being soiled by her tormentor's putrid flesh should have been enough, but even worse was that a pathetic, puffed up bigot would be the last man inside her.

'Hell hath no fury...' Shana's close seafaring friend, Irish had told her as he comforted her in his arms when he had found her in a wretched state... the day that her only child, Patrick had been conceived when she had been brutally raped aboard the Banshee. Her crying had lasted for days but the hatred and loathing of importunate men festered inside her heart for the rest of her life. She determined that no male child of hers would ever treat women with the disrespect and abuse that she had suffered.

Many years later Shana often told her son, Patrick who was more like a brother to her than a son, 'Tis naught to be ashamed of for a grown man to cry.' These were the last memories to pass through Miss Sushana Culley's deep and focused mind as she saw the stranger with the most beautiful ocean blue eyes crying for her… memories of words of wisdom that she had spoken to her fine and intelligent son. Her son had heeded them well and was now waiting for his mother's return. He was so far away and it broke her heart to think that she had to make this huge sacrifice for Patrick to take over her role as the greatest, most revered pyrate leader. The infamous and terrible pyrate queen who had ruled vast seas for ten years adored her only son and her heart was heavy on the day she died, in the knowledge that she would never see her Patrick again.

Early next morning the sound of metal on metal rang through the narrow streets of Plymouth as the hustle and bustle of daily life began. Anthony, the blacksmith's son would sleep heavily again that night and remember the wonderful love that he had glimpsed in the woman's eyes before she flung herself to her own carefully planned death. A massive riot had broken out on the day of Miss Culley's execution. Word was that the damage caused by the disappointed and unruly crowd would take months to repair. Apparently the executioner had behaved inappropriately towards a female prisoner, but had got his comeuppance. The town crier reported events loud and clear...

'Executioner's final drop!'

These were the words that the crier had chosen to describe the humiliation of Master Olaf who had been blinded by a woman scorned... The infamous queen of the most loyal crew of Elizabethan pyrates had even had the effrontery to rob him of his final execution! The crowd had been confused by the bleeding executioner reeling on the platform, clutching at the bloodied pulps that were once his eyes. A hush had fallen around the square at the sudden unexpected sound of whiplash from the thick, too long rope. It was said that grown men cried as they witnessed the infamous pyrate queen's spectacular leap to her own death...

'Pyrate queen has the last 'Olaugh!'

Early risers sniggered as they heard the town crier's humour. Old Tom Corbett was always witty with his cries of news. Tom had plenty to cry about with this latest story- the passing of a legend and the end of a sadistic pervert's exploitative career. Tom was determined to have a field day with this yarn!

'Misjudged rope pulls pyrate's pretty little head off!'

It was rumoured that Shana's ample bosom had caused her death plunge and ruined the reputation of the queen's fearsome Master Executioner. He had literally sealed his own fate for he would never work again and had become a laughing stock. To add insult to injury, the town crier gleefully roared a well thought out line about the pyrate queen's precious gold, pearl and ruby necklace disappearing together with her head!

'Spin a coin... heads or tails? Tales abound of pyrate queen's ghostly body searching for its missing head and valuable jewels!'

Shana had even managed to rob the executioner of his final takings and word was spreading that her head appeared the night after her death, floating above the gallows with the precious necklace that she had worn clenched tightly between her teeth! Local taverns were packed full of eager folk keen to hear the latest news of the weird apparition... by pure coincidence the drinking dens that Master Corbett frequented were those where the tales had originated.

The blacksmith's son, Anthony smiled to himself at the irony of the whole affair. His dream queen had gone but her life and death story would live on for decades. The crier's words rang in his ears as he fingered the beautiful necklace deep in his pocket. He vowed one day to deliver the legacy to its rightful owner, Patrick Culley. The tall, bronzed, muscular man's smile faded as he thought of how the poor lad would receive the news of his mother's death. That was the least of Anthony's worries as he gazed at the freshly turned earth in the cemetery of Saint Xaviers Church. He smiled grimly to himself as he brushed soil from his clothes and wondered if anyone would ever discover the bizarre double-skulled skeleton of Isaac Bromley who had been buried that Saturday afternoon in July 1578.

At the end of the day, weary with toil, the smith's son and apprentice returned to his cramped, candlelit home.

He retired to his sleeping quarters and pulled the ropes on the wooden bed frame tight before he dragged over his straw stuffed mattress. Feeling no guilt whatsoever he prepared himself for a restless night of wild and imaginative thoughts.

Anthony was an intelligent boy who had grown worldly wise during his few years working at the forge. However the day of Miss Sushana Culley's execution had shocked him, especially when the clumsy executioner had caught his hand in her fine silk blouse just as she jumped forward. Anthony reached under his clothes to satisfy his desires as he became hard from the memory of the fine and brave working class wench who had become a legend unlikely to be forgotten. His hand tightened around his erect penis as Anthony pleasured himself beyond anything he had ever experienced. He recalled the scene when his dream woman, who in her leap for freedom unintentionally exposed her beautiful, ample and heavy chest of dreams. Those dreams had certainly been fulfilled and ensured that the incredible, notorious child-woman's life would become one to be documented and envied for many years to follow.

Ironically the day of her death was Miss Culley's fortieth birthday. Unbeknown to her, that very year Francis Drake would be commissioned by the queen of England to 'rob by command' the Spanish ship 'Nuestra Senora de la Conception', en route from Lima to Panama. The doomed ship had aptly been given the vulgar name 'Cacfuego', which translated as 'Shitfire', by Drake's witty and original privateers. The craft was so heavily laden with guns and a precious cargo of vast treasure that it proved a relatively easy target for Captain Drake and his experienced crew to overcome. It sat low in the water and was a sitting duck. In these rough and unruly times the queen's Privateers, who robbed on behalf of the crown, were renowned and mostly successful but pyracy was also rife. Pyrates risked their necks rather than share their booty with the queen. The Spanish feared Sir Francis Drake, now a famous privateer who had been knighted for his bravery and devoted service to his queen. The notoriously jealous queen would not have been amused to discover that her favourite was blood cousin to the lover of the infamous and most exotic erotic pyrate queen, Sushana Culley.

Thus ends the closely guarded tale of Shana Culley the pyrate queen and her uncanny link with Queen Elizabeth, arguably the most successful pyrate of all time! These two strong minded women led men to steal, on their behalf, from ships on the seas and waters surrounding 'The New World'. They took their bounty from vessels transporting huge hauls of treasure already stolen from a people that sadly no longer exist in our New World.